U0085046

本書的特色是

不要背，只要聽。

不必專心，無形中就背下單字。

英文唸兩遍，中文唸一遍，
中英文同時學。

只要聽、聽、聽，
聽了英文就知道中文，
聽了中文就知道英文。

英文不要學，只要聽，
本書由名美籍播音員錄音，
中文說得比中國人好，
英文說得比美國人好。

修編序

　　學習英文最常遇到的一個問題，便是字彙不足。一個字彙不足的人，在英文聽、寫、說各方面的能力都會受到嚴重的限制。因此往往無法適當地與英美人士溝通意見；在參加考試時，更經常因爲看不懂題目，而不知從何作答。

　　我們有鑑於此，特別爲全國廣大的英文讀者編排了一系列的字彙叢書。從最基本的 **Vocabulary Fundamental**，到足以應付留學考試之需的 **Vocabulary 22000**，爲您紮實地打好字彙基礎。無論您目前在校求學或已步入社會，都會發現本系列書籍即是您苦尋已久，增強英文實力的最佳利器。學校老師更可採用本系列書籍爲輔助教材，以補平日上課內容之不足。

　　一般均認爲背單字是件既吃力，又往往成效不彰的苦差事，因而總是望之卻步。本系列書籍的問世恰可打破以上觀念。以下列出字彙系列叢書的各項特點：

1. 以「課」爲單元，容易安排學習進度，也避免了背字典式學習方法的冗長與雜亂無章。

2. 新的排版，**左邊英文，右邊中文**，可以遮住英文部分，測驗中文，也可以遮住中文部分，測驗英文。

3. 適當列出各單字的衍生字、同義字及反義字，困難的字彙有「記憶技巧」，包含字根分析、諧音法，以及相似字彙聯想，可收舉一反三，事半功倍之效。

4. 以例句說明單字的用法，各例句並附有中譯，以便參考。

5. 每一部份後均有習題，以加深對所學單字的印象；每一課後面更附有成果測驗，以評量對所學單字的了解程度，並增進活用單字的能力。

字彙的增加絕非一蹴可及的，但是若能採用有系統的方法，依舊可縮短增加字彙所需的時間。因此，本系列叢書的讀者，只要按部就班，循序漸進，必可在最短的期間內，獲得最大的成效。並請切記隨時要活用所學的單字，唯有如此，這些字彙才會確確實實地成為你自己的。

Vocabulary Fundamental

1. 本書所列單字共計一千三百個，加上各字的衍生字、同義字及反義字，則實際收錄約三千字。均為平日最常用，最容易接觸到的單字。

2. 詳細列出各字的 kk 音標、詞性說明及中文解釋，省卻查字典的麻煩。中文解釋是以該字最常用的意義為主，一字若有一種以上的常用解釋或詞性，則亦一併列出。單字後面附有例句，以說明該字的用法；例句並有中文翻譯，以便對照參考。

3. 每一課分為五個部份，以便於分段記憶。每一部份之後有習題，課後並有成果測驗；可藉著重覆測驗來加深對單字的印象，並學習如何活用單字。

4. 本書共分為 24 課，建議進度為一天一課，如此便可在一個月內增加 3,000 個字彙。

編者　謹識

CONTENTS 目 錄

VOCABULARY FUNDAMENTAL

一封感人的來信

學習出版社，您好：

　　我是貴社出版書籍的愛用者，畢業於台大電機系，入伍服預官役，於今年六月一日退伍。退伍後打定出國繼續深造的心意，首先面臨的就是托福及 GRE 測驗，在一個偶然的機會下，在書局發現貴社 Vocabulary Fundamental～22000 這一系列的字彙進階書，其內容紮實，循序漸進的編排方式甚合我的需要，於是直接到許昌街門市購買了 Vocabulary 5000 及 Vocabulary 10000 兩套，以此二套書來準備托福考試，果然於 8 月 1 日的托福考試中獲得 610 分的理想分數；接下來為了 GRE 考試的需要，我又購買 Vocabulary 22000 這一套及 GRE 字彙進階一書，經過充分研讀之後，於 10 月 11 日充滿信心的走入考場。前幾天我收到了 GRE 成績單：語文 570，計量 800，分析 760，總分 2130，這個成績是我原先作夢都不敢夢到的，尤其語文部分 570 分更可說貴社的書籍功不可沒。目前我正在進行美國碩士班的申請，在欣喜之餘，特地提筆向貴社致上我最誠懇的謝意，並盼望貴社本著一貫的高水準，繼續造福有志學好英文的莘莘學子。

最後謹祝

　　編安

　　　　　　　　　　　　　　　　　　　×××　上

Lesson 1

用手機掃瞄聽錄音

Lesson 1

✦ **第一部分**

abroad
〔əˋbrɔd〕

He lived ***abroad*** for many years; he knows several foreign languages.
他在國外住了許多年；他知道幾種外國語言。

adv. 在國外；
　　　到國外
同 overseas

【記憶技巧】
ab (away) + ***road*** (way)（離開平常走的路，就是「到國外」）

affect
〔əˋfɛkt〕

The small amount of rain last year ***affected*** the growth of crops.
去年雨量少，影響農作物的生長。

v. 影響
同 influence

attend
〔əˋtɛnd〕

All children over seven must ***attend*** school. 七歲以上的小孩都必須上學。

v. 上 (學)；參加
名 attendance

【記憶技巧】
at (to) + ***tend*** (stretch)（往有人的地方伸展，就是「上 (學)；參加」）

blame
〔blem〕

Don't ***blame*** me. It's not my fault.
不要責備我。這不是我的錯。

v. 責備
反 praise;
　　 compliment

bubble
〔ˋbʌbl̩〕

Children like to make ***bubbles*** with soap and water.
孩子們喜歡用肥皂水做泡泡。

n. 泡泡

Lesson 1

cemetery
〔ˋsɛmə͵tɛrɪ〕

There are many tombs in the ***cemetery***. 墓地裡有許多墳墓。

【記憶技巧】
cemet (sleep) + ***ery*** (*n.*) (安息地，也就是「墓地」)

n. 墓地
同 graveyard

commendation
〔͵kɑmənˋdeʃən〕

He was given a ***commendation*** for bravery after he saved the little children from the fire. 他從火災中救出孩子們後，因為勇氣可嘉而受到稱讚。

n. 稱讚
同 praise; compliment
反 blame

conflict
〔ˋkɑnflɪkt〕

Some people think that there is a great deal of ***conflict*** between religion and science. 有些人認為宗教與科學之間有很大的衝突。

【記憶技巧】
con (together) + ***flict*** (strike) (彼此毆打，也就是有「衝突」)

n. 衝突；爭鬥
同 fight; struggle
反 reconciliation

cooperate
〔koˋɑpə͵ret〕

The children ***cooperated*** with their teachers in keeping their classrooms clean. 孩子們與老師合作保持教室清潔。

【記憶技巧】
co (together) + ***oper*** (work) + ***ate*** (*v.*) (一起工作，就是「合作」)

v. 合作
名 cooperation
形 cooperative

curious
〔ˋkjʊrɪəs〕

I am ***curious*** to know what my teacher said to my mother. 我很好奇想知道老師跟我母親說些什麼。

adj. 好奇的
同 inquisitive
反 indifferent

Exercise 1.1   從第一部分中選出最適當的一個英文字，填入空格內。

1. The news of his mother's death _____ him deeply.

2. A _____ is a place for burying the dead.

3. He is planning to go _____ next year for his studies.

4. He doesn't _____ church very often.

5. If a child is _____, he is always asking questions.

> 【解答】
> 1. affected   2. cemetery   3. abroad   4. attend   5. curious

✦ 第二部分

delicious
〔dɪˈlɪʃəs〕

We had some ***delicious*** cake after dinner.
我們在晚飯後吃了一些美味的蛋糕。

> 【記憶技巧】
> *de* (intensive) + *lic* (entice 引誘) +
> *ious* (*adj.*) (食物有著強烈的誘惑，表示
> 「美味的」)

adj. 美味的
同 tasty

direct
〔dəˈrɛkt〕

Which is the most ***direct*** way to London?
去倫敦最直接的路是哪一條？
There was nobody to ***direct*** the workmen.
沒有人指導工人。

adj. 直接的
反 indirect
v. 指導；監督
同 conduct;
    command

draw
〔drɔ〕

Draw your chair nearer to the table.
把你的椅子往桌子拉近一點。

v. 拉；畫
同 drag; haul

empire
〔'ɛmpaɪr〕

The United States was once a part of the British *Empire*.
美國曾經是大英帝國的一部分。

n. 帝國
同 realm

【記憶技巧】
em (in) + *pire* (order)

event
〔ɪ'vɛnt〕

The discovery of America was a great *event*.
發現美洲是一件大事。

n. 事件；(大型)活動
同 incident;
   happening

failure
〔'feljɚ〕

Success came after many *failures*.
成功在多次的失敗之後到來。

n. 失敗；失敗的人
反 success

file
〔faɪl〕

Please put these letters in the main *file*. 請將這些信件放入主要卷宗中。
The secretary *filed* the cards in order. 秘書將卡片依序歸檔。

n. 檔案；卷宗

v. 歸檔

frank
〔fræŋk〕

He was *frank* in admitting that he had not studied the lesson.
他坦白承認沒有唸那一課。

adj. 坦白的
同 candid; honest
反 deceitful;
   dishonest

generate
〔'dʒɛnə,ret〕

We know that heating water can *generate* steam.
我們知道將水加熱可以產生蒸氣。

v. 產生
同 produce;
   make

【記憶技巧】
gener (produce) + *ate* (v.)

halt
〔hɔlt〕

The soldiers *halted* for a rest.
士兵們停下來休息片刻。

v. 停止
同 stop

Exercise 1.2 從第二部分中選出最適當的一個英文字，填入空格內。

1. Her graduation from college was a(n) _____ I did not want to miss.

2. What _____ food you've cooked!

3. The picnic was a _____ because it rained.

4. If you want my _____ opinion, I don't think the plan will succeed.

5. The company _____ operations during the strike.

> 【解答】
> 1. event   2. delicious   3. failure   4. frank   5. halted

✦ 第三部分

horn〔hɔrn〕	A goat has two ***horns*** on its head. 山羊的頭上有兩隻角。	*n.* 角
individual〔͵ɪndə'vɪdʒʊəl〕	A teacher cannot give ***individual*** attention if his class is large. 如果班上的人數衆多，老師就不能個別地注意到每一個學生。	*adj.* 個別的
	The rights of the ***individual*** are more important than the rights of society as a whole. 個人的權利比整個社會的權利要重要得多。	*n.* 個人 同 person

> 【記憶技巧】
> ***in*** (not) + ***divid*** (divide) + ***ual*** (*adj.*) (不能再分割，表示已經是獨立的個體)

interval
〔ˈɪntɚvḷ〕

There was a long *interval* before he replied.
他隔了一段很長的時間才回答。

【記憶技巧】
inter (between) + *val* (wall)（牆與牆之間的空間就是「間隔」）

n.（時間的）間隔；
休息時間
同 break; pause

knot
〔nɑt〕

The *knots* on your package must be tied tightly.
你包裹上的結必須綁緊。

【記憶技巧】
k + *not*（打不開的東西，就是「結」）

n. 結

liberal
〔ˈlɪbərəl〕

He is *liberal* in his views on marriage and divorce.
他對結婚和離婚的看法很開明。
They want their children to have a *liberal* education.
他們要他們的孩子接受通才教育。

adj. 1. 開明的

2. 通才的
反 professional

magnificent
〔mægˈnɪfəsṇt〕

The king was wearing a *magnificent* gold crown.
國王戴著華麗的金冠。

【記憶技巧】
magn (great) + *ific* (do) + *ent* (*adj.*)

adj. 壯麗的
同 grand;
splendid
名 magnificence

mental
〔ˈmɛntḷ〕

Maintaining *mental* health is very important in modern society. 在現代社會中，維護心理健康是非常重要的。

【記憶技巧】
ment (mind) + *al* (*adj.*)

adj. 心理的
反 physical

momentary
〔'momən,tɛrɪ 〕

Her feeling of danger was only ***momentary***; it soon passed.
她的危險感只是暫時的；很快就消失了。

adj. 暫時的
同 transient
反 everlasting

neutral
〔'njutrəl 〕

He remained ***neutral*** in the argument between his two friends.
他在兩個朋友的爭論中保持中立。

adj. 中立的
同 impartial

【記憶技巧】
neutr (neither) + ***al*** (*adj.*)（不介入兩方，表示立場是「中立的」）

omit
〔 o'mɪt , ə'mɪt 〕

He made many mistakes in spelling by ***omitting*** letters. 他因漏掉字母而犯了許多拼字上的錯誤。

v. 省略；遺漏

【記憶技巧】
o (away) + ***mit*** (send)（把東西送走，忘了帶，就是「遺漏」）

Exercise 1.3 從第三部分中選出最適當的一個英文字，填入空格內。

1. We didn't think that you would come here, because your name was ＿＿＿＿ from the list.

2. The judge in a court must be ＿＿＿＿ in a trial.

3. Each ＿＿＿＿ leaf on the tree is different.

4. There is a(n) ＿＿＿＿ of a week between Christmas and New Year's Day.

5. There are probably as many kinds of ＿＿＿＿ illnesses as there are kinds of physical illnesses.

【解答】
1. omitted　2. neutral　3. individual　4. interval　5. mental

✦ 第四部分

peacock
〔ˈpiˌkɑk〕

A ***peacock*** can fly only short distances. 孔雀只能飛很短的距離。

【記憶技巧】
pea（豌豆）+ ***cock***（公雞）

n. 孔雀

pioneer
〔ˌpaɪəˈnɪr〕

John Glenn was a ***pioneer*** in space travel.
約翰‧葛倫是太空旅行的先驅。

n. 先驅
同 forerunner

pray
〔pre〕

I will ***pray*** to God for your safe return.
我會向上帝祈禱你的平安歸來。

v. 祈禱

pronounce
〔prəˈnaʊns〕

The teacher ***pronounced*** each word slowly.
老師每一個字都慢慢發音。
The doctor ***pronounced*** the man dead. 醫生宣告那男人死了。

【記憶技巧】
pro（out）+ ***nounce***（announce）
（向外宣佈，就是「發音；宣告」）

v. 1. 發音
名 pronunciation

2. 宣告
名 pronouncement

race
〔res〕

Many government forms ask you for your ***race***, for example, Caucasian, Hispanic, or Asian.
很多政府的表格會問你的種族是什麼，例如：白種人、西班牙裔美國人，或是亞洲人。
Please tell me which horse won the ***race***. 請告訴我哪一匹馬贏得比賽。

n. 1. 種族

2. 比賽

Lesson 1

relative
〔'rɛlətɪv〕

He has many *relatives* in the United States. 他在美國有很多親戚。

n. 親戚

East is a *relative* term; for example, France is east of England but west of Italy. 東方是個相對的名詞；譬如說，法國在英國的東方，但卻在義大利的西方。

adj. 相對的
反 absolute

resort
〔rɪ'zɔrt〕

In the end, the police *resorted* to force. 最後警方訴諸於武力。

v. 1. 訴諸於

When we were high school students, we *resorted* to the restaurant. 當我們是高中生時，常去這家餐廳。

2. 常去

Aspen is a famous ski *resort* in Colorado. 阿斯彭是科羅拉多州一個有名的滑雪勝地。

n. 度假勝地

【記憶技巧】
re (again, back) + *sort* (go out)（「度假勝地」會讓人「常去」）

rub
〔rʌb〕

He *rubbed* his hands together to warm up. 他摩擦雙手以取暖。

v. 摩擦

shadow
〔'ʃædo〕

The building cast its *shadow* across the street. 這棟大樓的影子投射在對街。

n. 陰影
同 shade

situation
〔ˌsɪtʃu'eʃən〕

I'm in a difficult *situation* and I don't know what to do. 我處在一個困難的情況中，不知道該怎麼辦。

n. 情況
同 condition;
case

【記憶技巧】
sit（坐）+ *uation* (*n.*)（坐的地方就是「情況」）

Exercise 1.4 從第四部分中選出最適當的一個英文字，填入空格內。

1. People of many _____ settled in the United States.

2. My uncle is my nearest _____.

3. With the light behind him, his _____ could be seen on the wall.

4. The doctor is regarded as a(n) _____ in operating on human hearts.

5. There is nothing that we can do now but _____ to God for help.

```
【解答】
1. races   2. relative   3. shadow   4. pioneer   5. pray
```

✦ 第五部分

sore〔 sor 〕	His *sore* leg made walking difficult. 疼痛的腿使他步行困難。	*adj.* 疼痛的 同 aching; painful
spread〔 sprɛd 〕	His sister *spread* a cloth on the table. 他的姊姊把一塊桌布舖在桌上。	*v.* 散播； 舖（桌布）
stomach〔'stʌmək 〕	It is unwise to swim on a full *stomach*. 肚子飽時游泳是不明智的。	*n.* 胃；腹部
suitcase〔'sut͵kes 〕	He took two *suitcases* with him on the trip. 他旅行時帶著兩個手提箱。	*n.* 手提箱

```
【記憶技巧】
suit（一套衣服）＋ case（箱子）（「手提箱」約
可裝一套衣服）
```

Lesson 1

talent
〔ˈtælənt〕

The girl has a *talent* for music.
那女孩有音樂的才能。

n. 才能

throne
〔θron〕

He was only 15 years old when he came to the *throne*.
當他登基時，只有十五歲。

n. 王位

transfer
〔træns'fɝ〕
〔ˈtrænsfɝ〕

The football player is hoping to *transfer* to another team soon.
該足球員希望不久能調到另一隊。

v. 轉移

He has asked for a *transfer* to another job. 他已要求調職。

n. 調職

---【記憶技巧】---
trans (across) + *fer* (carry)（越過某地運送，就是「轉移」）

usage
〔ˈjusɪdʒ〕

Machines soon wear out under rough *usage*. 機器使用不小心很快就會磨損。

n. 用法；使用

vowel
〔ˈvaʊəl〕

The *vowels* in the English language are represented by a, e, i, o, u, and, sometimes, y. 英文中的母音以 a, e, i, o, u 為代表，有時再加上 y。

n. 母音
反 consonant

withdraw
〔wɪð'drɔ〕

He quickly *withdrew* his hand from the hot stove.
他迅速地把手從熱火爐上縮回。

v. 撤退；縮回
反 advance

---【記憶技巧】---
with (back) + *draw*（拉）

Exercise 1.5 從第五部分中選出最適當的一個英文字，填入空格內。

1. _____ are more difficult to pronounce than consonants.

2. It is not wise to work on an empty _____.

3. The general decided to _____ the troops from the present position.

4. The boy showed a real _____ for painting.

5. He has been _____ to another branch in Boston.

> 【解答】
> 1. Vowels   2. stomach   3. withdraw   4. talent   5. transferred

成果測驗

I. 找出一個與其他三個不相關的字：

( ) 1. (A) compliment   (B) commendation
       (C) approach   (D) praise

( ) 2. (A) attend   (B) draw   (C) haul   (D) drag

( ) 3. (A) candid   (B) curious   (C) frank   (D) honest

( ) 4. (A) interval   (B) omit   (C) break   (D) pause

( ) 5. (A) splendid   (B) neutral
       (C) magnificent   (D) grand

( ) 6. (A) race   (B) situation   (C) condition   (D) case

( ) 7. (A) aching   (B) painful   (C) delicious   (D) sore

( ) 8. (A) conflict   (B) event   (C) struggle   (D) fight

( ) 9. (A) obey   (B) command   (C) conduct   (D) direct

( ) 10. (A) happening   (B) event   (C) incident   (D) pioneer

Ⅱ. 找出一個與題前中文意思相同的英文字：

( ) 1. 影響
    (A) conflict   (B) cooperate
    (C) affect   (D) attend

( ) 2. 責備
    (A) blame   (B) responsibility
    (C) stomach   (D) talent

( ) 3. 美味的
    (A) curious   (B) delicious
    (C) dull   (D) candid

( ) 4. 先驅
    (A) bubble   (B) consonant
    (C) peacock   (D) pioneer

( ) 5. 親戚
    (A) neutral   (B) relative
    (C) uncle   (D) resort

Lesson 1

Ⅲ. 找出一個與斜體字意義相反的單字：

( ) 1. *compliment*
    (A) conflict   (B) blame   (C) success   (D) failure

( ) 2. *indifferent*
    (A) delicious   (B) dull
    (C) curious   (D) magnificent

( ) 3. *deceitful*
    (A) dull   (B) grand   (C) neutral   (D) frank

( ) 4. *momentary*
    (A) everlasting   (B) transient
    (C) liberal   (D) important

( ) 5. *withdraw*
    (A) haul   (B) draw
    (C) advance   (D) cooperate

Ⅳ. 完整拼出下列各句中所欠缺的單字，每一格代表一個字母：

1. Although he was a f_ _ _ _ _e at school, he became a successful man later. (失敗的人)

2. He was so c_ _ _ _ _s to know what was in the letter that he opened it, even though it was addressed to his sister. (好奇的)

3. Will you be quite f_ _ _k with me about this matter? (坦白的)

4. In their school they have an i_ _ _ _ _ _l of ten minutes for recess. (時間的間隔)

5. The police watched the café to which the robber was known to r_ _ _ _t. (常去)

V. 找出一個與句中斜體字意義最接近的單字：

( ) 1. Steam can *generate* electricity by turning an electric generator.
    (A) change   (B) produce
    (C) stop   (D) spread

( ) 2. He earned high *commendation* from the people for his bravery.
    (A) reward   (B) pride
    (C) praise   (D) consideration

( ) 3. The policeman *halted* the speeding car to see if the driver was drunk.
    (A) stopped   (B) found
    (C) chased   (D) caught

( ) 4. I have a *sore* throat because I have a cold.
    (A) strong   (B) weak
    (C) clear   (D) painful

( ) 5. I will show you the *magnificent* palace of the king.
    (A) grand   (B) ancient
    (C) colorful   (D) dull

Lesson 1

---- 【解答】 --
I. 1. C 2. A 3. B 4. B 5. B 6. A 7. C 8. B 9. A 10. D
II. 1. C 2. A 3. B 4. D 5. B
III. 1. B 2. C 3. D 4. A 5. C
IV. 1. failure 2. curious 3. frank 4. interval 5. resort
V. 1. B 2. C 3. A 4. D 5. A

Lesson 2

✦ 第一部分

Lesson 2

absolute （'æbsə,lut）	He is a man of ***absolute*** honesty. 他是個絕對誠實的人。	*adj.* 絕對的 反 relative

┌─【記憶技巧】─────────┐
諧音：惡霸收入，「絕對的」多。
└───────────────┘

agency （'edʒənsɪ）	The Ford Company has ***agencies*** all over the country. 福特公司在全國都有經銷處。	*n.* 代辦處； 經銷處
attitude （'ætə,tjud）	He took a sympathetic ***attitude*** toward my situation. 他對我的情況抱持同情的態度。	*n.* 態度
blank （blæŋk）	Please write your name in the ***blank*** space at the top of the page. 請把你的名字寫在此頁上頭的空白處。	*adj.* 空白的 同 empty
bulk （bʌlk）	The ***bulk*** of the coal is still stored in the basement. 大部份的煤仍儲存在地下室。	*n.* 大部份； 容量；體積 同 volume
ceremony （'sɛrə,monɪ）	Their marriage ***ceremony*** was performed in the church. 他們的結婚典禮在教堂舉行。	*n.* 典禮
commerce （'kɑmɝs）	Our country has grown rich because of its ***commerce*** with other nations. 我國由於與他國間的貿易而致富。	*n.* 商業；貿易 形 commercial 同 trade

┌─【記憶技巧】─────────┐
com (together) + ***merce*** (trade)（共同交易，就是「商業；貿易」）
└───────────────┘

confuse 〔 kənˈfjuz 〕	Their own mother sometimes *confused* the twins. 雙胞胎自己的母親，有時候也會混淆。	*v.* 使困惑；混淆 名 confusion 同 puzzle; baffle; bewilder

【記憶技巧】
con (together) + *fuse* (pour)（太多事情同時注入，會「使困惑；混淆」）

copper 〔ˈkɑpɚ 〕	*Copper* is easily shaped into a thin sheet or fine wire. 銅易於塑成薄板或細線。	*n.* 銅
curse 〔 kɝs 〕	In the story, the witch put a *curse* on the princess. 在這個故事中，巫婆對公主下了詛咒。	*v. n.* 詛咒；咒罵

Lesson 2

Exercise 2.1 從第一部分中選出最適當的一個英文字，填入空格內。

1. He stood there in a threatening _____.

2. _____ is an excellent conductor of heat and electricity.

3. He _____ when a car almost hit him.

4. Long ago some rulers had _____ power.

5. If you try to learn too many things at the same time you may get _____.

【解答】
1. attitude   2. Copper   3. cursed   4. absolute   5. confused

✦ 第二部分

Lesson 2

delight
〔 dɪˈlaɪt 〕

Movies give great ***delight*** to millions of people.
電影提供數以百萬計的人們很大的娛樂。

n. 愉快
同 pleasure

disappear
〔 ˌdɪsəˈpɪr 〕

The little boy ***disappeared*** around the corner.
那小男孩在街角處消失。

v. 消失
同 vanish
反 appear

drift
〔 drɪft 〕

The boat was ***drifting*** down the stream.　那艘船順著溪流往下漂。

v. 漂流

employ
〔 ɪmˈplɔɪ 〕

That big factory ***employs*** many workers.　那家大工廠雇用許多工人。

v. 雇用
同 hire

evidence
〔 ˈɛvədəns 〕

When the police arrived, he had already destroyed all the ***evidence***.
當警方到達時，他已毀滅所有的證據。

n. 證據
形 evident
副 evidently

┌─【記憶技巧】─────────┐
e (out) + *vid* (see) + *ence* (*n.*) (外面看得
到，變成「證據」)
└──────────────────────┘

faculty
〔 ˈfækḷtɪ 〕

John has the ***faculty*** to learn languages easily.
約翰有迅速學會語言的能力。
That will be discussed at the next ***faculty*** meeting.
那將會在下一次的教職員會議中討論。

n. 1. 能力
同 capability

2. 全體教職員

┌─【記憶技巧】─────────┐
fac (make) + *ulty* (*n.*) (做事情要有「能
力」，才能成爲「教職員」)
└──────────────────────┘

financial
〔 faɪˈnænʃəl 〕

Before he decides to study abroad, he has to solve some ***financial*** problems.　在他決定出國唸書前，必須先解決一些財務問題。

adj. 財務的
名 finance

freight
〔 fret 〕

This aircraft company deals with ***freight*** only; it has no passenger service. 這家航空公司只經營貨運；它沒有乘客服務。

n. 貨物
同 cargo

> ┌── 【記憶技巧】
> │ 先記 weight (重量)，字首再改成 fr，因為
> │ 「貨物」都有重量。

generous
〔'dʒɛnərəs 〕

It was very ***generous*** of them to share their meal with their poor neighbors. 他們願意讓貧苦的鄰居共享餐食，甚為慷慨。

adj. 慷慨的；
　　　 寬厚的
反 stingy
名 generosity

handy
〔'hændɪ 〕

There were ***handy*** shelves near the kitchen sink.
廚房的水槽邊有便利的架子。

adj. 便利的
同 convenient

Exercise 2.2 從第二部分中選出最適當的一個英文字，填入空格內。

1. He was very _____ in his treatment of the captives.

2. He has a great _____ for arithmetic.

3. The city of London is a great _____ center in Europe.

4. The steel manufacturing company _____ most of the young men in town.

5. This _____ must be carefully handled when being loaded.

> ┌── 【解答】
> │ 1. generous   2. faculty   3. financial   4. employs   5. freight

Lesson 2

✦ 第三部分

Lesson 2

horrible
〔'hɑrəbḷ 〕

I have never seen such a ***horrible*** car accident.
我從未見過如此可怕的車禍。

adj. 可怕的
同 ghastly
名 horror

industrious
〔 ɪn'dʌstrɪəs 〕

An ***industrious*** student usually has good grades.
勤勉的學生通常有好成績。

adj. 勤勉的
同 diligent;
　　hardworking

【記憶技巧】
industry（工業；勤勉）有兩個形容詞，另一個是 industrial（工業的）。

intimate
〔'ɪntəmɪt 〕

Although my brother knew many people, he had few ***intimate*** friends.
雖然我兄弟認識許多人，但親密的朋友卻很少。

adj. 親密的
名 intimacy
副 intimately

knowledge
〔'nɑlɪdʒ 〕

A baby has no ***knowledge*** of good and evil. 嬰兒不了解善惡。

n. 知識；了解

liberty
〔'lɪbɚtɪ 〕

They fought to defend their ***liberty*** against the invaders.
他們爲保衛自由而抵抗侵略者。

n. 自由

majesty
〔'mædʒəstɪ 〕

They were inspired by the ***majesty*** of the snow-covered mountains.
他們由積雪山脈的雄偉氣氛中獲得啓示。

n. 莊嚴；雄偉
同 dignity;
　　greatness;
　　grandeur

【記憶技巧】
想到 <u>maj</u>or（主要的；重大的），就能聯想到 <u>maj</u>esty（莊嚴；雄偉）了。

mention
〔'mɛnʃən 〕

Do not ***mention*** the terrible accident in front of the little children.
在小孩面前，不要提到那件可怕的意外。

v. 提到

monument (ˈmɑnjəmənt)	The ruins of the castle are an ancient ***monument***, which the government pays money to preserve. 城堡的廢墟是古代的紀念物，政府有花錢保存。	*n.* 紀念碑； 紀念物 同 memorial

【記憶技巧】
monu (remind) + ***ment*** (*n.*) (「紀念碑」會讓人想起過去發生的事)

nickname (ˈnɪkˌnem)	He got the ***nickname*** "Fatty" because he was very fat. 他非常胖，因而得到「胖子」的綽號。	*n.* 綽號

onion (ˈʌnjən)	***Onion*** has a very strong smell and taste. 洋蔥有非常強烈的氣味和味道。	*n.* 洋蔥

Exercise 2.3　從第三部分中選出最適當的一個英文字，填入空格內。

1. He is a(n) _____ student and deserves good grades.

2. The _____ of the Niagara Falls attracts a lot of visitors.

3. I heard many _____ stories from my grandfather when I was young.

4. She opened the cage and gave the bird its _____.

5. He has a good _____ of French history.

【解答】
1. industrious   2. majesty   3. horrible   4. liberty   5. knowledge

✦ 第四部分

peak 〔 pik 〕	The mountain **peak** is covered with snow all year round. 山頂終年覆蓋著雪。	*n.* 山頂 同 summit 反 foot
pit 〔 pɪt 〕	He was covered from head to toe in coal dust, like a miner coming up from the **pit**. 他從頭到腳全是煤灰，就像一個礦工剛從坑道裡出來一樣。	*n.* 洞；坑 同 hole
preach 〔 pritʃ 〕	Many people went to church to hear him **preach**. 許多人到教堂聽他傳教。	*v.* 說教；傳教

【記憶技巧】
p + **reach**（達到）

proof 〔 pruf 〕	We must wait for better **proof** before we believe. 在我們相信以前，必須等待更有力的證據。	*n.* 證據 動 prove 同 evidence
rag 〔 ræg 〕	She wiped her boots with a **rag**. 她用一塊破布擦她的靴子。	*n.* 破布 形 ragged
release 〔 rɪ'lis 〕	After he was **released** from prison, he came home directly. 他被釋放出獄後，立刻回家。	*v.* 釋放 反 hold

【記憶技巧】
re + **l** + **ease**（放鬆）

responsibility 〔 rɪ͵spɑnsə'bɪlətɪ 〕	Now that you are 13, you should have a greater sense of **responsibility**. 既然你已十三歲，就應有更多的責任感。	*n.* 責任 形 responsible

Lesson 2

rude 〔 rud 〕	It is **rude** to stare at people or to point with a finger. 瞪眼看人或用手指人，都是不禮貌的。	*adj.* 無禮的 同 impolite 反 polite
scorn 〔 skɔrn 〕	We feel **scorn** for a traitor. 我們輕視背叛者。 ---【記憶技巧】--- **s + corn**（玉米）	*n.* 輕視　*v.* 瞧不起； 　　　　　不屑；輕視 同 contempt 反 respect
shallow 〔'ʃælo 〕	The lake is too **shallow** for swimming. 那湖太淺無法游泳。	*adj.* 淺的 反 deep

Exercise 2.4 從第四部分中選出最適當的一個英文字，填入空格內。

1. Do you have any _____ that you weren't there at nine o'clock last night?

2. The nurse will be _____ from duty at seven o'clock.

3. Most pupils feel _____ for those who cheat in an exam.

4. He _____ that God would soon destroy the evil world.

5. Don't be so _____ to your teacher.

---【解答】---
1. proof　2. released　3. scorn　4. preached　5. rude

✦ 第五部分

soul 〔 sol 〕	They were praying for the **souls** of the dead. 他們正為死者的靈魂祈禱。	*n.* 靈魂 同 spirit 反 body

sprinkle
〔'sprɪŋkl̩〕

He *sprinkled* sand along the icy path. 他沿著結冰的路撒砂子。

v. 撒；灑
同 scatter

【記憶技巧】
先記 spring（春天），字尾改成 kle，
因為春天會「撒」水給大地。

stoop
〔stup〕

He *stooped* to pick up the paper.
他彎腰撿紙。

v. 彎腰
同 bend

【記憶技巧】
先記 stop（停止）＋o，「彎腰」前要先
停下來。

sum
〔sʌm〕

He paid the *sum* of $10 for a new bag. 他以十元的價格買一個新袋子。
The *sum* of 2 and 3 is 5.
二加三的和是五。

n. 1. 金額

2. 和；總和
同 amount

talkative
〔'tɔkətɪv〕

No man likes *talkative* women.
沒有男人喜歡愛說話的女人。

adj. 愛說話的

throughout
〔θru'aʊt〕

His name is famous *throughout* the world. 他的名字聞名全世界。

prep. 遍及

transport
〔træns'port〕

Wheat is *transported* from the farms to the mills.
小麥被從農場運送至麵粉廠。

v. 運送
名 transportation

utter
〔'ʌtɚ〕

He was gone before she could *utter* a word.
她還未開口說一句話，他就走了。
She is an *utter* stranger to me.
對我來說，她完全是一個陌生人。

v. 說出
名 utterance

adj. 完全的
同 complete

Lesson 2

voyage
〔'vɔɪ·ɪdʒ 〕

The *voyage* from England to India used to take six months.

過去從英國航行到印度，要花六個月的時間。

n. 航行
同 navigation

--- 【記憶技巧】---
voy (way) + *age* (n.) (順著海的路線行走，也就是「航行」)

wither
〔'wɪðɚ 〕

The grass *withered* in the sun.

草在陽光下枯萎了。

v. 枯萎
同 fade

Exercise 2.5 　從第五部分中選出最適當的一個英文字，填入空格內。

1. Many people believe in the immortality of the _____.

2. The flowers _____ in the cold.

3. She _____ to get into the car.

4. We _____ ashes on the icy sidewalk this morning.

5. The goods were _____ by rail and ship.

--- 【解答】---
1. soul　2. wither(ed)　3. stooped　4. sprinkled　5. transported

Lesson 2

成果測驗

I. 找出一個與斜體字的意義最接近的單字：

( ) 1. a great *faculty* for music
    (A) member   (B) capability
    (C) audience   (D) knowledge

( ) 2. clear *evidence*
    (A) proof   (B) knowledge   (C) situation   (D) agency

( ) 3. a bulk of *freight*
    (A) weight   (B) surprise   (C) failure   (D) cargo

( ) 4. a *handy* little box
    (A) relative   (B) heavy   (C) convenient (D) cheap

( ) 5. a *horrible* accident
    (A) dangerous (B) ghastly   (C) sore   (D) big

( ) 6. the *majesty* of the mountains
    (A) grandeur (B) faculty   (C) monument (D) honor

( ) 7. the *peak* of a mountain
    (A) foot   (B) summit   (C) height   (D) horn

( ) 8. *rude* remarks
    (A) loud   (B) impolite   (C) direct   (D) candid

( ) 9. to *sprinkle* water on the road
    (A) scatter   (B) draw   (C) drink   (D) gather

( ) 10. large *sum* of money
    (A) spending (B) peak   (C) amount   (D) resort

II. 找出一個與題前中文意思相同的英文字：

(　) 1. 撒；灑
　　(A) pour　　　　(B) halt　　　(C) scorn　　　(D) sprinkle

(　) 2. 枯萎
　　(A) rub　　　　(B) utter　　　(C) wither　　　(D) resort

(　) 3. 商業
　　(A) commerce　(B) industry　(C) finance　　(D) freight

(　) 4. 詛咒
　　(A) release　　(B) curse　　　(C) blame　　　(D) pray

(　) 5. 說教
　　(A) utter　　　(B) mention　　(C) preach　　(D) affect

III. 找出一個與斜體字意義相反的單字：

(　) 1. *disappear*
　　(A) vanish　　(B) spread　　(C) appear　　　(D) attend

(　) 2. *generous*
　　(A) liberal　　(B) mean　　　(C) special　　(D) common

(　) 3. *industrious*
　　(A) handy　　(B) diligent　(C) lazy　　　(D) agricultural

(　) 4. *release*
　　(A) hold　　　(B) work　　　(C) withdraw　(D) draw

(　) 5. *rude*
　　(A) frank　　(B) low　　　(C) peak　　　(D) polite

(　) 6. *scorn*
　　(A) contempt　(B) wet　　(C) cooperation　(D) respect

( ) 7. *shallow*
    (A) delightful (B) shade (C) deep   (D) delicious

( ) 8. *soul*
    (A) straight (B) body (C) haul   (D) grand

( ) 9. *absolute*
    (A) relative (B) present (C) intimate (D) diligent

( ) 10. *delight*
    (A) pleasure (B) sorrow (C) horror   (D) scorn

IV. 完整拼出下列各句中所欠缺的單字，每一格代表一個字母：

1. It is r_ _e to say you don't like the food when she spent so long preparing it. (無禮的)

2. He seemed to s_ _ _n women, and never married. (瞧不起)

3. He becomes very t_ _ _ _ _ _ _e when he gets drunk. (愛說話的)

4. His a_ _ _ _ _ _e toward school changed from one of dislike to one of great enthusiasm. (態度)

5. He is a member of the college f_ _ _ _ _y. (全體教職員)

V. 選出最適合句意的一個單字：

( ) 1. Despite his great _____, he was able to fit into the small car.
    (A) empire   (B) pit   (C) bubble   (D) bulk

( ) 2. To his great _____, he passed the examination easily.
    (A) delight   (B) despair
    (C) faculty   (D) convenience

(   ) 3. There was not enough _____ to prove him guilty of the crime.

    (A) faculty   (B) evidence   (C) conflict   (D) police

(   ) 4. Though he didn't have much money to give, he was very _____ with his money.

    (A) curious   (B) magnificent

    (C) generous   (D) neutral

(   ) 5. They built a _____ in memory of Abraham Lincoln.

    (A) monument   (B) cemetery

    (C) freight   (D) majesty

VI. 將題前的斜體字轉換爲適當詞性，填入空格中：

1. *horrible*   The little girl has a _____ of snakes and spiders.

2. *intimate*   The _____ with which the two friends talked showed how fond they were of each other.

3. *confuse*   If you write more clearly, you will prevent _____ among your readers.

4. *utter*   His crazy _____ disappointed everyone around him.

5. *proof*   In order to _____ the servant's honesty, she left a bag containing money on the table.

【解答】

  I. 1. B   2. A   3. D   4. C   5. B   6. A   7. B   8. B   9. A   10. C

  II. 1. D   2. C   3. A   4. B   5. C

  III. 1. C   2. B   3. C   4. A   5. D   6. D   7. C   8. B   9. A   10. B

  IV. 1. rude   2. scorn   3. talkative   4. attitude   5. faculty

  V. 1. D   2. A   3. B   4. C   5. A

  VI. 1. horror   2. intimacy   3. confusion   4. utterance   5. prove

Lesson 2

Lesson 3

✦ 第一部分

academic
〔,ækə'dɛmɪk 〕
The ***academic*** year begins when school opens in September.
學年是從學校九月開學時開始。
adj. 學術的
同 scholastic

ahead
〔 ə'hɛd 〕
Tom was a quick walker, so he soon got ***ahead*** of the others.
湯姆是個走路很快的人，所以他不久就走在別人前面了。
adv. 在前地

【記憶技巧】
a + ***head*** (頭)

attraction
〔 ə'trækʃən 〕
He cannot resist the ***attraction*** of the sea in hot weather. 在炎熱的天氣中，他無法抵抗海的吸引力。
n. 吸引力
動 attract

blaze
〔 blez 〕
I put some wood on the fire and it soon burst into a ***blaze***. 我放一些木柴在火中，很快就發出火焰。
n. 火焰
同 flame

challenge
〔'tʃælɪndʒ 〕
I ***challenged*** him to a game of tennis. 我向他挑戰比網球比賽。
v. 挑戰

commit
〔 kə'mɪt 〕
A man who steals ***commits*** a crime. 偷竊的人犯罪。
He ***committed*** himself to the doctor's care.
他將自己委託給醫生照顧。
v. 1. 犯 (罪)

2. 委託
名 commitment

【記憶技巧】
com (together) + ***mit*** (let go) (叫別人帶著一起走，即是「委託」，帶了東西，易見財起意，就會「犯罪」)

congress
〔'kɑŋgrəs 〕

In some countries, the *congress* is composed of a senate and a house of representatives. 有些國家的國會是由參議院和衆議院組成。

n. 議會；會議；國會
同 parliament; assembly

> 【記憶技巧】
> *con* (together) + *gress* (walk) (參加「會議」時，大家會一同走去開會的地方)

correction
(kə'rɛkʃən)

Teachers usually make *corrections* in red ink. 老師通常用紅墨水批改。

n. 改正
動 correct

damp
(dæmp)

If you sleep between *damp* sheets, you will probably catch cold. 如果你睡在潮濕的被單裏，可能會著涼。

adj. 潮濕的
同 wet; moist

demand
(dɪ'mænd)

This sort of work *demands* great patience. 這種工作需要很大的耐心。

v. 要求；需要

> 【記憶技巧】
> *de* (completely) + *mand* (order) (完全以下令的方式，就是「要求」)

Lesson 3

Exercise 3.1 從第一部分中選出最適當的一個英文字，填入空格內。

1. Our school _____ the neighboring school's team to a game of football last week.

2. In the U.S.A., the _____, consisting of the Senate and the House of Representatives, is the law-making body.

3. If you fall into a river, your clothes will be wet; if you walk in the rain for a short time, they will be _____.

4. History and French are _____ subjects; typewriting and bookkeeping are commercial subjects.

5. Columbus was _____ of his times in his belief that the world was round.

> 【解答】
>
> 1. challenged　2. Congress　3. damp　4. academic　5. ahead

✦ 第二部分

disappoint
〔͵dɪsə'pɔɪnt〕

I was *disappointed* when I heard you couldn't come to the party. 當我聽到你不能來參加派對時，感到很失望。

v. 使失望
名 disappointment

> 【記憶技巧】
> *dis*（undo）+ *appoint*（指派）（沒有達成指派的任務，就是「使失望」）

drown
〔draʊn〕

The fisherman almost *drowned* when his boat was overturned. 當漁夫的船翻覆時，他差點淹死。

v. 淹死

encourage
〔ɪn'kɝɪdʒ〕

The teacher's praise *encouraged* the students to study hard. 老師的稱讚鼓勵了學生們用功讀書。

v. 鼓勵
同 inspire

Lesson 3

evident
(ˈɛvədənt)

It is now ***evident*** that, if I don't study hard, I'll fail the course.
現在情形很明顯，如果我不努力用功，我這一科就會不及格。

adj. 明顯的
名 evidence

【記憶技巧】
e (out) + *vid* (see) + *ent* (*adj.*) (可以看到外面的，表示「明顯的」)

fable
(ˈfebḷ)

He read stories to the children from an old book of ***fables***. 他唸一本舊的寓言書裏的故事給孩子們聽。

n. 寓言

firm
(fɝm)

We build houses on ***firm*** ground.
我們在堅硬的土地上蓋房子。

adj. 堅定的；
　　　堅硬的

frequent
(ˈfrikwənt)

Sudden rainstorms are ***frequent*** on this coast.
此處的海岸常有突然的暴風雨。

adj. 經常的
名 frequency

genius
(ˈdʒinjəs)

Important discoveries and inventions are usually made by men of ***genius***.
重要的發現和發明通常是有天才的人所爲。

n. 天才

harbor
(ˈhɑrbɚ)

The ship is in the ***harbor*** of New York.
那船停在紐約港中。

n. 港口

howl
(haʊl)

The dogs were ***howling*** at the stranger.
狗正向著那陌生人咆哮著。

v. 咆哮
同 yell; shout

【記憶技巧】
how + ***l***，擬聲音，唸起來像「好喔」)

Lesson 3

Exercise 3.2　從第二部分中選出最適當的一個英文字，填入空格內。

1. He jumped into the river and saved the _____ man.

2. It is not a(n) _____ but a real story.

3. The cheers of their schoolmates _____ the players to try to win the game for the school.

4. He was very _____ when I said he had to stay at home on Sunday.

5. The little girl's joy was _____ when she saw the present her father had bought her.

【解答】
1. drowning　2. fable　3. encouraged　4. disappointed　5. evident

✦ 第三部分

infamous
〔ˈɪnfəməs〕

Nobody likes him because he is an ***infamous*** liar.
每個人都不喜歡他，因為他是個聲名狼藉的騙子。

adj. 聲名狼藉的
回 notorious

introduce
〔ˌɪntrəˈdjus〕

The chairman ***introduced*** the speaker to the audience.
主席將演講人介紹給聽眾。

v. 介紹
名 introduction
形 introductory

【記憶技巧】
intro (inward) + ***duce*** (lead) (「介紹」別人的時候，通常會把他帶領到人群中讓大家看清楚)

Lesson 3

labor
〔'lebɚ〕

The majority of men earn their living by manual ***labor***.
大多數的人靠雙手勞動來謀生。

n. 勞動
形 laborious

lid
〔 lɪd 〕

Do not open the ***lid*** of the stove.
不要打開爐蓋。

n. 蓋子
同 cover

majority
〔 mə'dʒɔrətɪ 〕

The ***majority*** of people prefer peace to war.
大多數的人喜愛和平，不喜歡戰爭。

n. 大多數

mercy
〔'mɝsɪ 〕

He showed ***mercy*** to his enemies and let them live.
他對敵人展現了慈悲，讓他們活著。

n. 慈悲
形 merciful

moral
〔'mɔrəl 〕

The teacher felt a ***moral*** responsibility for the student's crime.
老師對那學生所犯的罪，感到有道義上的責任。

adj. 道德的
名 morality

【記憶技巧】
mor (custom) + ***al*** (*adj.*) (「道德」標準會因風俗習慣不同而產生差異)

nod
〔 nad 〕

The president ***nodded*** and everyone sat down around the table.
董事長點了頭，每個人就圍著桌子坐下。

v. 點頭

operate
〔'apə‚ret 〕

The machine ***operates*** day and night.
機器日夜地運作。

v. 操作；運作
名 operation

【記憶技巧】
oper (work) + ***ate*** (*v.*) (工作就是需要動手「操作」)

Lesson 3

painful
〔'penfəl〕
He had a *painful* cut on his thumb.　　*adj.* 疼痛的
他大拇指上有疼痛的割傷。

Exercise 3.3　從第三部分中選出最適當的一個英文字，填入空格內。

1. He tried to _____ a sewing machine.

2. Tobacco was _____ into Europe from America.

3. To win an election, a candidate must receive the _____ of the votes.

4. Land, _____, and capital are the three principal factors of production.

5. They showed little _____ to their enemies.

---【解答】---
1. operate　2. introduced　3. majority　4. labor　5. mercy

✦ 第四部分

pearl
〔 pɝl 〕
A natural *pearl* is much more expensive than a cultured one.　*n.* 珍珠
天然的珍珠比養珠要昂貴得多。

pitch
〔 pɪtʃ 〕
Every child likes to *pitch* stones into a lake. 每個孩子都喜歡將石頭拋入湖中。　*v.* 1. 投擲；拋
We *pitched* our tent under the tree.
我們在樹下紮營。　　　　2. 搭；紮

precious
（'prɛʃəs）

Time is *precious*; do not waste it on worthless deeds. 時間是寶貴的，不要把它浪費在無價值的行動上。

adj. 珍貴的；寶貴的

同 valuable

---【記憶技巧】---
preci (price) + *ous* (*adj.*)

property
（'prɑpətɪ）

The police found some stolen *property* hidden in the thief's house. 警察發現一些失竊物被藏在小偷的房子裏。

n. 財產；地產

rage
（redʒ）

He flew into a *rage* when he found they had gone without him. 當他發現他們已不告而別時，大為憤怒。

n. 憤怒

同 anger; fury

relieve
（rɪ'liv）

The medicine will soon *relieve* your headache. 那藥很快就會減輕你的頭疼。
We were *relieved* to hear that you had arrived safely.
聽到你已安全抵達，我們都放心了。

v. 1. 減輕
名 relief
2. 使放心；使鬆了一口氣

---【記憶技巧】---
re (again) + *lieve* (lift)（再拿起來，表示負擔「減輕」了）

restless
（'rɛstlɪs）

He couldn't sit still; he was very *restless*. 他無法坐著不動；他很不安。

adj. 不安的

rug
（rʌg）

There are several small *rugs* in the living room. 客廳裏有幾條小地毯。

n. 小塊地毯

同 carpet

scout
（skaut）

The *scouts* went out during the night. 偵察兵夜間出來。

n. 偵察員；偵察

---【記憶技巧】---
sc + *out*（到外面去看看，就是「偵察」）

Lesson 3

shame 〔ʃem〕	She felt *shame* at having been so thoughtless. 她對自己曾經如此疏忽感到羞恥。	*n.* 羞恥 同 humiliation 反 boldness

Exercise 3.4 從第四部分中選出最適當的一個英文字，填入空格內。

1. In his _____ at being scolded, he broke the teacher's vase.

2. The child blushed with _____ when he was caught stealing candy.

3. She received a beautiful necklace of _____ on her birthday.

4. The city is growing and _____ in the center is becoming more valuable.

5. The sick child passed a _____ night.

> 【解答】
> 1. rage　2. shame　3. pearls　4. property　5. restless

✦ 第五部分

sketch 〔skɛtʃ〕	He gave me a *sketch* of his plans for the expedition. 他給我一份他探險計畫的草案。	*n.* 素描；草案
sound 〔saʊnd〕	They heard the *sound* of the train whistle. 他們聽到火車的汽笛聲。 He has a *sound* body; he is in healthy condition. 他有健康的身體；他的健康情況良好。	*n.* 聲音 *adj.* 健全的

spy 〔 spaɪ 〕	The *spy* reported the development of a new weapon.　間諜報告新武器的進展。	*n.* 間諜
	His job was to *spy* on the enemy. 他的工作是偵察敵軍。	*v.* 偵察
storage 〔ˈstorɪdʒ 〕	A cold *storage* is used to keep eggs and meat from spoiling. 冷藏庫是用來防止蛋和肉腐壞。	*n.* 貯藏； 　　貯藏庫
summon 〔ˈsʌmən 〕	They were *summoned* to the bedside of their dying father. 他們被召喚至垂死父親的床邊。	*v.* 召喚

【記憶技巧】
sum (under) + *mon* (advise)（聽到通知而前來，表示受到「召喚」）

tame 〔 tem 〕	It is not difficult to ride a *tame* horse. 騎一匹溫馴的馬並不難。	*adj.* 溫馴的
	He *tamed* the lions for the circus. 他爲馬戲團馴服獅子。	*v.* 馴服
thrust 〔 θrʌst 〕	Jack *thrust* his hands into his pockets. 傑克把兩手插進口袋裏。	*v.* 插入

【記憶技巧】
想到 trust（信任）+ *h* = *thrust*，信任要「插入」人心。

trap 〔 træp 〕	The police set a *trap* to catch the escaped prisoner. 警方設下陷阱以逮捕逃犯。	*n.* 陷阱 同 snare
vaccinate 〔ˈvæksn̩ˌet 〕	He was *vaccinated* against several diseases at one time. 他接種疫苗，一次可抵抗好幾種疾病。	*v.* 接種疫苗
wage 〔 wedʒ 〕	His *wage* is $30 a week. 他的工資一星期三十元。	*n.* 工資

Lesson 3

witness
(ˈwɪtnɪs)

He made the remark in the presence of several **witnesses**.
他在幾個證人面前說了那些話。
The boy **witnessed** the accident.
那男孩目睹了意外事故。

n. 目擊者；
證人

v. 目睹

Exercise 3.5 從第五部分中選出最適當的一個英文字，填入空格內。

1. They were asking for a _____ increase of $5 a week.

2. She made a _____ of the landscape in pencil before painting it.

3. His furniture is in _____ while he looks for a new house.

4. The birds are so _____ that they eat from our hands.

5. I was _____ against typhus last month.

--------【解答】--------
1. wage   2. sketch   3. storage   4. tame   5. vaccinated

成果測驗

I. 找出一個與其他三個不相關的字：

(　) 1. (A) wet   (B) curious   (C) moist   (D) damp

(　) 2. (A) sum   (B) wage   (C) salary   (D) pay

(　) 3. (A) require   (B) demand   (C) claim   (D) desire

(　) 4. (A) sketch   (B) bulk   (C) outline   (D) plan

(　) 5. (A) dishonor (B) shame   (C) witness   (D) humiliation

(　) 6. (A) firm　　(B) hard　　(C) solid　　(D) damp

(　) 7. (A) notorious　　　　(B) infamous
　　　(C) horrible　　　　(D) disreputable

(　) 8. (A) rage　　(B) fury　　(C) anger　　(D) scorn

(　) 9. (A) common　　　　(B) unusual
　　　(C) numerous　　　　(D) frequent

(　) 10. (A) evident　　(B) absolute　　(C) clear　　(D) obvious

II. 找出一個與題前中文意思相同的英文字：

(　) 1. 溫馴的
　　　(A) rude　　(B) generous　　(C) tame　　(D) fame

(　) 2. 點頭
　　　(A) vanish　　(B) spy　　(C) haul　　(D) nod

(　) 3. 憤怒
　　　(A) wage　　(B) voyage　　(C) pitch　　(D) rage

(　) 4. 犯（罪）；委託
　　　(A) commit　　(B) relieve　　(C) release　　(D) scorn

(　) 5. 淹死
　　　(A) wage　　(B) drown　　(C) vaccinate　　(D) trap

III. 找出一個與斜體字意義相反的單字：

(　) 1. *evident*
　　　(A) firm　　(B) ambiguous　　(C) excellent　　(D) plain

(　) 2. *demand*
　　　(A) direct　　(B) command　　(C) request　　(D) grant

Lesson 3

(   ) 3. *encourage*
    (A) disappoint   (B) relieve
    (C) affect   (D) wither

(   ) 4. *frequent*
    (A) shallow   (B) evident   (C) rude   (D) rare

(   ) 5. *shame*
    (A) charm   (B) rug
    (C) boldness   (D) challenge

IV. 完整拼出下列各句中所欠缺的單字，每一格代表一個字母：

1. He is the only w_ _ _ _ _s of the accident. （證人）

2. I saw him t_ _ _ _t the tent pole into the ground. （插入）

3. Aspirin will r_ _ _ _ _e your headache. （減輕）

4. Children usually like to read old f_ _ _es. （寓言）

5. Einstein was a mathematical and scientific g_ _ _ _s. （天才）

V. 找出一個與句中斜體字意義最接近的單字：

(   ) 1. We could see the *blaze* of a cheerful fire through the window.
    (A) pitch   (B) rage   (C) fury   (D) flames

(   ) 2. My parents will be *disappointed* if I fail the examination again.
    (A) saddened   (B) disappeared
    (C) vanished   (D) released

(   ) 3. They put meat in the *trap* to attract the lion.
    (A) rug   (B) rag   (C) snare   (D) freight

Lesson 3

(　) 4. The church bells *summon* people to worship.

    (A) call　　(B) commit　　(C) pray　　(D) attract

(　) 5. The dog seemed *restless,* as if he sensed some danger.

    (A) shallow　　　　　(B) uneasy

    (C) generous　　　　　(D) painful

(　) 6. Your friendship is most *precious* to me.

    (A) firm　　(B) evident　　(C) rude　　(D) valuable

(　) 7. We heard a wolf *howl* near the house.

    (A) disappear　(B) yell　　(C) drown　　(D) thrust

(　) 8. He refused to join the army, believing that he had no *moral* right to kill.

    (A) ethical　　(B) normal　　(C) sound　　(D) bold

(　) 9. The car is my *property*; you can't use it without my permission.

    (A) faculty　　　　　(B) possession

    (C) resort　　　　　(D) responsibility

(　) 10. The doctor said that the patient's heart was *sound*.

    (A) healthy　　(B) curious　　(C) candid　　(D) neutral

Lesson 3

【解答】

  I. 1. B　2. A　3. D　4. B　5. C　6. D　7. C　8. D　9. B　10. B

  II. 1. C　2. D　3. D　4. A　5. B

  III. 1. B　2. D　3. A　4. D　5. C

  IV. 1. witness　2. thrust　3. relieve　4. fables　5. genius

  V. 1. D　2. A　3. C　4. A　5. B　6. D　7. B　8. A　9. B　10. A

Lesson 4

✦ 第一部分

Lesson 4

---

accentuate
〔 æk'sɛntʃʊˌet 〕

The dark frame *accentuates* the brightness of the picture.
暗框使畫的亮度更明顯。

v. 強調；使更爲明顯
同 emphasize

> 【記憶技巧】
> *accent*（口音）+ *uate* (v.)（口音會「使」特徵「更爲明顯」）

---

aim
〔 em 〕

He *aimed* at the lion, fired, and killed it. 他瞄準獅子，開槍，然後把牠打死了。

v. 瞄準

The hunter took *aim* at the lion.
那獵人瞄準獅子。

n. 瞄準

---

audience
〔'ɔdɪəns 〕

The *audience* was very excited by the show.
觀衆因表演而非常興奮。

n. 觀衆

> 【記憶技巧】
> *audi* (hear) + *ence* (n.)（聆聽觀看的人，就是「觀衆」）

---

bless
〔 blɛs 〕

They brought the children to church, and the priest *blessed* them. 他們帶孩子到教堂，牧師爲他們祝福。

v. 祝福
反 damn; curse

---

bundle
〔'bʌndḷ 〕

We sent her a large *bundle* of presents on her birthday.
我們在她生日時送她一大包禮物。

n. 一大堆；包；包裹

---

characteristic
〔ˌkærɪktə'rɪstɪk 〕

What are the *characteristics* that distinguish the Chinese from the Japanese? 區別中國人和日本人的特徵是什麼？

n. 特性
動 characterize

communicate
〔 kə'mjunə‚ket 〕

We can now ***communicate*** with people in Europe and America by telephone.
我們現在可以藉著電話和在歐洲及美洲的人溝通。

Radio, television, and newspapers quickly ***communicate*** news to all parts of the world.
收音機、電視機,和報紙能迅速地傳達消息到全世界。

v. 1. 溝通

2. 傳達
名 communication

connect
〔 kə'nɛkt 〕

The two towns are ***connected*** by a railway.
這兩個城鎮由鐵路連接。

v. 連接
名 connection

【記憶技巧】
con (together) + ***nect*** (bind)
(連結在一起,即「連接」)

correspond
〔 ‚kɔrə'spɑnd 〕

Janet and Bob ***corresponded*** for many years before they met.
珍妮特和鮑伯在見面前已通信了好幾年。

The house exactly ***corresponds*** with my needs.
這棟房子正好符合我的需求。

v. 1. 通信

2. 符合
名 correspondence

【記憶技巧】
cor (together) + ***respond*** (answer) (相互回信,即「通信」)

Lesson 4

darken
〔'dɑrkṇ 〕

The sky quickly *darkened* after sunset.
日落後，天空很快地變暗。

v. 變暗；變黑
〔形〕 dark

Exercise 4.1 從第一部分中選出最適當的一個英文字，填入空格內。

1. The priest _____ the bread and wine in preparation for the ceremony.

2. His face _____ with anger when he heard the bad news.

3. A popular television program may have a(n) _____ of several million people.

4. A useful _____ of the cat is its ability to catch and kill mice.

5. His expenses do not _____ to his income.

> 【解答】
> 1. blessed　2. darkened　3. audience　4. characteristic　5. correspond

✦ 第二部分

deny
〔 dɪ'naɪ 〕

Their employer *denied* them an increase in wages. 他們的老闆拒絕給他們加薪。

v. 否認；拒絕
〔名〕 denial

discharge
〔 dɪs'tʃɑrdʒ 〕

The servant was *discharged* for being dishonest. 這僕人因不誠實而被解雇。
Factory chimneys *discharge* smoke into the atmosphere and make it dirty.
工廠的煙囪排煙到空氣裏，造成空氣污染。

v. 1. 解雇
〔同〕 dismiss
2. 排出

> 【記憶技巧】
> *dis* (not) + *charge* (收費)（ 不再向老闆收費，因為被「解雇」)

dull
〔 dʌl 〕

The blade of this knife is so *dull* that it will not cut a radish.
這把刀的刀刃太鈍，不能切小蘿蔔。

adj. 鈍的；
暗淡的
同 blunt; dim

endeavor
〔 ɪn'dɛvɚ 〕

He made an *endeavor* to save the drowning girl.
他努力去救那快要淹死的女孩。
The sick man did not *endeavor* to get better.
那病人沒有努力使自己的病況好一點。

n. 努力
同 effort

v. 努力

【記憶技巧】
en (in) + *deavor* (duty)（盡自己的責任，也就是要「努力」）

excellence
〔'ɛksḷəns 〕

His teacher praised him for the *excellence* of his report.
他的老師因他傑出的報告而稱讚他。

n. 優秀
形 excellent

【記憶技巧】
excel（勝過；擅長）+ *lence* (*n.*)

fade
〔 fed 〕

The flowers in the garden *faded* at the end of summer.
花園裏的花在夏末時枯萎。

v. 褪色；枯萎；凋謝
同 wither

fist
〔 fɪst 〕

He raised his *fist* and threatened to hit me. 他舉起拳頭威脅要打我。

n. 拳頭

frighten
〔'fraɪtṇ 〕

She was *frightened* to look down from the top of the tall building.
她害怕從高樓的頂端往下看。

v. 使害怕
名 fright

ghost
〔 gost 〕

They claim that the *ghost* of the murdered man appears every night.
他們聲稱被謀殺的死者的鬼魂每晚出現。

n. 鬼；鬼魂
同 apparition

Lesson 4

hardship
〔'hɑrdʃɪp〕

Hunger, cold, and sickness were among the **hardships** of pioneer life. 飢餓、寒冷，和疾病都是拓荒者艱難生活中的一部份。

n. 艱難
反 comfort

----【記憶技巧】----
-ship 為表「樣子」的字尾。

Exercise 4.2 從第二部分中選出最適當的一個英文字，填入空格內。

1. The old man's hearing has become _____, and you must speak loudly to him.

2. The Yellow River _____ its water into the Yellow Sea.

3. Everything is clear; how can we _____ the truth of his statement?

4. All memories of her childhood had _____ from her mind.

5. Thunder and lightning _____ most children and many adults.

----【解答】----
1. dull   2. discharges   3. deny   4. faded   5. frighten

✦ 第三部分

huge
〔hjudʒ〕

Samson was a man of **huge** physical strength. 參孫是個力量極大的人。

adj. 巨大的
同 enormous

inferior
〔ɪn'fɪrɪɚ〕

His grades are **inferior** to mine this semester. 這學期他的分數比我差。

adj. 較差的
反 superior

invent
〔 ɪn'vɛnt 〕

Alexander Graham Bell *invented* the telephone in 1876. 亞歷山大・格雷安・貝爾在一八七六年發明電話。

v. 發明
同 devise
名 invention

- 【記憶技巧】
in (upon) + *vent* (come)（「發明」東西，就是靈感突然跑來腦中）

lighten
〔'laɪtn̩ 〕

A candle *lightened* the darkness of the great hall.
一枝蠟燭照亮了黑暗的大廳。

v. 照亮

male
〔 mel 〕

Boys and men are *males*; girls and women are females　男孩和男人是男性；女孩和女人是女性。

n. 男性
反 female

merit
〔'mɛrɪt 〕

Each child will get a mark according to the *merit* of his work.　每個孩子都會依其工作的表現而被評分。

n. 優點；價值
同 worth

mortal
〔'mɔrtl̩ 〕

He received a *mortal* wound soon after the battle began.
戰爭才開始不久，他就得了致命傷。
It's beyond *mortal* power to bring a dead man back to life.
使死人復生是人力所不能及的。

adj. 1. 必死的

2. 人類的
名 mortality

- 【記憶技巧】
mort (dead) + *al* (*adj.*)

opportunity
〔,ɑpɚ'tjunətɪ 〕

I am glad to have this *opportunity* of speaking to you.
我很高興有和你說話的機會。

n. 機會
同 chance

- 【記憶技巧】
op (toward) + *portun* (harbor) + *ity* (*n.*)
（風吹進港口，就是「機會」來了）

Lesson 4

palace
〔'pælɪs〕

His home is a *palace* compared with our poor little house. 他家和我們貧窮的小房子比起來，可算是個宮殿。

n. 宮殿

---【記憶技巧】---
place 多加個 a，就是「宮殿」。

peasant
〔'pɛznt〕

Many *peasants* were needed to help with the harvest.
這農夫需要許多農人來幫忙採收。

n. 農夫
同 farmer

---【記憶技巧】---
將 pleasant（令人愉快的）中的 l 去掉，就是 peasant（農夫）。

Exercise 4.3 從第三部分中選出最適當的一個英文字，填入空格內。

1. They are building a new _____ for their king.

2. In most bird species, the _____ is bigger and more brightly colored than the female.

3. I have had no _____ to give him your message because I have not seen him.

4. Edison didn't _____ many useful things for money.

5. Whales and elephants are _____ animals.

---【解答】---
1. palace　2. male　3. opportunity　4. invent　5. huge

Lesson 4

✦ 第四部分

pity
〔'pɪtɪ 〕

I gave the beggar some money, feeling **pity** for him.
我同情那乞丐而給了他一些錢。

n. 同情
形 pitiful

---

preface
〔'prɛfɪs 〕

What did the writer say in the **preface** of the book?
作者在這本書的序言裏說了什麼？

n. 序言

┌ 【記憶技巧】
pre (before) + **face** (speak) (一本書開頭
說的話，就是「序言」)

---

proportion
〔 prə'porʃən 〕

The **proportion** of sunny days to rainy days last month was four to one.
上個月晴天和雨天的比例是四比一。

n. 比例

┌ 【記憶技巧】
pro (for) + **portion** (部分)(要分割成很多
部分，要按「比例」)

---

range
〔 rendʒ 〕

The power of God is outside the **range** of human understanding.
上帝的力量是超過人類所能理解的範圍。

n. 範圍
同 scope;
extent

---

religious
〔 rɪ'lɪdʒəs 〕

Religious services are held here every Sunday.
每週日都在此舉行宗教儀式。

adj. 宗教的
名 religion

---

resume
〔 rɪ'zum 〕

We **resumed** our journey after a short rest. 休息片刻後，我們繼續旅行。

v. 再繼續
名 resumption

┌ 【記憶技巧】
re (again) + **sume** (take) (再做一樣的動
作，也就是「再繼續」)

Lesson 4

ruin
〔'ruɪn 〕

Proper care protects our property from *ruin*. 適當的照顧可保護我們資產免於損壞。
She poured water all over my painting and *ruined* it.
她把水倒在我整張畫上，破壞了它。

n. 破壞
同 destruction
v. 破壞
同 destroy;
spoil

┌─【記憶技巧】─────────┐
│ 諧音：奴役，奴役「破壞」人權。 │
└──────────────────┘

scrape
〔 skrep 〕

The boy *scraped* the mud from his shoes.
那男孩刮掉他鞋子上的泥巴。

v. 刮；擦去

sharp
〔 ʃɑrp 〕

She cut the meat with a *sharp* knife.
她用銳利的刀切肉。
The meeting starts at two o'clock *sharp*; don't be late. 會議兩點整開始；不要遲到。

adj. 銳利的
反 blunt
adv. 整；準
同 exactly

skill
〔 skɪl 〕

The teacher managed her pupils with wonderful *skill*.
這位老師熟練地管理她的學生。

n. 技巧；技能；
熟練

Exercise 4.4 從第四部分中選出最適當的一個英文字，填入空格內。

1. Too much smoking and drinking will _____ your health.

2. Mix water and orange juice in the _____ of three to one.

3. After two weeks' vacation, he _____ his work.

4. The policeman felt _____ for the lost and crying child.

5. Everyone within the _____ of his voice heard the remark and laughed.

┌─【解答】────────────────────────────┐
│ 1. ruin   2. proportion   3. resumed   4. pity   5. range │
└────────────────────────────────────┘

✦ 第五部分

sour
〔saʊr〕

Some people do not like lemon juice; it tastes *sour*. 有些人不喜歡檸檬汁，因為它的味道很酸。

adj. 酸的
同 acid

square
〔skwɛr〕

A *square* has four equal sides and four 90-degree angles. 正方形有四個等邊和四個九十度的角。

n. 正方形

stout
〔staʊt〕

He was too *stout* to fit into his old clothes. 他太胖，以致於穿不下舊衣服。

adj. 肥胖的
同 fat
反 slender

【記憶技巧】
st + *out* (向外)，「肥胖的」人體型向外擴大

superintendent
〔ˌsuprɪnˈtɛndənt〕

He is the *superintendent* of this school. 他是此校的督學。

n. 監督者

tangle
〔ˈtæŋgl̩〕

I don't like to sew with thread that *tangles* easily. 我不喜歡用容易糾結的線縫。

v. 糾纏；糾結
同 entangle
反 disentangle

【記憶技巧】
t + *angle* (角度)，角度不同會「糾結」在一起

thumb
〔θʌm〕

He accidentally hit his *thumb* with the hammer. 他不小心用鐵鎚敲到了拇指。

n. 大拇指

treaty
〔ˈtritɪ〕

The peace *treaty* was signed in Paris last summer. 和平條約於去年夏天在巴黎簽訂。

n. 條約
同 agreement

Lesson 4

vanish 〔'vænɪʃ 〕	Their fear ***vanished*** when the storm ended. 當暴風雨結束時，他們的恐懼就消失了。	*v.* 消失 同 disappear 反 appear

> 【記憶技巧】
> ***van*** (empty) + ***ish*** (*v.*) (空間變空了，表示東西都「消失」了)

warfare 〔'wɔr‚fɛr 〕	Civilians as well as soldiers take part in modern ***warfare***. 現代戰爭中，平民和士兵一樣要參加。	*n.* 戰爭 同 war
witty 〔'wɪtɪ 〕	A ***witty*** person makes ***witty*** remarks. 機智的人說話很風趣。	*adj.* 機智的； 詼諧的

Exercise 4.5 從第五部分中選出最適當的一個英文字，填入空格內。

1. The thief ran into the crowd and _____.

2. That trade _____ was signed by five countries.

3. Most green grapes and green apples taste _____.

4. Your glove has a hole in the _____.

5. The _____ of our school is responsible for our education.

> 【解答】
> 1. vanished   2. treaty   3. sour   4. thumb   5. superintendent

Lesson 4

🚗 成果測驗

I. 找出一個與斜體字的意義最接近的單字：

( ) 1. a *bunch* of flowers
    (A) field   (B) sum   (C) bundle   (D) file

( ) 2. major *characteristics* of the animal
    (A) features   (B) realms
    (C) knots   (D) testimonies

( ) 3. to *deny* one's offer
    (A) preach   (B) reject   (C) curse   (D) accept

( ) 4. a *dull* color
    (A) keen   (B) ghastly   (C) horrible   (D) dim

( ) 5. to make every *endeavor*
    (A) effort   (B) evidence   (C) incident   (D) skill

( ) 6. the *faded* flowers
    (A) rubbed   (B) vanished
    (C) uttered   (D) withered

( ) 7. a limited *range* of ideas
    (A) charm   (B) scope   (C) snare   (D) aim

( ) 8. to *invent* a machine
    (A) bend   (B) hire   (C) devise   (D) repair

( ) 9. a certificate of *merit*
    (A) worth   (B) ceremony
    (C) summit   (D) commerce

Lesson 4

( ) 10. a peace *treaty*
    (A) testimony   (B) agreement
    (C) trade   (D) peasant

Ⅱ. 找出一個與題前中文意思相同的英文字：

( ) 1. 排出
    (A) deny   (B) frighten
    (C) vanish   (D) discharge

( ) 2. 拳頭
    (A) bunch   (B) fist   (C) thumb   (D) finger

( ) 3. 必死的
    (A) keen   (B) sharp   (C) mortal   (D) huge

( ) 4. 破壞
    (A) ruin   (B) despair
    (C) cemetery   (D) curse

( ) 5. 督學
    (A) excellence   (B) superintendent
    (C) faculty   (D) palace

Ⅲ. 找出一個與斜體字意義相反的單字：

( ) 1. *sharp*
    (A) huge   (B) shallow   (C) blunt   (D) lazy

( ) 2. *slender*
    (A) stout   (B) dull   (C) tame   (D) flimsy

Lesson 4

(   ) 3. *vanish*

    (A) draw   (B) appear   (C) wither   (D) deny

(   ) 4. *bless*

    (A) confuse   (B) stoop   (C) sprinkle   (D) damn

(   ) 5. *comfort*

    (A) peak   (B) trap   (C) hardship   (D) mercy

IV. 完整拼出下列各句中所欠缺的單字，每一格代表一個字母：

1. There was a large a_ _ _ _ _ _e at the theater. (觀眾)

2. Would you like to c_ _ _ _ _ _ _ _d with an English boy?
(通信)

3. His e_ _ _ _ _ _r to persuade her to go with him failed. (努力)

4. When he returns, he will r_ _ _ _e his previous job. (再繼續)

5. You'd better use a ruler to draw a s_ _ _ _e. (正方形)

V. 找出一個與句中斜體字意義最接近的單字：

(   ) 1. She became *stout* as she grew older.

    (A) tall   (B) fat   (C) stiff   (D) rude

(   ) 2. We *scraped* the old paint from the furniture.

    (A) rubbed   (B) resumed

    (C) rejected   (D) released

(   ) 3. He won a *huge* sum of money in the horse race.

    (A) generous   (B) enormous

    (C) grand   (D) splendid

Lesson 4

(   ) 4. Her white dress *accentuated* the redness of her sunburned arms.

(A) lightened   (B) affirmed

(C) encouraged   (D) emphasized

(   ) 5. Most foods are not good to eat when they have a *sour* taste.

(A) sore   (B) rotten   (C) bitter   (D) acid

VI. 將題前的斜體字轉換爲適當詞性，填入空格中：

1. *invent*   Necessity is the mother of _____.

2. *deny*   The minister asked the newspaper to print a _____ of the true story.

3. *correspond*   The library bought all the _____ between Queen Victoria and her daughters.

4. *communicate*   Radio and television are important means of _____.

5. *mortal*   If this disease spreads in the country, the doctors fear that there'll be a high _____.

【解答】

I. 1. C   2. A   3. B   4. D   5. A   6. D   7. B   8. C   9. A   10. B

II. 1. D   2. B   3. C   4. A   5. B

III. 1. C   2. A   3. B   4. D   5. C

IV. 1. audience   2. correspond   3. endeavor   4. resume
     5. square

V. 1. B   2. A   3. B   4. D   5. D

VI. 1. invention   2. denial   3. correspondence
     4. communication   5. mortality

Lesson 4

Lesson 5

✦ 第一部分

accept
(əkˈsɛpt)

She asked me to go to the party and I *accepted* her invitation.　她請我去派對，而我接受了她的邀請。

v. 接受
同 receive

【記憶技巧】
ac (to) + *cept* (take) (把東西拿過來，就是「接受」)

---

alarm
(əˈlarm)

Earthquakes are so common here that people don't feel much *alarm* at them. 一些地震在此常發生，因此人們對它們並不感到很驚慌。

v. 使驚慌
n. 驚慌；警報；鬧鐘
同 fear

【記憶技巧】
al (to) + *arm* (weapons) (拿著武器，會使別人「驚慌」)

---

author
(ˈɔθɚ)

Do you know who the *author* of this novel is?　你知道這本小說的作者是誰嗎？

n. 作者

【記憶技巧】
auth (make to grow) + *or* (人) (使事物產生的人，即「作者」)

---

blind
(blaɪnd)

The deaf and the *blind* deserve sympathy and help.　聾人和盲人應該得到同情和幫助。

adj. 瞎的；盲目的

---

burden
(ˈbɝdn̩)

She had too heavy a *burden* and became sick.　她負擔太重，因而生病。
The mule was *burdened* with the heavy load.　那騾子負著重擔。

n. 負擔

v. 使負重擔
反 unload

charitable
〔'tʃærətəbḷ〕

He was a ***charitable*** man who used his wealth to help the poor and sick. 他是個慈善的人，會用他的財富去幫助窮人和病人。

adj. 慈善的
同 benevolent
反 cruel
名 charity

companion
〔kəm'pænjən〕

John traveled around the world with me as my ***companion***.
約翰和我結伴一起環遊世界。

n. 同伴

> 【記憶技巧】
> ***com*** (together) + ***pan*** (bread) + ***ion*** (*n.*) (貧困的時候，願意把麵包拿出來分享的人，就是「同伴」)

conquer
〔'kɑŋkɚ〕

Scientists are seeking ways to ***conquer*** cancer.
科學家正在尋找方法以征服癌症。

v. 征服；克服

> 【記憶技巧】
> ***con*** (wholly) + ***quer*** (seek) (完全求得，就是「征服」)

costume
〔'kɑstjum〕

The professor was in academic ***costume*** when I saw him yesterday. 我昨天看到教授時，他正穿著大學服。

n. 服裝
同 dress

dash
〔dæʃ〕

In a moment of anger he ***dashed*** the glass against the door.
他一時氣憤而將玻璃杯摔到門上。

v. 猛衝；投擲
同 hurl; throw

Exercise 5.1 從第一部分中選出最適當的一個英文字，填入空格內。

1. The Romans _____ much of the ancient world.

2. The guides at the museum were dressed in Chinese _____.

3. The design of the new car was not _____ by the public.

4. Tom helped the _____ man across the road.

5. A person who lives or travels with you as a friend and helper is your _____.

【解答】
1. conquered 2. costume 3. accepted 4. blind 5. companion

✦ 第二部分

deposit
〔 dɪ'pazɪt 〕

He *deposited* quite a lot of money in the bank. 他把相當多的錢存在銀行裏。
There is often a *deposit* of sand and mud at the mouth of a river.
河口常有沙泥的沉澱。

v. 存（款）

n. 沉澱物；
(*pl.*) 礦藏

【記憶技巧】
de (down) + *posit* (put)（將錢放置在銀行，就是「存（款）」）

disclose
〔 dɪs'kloz 〕

The lifting of the curtain *disclosed* a beautiful painting.
簾幕開啟後，就顯露出一幅美麗的畫。

v. 洩露；露出
同 reveal
反 conceal

Lesson 5

dumb
〔 dʌm 〕

The class remained *dumb* when the teacher asked a difficult question.
當老師問了一個難題時，全班啞口無言。

adj. 啞的；
　　沉默的
同 mute

endure
〔 ɪn'djʊr 〕

Be quiet! I can't *endure* that noise any longer.
安靜！我再也忍受不了那個噪音了。

v. 忍受
同 bear
名 endurance

【記憶技巧】
en (in) + *dure* (last)（處於持續狀態，表示「忍受」）

exception
〔 ɪk'sɛpʃən 〕

You all must take the examination; I can make no *exception*. 你們全都必須參加考試，我不允許有例外。

n. 例外
形 exceptional

【記憶技巧】
except（除…之外）+ *ion* (n.)

extreme
〔 ɪk'strim 〕

The *extreme* penalty of the law is punishment by death.
法律上的極刑是死刑。

adj. 極度的
名 extremity

flame
〔 flem 〕

The whole village was in *flames* when we got there.
我們到那裏時，整個村子都陷入火海。

n. 火焰

glance
〔 glæns 〕

I *glanced* out of the window to see if the rain had stopped.
我從窗口向外看雨是否已停。
He looked over the newspapers with a hasty *glance*. 他匆匆地看過報紙。

v. 看一眼；
　　掃視

n. 看一眼
同 glimpse

hardware
〔 'hɑrd,wɛr 〕

He bought a hammer and other *hardware* at the store. 他在那家店裏買了一支鐵鎚和其他的五金工具。

n. 硬體；五金工具【集合名詞】
反 software

humble
〔ˈhʌmbḷ〕

The vastness of the universe makes a person feel **humble**.
宇宙的浩瀚使人覺得自身卑微。
Lincoln was born in a **humble** log cabin.
林肯在一個簡陋的小木屋裏出生。

adj. 1. 謙卑的；
卑微的
同 modest
反 proud
2. 簡陋的

Exercise 5.2 從第二部分中選出最適當的一個英文字，填入空格內。

1. You must answer all the questions without _____.

2. Helen Keller learned to speak; she was blind and deaf but not _____.

3. There are rich _____ of gold in those hills.

4. The _____ of the burning candle was yellow.

5. Locks, nails, screws, knives, and tools are _____.

【解答】
1. exception   2. dumb   3. deposits   4. flame   5. hardware

✦ 第三部分

influence
〔ˈɪnfluəns〕

His **influence** made me a better man.
他的影響使我成為一個更好的人。
Don't let me **influence** your decision. 不要讓我影響你的決定。

n. 影響
形 influential

v. 影響
同 affect

Lesson 5

investigate
〔 ɪn'vɛstə,get 〕

The police ***investigated*** the causes of a railway accident.
警察調查火車意外的原因。

【記憶技巧】
in (in) + ***vestig*** (trace) + ***ate*** (*v.*) (往內追蹤，就是「調查」)

v. 調查
同 examine
名 investigation

lack
〔 læk 〕

The plants died for ***lack*** of water. 那些植物死於缺水。

n. v. 缺乏
同 shortage; want

lightning
〔 'laɪtnɪŋ 〕

Lightning is usually followed by thunder.
在閃電之後通常有雷聲。

n. 閃電

mammal
〔 'mæml̩ 〕

A whale is not a fish, but a ***mammal***.
鯨魚不是魚，而是哺乳類動物。

n. 哺乳類動物

motion
〔 'moʃən 〕

Avoid unnecessary ***motion*** of your hand while you are writing. 當你寫字時，要避免不必要的手部動作。

n. 動作
同 movement

normal
〔 'nɔrml̩ 〕

The ***normal*** temperature of the human body is 36.5 degrees centigrade. 人體正常的溫度是攝氏三十六點五度。

adj. 正常的
同 regular
反 abnormal

oppose
〔 ə'poz 〕

I am very much ***opposed*** to your going abroad. 我極力反對你出國。

【記憶技巧】
op (against) + ***pose*** (put)

v. 反對
同 resist
反 agree

Lesson 5

palm
〔 pɑm 〕

She put a coin in the *palm* of the beggar's hand. 她將一枚硬幣放在乞丐的手掌中。

n. 手掌

peck
〔 pɛk 〕

The bird *pecked* a hole in the tree.
那隻鳥在樹上啄個洞。

v. 啄

Exercise 5.3 從第三部分中選出最適當的一個英文字，填入空格內。

1. A(n) _____ feeds its young with milk from the breast.

2. Detectives _____ crimes to find out who did them.

3. In the backyard I saw many hens _____ at the corn.

4. If a thing is in _____, it is not at rest.

5. Many people _____ building a new highway because of the cost.

┌─ 【解答】 ─────────────────────────────┐
  1. mammal   2. investigate   3. pecking   4. motion   5. oppose(d)
└────────────────────────────────────┘

✦ 第四部分

planet
〔 ˈplænɪt 〕

The earth is one of the *planets* that move around the sun.
地球是繞太陽轉的行星之一。

n. 行星

preparation
〔 ˌprɛpəˈreʃən 〕

We are getting things together in *preparation* for the trip.
我們為準備旅行而把東西放在一起。

n. 準備
動 prepare

Lesson 5

proposal 〔 prə'pozḷ 〕	He has made a *proposal* that she should take a rest for a while. 他建議她應該休息一會兒。	*n.* 提議；建議 同 suggestion 動 propose
rapid 〔'ræpɪd 〕	The *rapid* development of Taiwan surprised all other countries. 台灣的迅速發展，使所有其他的國家感到驚訝。	*adj.* 快速的； 迅速的 同 fast; swift
remarkable 〔 rɪ'mɑrkəbḷ 〕	She is *remarkable* for her sweet temper. 她溫和的性情使她氣質出眾。 【記憶技巧】 *re*（重覆）+ *mark*（標記）+ *able* (*adj.*)，「出眾的」人才會被反覆標記出來	*adj.* 出色的； 出眾的； 引人注目 的
retain 〔 rɪ'ten 〕	She *retains* a clear memory of her school days. 她仍清楚記得她的學生時代。 【記憶技巧】 *re* (back) + *tain* (hold)（把東西拿到後面，就是「保留」）	*v.* 保留
rust 〔 rʌst 〕	The unpainted metal tools were covered with *rust*. 未上漆的金屬工具佈滿了銹。	*n.* 生銹；銹
scratch 〔 skrætʃ 〕	The man *scratched* a match on the wall. 那人在牆上劃亮一根火柴。 He has a deep *scratch* on his face. 他的臉上有道很深的抓痕。	*v.* 抓；劃 *n.* 抓痕
shave 〔 ʃev 〕	Do you *shave* yourself or go to the barber's? 你是自己刮鬍子，還是去理髮廳？	*v.* 刮鬍子
slant 〔 slænt 〕	The *slant* of the roof is too steep to climb. 屋頂的斜面太陡，無法攀爬。	*n.* 傾斜；斜面 同 slope

Exercise 5.4 從第四部分中選出最適當的一個英文字，填入空格內。

1. Man's landing on the moon is the most _____ event in all human history.

2. The champion has _____ his championship title longer than anyone else.

3. Plans for selling the new products are now in _____.

4. The _____ on your hand will soon be well.

5. Please rub the _____ off the old helmet.

【解答】
1. remarkable　2. retained　3. preparation　4. scratch　5. rust

✦ 第五部分

sow 〔 so 〕	The farmer *sowed* the field with wheat. 那農夫在田裡播下小麥種子。	*v.* 播種 反 harvest
squirrel 〔'skwɜəl 〕	The *squirrels* were very busy gathering nuts for the winter. 松鼠正忙著為冬天採集堅果。	*n.* 松鼠
strain 〔 stren 〕	He *strained* every muscle to lift the heavy rock.　他竭盡全力來舉起那塊很重的石頭。	*v.* 拉緊； 竭力
supreme 〔 sə'prim 〕	He showed *supreme* courage in his decision.　他的決定展現了最大的勇氣。	*adj.* 最高的； 最大的

【記憶技巧】
sup(e)r (above) + *eme* (表最高級的字尾)

tap
〔 tæp 〕

He *tapped* me on the shoulder.
他輕拍我的肩膀。
Hot water flowed from the *tap*.
熱水從水龍頭中流出。

v. 輕拍

n. 水龍頭

thunder
〔'θʌndə 〕

We have had a lot of *thunder* this
summer. 今年夏天經常打雷。

n. 雷；打雷

┌─【記憶技巧】─────────────────────
│ *th* + *under* (在…之下)，「打雷」會擊中下面的人
└──────────────────────────────

tremble
〔'trɛmbl̩ 〕

She *trembled* when she heard the bad
news. 她聽到壞消息時，顫抖了起來。

v. 發抖；
　　顫抖

vapor
〔'vepə 〕

Strange *vapors* rose from the dark lake.
奇怪的蒸氣自黑暗的湖中升起。

n. 蒸氣

warrior
〔'wɔrɪə 〕

The *warriors* couldn't defeat their enemy
with only their spears.
戰士們無法只以他們的矛來擊敗敵人。

n. 戰士

同 soldier

┌─【記憶技巧】─────────────────────
│ 想到 war (戰爭)，字尾 or 表示「人」。
└──────────────────────────────

woe
〔 wo 〕

Sickness and poverty are common *woes*.
疾病和貧窮是常見的災禍。

n. 悲哀；災禍

同 distress

Exercise 5.5 從第五部分中選出最適當的一個英文字，填入空格內。

1. The President is the _____ commander of the armed forces.

2. After the lightning came the _____.

3. The farmer will _____ the wheat next week.

4. The children _____ with fear when they saw the accident.

5. _____ can easily climb trees.

【解答】

1. supreme　2. thunder　3. sow　4. trembled　5. Squirrels

成果測驗

I. 找出一個與其他三個不相關的字：

(　) 1. (A) soldier　　(B) peasant　　(C) warrior　　(D) fighter

(　) 2. (A) lack　　　(B) shortage　(C) want　　　(D) ruin

(　) 3. (A) grief　　　(B) flame　　　(C) woe　　　(D) distress

(　) 4. (A) shake　　　(B) scratch　　(C) rub　　　(D) scrape

(　) 5. (A) rapid　　　(B) slender　　(C) swift　　　(D) quick

(　) 6. (A) subjugate　　　　　　(B) conquer
　　　(C) vanish　　　　　　　(D) vanquish

(　) 7. (A) reject　　　(B) object　　(C) oppose　　(D) defeat

(　) 8. (A) endure　　　　　　　(B) endeavor
　　　(C) stand　　　　　　　(D) bear

(　) 9. (A) keep　　　(B) hold　　　(C) retain　　(D) resume

(　) 10. (A) close　　　　　　　(B) show
　　　(C) reveal　　　　　　　(D) disclose

Lesson 5

II. 找出一個與題前中文意思相同的英文字：

(　　) 1. 沉默的
    (A) dull　　　　(B) dumb　　　　(C) dim　　　　(D) damp

(　　) 2. 火焰
    (A) flame　　　　(B) fame　　　　(C) shame　　　　(D) tame

(　　) 3. 哺乳類動物
    (A) plant　　　　　　　　(B) squirrel
    (C) fable　　　　　　　　(D) mammal

(　　) 4. 輕拍
    (A) nod　　　　(B) tap　　　　(C) tangle　　　　(D) rub

(　　) 5. 蒸氣
    (A) rust　　　　(B) fist　　　　(C) vapor　　　　(D) feature

III. 找出一個與斜體字意義相反的單字：

(　　) 1. *cruel*
    (A) dull　　　　　　　　(B) religious
    (C) charitable　　　　　　(D) restless

(　　) 2. *conceal*
    (A) discharge　　(B) disclose　　(C) reject　　(D) vanish

(　　) 3. *humble*
    (A) proud　　　　(B) cheap　　　　(C) huge　　　　(D) firm

(　　) 4. *burden*
    (A) scrape　　　　(B) unload　　　　(C) tangle　　　　(D) connect

(　　) 5. *sow*
    (A) harvest　　　　(B) plant　　　　(C) bless　　　　(D) strain

IV. 完整拼出下列各句中所欠缺的單字，每一格代表一個字母：

1. Please don't leave the t_p running. （水龍頭）

2. Two persons were killed by the l_ _ _ _ _ _ _g last night. （閃電）

3. The w_ _ _ _ _rs agreed to defend their castle to the last man.
   （戰士）

4. The stars' i_ _ _ _ _ _ _e on men has not been proved. （影響）

5. Before writing your check, you must d_ _ _ _ _t some of your
   money in the bank. （存（款））

V. 找出一個與句中斜體字意義最接近的單字：

( ) 1. Grandfathers are usually *charitable* toward the mistakes of
      their grandchildren.
   (A) cruel   (B) benevolent
   (C) enormous   (D) ambitious

( ) 2. She was gathering flowers with her *companions* in the
      valley.
   (A) challenges   (B) warriors
   (C) trades   (D) colleagues

( ) 3. If you go to Scotland, you may see people in Highland
      costume.
   (A) dress   (B) parcel
   (C) custom   (D) charm

( ) 4. The waves *dashed* the boat against the rocks.
   (A) pulled   (B) rejected
   (C) hurled   (D) resumed

Lesson 5

(　) 5. If help does not come, we must *endure* to the end.

    (A) bear   (B) endeavor

    (C) retain   (D) strain

(　) 6. I could recognize the old car at a *glance*.

    (A) square   (B) feature

    (C) flame   (D) glimpse

(　) 7. What *influenced* you to do it?

    (A) affirmed   (B) affected

    (C) invited   (D) interested

(　) 8. They soon began to *investigate* the cause of the fire.

    (A) affirm   (B) invent

    (C) examine   (D) deny

(　) 9. The farmers worried about the *lack* of rain.

    (A) shortage   (B) drift

    (C) woe   (D) burden

(　) 10. Japan made a *proposal* to Korea for increasing trade between the two countries.

    (A) preparation   (B) exception

    (C) suggestion   (D) companion

【解答】

I. 1. B   2. D   3. B   4. A   5. B   6. C   7. D   8. B   9. D   10. A

II. 1. B   2. A   3. D   4. B   5. C

III. 1. C   2. B   3. A   4. B   5. A

IV. 1. tap   2. lightning   3. warriors   4. influence   5. deposit

V. 1. B   2. D   3. A   4. C   5. A   6. D   7. B   8. C   9. A   10. C

Lesson 6

 Lesson 6

✦ 第一部分

accidental 〔͵æksəˋdɛntḷ〕	We became friends after our *accidental* meeting at the Christmas party. 在聖誕派對偶然的相遇後，我們成為朋友。	*adj.* 意外的； 　　偶然的 同 unexpected; 　　casual

ambition
〔æmˋbɪʃən〕

One of his *ambitions* is to become a famous politician. 成為一個有名的政治家是他的抱負之一。

n. 抱負；雄心
形 ambitious

> 【記憶技巧】
> *amb* (about) + *it* (go) + *ion* (n.)（為了「抱負」，就要到處奔波）

authority
〔əˋθɔrətɪ〕

A policeman has the *authority* to arrest speeding drivers.
警察有權力拘捕超速的駕駛人。

n. 權威；權力
動 authorize

> 【記憶技巧】
> *author*（作者）+ *ity* (n.)（作者有寫作的「權力」）

blossom
〔ˋblɑsəm〕

The cherry trees are in full *blossom* now. 櫻花樹現正盛開中。
All the orchards *blossom* in spring.
所有的果樹都在春天開花。

n. 花；開花的
　　狀態或時期
v. 開花
同 flower;
　　bloom

bureau
〔ˋbjʊro〕

An information *bureau* collects and keeps various facts.
新聞局收集和保存多方面的事實。

n. 局
同 office

charm
〔 tʃɑrm 〕

His essays have a *charm* of style that cannot be found in those of other writers.

他的文章有一種迷人的風格，這在其他作家是找不到的。

n. 魅力；迷人
同 attraction
反 ugliness

comparison
〔 kəm'pærəsn̩ 〕

The buildings in Taipei are small in *comparison* with the skyscrapers in New York.

台北的建築物和紐約的摩天大樓相比，算是小的。

n. 比較；比喻
動 compare
形 comparative

conscience
〔'kɑnʃəns 〕

Jean has no *conscience*; she'd steal anything from anybody.

琴沒有良心；她會偷任何人的東西。

--- 【記憶技巧】 ---
con (with) + *sci* (know) + *ence* (n.)
（「良心」就是懂得分辨是非）

n. 良心
形 conscientious

cottage
〔'kɑtɪdʒ 〕

He lives in a *cottage* in the woods. 他住在森林裏的小屋。

n. 農舍；小屋
同 cabin

dawn
〔 dɔn 〕

We started our trip at *dawn* in order to get there before noon.

為了在中午前到達那裡，我們黎明即動身上路。

n. 黎明
同 daybreak
反 dusk

Exercise 6.1 從第一部分中選出最適當的一個英文字，填入空格內。

1. If you have a guilty _____, you feel or know you have done wrong.

2. They worked hard from _____ till dusk.

3. It was _____ that we arrived at the party at the same time.

4. Because he was filled with _____, he worked after school and on Saturday.

5. The teacher's _____ of the heart to a pump helped the students to understand its action.

【解答】

1. conscience   2. dawn   3. accidental   4. ambition   5. comparison
---

✦ 第二部分

depress
〔 dɪ'prɛs 〕

The rainy season always **depresses** me. 雨季總使我沮喪。
When business is **depressed**, many workers lose their positions.
商業蕭條時，許多人失業。

v. 1. 使沮喪

2. 使蕭條
同 boost

【記憶技巧】

de (down) + *press*（壓）（壓到谷底，就是「使沮喪」）
---

discourage
〔 dɪs'kɝɪdʒ 〕

Try again! Don't let one failure **discourage** you.
再試試！不要因一次失敗就使你氣餒。
We tried to **discourage** him from climbing the mountain without a guide.
我們設法勸他不要沒有嚮導就去爬山。

v. 1. 使氣餒
同 depress

2. 勸阻
同 dissuade

【記憶技巧】

dis (deprive of) + *courage*（勇氣）（剝奪勇氣，會「使人氣餒」）
---

dusk
〔 dʌsk 〕

The buildings over there are scarcely visible in the *dusk*.
傍晚時，那裏的建築物幾乎看不見。

n. 傍晚；黃昏
同 twilight

exchange
〔 ɪksˈtʃendʒ 〕

Exchange of prisoners during a war is not very common.
戰爭中交換戰俘不是很常見。

n. v. 交換
同 interchange

【記憶技巧】
ex (fully) + *change* (改變) (完全變換，就是「交換」)

extraordinary
〔 ɪkˈstrɔrdn̩ˌɛrɪ 〕

Eight feet is an *extraordinary* height for a man.
一個人身高八呎是驚人的。

adj. 不尋常的；
驚人的
同 exceptional

【記憶技巧】
extra + *ordinary* (普通的) (超出普通的範圍，即「驚人的」)

faint
〔 fent 〕

She called for help in a *faint* voice. 她以微弱的聲音求助。

adj. 微弱的
同 strong

flash
〔 flæʃ 〕

The lightning *flashed* across the sky. 閃電閃過天空。

n. 閃光 *v.* 閃現
同 sparkle

frost
〔 frɔst 〕

Frost has killed several of our young plants.
霜已摧毀了我們好幾株的幼苗。

n. 霜
形 frosty

gleam
〔 glim 〕

A *gleam* of light shone through the partly opened door.
微弱的光線從半開的門射進來。

n. 閃爍；微弱
的光
同 flash; glow

harness
〔'hɑrnɪs 〕

The saddle is a part of a horse's ***harness***.   *n.* 馬具
坐鞍是馬具的一部分。
We can ***harness*** water in a river to produce   *v.* 利用
electric power.
我們可以利用河中的水產生電力。

Exercise 6.2 從第二部分中選出最適當的一個英文字，填入空格內。

1. The scientist is a man of _____ genius.

2. The young buds on the tree have been damaged by the late
   _____.

3. There have been numerous _____ of views between the two
   countries.

4. The wet weather _____ people from going to the sports
   meeting.

5. I was _____ after reading the newspaper, which was filled with
   news of accidents.

【解答】

1. extraordinary 2. frost 3. exchanges 4. discouraged 5. depressed

✦ 第三部分

hymn
〔 hɪm 〕

The people joined together in singing a   *n.* 聖歌
hymn. 人們聚在一起唱聖歌。
They ***hymned*** their thanks to God.   *v.* 唱讚美歌
他們唱讚美歌以表達對上帝的感謝。

inform
〔 ɪn'fɔrm 〕

Can you *inform* me when he arrives?
他到達的時候，你可以通知我嗎？

v. 通知
名 information

【記憶技巧】
in (into) + *form* (form) (事先的「通知」就是讓人心中有個底)

invite
〔 ɪn'vaɪt 〕

She *invited* her friends to her birthday party. 她邀請朋友參加她的生日派對。

v. 邀請
名 invitation

ladder
〔 'lædɚ 〕

The boys climbed the *ladder* to get into their tree house.
男孩們爬梯子進入他們的樹屋。

n. 梯子

limb
〔 lɪm 〕

That man with one arm lost his *limb* in an airplane crash. 那獨臂男人是在一次墜機中失去一條手臂的。

n. (四) 肢；臂；腳

【記憶技巧】
lamb (羔羊) 是 animal (動物)，不要搞混。

manage
〔 'mænɪdʒ 〕

They hired a young man to *manage* their business.
他們雇用一個年輕人來管理他們的業務。
He couldn't *manage* his horse, and it threw him to the ground.
他駕馭不住馬，被牠摔到地上。

v. 1. 管理
同 conduct

2. 操控
同 handle

method
〔 'mɛθəd 〕

Jonas Salk found a new *method* of teaching music.
約納斯・沙克找到一個教音樂的新方法。

n. 方法
同 way

motive
〔 'motɪv 〕

We despise those who act from low or selfish *motives*. 我們輕視那些行爲出自下流或自私動機的人。

n. 動機
同 cause

nostril
(ˈnɑstrəl)

The princess wore a diamond in her right ***nostril***.

那位公主在右鼻孔中戴了一顆鑽石。

n. 鼻孔

> 【記憶技巧】
> ***nos*** (nose) + ***tril*** (hole)

oral
(ˈɔrəl)

She gave us an ***oral*** report instead of a written report.

她以口頭而非書面向我們報告。

adj. 口頭的

Exercise 6.3 從第三部分中選出最適當的一個英文字，填入空格內。

1. We were _____ that the prisoner had escaped.

2. We _____ all our relatives to my grandfather's sixtieth birthday party.

3. She knows how to _____ her husband when he is angry.

4. A(n) _____ agreement is not enough; we must have a written promise.

5. A rope _____ was hung over the ship's side.

> 【解答】
> 1. informed 2. invited 3. manage 4. oral 5. ladder

✦ 第四部分

pang
(pæŋ)

It is hard to stand the ***pangs*** of a toothache.

一陣陣的牙疼很難忍受。

n. 劇痛；一陣突然的痛苦

peculiar
〔 pɪˈkjuljɚ 〕

All creatures seem to have *peculiar* customs.

所有的生物似乎都有獨特的習慣。

adj. 獨特的；
特有的

名 peculiarity

plate
〔 plet 〕

In America, food is usually served on *plates*.

在美國，食物通常裝在盤子裏。

n. 盤子

同 dish

preserve
〔 prɪˈzɝv 〕

The city decided to *preserve* the beautiful old building as a museum. 該市決定保存那棟漂亮的古老建築物作爲博物館。

v. 保存

名 preservation

【記憶技巧】
pre (before) + *serve* (keep) (保持在以前的狀態，就是「保存」)

prospect
〔ˈprɑspɛkt 〕

I see no *prospect* of his recovery from the disease.

我看他沒有希望能從疾病中康復。

From the top of the hill there is a beautiful *prospect* over the city.

從山頂可以看到這座成市美麗的景色。

n. 1. 期望；希望
同 expectation; hope

2. 景色
同 view; scene

【記憶技巧】
pro (forward) + *spect* (look at) (向前看，表示心中充滿「希望」)

rare
〔 rɛr 〕

Today tigers are *rare* animals in Taiwan.

現在老虎在台灣是稀有動物。

I want my steak very *rare*, please.

我的牛排要生一點，謝謝。

adj. 1. 罕見的；
稀有的

2.（指肉）
半熟的

remedy (ˈrɛmədɪ)	This pill is a good ***remedy*** for a headache or toothache. 這藥丸是治頭痛或牙痛的良藥。	*n.* 治療法； 補救方法 同 cure

> 【記憶技巧】
> ***re*** (加強語氣的字首) + ***med*** (heal) + ***y*** (*n.*)

retire (rɪˈtaɪr)	My father ***retired*** from his job at the age of 60. 我父親於六十歲時退休。	*v.* 退休 名 retirement

> 【記憶技巧】
> 先背 tire「使疲倦」。

scream (skrim)	A ***scream*** for help came from inside the building. 從那棟建築物內傳出一聲呼救的尖叫聲。	*n. v.* 尖叫

shed (ʃɛd)	The garden tools are in that ***shed***. 園藝用具在那間小屋內。 We ***shed*** our blood for our country. 我們為國家灑熱血。	*n.* 小屋；棚 *v.* 流出

Exercise 6.4 從第四部分中選出最適當的一個英文字，填入空格內。

1. That way of speaking is _____ to people in this part of the country.

2. They built a new school as a _____ for crowded classrooms.

3. Ancient Egyptians knew how to _____ dead bodies from decay.

4. She helped her mother wash the _____ in the kitchen.

5. Seeing no _____ of success, we quit the attempt to climb the mountain.

【解答】
1. peculiar　2. remedy　3. preserve　4. plates　5. prospect

✦ 第五部分

slavery 〔'slevərɪ〕	Many men fought for the abolition of *slavery*. 許多人為廢除奴隸制度而奮鬥。	*n.* 奴隸制度 *cf.* slave
spacious 〔'speʃəs〕	The rooms of the palace were *spacious*. 這座宮殿的房間很寬敞。 【記憶技巧】 *space*（空間）– *e* + *ious* (*adj.*)	*adj.* 寬敞的 同 roomy
staff 〔stæf〕	The teaching *staff* of the school is excellent. 該校的教員很優秀。	*n.* 全體職員 【集合名詞】
straw 〔strɔ〕	The farmers covered the barn floor with *straw*. 農夫們以稻草覆蓋在穀倉的地板上。	*n.* 稻草；吸管
surface 〔'sɝfɪs〕	Leaves were floating on the *surface* of the pond. 葉子漂浮在池塘的水面。 【記憶技巧】 *sur* (above) + *face*	*n.* 表面；水面 反 bottom
tick 〔tɪk〕	The silence was broken only by the *tick* of the clock. 只有時鐘的滴答聲打破了寂靜。	*n.* 滴答聲 *v.* 滴答響

tremendous
(trɪˈmɛndəs)

The army suffered a *tremendous* defeat in that battle.
在那次戰役中，他們的軍隊慘敗。

adj. 巨大的；
可怕的
同 huge;
dreadful

【記憶技巧】
諧音：出門待死，這是「巨大的」不幸。

variety
(vəˈraɪətɪ)

The store over there has a great *variety* of toys.
那邊那家商店有各式各樣的玩具。

n. 多樣性
反 monotony

waterfall
(ˈwɔtɚˌfɔl)

The Niagara Falls is one of the most beautiful *waterfalls* in the world.
尼加拉瀑布是世界上最美麗的瀑布之一。

n. 瀑布

worm
(wɝm)

The *worm* turns the soil.
那隻蟲把土翻起來。

n. 蟲

Exercise 6.5 從第五部分中選出最適當的一個英文字，填入空格內。

1. A _____ hat protects us from the hot sun.

2. On the _____ the two men seemed friendly.

3. The President has _____ responsibilities for the nation.

4. Many Africans were captured and sold into _____.

5. We demanded more _____ in our food.

【解答】
1. straw　2. surface　3. tremendous　4. slavery　5. variety

成果測驗

I. 找出一個與斜體字的意義最接近的單字：

( ) 1. her *method* of teaching children

    (A) effort   (B) way   (C) ability   (D) opinion

( ) 2. a *prospect* of victory

    (A) proposal (B) hope   (C) motive   (D) woe

( ) 3. a humanistic *motive*

    (A) suggestion   (B) conscience

    (C) cause   (D) mercy

( ) 4. to *shed* tears of sorrow

    (A) wash   (B) drop   (C) hurl   (D) retain

( ) 5. an *accidental* happening

    (A) casual   (B) unusual   (C) usual   (D) special

( ) 6. a *spacious* hall

    (A) roomy   (B) tremendous (C) magnificent (D) special

( ) 7. an *extraordinary* power

    (A) military   (B) exceptional (C) foreign   (D) human

( ) 8. a *remedy* for cancer

    (A) harness   (B) cause   (C) cure   (D) pang

( ) 9. a *gleam* of firelight

    (A) blossom   (B) bureau

    (C) glow   (D) frost

(   ) 10. at a *tremendous* speed

         (A) normal   (B) dreadful

         (C) slow   (D) specified

II. 找出一個與題前中文意思相同的英文字：

(   ) 1. 表面

         (A) deposit   (B) surface   (C) planet   (D) slant

(   ) 2. 良心

         (A) conscience   (B) mammal   (C) motive   (D) pang

(   ) 3. 蟲

         (A) straw   (B) limb   (C) worm   (D) dawn

(   ) 4. （四）肢

         (A) limb   (B) tick   (C) fist   (D) thumb

(   ) 5. 魅力

         (A) prospect   (B) charm   (C) cottage   (D) palm

III. 找出一個與斜體字意義相反的單字：

(   ) 1. *surface*

         (A) bottom   (B) conscience   (C) bureau   (D) hymn

(   ) 2. *monotony*

         (A) ambition   (B) hardship   (C) variety   (D) nonsense

(   ) 3. *dawn*

         (A) dusk   (B) daybreak

         (C) authority   (D) blossom

( ) 4. *rare*

    (A) huge   (B) common (C) religious   (D) humble

( ) 5. *faint*

    (A) dumb   (B) notable   (C) rare   (D) strong

IV. 完整拼出下列各句中所欠缺的單字，每一格代表一個字母：

1. He explained the new policy to the editorial s_ _ _f. (全體職員)

2. We heard someone s_ _ _ _m in fright. (尖叫)

3. She didn't like the work because it lacked v_ _ _ _ _y. (多樣性)

4. The child put the watch to his ear and listened to its t_ _k.
(滴答聲)

5. The doctor put some medicine in each n_ _ _ _ _l. (鼻孔)

V. 選出最適合句意的一個單字：

( ) 1. I want to run away, but my _____ bothers me.
    (A) pang   (B) remedy
    (C) rust   (D) conscience

( ) 2. A boy who is filled with _____ always works hard.
    (A) vapor   (B) ambition (C) harness   (D) burden

( ) 3. He doesn't work in the office any longer; he _____ from
his job several years ago.
    (A) retired   (B) retained
    (C) strained   (D) resumed

(   ) 4. Her letter _____ us as to how and when she expected to arrive.

    (A) faded   (B) blessed

    (C) informed   (D) managed

(   ) 5. I gave him my old textbooks and received a dictionary in _____.

    (A) exchange   (B) preparation

    (C) proposal   (D) proportion

Ⅵ. 將題前的斜體字轉換爲適當詞性，填入空格中：

1. *ambition*   Jack is an _____ boy; he wants to become as famous as Edison.

2. *authority*   I have _____ him to act for me while I am abroad.

3. *inform*   Can you give me any _____ about this matter?

4. *retire*   There have been several _____ recently.

5. *invite*   I received an _____ card to her birthday party.

【解答】

  Ⅰ. 1. B   2. B   3. C   4. B   5. A   6. A   7. B   8. C   9. C   10. B

  Ⅱ. 1. B   2. A   3. C   4. A   5. B

  Ⅲ. 1. A   2. C   3. A   4. B   5. D

  Ⅳ. 1. staff   2. scream   3. variety   4. tick   5. nostril

  Ⅴ. 1. D   2. B   3. A   4. C   5. A

  Ⅵ. 1. ambitious   2. authorized   3. information   4. retirements

     5. invitation

Lesson 7

Lesson 7

✦ 第一部分

accompany
〔 ə'kʌmpənɪ 〕

He *accompanied* his girlfriend to the airport. 他陪著女朋友到機場。
She *accompanied* the singer on the piano. 她為演唱者擔任鋼琴伴奏。

v. 1. 陪伴

2. 伴奏

---【記憶技巧】---
ac (to) + *company*（同伴）（去當別人的
同伴，就是「陪伴」）

---

amuse
〔 ə'mjuz 〕

The storyteller's jokes *amused* the children. 說書人的笑話逗笑了孩子。

v. 娛樂；使發笑
名 amusement
形 amusing

---【記憶技巧】---
a + *muse*（Muse 繆斯女神，掌管音樂、美
術等，有「娛樂」性質的學問）

---

avoid
〔 ə'vɔɪd 〕

Children should try to *avoid* crossing the road except when a policeman stops the traffic.
孩子們應避免穿越馬路，除非有警察
禁止車輛通行。

v. 避免
名 avoidance

---

bomb
〔 bɑm 〕

A time *bomb* explodes some time after it is placed in position.
定時炸彈被放置於定位後，會在一段
時間後爆炸。

n. 炸彈

---

burial
〔 'bɛrɪəl 〕

The *burial* of the dead sailor was performed at sea.
那死去船員的葬禮在海上舉行。

n. 埋葬；葬禮

chase 〔 tʃes 〕	The old lady saw the thief running up the street and *chased* him on her bicycle. 老婦人看見小偷跑到街上，於是騎著腳踏車去追他。	*v.* 追趕 反 flee
compel 〔 kəmˈpɛl 〕	He was *compelled* by illness to give up his studies. 他因病被迫放棄學業。 ----【記憶技巧】---- *com* (with) + *pel* (drive)（驅使別人去做不想做的事，算是「強迫」）	*v.* 強迫
consent 〔 kənˈsɛnt 〕	He asked the girl to marry him and she *consented*. 他請求那女孩嫁給他，她答應了。 ----【記憶技巧】---- *con* (together) + *sent* (feel)（有共同的感覺，表示「同意」）	*v.* 同意
counterpart 〔ˈkaʊntɚˌpɑrt 〕	The Chinese foreign minister met his Korean *counterpart*. 中國外交部長接見韓國外交部長。 Your right hand is the *counterpart* of your left hand. 你的右手和你左手互相配對。	*n.* 1. 相對應的人或物 2. 配對物；對照物
deafen 〔ˈdɛfən 〕	A sudden explosion *deafened* us for a moment. 突然的爆炸聲使我們耳聾了一會兒。	*v.* 使聾 形 deaf

Lesson 7

Exercise 7.1　從第一部分中選出最適當的一個英文字，填入空格內。

1. The rain _____ us to stop our ball game.

2. As soon as we saw the enemy ship, we began to _____ it.

3. _____ may be filled with a chemical substance and are sometimes dropped from aircraft.

4. The children _____ themselves by playing games while their parents talked.

5. The warships _____ the merchant ships through the Mediterranean.

【解答】

1. compelled　2. chase　3. Bombs　4. amused　5. accompanied

✦ 第二部分

derive
〔dəˋraɪv〕

The word "deride" is **derived** from the Latin "de" (down) and "riddere" (to laugh).
deride 這個字是起源於拉丁文 de（向下）和 riddere（笑）。

We have **derived** benefit from the new method of generating electricity.
我們已從新的發電法獲得益處。

v. 1. 起源

2. 獲得

【記憶技巧】
de (from) + *rive* (stream)（從哪個地方流進來，就是「源自」哪裡）

display
〔 dɪs'ple 〕

Department stores ***display*** their goods in the windows.
百貨公司在櫥窗展示他們的商品。

v. 展示
同 show;
  reveal

【記憶技巧】
dis (apart) + ***play*** (fold) (將摺疊的東西展開來，讓別人看到，就是「展示」)

dust
〔 dʌst 〕

There was half an inch of ***dust*** on the books before I cleaned them. 在我清理這些書之前，有半吋的灰塵積在上面。

n. 灰塵
形 dusty

energetic
〔 ,ɛnɚ'dʒɛtɪk 〕

Cool autumn days make us feel ***energetic***.
涼爽的秋天使我們感到精力充沛。

adj. 精力充沛的

extent
〔 ɪk'stɛnt 〕

I was amazed at the ***extent*** of his knowledge.
我對他知識的廣博極爲驚異。

n. 程度；廣闊

【記憶技巧】
ex (out) + ***tent*** (帳棚)(帳棚要夠「廣闊」)

fairy
〔 'fɛrɪ 〕

The ***fairy*** promised to grant the child's wish.
小仙子答應允諾那孩子的願望。

n. 仙女；小仙子

flatter
〔 'flætɚ 〕

He ***flattered*** her with flowers and expensive gifts.
他用花和昂貴的禮物來奉承她。

v. 奉承

frown
〔 fraʊn 〕

Mary wanted to go to Europe by herself, but her parents ***frowned*** on the idea. 瑪麗想要單獨去歐洲，可是她的父母不同意這個想法。

v. 皺眉頭；不悅
同 scowl
反 smile

Lesson 7

glimpse
〔 glɪmps 〕

I caught a *glimpse* of the falls as our train went by.
當我們的火車經過時，我瞥見了瀑布。

n. 看一眼；
一瞥

harvest
〔 ˈhɑrvɪst 〕

Many men were needed to help the farmer with the *harvest*.
那農夫需要許多人幫忙採收。

n. 收穫
同 crop

┌─ 【記憶技巧】─────────
│ *har* + *vest* (背心)
└──────────────────

Exercise 7.2 從第二部分中選出最適當的一個英文字，填入空格內。

1. He ＿＿＿＿＿＿ much pleasure from reading adventure stories.

2. The motor car raised a terrible ＿＿＿＿＿＿ as it passed us.

3. I agree with your plans, but only to a certain ＿＿＿＿＿＿.

4. He was only ＿＿＿＿＿＿ her when he said that she sang well; he didn't really mean it.

5. My grandmother always ＿＿＿＿＿＿ when she's putting thread into a needle.

┌─ 【解答】────────────────────────────────
│ 1. derives　2. dust　3. extent　4. flattering　5. frowns
└──

✦ 第三部分

inhabit
〔 ɪnˈhæbɪt 〕

The earth we *inhabit* is a point in space.
我們居住的地球只是太空中的一點。

v. 居住於
名 inhabitant

involve
〔 ɪn'vɑlv 〕

Housekeeping ***involves*** cooking, washing dishes, sweeping, and cleaning. 家務包含烹飪、洗碗、打掃，及清洗。

> 【記憶技巧】
> ***in*** (in) + ***volve*** (roll)（捲入其中，就是「使牽涉；包含」）

v. 使牽涉；
包含
同 include
反 exempt;
exclude

---

lamb
〔 læm 〕

The ***lambs*** were playing on the hillside. 小羊在山坡上玩耍。

> 【記憶技巧】
> lamb（羔羊）就是羊 <u>b</u>aby，而 lam<u>e</u>（跛腳的）就是腳（<u>feet</u>）有問題。

n. 羔羊；
小羊

---

liquid
〔'lɪkwɪd 〕

Water, oil, and milk are ***liquids***. 水、油，和牛奶都是液體。
The sick man could eat only ***liquid*** foods.　那病人只能吃流質食物。

n. 液體

adj. 流體的

---

mighty
〔'maɪtɪ 〕

The ***mighty*** battleship was so badly damaged that it could not be used again. 強大的戰艦受到嚴重的損害，無法再使用。

adj. 強有力的
同 powerful
名 might

---

mount
〔 maʊnt 〕

He ***mounted*** the bicycle and rode away. 他登上腳踏車後騎走了。
The soldiers ***mounted*** fine black horses.　士兵們騎上漂亮的黑馬。

v. 1. 登上
同 climb
2. 騎上；
使騎上

---

notify
〔'notə,faɪ 〕

Our teacher ***notified*** us that there would be a test on Monday. 老師通知我們星期一要考試。

> 【記憶技巧】
> ***not*** (note) + ***ify*** (make)（使人注意到，就是「通知」）

v. 通知
同 inform

orbit
〔ˈɔrbɪt〕

The moon travels in an *orbit* around the earth. 月球繞著地球的軌道運行。

n. 軌道

paradise
〔ˈpærəˌdaɪs〕

The island was a *paradise* of birds and flowers.
此島是鳥和花的天堂。

n. 天堂
同 heaven
反 hell

peer
〔pɪr〕

She *peered* through the mist, trying to find the right way.
她透過霧中細看，想找到正確的路。

v. 凝視；細看
同 stare

┌── 【記憶技巧】──────────────┐
│ 想到 *pear*（西洋梨），會一直 peer（細看）。│
└──────────────────────────────┘

Exercise 7.3 從第三部分中選出最適當的一個英文字，填入空格內。

1. A person as good as he deserves to go to _____.

2. He lifted up his little son, and _____ him on the donkey.

3. Jelly is not _____ but solid.

4. When my guest arrives, please _____ me.

5. The United States of America is one of the _____ nations in the world.

┌── 【解答】──────────────────────────┐
│ 1. paradise   2. mounted   3. liquid   4. notify   5. mightiest │
└──────────────────────────────────────┘

✦ 第四部分

pledge
〔plɛdʒ〕

I give my *pledge* that I will continue to help you. 我保證會繼續幫助你。
They *pledged* themselves never to tell the secrets. 他們發誓絕不洩密。

n. 保證

v. 發誓；使發誓
同 promise; vow

pressure
〔ˊprɛʃə〕

The air ***pressure*** at sea level is nearly 15 pounds for each square inch. 海平面上的大氣壓力每一平方英吋約有十五磅。

n. 壓力
動 press

prosper
〔ˊprɑspə〕

His business ***prospered*** at its new location. 他在新地點的生意興隆。

v. 繁榮;興隆

> 【記憶技巧】
> 背這個字要先背 proper (適當的),中間再加 s。

raw
〔rɔ〕

Children like to eat ***raw*** fruits. 孩子們喜歡吃生的水果。

adj. 生的
同 uncooked

remind
〔rɪˊmaɪnd〕

This picture ***reminds*** me of the story I heard before. 這幅畫使我想起以前聽過的故事。

v. 提醒;使想起

retreat
〔rɪˊtrit〕

The enemy ***retreated*** before the advance of our soldiers. 敵軍在我們士兵進攻之前就撤退了。

v. 撤退
同 withdraw
反 advance

> 【記憶技巧】
> 先背 treat (對待)。

sacred
〔ˊsekrɪd〕

The Bible and Koran are ***sacred*** writings. 聖經和可蘭經都是聖典。

adj. 神聖的
反 profane

screen
〔skrin〕

We have ***screens*** at the windows to keep out flies. 我們的窗戶上有紗窗以防蒼蠅。

n. 銀幕;紗窗

Lesson 7

shelf
〔 ʃɛlf 〕

I kept that book on the bottom *shelf*.
我把那本書放在底層的書架上。
The wrecked ship rested on a *shelf* at the
bottom of the sea.
遭遇船難的船隻擱置在海底的暗礁上。

n. 1. 架子；書架

2. 暗礁

sleeve
〔 sliv 〕

The *sleeves* of his coat were too long.
他外套的袖子太長。

n. 袖子

【記憶技巧】
諧音：撕禮服，從「袖子」開始撕。

Exercise 7.4 從第四部分中選出最適當的一個英文字，填入空格內。

1. I've forgotten what you said; will you _____ me of it?

2. The defeated army had to _____ hastily from the battlefield.

3. In India, the cow is a _____ animal.

4. The tailor shortened the _____ of his shirt.

5. The windows were covered with _____ to keep out insects.

【解答】
1. remind   2. retreat   3. sacred   4. sleeves   5. screens

✦ 第五部分

spare
〔 spɛr 〕

She is looking for something to read in
her *spare* time.
她正在找些能在空閒時間讀的東西。
Take my money but *spare* my life!
拿我的錢，但請饒了我的命！

adj. 空閒的

v. 饒恕

stability
(stə'bɪlətɪ)

A concrete wall has more *stability* than a wooden fence.
水泥牆比木製柵欄穩固得多。

【記憶技巧】
st + *ability*（能力）

n. 穩定；穩固
形 stable

strawberry
('strɔ,bɛrɪ)

We had *strawberries* and ice cream for dessert.
我們以草莓和冰淇淋做爲甜點。

n. 草莓

surgeon
('s3dʒən)

A *surgeon* took out Fred's tonsils.
一位外科醫生切除了佛瑞德的扁桃腺。

n. 外科醫生

task
(tæsk)

The President has to perform many *tasks*.
總統必須執行許多任務。

n. 任務；工作
同 assignment; job

tide
(taɪd)

They liked to walk along the beach at low *tide*.
他們喜歡在退潮時沿著海灘散步。

n. 潮水；潮汐
cf. ebb

trial
('traɪəl)

She learned to cook by *trial* and error. 她藉著嘗試錯誤法學會烹飪。
In the *trial*, she changed her previous statement.
在審判時，她改變了先前的陳述。

n. 1. 試驗
同 testing
2. 審判

vast
(væst)

Texas and Alaska cover *vast* territories.
德州和阿拉斯加佔地極大。

adj. 巨大的；廣大的
同 tiny

waterproof
('wɔtɚ'pruf)

Put on your *waterproof* coat before you go out in the rain.
下雨外出前，穿上你的防水外套。
These hiking shoes have been *waterproofed*.
這些健走鞋有經過防水處理。

【記憶技巧】
proof（防~的）

adj. 防水的

v. 使不透水

worsen
〔'wɜsn̩〕

The rain *worsened* our difficulties.
雨使我們的困境變得更糟。

【記憶技巧】
worse（更糟的）+ *n*

v. 使惡化；使變壞

Exercise 7.5 從第五部分中選出最適當的一個英文字，填入空格內。

1. The prisoner asked the judge to _____ his life.

2. The political situation of the country has _____ since its independence.

3. A billion dollars is a _____ amount of money.

4. Many thieves were caught and brought to _____.

5. The _____ of the government is required to overcome the present hardship.

【解答】
1. spare　2. worsened　3. vast　4. trial　5. stability

成果測驗

I. 找出一個與其他三個不相關的字：

(　) 1. (A) live　　(B) inhabit　　(C) dwell　　(D) reject

(　) 2. (A) display　(B) discourage　(C) show　　(D) reveal

(　) 3. (A) defeat　(B) consent　　(C) agree　　(D) assent

(　) 4. (A) compel　(B) force　　　(C) impel　　(D) reject

(　) 5. (A) vast　　(B) immense　　(C) stable　　(D) huge

Lesson 7

( ) 6. (A) pledge   (B) promise   (C) preserve   (D) vow

( ) 7. (A) energetic   (B) swift   (C) active   (D) vigorous

( ) 8. (A) job   (B) task   (C) assignment   (D) bureau

( ) 9. (A) extent   (B) range   (C) burial   (D) scope

( ) 10. (A) raw   (B) solemn   (C) sacred   (D) holy

II. 找出一個與題前中文意思相同的英文字：

( ) 1. 小仙女
     (A) twilight   (B) charm   (C) fairy   (D) squirrel

( ) 2. 袖子
     (A) staff   (B) sleeve   (C) straw   (D) slant

( ) 3. 外科醫生
     (A) surgeon   (B) physician
     (C) suggestion   (D) colleague

( ) 4. 空閒的
     (A) sour   (B) stout   (C) spacious   (D) spare

( ) 5. 娛樂
     (A) amuse   (B) prosper   (C) tap   (D) peck

III. 找出一個與斜體字意義相反的單字：

( ) 1. *profane*
     (A) secular   (B) sacred   (C) peculiar   (D) extreme

( ) 2. *flee*
     (A) chase   (B) discharge   (C) lose   (D) vanish

(   ) 3. *exempt*

    (A) retire   (B) notify   (C) involve   (D) faint

(   ) 4. *advance*

    (A) ensure   (B) retreat   (C) affect   (D) reveal

(   ) 5. *tiny*

    (A) vast   (B) witty   (C) dumb   (D) dim

IV. 完整拼出下列各句中所欠缺的單字，每一格代表一個字母：

1. The air is a fluid but not a l_ _ _ _d. （液體）

2. The b_ _ _ _l ceremony of the late President was held yesterday.
   （葬禮）

3. Please r_ _ _ _d me to take my medicine in the morning.（提醒）

4. Don't try to f_ _ _ _ _r her with praises.（奉承）

5. I only caught a g_ _ _ _ _e of the parcel, so I can't guess what
   was inside it.（看一眼）

V. 找出一個與句中斜體字意義最接近的單字：

(   ) 1. John likes to have *raw* vegetables.

    (A) soft   (B) cheap   (C) rotten   (D) uncooked

(   ) 2. He *pledged* to marry her when he returned from England.

    (A) devised   (B) denied

    (C) vowed   (D) flattered

(   ) 3. Our soldiers *displayed* no fear under the enemy's fire.

    (A) revealed   (B) vanquished

    (C) discharged   (D) informed

(   ) 4. This year's wheat *harvest* was very small because of bad weather.

    (A) peasant   (B) crop   (C) deposit   (D) bunch

(   ) 5. We will *notify* you when the books arrive.

    (A) inform   (B) reveal   (C) request   (D) guess

(   ) 6. When I asked him a question, the old man *peered* at me over his glasses.

    (A) pecked   (B) stared

    (C) screamed   (D) scratched

(   ) 7. The soldiers stood beside their horses, waiting for the order to *mount*.

    (A) relieve   (B) run   (C) dismiss   (D) climb

(   ) 8. Seeing the big dog, the boys *retreated* rapidly.

    (A) advanced   (B) screamed

    (C) withdrew   (D) vanished

(   ) 9. He gave the machine another *trial* to see if it would work.

    (A) motion   (B) testing   (C) pressure   (D) flame

(   ) 10. Jane's *task* is to set the table.

    (A) assignment   (B) distress

    (C) tide   (D) rust

【解答】

I. 1. D   2. B   3. A   4. D   5. C   6. C   7. B   8. D   9. C   10. A

II. 1. C   2. B   3. A   4. D   5. A

III. 1. B   2. A   3. C   4. B   5. A

IV. 1. liquid   2. burial   3. remind   4. flatter   5. glimpse

V. 1. D   2. C   3. A   4. B   5. A   6. B   7. D   8. C   9. B   10. A

Lesson 7

Lesson 8

Lesson 8

✦ 第一部分

accomplish
〔 ə'kɑmplɪʃ 〕

How many years did it take to *accomplish* your purpose? 你爲達到目的花費了多少年？

v. 完成；達到
名 accomplishment

anchor
〔 'æŋkɚ 〕

The *anchor* caught in the mud of the lake bottom and kept the boat from moving. 錨卡在湖底的泥巴裏，使船無法移動。

n. 錨

┌─【記憶技巧】────────
諧音：岸可，岸可下「錨」。
└──────────────────

awaken
〔 ə'wekən 〕

The sun was shining when I *awakened* this morning. 我今早醒來時，太陽正閃耀著。

v. 喚醒；醒來
同 awake

┌─【記憶技巧】────────
awake（醒的）+ *n*
└──────────────────

blush
〔 blʌʃ 〕

She *blushed* as red as a rose with shame. 她因羞愧臉紅得像玫瑰一樣。

v. 臉紅

bush
〔 buʃ 〕

He came out of the shadow of the *bush* and blinked in the sun. 他從灌木蔭下出來，在陽光下眨著眼。

n. 灌木叢

cheat
〔 tʃit 〕

The boy doesn't study hard, and he always *cheats* in examinations. 那男孩不用功，總是在考試時作弊。

v. 欺騙
同 deceive

compete 〔kəm'pit〕	The rival schools ***competed*** for the football trophy. 各參賽學校為足球獎而競爭。 ---【記憶技巧】--- ***com*** (together) + ***pete*** (strive) (一起爭鬥，即「競爭」)	*v.* 競爭 同 contend 名 competition
consequence 〔'kɑnsə,kwɛns〕	He fell ill and the ***consequence*** was that he lost his position. 他生病的結果是失業。 ---【記憶技巧】--- ***con*** (with) + ***sequ*** (follow) + ***ence*** (*n.*)	*n.* 後果；結果 同 outcome 反 cause 形 consequent
courage 〔'kɝɪdʒ〕	***Courage*** is the ability to control fear, not the absence of fear. 勇氣是指克制恐懼的能力，而非全然無懼。	*n.* 勇氣 反 cowardice 形 courageous
debate 〔dɪ'bet〕	The question of whether war can be abolished has often been ***debated***. 戰爭能否廢除的問題常被討論。 ---【記憶技巧】--- ***de*** (down) + ***bate*** (beat) (「辯論」就是要打倒對方)	*v.* 辯論；討論 同 argue; 　　discuss

Lesson 8

Exercise 8.1　從第一部分中選出最適當的一個英文字，填入空格內。

1. He _____ the old woman by making her sign a paper she didn't understand.

2. The man was highly praised for having the _____ to go into the burning house to save the little girl.

3. We were _____ whether to go to the mountains or to the seaside for our summer holidays.

4. The horse was _____ against many fine horses for the first prize.

5. The _____ of the heavy rain was the flooding of large areas of land.

【解答】

1. cheated　2. courage　3. debating　4. competing　5. consequence

---

✦ 第二部分

descend 〔 dɪ'sɛnd 〕	The sun slowly ***descended*** over the western hills. 太陽慢慢落於西邊的山頭。 【記憶技巧】 *de* (down) + *scend* (climb) (往下爬，就是「下降」)	*v.* 下降 反 ascend
dispose 〔 dɪ'spoz 〕	You'd better ***dispose*** of the rubbish before you go out. 在你外出前，最好把垃圾處理掉。 The general ***disposed*** soldiers for the coming battle. 將軍爲即將來臨的戰役部署士兵。	*v.* 1. 處置； 　　　處理 　　2. 部署
earnest 〔 'ɝnɪst 〕	He made an ***earnest*** attempt to persuade her. 他認眞嘗試想說服她。	*adj.* 認眞的 同 sincere

enforce
〔 ɪn'fors 〕

Policemen and judges will *enforce* the laws of the city.
警察和法官將執行都市法規。

【記憶技巧】
en (in) + *force* (strong)（用力做事，就是「執行」）

v. 執行
名 enforcement

---

extend
〔 ɪk'stɛnd 〕

An imperialistic country *extends* its power and influence into neighboring countries. 帝國主義的國家將它的勢力和影響擴展至鄰近國家。
He refused to take the hand I *extended* in friendship.
他拒絕握我那基於友善而伸出的手。

【記憶技巧】
ex (out) + *tend* (stretch)

v. 1. 延伸；擴展
同 enlarge
名 extension

2. 伸出

---

faithful
〔 'feθfəl 〕

Dogs are always *faithful* to their masters. 狗總是對牠們的主人忠實。

adj. 忠實的
反 insincere

---

flavor
〔 'flevɚ 〕

Chocolate and vanilla have different *flavors*. 巧克力和香草的味道不同。

n. 口味；味道
同 taste

---

frustrate
〔 'frʌstret 〕

His indifference *frustrated* the teacher's efforts.
他的漠不關心使老師的努力受挫。

【記憶技巧】
frustr (in vain) + *ate* (*v.*)（所做的一切都白費，會使人感到挫折）

v. 使受挫
同 disappoint
名 frustration

---

glorious
〔 'glorɪəs 〕

A *glorious* victory could be attained only by effort and patience. 光榮的勝利只有藉著努力和耐心才能獲得。

adj. 光榮的
名 glory

| **haste** | Make *haste* or you will miss the train again. | *n.* 匆忙 |
| 〔 hest 〕 | 快一點，否則你會再次錯過那一班火車。 | 形 hasty |

Exercise 8.2 從第二部分中選出最適當的一個英文字，填入空格內。

1. All his _____ was of no use; he missed the last train.

2. The sun _____ behind the hills and it was dark everywhere.

3. The _____ student tried very hard to do his best.

4. A _____ friend is reliable and can be depended on to do his work.

5. The bad weather _____ our plans for a picnic.

```
┌─── 【解答】 ────────────────────────────────
│ 1. haste  2. descended  3. earnest  4. faithful  5. frustrated
└────────────────────────────────────────────
```

✦ 第三部分

identify	Can you *identify* a composer by listening to his music?	*v.* 辨認；認出
〔 aɪˈdɛntəˌfaɪ 〕	你能聽音樂就認出作曲家嗎？	同 recognize
		名 identification

> ---【記憶技巧】---
> *identi* (the same) + *fy* (v.) (看看是不是一樣的，就是「辨認」)

| **injure** | She was *injured* badly in the car accident yesterday. | *v.* 傷害 |
| 〔ˈɪndʒɚ 〕 | 她在昨天的車禍中受重傷。 | 同 harm |

> ---【記憶技巧】---
> *in* (not) + *jure* (right) (「傷害」別人是不正當的行爲)

Lesson 8

irregular
〔 ɪ'rɛgjələ 〕

The train schedules were ***irregular*** during the flood.
水災期間，火車班次不規則。

【記憶技巧】
ir (not) + ***regular*** (規律的)

adj. 不規則的
同 random

---

lame
〔 lem 〕

The soldier is not able to walk normally because he is ***lame*** from an old wound.　那士兵無法正常地行走，因為他的舊傷使他跛腳。

adj. 跛腳的
同 crippled

---

liquor
〔'lɪkə 〕

Does this restaurant have a license to serve ***liquor***?
這家餐廳有賣酒的執照嗎？

【記憶技巧】
諧音：立刻，喝了「酒」立刻就醉。

n. 烈酒；酒類

---

manly
〔'mænlɪ 〕

My aunt was a lady of strong mind and great resolution; she was a very ***manly*** woman.
我的阿姨是位意志堅強，非常有決心的女士；她是一個很有男子氣概的女人。

adj. 有男子氣概的
反 womanly;
　　womanish

---

mild
〔 maɪld 〕

The thief was given a ***milder*** punishment than he deserved.
那小偷受到較他應得為輕的懲罰。

adj. 溫和的；輕的
同 gentle; kind

---

mourn
〔 mɔrn 〕

All the people ***mourned*** the loss of their president.
所有的人都為總統的去世而哀悼。

v. 哀悼

---

notion
〔'noʃən 〕

Your head is full of silly ***notions***.
你腦子裏充滿愚蠢的想法。

n. 觀念；想法

---

order
〔'ɔrdə 〕

He gave ***orders*** that the work should be done at once.
他下命令，工作應該立刻進行。

n. v. 命令

Exercise 8.3　從第三部分中選出最適當的一個英文字，填入空格內。

1. John could easily ＿＿＿＿＿＿＿ his own son among many boys.

2. A soldier who doesn't obey ＿＿＿＿＿＿＿ will be in serious trouble.

3. He ＿＿＿＿＿＿＿ his leg when he fell over the big stone.

4. It was her ＿＿＿＿＿＿＿ that planes were safer than trains.

5. He was ＿＿＿＿＿＿＿ the loss of his best friend.

【解答】

1. identify　2. orders　3. injured　4. notion　5. mourning

✦ 第四部分

paragraph〔ˈpærəˌgræf〕	A new ***paragraph*** always begins on a new line. 新的一段總是換行開始。	*n.* 段落

【記憶技巧】

para (beside) + ***graph*** (write)（不相關的內容寫在不同的「段落」）

penalty〔ˈpɛnḷtɪ〕	The ***penalty*** for his offense was five years in prison. 他犯罪的刑罰是監禁五年。	*n.* 刑罰

【記憶技巧】

pen (punish) + ***al*** (*adj.*) + ***ty*** (*n.*)（處罰罪犯就是給予「刑罰」）

pluck〔plʌk〕	Do not ***pluck*** the flowers in the garden, please. 請勿摘花園中的花。	*v.* 摘（花）；採

pretend
〔 prɪˈtɛnd 〕

He **pretended** to be asleep when his mother called him.

他母親叫他時，他假裝睡著。

【記憶技巧】
pre (before) + **tend** (stretch) (在別人面前展開另一種面貌，就是「假裝」)

v. 假裝
名 pretence

protect
〔 prəˈtɛkt 〕

We keep our army to **protect** our country from the enemy. 我們保有軍隊，以保衛國家免受敵人侵犯。

v. 保護
名 protection

realize
〔ˈriəˌlaɪz 〕

He didn't **realize** how cold it was until he went outside.

直到他走到外面，才了解到天氣有多冷。

He **realized** his dreams when he became a doctor.

當他成為醫生時，實現了他的夢想。

v. 1. 了解

2. 實現
名 realization

remove
〔 rɪˈmuv 〕

She could not **remove** the spot from the carpet. 她無法除去地毯上的斑點。

Our office has **removed** from New York to Chicago.

我們的辦公室已從紐約遷移到芝加哥。

v. 1. 除去
同 eliminate
2. 遷移；移開

reveal
〔 rɪˈvil 〕

Can you promise never to **reveal** my secret?

你能答應絕不會洩漏我的祕密嗎？

【記憶技巧】
re (opposite of) + **veal** (to veil) (取下面紗，表示將隱藏在下面的東西「顯示」出來)

v. 顯示；洩漏
同 disclose
反 conceal
名 revelation

Lesson 8

sacrifice
〔'sækrə,faɪs 〕

A mother will *sacrifice* her life for her children.
母親會為她的孩子犧牲生命。

v. 犧牲

Success is not worth the *sacrifice* of your health.
成功不值得犧牲你的健康。

n. 犧牲

> 【記憶技巧】
> *sacr* (sacred) + *ifice* (make) (「犧牲」是一種神聖的行為)

screw
〔 skru 〕

Turn the *screw* to the right to tighten it. 將螺絲釘向右旋轉扭緊它。

n. 螺絲釘

The carpenter *screwed* a lock on the door.
木匠用螺絲釘將鎖釘在門上。

v. 用螺絲釘釘住

screw

Exercise 8.4 從第四部分中選出最適當的一個英文字，填入空格內。

1. She suddenly _____ the fact that she was not married.

2. Please _____ the mud from your shoes before you go into the hall.

3. She _____ her dream of becoming an actress.

4. He raised his arm in order to _____ his face from the blow.

5. She wasn't really crying; she was only _____.

> 【解答】
> 1. revealed 2. remove 3. realized 4. protect 5. pretending

✦ 第五部分

shell 〔ʃɛl〕	The cook broke the ***shell*** of an egg. 廚師將蛋殼打破。	*n.* 殼 反 core
slender 〔'slɛndɚ〕	She is a very ***slender*** blonde. 她是個非常苗條的金髮女郎。	*adj.* 苗條的 同 thin
sparkle 〔'spɑrkl̩〕	The lake ***sparkled*** in the sunshine. 湖水在陽光下閃閃發光。	*v.* 閃耀

> 【記憶技巧】
> ***spark***（閃光）+ ***le***

stain 〔sten〕	He has ink ***stains*** on his shirt. 他的襯衫上有墨水污漬。 The tablecloth is ***stained*** where food has been spilled. 在食物灑出的地方，桌布被弄髒了。	*n.* 污漬；污點 同 spot *v.* 弄髒
stream 〔strim〕	They walked along the bank of the ***stream***. 他們沿著溪流的岸邊走。	*n.* 溪流
surrender 〔sə'rɛndɚ〕	We advised the bandits to ***surrender*** themselves to the police. 我們勸強盜向警方自首。	*v.* 投降 同 yield

> 【記憶技巧】
> ***sur*** (upon) + ***render***（給予）（願意把東西交給別人，表示「投降」）

tasty 〔'testɪ〕	All of us had a very ***tasty*** meal yesterday. 我們昨天都享受了非常美味的一餐。	*adj.* 美味的 名 taste

Lesson 8

tight
〔 taɪt 〕

The drawer is so ***tight*** that I can't open it.
抽屜太緊，我打不開。

adj. 緊的
adv. 緊緊地
動 tighten

tribe
〔 traɪb 〕

America was once the home of many Indian ***tribes***.
美洲曾經是許多印地安部落的家。

n. 部落

weapon
〔'wɛpən 〕

The soldiers were cleaning their ***weapons***.
士兵們在清理他們的武器。

n. 武器

--- 【記憶技巧】
諧音：外噴，「武器」會向外噴火。

wreck
〔 rɛk 〕

The ***wreck*** of the ship was reported last night. 船隻的殘骸於昨晚被發現。
The building was ***wrecked*** because it was unsafe. 該棟建築物因為不安全而被拆毀。

n. 殘骸
v. 拆毀
同 destroy

Lesson 8

Exercise 8.5　從第五部分中選出最適當的一個英文字，填入空格內。

1. There were blood _____ at the scene of the murder.

2. We will never _____ to the enemy.

3. Pack the cases as _____ as possible.

4. Guns are of little use against modern _____ in war.

5. Most girls want to be _____.

--- 【解答】
1. stains　2. surrender　3. tight(ly)　4. weapons　5. slender

成果測驗

I. 找出一個與斜體字的意義最接近的單字：

( ) 1. a *slender* girl

　　(A) thin　　(B) faint　　(C) tiny　　(D) small

( ) 2. a sweet *flavor*

　　(A) blossom　　　(B) flower

　　(C) taste　　　　(D) pledge

( ) 3. to *compete* for prize

　　(A) spare　　(B) contend　　(C) impel　　(D) amuse

( ) 4. to *surrender* unconditionally

　　(A) conquer　(B) love　　(C) escape　　(D) yield

( ) 5. to *identify* the coat at once

　　(A) notify　　　(B) display

　　(C) disclose　　(D) recognize

( ) 6. to be *frustrated* by rain

　　(A) cheated　　(B) disappointed

　　(C) removed　　(D) compelled

( ) 7. to *injure* one's feelings

　　(A) harm　　(B) control　　(C) reveal　　(D) flatter

( ) 8. the *consequence* of war

　　(A) escape　　　(B) outcome

　　(C) trial　　　　(D) prospect

Lesson 8

( ) 9. an *earnest* man

    (A) sincere   (B) rich   (C) strong   (D) unusual

( ) 10. to *reveal* secrets

    (A) identify   (B) conceal   (C) disclose   (D) inform

II. 找出一個與題前中文意思相同的英文字：

( ) 1. 污漬

    (A) clan   (B) veil   (C) stain   (D) blush

( ) 2. 犧牲

    (A) sacrifice   (B) stare   (C) deserve   (D) derive

( ) 3. 處置

    (A) compete   (B) dispose

    (C) perform   (D) worsen

( ) 4. 實現

    (A) identify   (B) awaken   (C) realize   (D) stretch

( ) 5. 殘骸

    (A) woe   (B) screw   (C) shell   (D) wreck

III. 找出一個與斜體字意義相反的單字：

( ) 1. *courage*

    (A) punishment   (B) cowardice

    (C) injury   (D) instability

( ) 2. *conceal*

    (A) avoid   (B) debate   (C) deceive   (D) reveal

Lesson 8

(   ) 3. *consequence*

    (A) haste   (B) result

    (C) cause   (D) conscience

(   ) 4. *insincere*

    (A) faithful   (B) mighty   (C) extensive   (D) profane

(   ) 5. *ascend*

    (A) frustrate   (B) descend   (C) protect   (D) debate

IV. 完整拼出下列各句中所欠缺的單字，每一格代表一個字母：

1. For a moment he could not r_ _ _ _e his eyes from the face of the little girl. （移開）

2. Many children were swimming in the s_ _ _ _m. （溪流）

3. She saw the diamonds s_ _ _ _ _e in the bright light. （閃耀）

4. He has too m_ _d a nature to get angry, even if he has good cause. （溫和的）

5. It took three years to a_ _ _ _ _ _ _ _h his ambition. （達到）

V. 選出最適合句意的一個單字：

(   ) 1. In his attempt to escape, the prisoner was _____ by a watchful guard.

    (A) amused   (B) frustrated   (C) wrecked   (D) plucked

(   ) 2. Government makes laws and the police _____ them.

    (A) enforce   (B) stretch   (C) dispose   (D) chase

Lesson 8

( ) 3. The city _____ the road to the next town.
    (A) yield   (B) guarded
    (C) disposed   (D) extended

( ) 4. A _____ friend keeps his promises.
    (A) solemn   (B) splendid   (C) faithful   (D) lame

( ) 5. The sick man's heartbeat was _____.
    (A) irregular   (B) raw   (C) spare   (D) tiny

VI. 將題前的斜體字轉換爲適當詞性，填入空格中：

1. *haste*   His _____ decisions caused many mistakes.

2. *frustrate*   Life is full of _____ for most people.

3. *accomplish*   She is known for her _____ in improving the country's hospitals.

4. *pretend*   He often drops by my house without my permission under the _____ of friendship.

5. *courage*   It was _____ of you to try and save the drowning man.

> **【解答】**
> I. 1. A   2. C   3. B   4. D   5. D   6. B   7. A   8. B   9. A   10. C
> II. 1. C   2. A   3. B   4. C   5. D
> III. 1. B   2. D   3. C   4. A   5. B
> IV. 1. remove   2. stream   3. sparkle   4. mild   5. accomplish
> V. 1. B   2. A   3. D   4. C   5. A
> VI. 1. hasty   2. frustration(s)   3. accomplishment(s)
>   4. pretence   5. courageous

Lesson 8

Lesson 9

✦ 第一部分

accord 〔 ə'kɔrd 〕	What you have just said does not **accord** with what you told us yesterday. 你剛才說的和你昨天告訴我們的不一致。	*v.* 一致 同 concur; harmonize 反 discord

【記憶技巧】
ac (to) + *cord* (heart)（做事符合心裏的想法，就是「一致」）

award 〔 ə'wɔrd 〕	He was **awarded** the first prize in the speech contest. 他在演講比賽中被頒發頭獎。	*v.* 頒發 *n.* 獎

【記憶技巧】
award 和 reward 要一起背，口訣是：「頒發」「獎賞」）

boast 〔 bost 〕	He **boasted** about the big fish he had caught.　他誇耀他抓到的大魚。	*v.* 自誇；誇耀
butcher 〔'butʃə 〕	You can buy meat at the **butcher** shop.　你可以在肉店買肉。	*n.* 肉店老板； 屠夫
cheek 〔 tʃik 〕	Her **cheeks** went red after she broke the window.　她打破窗戶後，滿臉通紅。	*n.* 臉頰
competent 〔'kɑmpətənt 〕	He is not **competent** enough to do the job.　他無法勝任那件工作。 Before you can be a lawyer, you must have a **competent** knowledge of the law.　在你成為律師之前，必須具有充分的法律知識。	*adj.* 1. 能幹的； 　　 勝任的 　　 2. 充分的

Lesson 9

consist
〔 kən'sɪst 〕

The United Kingdom *consists* of
Great Britain and Northern Ireland.
英國是由大不列顛和北愛爾蘭所組成。
Happiness *consists* in contentment.
快樂在於知足。

v. 1. 由～組成；
　　包含
同 comprise
2. 在於

crack
〔 kræk 〕

There is a *crack* in the ice.　Don't
skate around here.
冰上有一道裂縫，不要在這附近溜冰。

n. 裂縫
同 crevice
v. 裂開

debt
〔 dɛt 〕

He was in *debt* when he was poor, but
has been out of *debt* since he got rich.
他貧窮時負債，可是自從他有錢後，已經
還清了債務。

n. 債務

describe
〔 dɪ'skraɪb 〕

The reporter *described* the accident
in detail.　記者詳盡地描述那場意外。

v. 描述
名 description

【記憶技巧】
de (fully) + *scribe* (write) (寫得很詳細，也
就是「描述」)

Exercise 9.1　從第一部分中選出最適當的一個英文字，填入空格內。

1. I owe him a(n) _____ of gratitude for all he has done to help
me.

2. His account of the accident seems to _____ with yours.

3. It is unpleasant to hear one _____ about his own abilities,
achievements, or possessions.

4. His horse was _____ the highest prize at the horse show.

5. Happiness _____ largely in being easily pleased or satisfied.

【解答】

1. debt   2. accord   3. boast   4. awarded   5. consists

✦ 第二部分

dispute
〔 dɪˈspjut 〕

They ***disputed*** for hours where to go for their picnic.
他們為去哪裏野餐爭論了好幾個小時。

v. 爭論

【記憶技巧】
dis (apart) + ***pute*** (think) (大家擁有不同的想法，就會開始「爭論」)

ease
〔 iz 〕

The soldiers marched twenty miles with ***ease***.
士兵們輕易地行進了二十哩。

n. 輕鬆
形 easy

engage
〔 ɪnˈgedʒ 〕

The old lady ***engaged*** herself in making clothes for her neighbor's children.
那老婦人忙於為鄰家的孩子做衣服。
She ***engaged*** a carpenter to repair the sofa and the table.
她雇用一個木匠來修理沙發和桌子。

v. 1. 忙於
反 dismiss
名 engagement

2. 雇用
同 employ

express
〔 ɪkˈsprɛs 〕

He is still unable to ***express*** himself in English.
他仍然無法用英語表達自己的意思。

v. 表達
名 expression

【記憶技巧】
ex (out) + ***press*** (壓) (將想法從腦子裡壓出去，即「表達」)

fancy
(ˈfænsɪ)

By the power of *fancy*, we may create an unreal world. 藉著想像力，我們可以創造一個虛幻不實的世界。

n. 幻想
同 illusion
形 fanciful

flee
(fli)

The enemy were defeated and *fled* in disorder.
敵軍潰敗而逃。

v. 逃跑
同 fly; escape
反 chase

fulfil(l)
(fʊlˈfɪl)

If you make a promise, you should *fulfil* it. 如果你許下諾言，就應該實踐它。

v. 履行；實踐

【記憶技巧】
ful(l) + *fill* (填滿)

grace
(gres)

The ballet dancer danced with much *grace*. 那芭蕾舞者的舞步極為優雅。

n. 優雅

haunt
(hɔnt)

People say that the old house is *haunted* by a ghost.
據說那棟舊宅裏有鬼魂出沒。

v. 鬼魂出沒於

innocent
(ˈɪnəsn̩t)

Is he guilty or *innocent* of the crime?
他是有罪還是無罪？

adj. 清白的；無罪的

【記憶技巧】
in (not) + *noc* (harm) + *ent* (adj.) (沒有傷害別人，表示這個人是「清白的」)

Lesson 9

Exercise 9.2 從第二部分中選出最適當的一個英文字，填入空格內。

1. The robbers tried to _____ but they were caught soon.

2. The old woman _____ a maidservant to clean her house.

3. His speech was full of _____ and wit.

4. A nurse has many duties to _____ in caring for the sick.

5. They were still _____ the rights and wrongs of the case at midnight.

【解答】
1. flee   2. engaged   3. grace   4. fulfil(l)   5. disputing

✦ 第三部分

issue
〔ˈɪʃʊ, ˈɪʃju〕

The government *issues* money and stamps. 政府發行鈔票和郵票。

v. 1. 發行

This book was *issued* in New York in 1972.
這本書於一九七二年在紐約出版。

2. 出版
同 publish

A lot of blood was *issuing* from the wound. 大量的血正從傷口流出。

3. 流出
n. 議題

landlord
〔ˈlænd,lɔrd〕

The *landlord* put a new stove in my room. 房東在我房間裏放了一個新爐子。

n. 房東

【記憶技巧】
land（土地）+ *lord*（主人）

literature
〔ˈlɪtərətʃ⋅〕

Many foreigners are studying Chinese *literature*.
許多外國人正在學習中國文學。

n. 文學
形 literary

manufacture
〔ˌmænjəˈfæktʃ⋅〕

The factory *manufactures* automobiles in large quantity by using machines.
該工廠使用機器大量製造汽車。

v. 製造
同 make;
    produce

The *manufacture* of watches is the chief business of Switzerland.
鐘錶製造是瑞士主要的產業。

n. 製造

【記憶技巧】
manu (hand) + *fact* (make) + *ure* (*n.*, *v.*)
（動手做，就是「製造」）

Lesson 9

Lesson 9

military
（'mɪlə,tɛrɪ）

In some countries every healthy young man must do two or three years' **military** service. 在某些國家，所有年輕健康的男子都必須服兩年或三年的兵役。

adj. 軍事的
反 civilian

【記憶技巧】
milit (soldier) + **ary** (*adj.*) (有關軍人的)

multiply
（'mʌltə,plaɪ）

The population of the city is **multiplying** rapidly.
該市人口正迅速地增加。

v. 繁殖；增加

numerous
（'njumərəs）

Children often ask **numerous** questions about the universe.
孩子經常問許多有關宇宙的問題。

adj. 極多的；
　　　許多的

【記憶技巧】
numer (number) + **ous** (*adj.*) (數量眾多，也就是「極多的」)

ordinary
（'ɔrdn̩,ɛrɪ）

His **ordinary** lunch consists of soup, a sandwich, and milk. 他平常的午餐包括湯，一個三明治，還有牛奶。

adj. 普通的；
　　　一般的

【記憶技巧】
ordin (order) + **ary** (*adj.*) (按照順序，就是「普通的」)

pardon
（'pɑrdn̩）

I beg your **pardon** for being late.
請你原諒我遲到。
We must **pardon** him for his little faults. 我們必須原諒他的小錯。

n. 原諒

v. 原諒
同 excuse;
　　forgive

【記憶技巧】
par (thoroughly) + **don** (give) (願意全力付出，表示「原諒」)

peninsula
〔pəˈnɪnsələ〕

Spain and Italy are *peninsulas*.
西班牙和義大利都是個半島。

n. 半島

【記憶技巧】
pen (almost) + *insula* (island)（幾乎可以成為一個島了）

Exercise 9.3 從第三部分中選出最適當的一個英文字，填入空格內。

1. The chimney _____ smoke from the fireplace.

2. As we climbed up the mountain, the dangers and difficulties

   _____.

3. At night we can see _____ stars in the sky.

4. Shakespeare is a great name in English _____.

5. I beg your _____, but I didn't hear you.

【解答】
1. issues   2. multiplied   3. numerous   4. literature   5. pardon

✦ **第四部分**

plunge
〔plʌndʒ〕

He *plunged* into the river and saved the boy. 他跳入河中救起那男孩。

v. 跳進；跳入

prevent
〔prɪˈvɛnt〕

A heavy rain *prevented* us from going on a picnic. 大雨使我們不能去野餐。

v. 預防；避免；阻止

【記憶技巧】
pre (before) + *vent* (come)（事情來臨前先做，即「預防；避免」）

Lesson 9

protest
(prə'tɛst)

Most of them ***protested*** against the new heavy tax. 他們大多數抗議新的重稅。

v. 抗議
同 object

> 【記憶技巧】
> ***pro*** + ***test***（測驗）

---

rear
(rɪr)

The people in the ***rear*** of the room could not hear the speaker.
房間後頭的人聽不到演說者的聲音。

n. 後面
同 back
反 front

> 【記憶技巧】
> ***r*** + ***ear***（耳朵）

---

rent
(rɛnt)

We don't own our house; we ***rent*** it from Mr. Gay.
我們住的房子不是自己的，是向蓋伊先生租的。
Rent for that three-bedroom apartment is $500 a month.
那間有三間臥室的公寓，每月租金五百元。

v. 租

n. 租金

---

revenge
(rɪ'vɛndʒ)

His mind was filled with ***revenge***.
他心中充滿復仇之意。

n. 報復；
　　復仇

---

saddle
('sædḷ)

It is difficult to ride a horse without a ***saddle***.
沒有馬鞍騎馬很困難。

n. 馬鞍

---

seal
(sil)

The paper had been stamped with the required official ***seal***.
這份文件已印有必需之官方封印。
The treaty was signed and ***sealed*** by both governments.
兩國政府都在條約上簽署蓋章。

n. 印章；
　　封印；
　　海豹

v. 蓋章

Lesson 9

shelter
（ˈʃɛltɚ）

The cave provided a good *shelter* for the ancient people.
洞穴為古人提供了一個良好的避難所。
The abandoned car *sheltered* them from the rain. 那部被丟棄的車子供他們躲雨。

n. 避難所
同 refuge

v. 遮蔽

> 【記憶技巧】
> *shel*（shield 盾牌）+ *ter* (strong)（軍隊用盾牌圍成堅固的避難所）

slice
〔slaɪs〕

He ate two *slices* of bread for his breakfast.
他早餐吃了兩片麵包。

n. 一片；
薄片

Exercise 9.4 從第四部分中選出最適當的一個英文字，填入空格內。

1. The _____ for the house was more than they could afford.

2. The garage is usually at the _____ of a house.

3. There was a large crowd in the street, _____ against the war.

4. Illness _____ him from taking the examination.

5. The fireman _____ into the burning house to rescue the baby in it.

> 【解答】
> 1. rent 2. rear 3. protesting 4. prevented 5. plunged

Lesson 9

✦ 第五部分

spear
〔 spɪr 〕

In Africa, *spears* are still used in hunting or fishing.
在非洲仍然用矛來打獵或捕魚。

n. 矛；魚叉

stake
〔 stek 〕

Stakes mark the boundary of his ranch. 木樁用來標示他農場的範圍。
As a partner, he has a *stake* in that business. 身為一個合夥人，他和那家公司有利害關係。
He *staked* all his money on the black horse. 他將所有的錢賭在那匹黑馬上。

n. 1. 木樁

2. 利害關係

v. 賭
同 bet

stretch
〔 strɛtʃ 〕

The beggar *stretched* out his hand for the money.
那乞丐伸出手要錢。

v. 拉長；伸出；伸展手腳
同 extend

surround
〔 sə'raʊnd 〕

The field is *surrounded* by a high fence. 那塊田被很高的籬笆所圍繞。

v. 圍繞；包圍
同 enclose
名 surroundings

【記憶技巧】
sur (over) + *round* (環繞)

tavern
〔'tævən 〕

They met at the *tavern* for a drink.
他們在酒館裏碰面喝酒。

n. 酒館；酒店；旅店

timber
〔'tɪmbə 〕

The fire destroyed thousands of acres of *timber*. 大火燒毀了數千英畝的森林。

n. 木材；森林
同 lumber

【記憶技巧】
諧音：挺拔，「森林」「木材」很挺拔。

trick
〔 trɪk 〕

The *tricks* of the magician delighted the children.
魔術師的戲法使孩子們很高興。
We were *tricked* into buying a poor car. 我們被騙買一部破車。

n. 把戲；戲法

v. 欺騙
同 cheat

Lesson 9

vein 〔 ven 〕	Blood poured from the cut ***vein***. 血從割開的靜脈中流出。	*n.* 靜脈 反 artery
weaken 〔'wikən 〕	The illness ***weakened*** her heart. 她的病使得她的心臟衰弱。	*v.* 使虛弱；使稀薄；沖淡 形 weak
wring 〔 rɪŋ 〕	I'll ***wring*** your neck if you don't behave well. 如果你不守規矩，我就掐死你。	*v.* 擰乾；扭；絞 同 twist

【記憶技巧】
w + ***ring***（戒指）

Exercise 9.5　從第五部分中選出最適當的一個英文字，填入空格內。

1. The bird _____ its wings when it wants to fly.

2. The soldiers _____ the enemy in the town.

3. _____ carry blood to the heart from all parts of the body.

4. She _____ as her illness grew worse.

5. _____ the water from your bathing suit.

【解答】
1. stretches　2. surrounded　3. Veins　4. weakened　5. Wring

成果測驗

I. 找出一個與其他三個不相關的字：

(   ) 1. (A) accomplish   (B) perform
          (C) stretch   (D) fulfil

(   ) 2. (A) make   (B) manufacture
          (C) produce   (D) wring

(   ) 3. (A) defeat   (B) express
          (C) reveal   (D) represent

(   ) 4. (A) twist   (B) squeeze   (C) yield   (D) wring

(   ) 5. (A) protection   (B) revenge   (C) refuge   (D) shelter

(   ) 6. (A) many   (B) plentiful
          (C) numerous   (D) extensive

(   ) 7. (A) concur   (B) harmonize
          (C) achieve   (D) accord

(   ) 8. (A) flee   (B) fly   (C) escape   (D) chase

(   ) 9. (A) ordinary   (B) useful   (C) common   (D) average

(   ) 10. (A) landlord   (B) host
          (C) rent   (D) innkeeper

II. 找出一個與題前中文意思相同的英文字：

(   ) 1. 優雅
         (A) reverse   (B) grace   (C) blush   (D) clean

Lesson 9

(　　) 2. 擰乾
    (A) wing　　　　(B) ring　　　　(C) wring　　　　(D) seal

(　　) 3. 鬼魂出沒於
    (A) haunt　　　　　　　　　(B) flee
    (C) multiply　　　　　　　(D) enclose

(　　) 4. 拉長
    (A) pretend　　　(B) fulfil　　　(C) spare　　　(D) stretch

(　　) 5. 把戲
    (A) seal　　　　(B) trick　　　(C) screw　　　(D) stain

Ⅲ. 找出一個與斜體字意義相反的單字：

(　　) 1. *chase*
    (A) assume　　(B) flee　　　(C) wreck　　(D) conceal

(　　) 2. *artery*
    (A) vein　　　　　　　　　(B) veil
    (C) manufacture　　　　　(D) literature

(　　) 3. *front*
    (A) revenge　　　　　　　(B) opposite
    (C) sleeve　　　　　　　　(D) rear

(　　) 4. *discord*
    (A) baffle　　　　　　　　(B) mourn
    (C) haunt　　　　　　　　(D) harmonize

(　　) 5. *dismiss*
    (A) discharge　　　　　　(B) engage
    (C) disclose　　　　　　　(D) find

Lesson 9

IV. 完整拼出下列各句中所欠缺的單字，每一格代表一個字母：

1. Hamlet wanted r_ _ _ _ e for his father's murder. （復仇）

2. He found a room for the night at a t_ _ _ _n. （旅店）

3. His peaceful words and violent actions do not a_ _ _ _d.
   （一致）

4. What kind of t_ _ _ _r was used for the frame of the house?
   （木材）

5. You can w_ _ _ _n tea by adding water. （沖淡）

V. 找出一個與句中斜體字意義最接近的單字：

( ) 1. He threw the mirror on the floor, but there was not a *crack*
        in it.
    (A) sound   (B) crevice
    (C) stake   (D) trick

( ) 2. That magazine is *issued* once a month.
    (A) sold   (B) bought
    (C) published   (D) shown

( ) 3. If you want to learn German, you must first find a
        competent teacher.
    (A) capable   (B) faithful
    (C) honorable   (D) sacred

( ) 4. Some husbands and wives are always *disputing*.
    (A) discharging   (B) disposing
    (C) competing   (D) arguing

(　) 5. Water *consists of* hydrogen and oxygen.
- (A) disposes
- (B) comprises
- (C) derives
- (D) involves

(　) 6. The children *protested* loudly when they were told to go to bed.
- (A) objected
- (B) protected
- (C) discorded
- (D) revenged

(　) 7. They *engaged* a man to paint their new house.
- (A) employed
- (B) forced
- (C) dismissed
- (D) pardoned

(　) 8. Did I really hear someone come in or was it only a *fancy*?
- (A) notion
- (B) flavor
- (C) grace
- (D) illusion

(　) 9. The old house is *enclosed* by trees.
- (A) protected
- (B) prevented
- (C) disclosed
- (D) surrounded

(　) 10. *Forgive* my mistakes. I'll try not to make the same mistakes.
- (A) mourn
- (B) deter
- (C) pardon
- (D) forget

Lesson 9

【解答】
I. 1. C　2. D　3. A　4. C　5. B　6. D　7. C　8. D　9. B　10. C
II. 1. B　2. C　3. A　4. D　5. B
III. 1. B　2. A　3. D　4. D　5. B
IV. 1. revenge　2. tavern　3. accord　4. timber　5. weaken
V. 1. B　2. C　3. A　4. D　5. B　6. A　7. A　8. D　9. D　10. C

Lesson 10

✦ 第一部分

account 〔 ə'kaʊnt 〕	The boy gave his father an ***account*** of the ball game. 那男孩向他父親敘述球賽的經過。	*n.* 帳戶；敘述

【記憶技巧】
ac (to) + *count* (count) (把所有事情計算清楚，就是「敘述」)

angle 〔'æŋgl̩ 〕	An ***angle*** of 90 degrees is called a right ***angle***. 九十度的角叫作直角。	*n.* 角度；角

【記憶技巧】
不要和 angel (天使) 搞混。

aware 〔 ə'wɛr 〕	I was too sleepy to be ***aware*** of how cold it was. 我太睏以致無法察覺出有多冷。	*adj.* 知道的； 察覺到的 名 awareness
bold 〔 bold 〕	Climbing the steep mountain is a ***bold*** act. 爬那座險峻的山是大膽的行爲。	*adj.* 大膽的 同 brave 反 cowardly
cabin 〔'kæbɪn 〕	The pioneers lived in a ***cabin*** in the woods. 拓荒者住在森林裏的一間小屋內。	*n.* 小屋
cheer 〔 tʃɪr 〕	Everyone was ***cheered*** by the news that peace had come. 和平到來的消息使每一個人都高興。	*v.* 使振作；使 高興；歡呼 同 applaud

complain
〔kəm'plen〕

She *complained* to the police about the barking of her neighbor's dog.
她向警方抱怨鄰居家的狗叫聲。

v. 抱怨
名 complaint

> 【記憶技巧】
> *com* (together) + *plain* (beat the breast) (想「抱怨」時，因為內心充滿怒火，會想要捶胸頓足)

consolation
〔ˌkɑnsə'leʃən〕

I got many letters of *consolation* when my mother died. 當我母親去世時，我收到許多慰問信。

n. 安慰
動 console

crash
〔kræʃ〕

He was killed in an aircraft *crash*. 他在一次飛機失事中喪生。
The bottles fell on the floor with a *crash*. 瓶子嘩啦一聲掉在地上。

n. 1. 墜毀；失事；
　　（雷）隆隆聲
　　2. 破碎聲

decay
〔dɪ'ke〕

Her teeth *decayed* because she ate too many sweets.
她的牙齒因吃太多甜食而蛀壞。

v. 腐爛
同 decline; rot

> 【記憶技巧】
> *de* (down) + *cay* (fall) (木頭「腐爛」，建築物會倒下)

Lesson 10

Exercise 10.1 從第一部分中選出最適當的一個英文字，填入空格內。

1. The two roads lie at a(n) _____ of 45 degrees.

2. When your teeth begin to _____ you should go to see a dentist at once.

3. Every time an American runner won a race, the crowd _____.

4. Are you _____ that you are sitting on my hat?

5. Please give me a(n) _____ of everything as it happened.

【解答】

1. angle　2. decay　3. cheered　4. aware　5. account

✦ 第二部分

deserve
〔 dɪˋzɝv 〕

If you do wrong, you **deserve** severe punishment.
如果你做錯事，應受嚴厲的處罰。

v. 應得（賞罰）

distinction
〔 dɪˋstɪŋkʃən 〕

She treated all the children alike without **distinction**.
她給孩子們同樣的待遇，沒有區分。

n. 區分
同 discrimination
動 distinguish

echo
〔ˋɛko 〕

Their voices **echoed** in the big hall. 他們的聲音在大廳裏回響著。

n. 回音
v. 發出回響

enormous
〔 ɪˋnɔrməs 〕

The war cost an **enormous** sum of money. 那場戰爭消耗大量的金錢。

adj. 巨大的

【記憶技巧】

e (out of) + *norm*（標準）+ *ous* (*adj.*)
（超出標準，即「巨大的」）

---

expose
〔 ɪkˋspoz 〕

Soldiers in an open field are **exposed** to the enemy's fire.
曠野中的士兵暴露在敵人的砲火下。
He threatened to **expose** the secret to the police. 他威脅要向警方揭穿祕密。

v. 1. 暴露

2. 揭穿
同 disclose
名 exposure

【記憶技巧】

ex (out) + *pose* (put)（放在外面，就是「暴露」）

Lesson 10

farewell
〔͵fɛr'wɛl〕

We shall have a *farewell* party before we leave.
在我們離開前，將會舉辦一場歡送會。

n. 告別；離別
同 goodbye

fleet
〔flit〕

The Sixth *Fleet* is moving toward our coast.
第六艦隊正朝著我們的海岸駛來。

n. 艦隊

function
〔'fʌŋkʃən〕

The brain performs a very important *function*; it controls the nervous system of the body. 大腦執行一項非常重要的功能；它控制身體的神經系統。

n. 功能
形 functional
動 function

> 【記憶技巧】
> *funct* (perform) + *ion* (*n.*)（能執行某件事，就是有某種「功能」）

gradual
〔'grædʒuəl〕

A child's growth into an adult is *gradual*.
兒童到成人的成長過程是逐漸的。

adj. 逐漸的
副 gradually
反 swift

> 【記憶技巧】
> *gradu* (step) + *al* (*adj.*)（一步一步來，即「逐漸的」）

hay
〔he〕

They usually keep the *hay* in the barn.
他們通常將乾草存放在穀倉中。

n. 乾草

Lesson 10

Exercise 10.2 從第二部分中選出最適當的一個英文字，填入空格內。

1. The murderer was hanged; he _____ his fate.

2. He gave all his servants the same wages, without making any
_____ .

3. The change was _____, but now it looks completely different.

4. The hill _____ back the noise of the gunshot.

5. During the last ten years, he has made a(n) _____ amount of money and become a millionaire.

【解答】
1. deserved 2. distinction(s) 3. gradual 4. echoed 5. enormous

✦ 第三部分

ignorant
〔ˈɪgnərənt〕

He is quite *ignorant*; he can't even read or write.
他很無知；他甚至連讀或寫都不會。

adj. 無知的

inquire
〔ɪnˈkwaɪr〕

I *inquired* of him what he wanted.
我問他想要什麼。

【記憶技巧】
in (into) + *quire* (seek) (深入尋求，就是「詢問」)

v. 詢問
同 ask
反 reply
名 inquiry

item
〔ˈaɪtəm〕

Meat, salad, and potatoes were three of the *items* on her shopping list.
肉、沙拉，還有馬鈴薯是她購物清單上的三個項目。

n. 項目；物品

landscape
〔ˈlændskep〕

From the church tower, we can overlook the beautiful *landscape* of the valley. 從教堂的塔上，我們可以俯瞰山谷美麗的風景。

n. 風景
同 scenery; view

Lesson 10

liver
(ˈlɪvɚ)

He was sent to hospital because of his bad *liver*.
他因肝病被送到醫院。

n. 肝臟

manuscript
(ˈmænjəˌskrɪpt)

He sent the *manuscript* to the printer yesterday.
他昨天將手稿送到印刷廠。

n. 手稿

【記憶技巧】
manu (hand) + *script* (write) (用手寫的紙張，也就是「手稿」)

millionaire
(ˌmɪljənˈɛr)

The man is a *millionaire*; he is a very rich man. 那人是個百萬富翁；他是一個非常富有的人。

n. 百萬富翁

【記憶技巧】
-aire 表「人」的字尾。

murder
(ˈmɝdɚ)

The man was guilty of *murder*; he killed someone.
那人犯了謀殺罪；他殺了人。

n. 謀殺

obey
(əˈbe)

Obey the law, or you will be punished.
要遵守從法律，否則你將會受罰。

v. 遵守；服從
反 violate
名 obedience

organization
(ˌɔrgənəˈzeʃən)

The human body has a very complex *organization*.
人體組織非常複雜。

n. 組織

Lesson 10

Exercise 10.3 從第三部分中選出最適當的一個英文字，填入空格內。

1. We could see the beautiful _____ of the English Lakes through the train window.

2. An army without _____ would be useless.

3. Soldiers should _____ orders immediately.

4. That _____ owns his own ship and helicopter.

5. A person who has not had much chance to learn may be _____.

【解答】

1. landscape　　2. organization　　3. obey　　4. millionaire　　5. ignorant

---

✦ 第四部分

parliament
（'pɑrləmənt）

Parliament is the lawmaking body in Great Britain.
國會是英國的立法機構。

【記憶技巧】
parlia（parley 商談）+ ***ment***（n.）（「國會」就是談國事的地方）

n. 國會
同 congress

pepper
（'pɛpə）

Pepper is used to make food taste better. 胡椒可使食物更美味。

n. 胡椒

poetry
（'po·ɪtrɪ）

The teacher praised her great efforts at ***poetry***. 老師稱讚她肯下苦工作詩。

n. 詩【集合名詞】

preview
〔'pri,vju 〕

Before the movie was shown to the students, there was a ***preview*** for the teachers. 在電影放映給學生看之前，有一場給老師看的試映。

n. 預告片；
　　試映；預習

【記憶技巧】
pre (before) + ***view*** (see)(之前先看，就是「試映；預習」)

---

provide
〔 prə'vaɪd 〕

The farm ***provided*** them with all the food they needed.
農場提供他們所有需要的食物。

v. 提供
同 supply;
　　furnish

---

reckless
〔'rɛklɪs 〕

Two children were killed by a ***reckless*** driver. 兩個孩子被魯莽的駕駛人撞死。

adj. 魯莽的
同 careless

【記憶技巧】
reck (顧慮) + ***less*** (*adj.*) (不顧慮後果的，即「魯莽的」)

---

repair
〔 rɪ'pɛr 〕

We'd better ***repair*** the house before we move into it.
在我們搬進去之前，最好先修理一下房子。

v. 修理
同 mend; fix

【記憶技巧】
re (again) + ***pair*** (prepare)

---

saint
〔 sent 〕

They named their child after the ***saint***.
他們用聖人的名字來為他們的孩子命名。

n. 聖人

---

search
〔 sɝtʃ 〕

We ***searched*** all day for the lost cat.
我們整日尋找那隻走失的貓。

v. 尋找

Lesson 10

sheriff (ˈʃɛrɪf)	The *sheriff* brought the captured criminal before the judge. 警長將被捕的罪犯帶到法官面前。	*n.* 警長

【記憶技巧】
sher (shire 郡) + *iff* (official))

Exercise 10.4 從第四部分中選出最適當的一個英文字，填入空格內。

1. The _____ in the United Kingdom is made up of the Queen, the Lords, and the elected representatives of the people.

2. Shakespeare and Milton were masters of English _____.

3. _____ driving causes many automobile accidents.

4. The _____ pursued the man who robbed the bank.

5. They will _____ the school building during the summer vacation.

【解答】
1. parliament   2. poetry   3. Reckless   4. sheriff   5. repair

---

✦ 第五部分

specialist (ˈspɛʃəlɪst)	The patient was advised to see a heart *specialist*. 有人勸那病患去看一個心臟專家。	*n.* 專家

stalk 〔 stɔk 〕	The hunter ***stalked*** the lion. 獵人潛行接近獅子。 With her head in the air, she ***stalked*** out of the room. 她趾高氣昂，大步地走出房間。 The trunk of a tree and the ***stalks*** of corn are stems. 樹幹和穀物的莖都屬於莖。	*v.* 1. 跟蹤；潛近 　 2. 大步走 *n.*【植物】莖； 　 幹；葉柄； 　 花梗 同 stem

【記憶技巧】
s + *talk*（說話）(「潛近」某人跟他說話)

Stalk

strict 〔 ˌstrɪkt 〕	They are very ***strict*** with their children. 他們對孩子非常嚴格。	*adj.* 嚴格的
survey 〔 sɚˋve 〕	He stood on the hill and ***surveyed*** the surrounding country. 他站在山丘上，眺望四周的鄉間。	*v.* 調查；眺望

【記憶技巧】
sur(over) + *vey*(see)（從上往下看，就是「調查；眺望」)

temper 〔 ˋtɛmpɚ 〕	He was in a good ***temper*** yesterday and smiled all day. 他昨天心情好，整天都面帶微笑。	*n.* 脾氣；心情 同 disposition
tin 〔 tɪn 〕	The house over there has a ***tin*** roof. 那邊的那幢房子，有個錫做的屋頂。	*n.* 錫
trim 〔 trɪm 〕	The student had his hair ***trimmed***. 那個學生修剪了頭髮。 The new house has a ***trim*** appearance. 那幢新房子的外觀整潔。	*v.* 修剪 *adj.* 整齊的

Lesson 10

venture
〔ˈvɛntʃɚ〕

If his business ***venture*** succeeds, he will be wealthy.
如果他的冒險事業成功，他將會富有。

He ***ventured*** his life to save her from drowning.
他冒著生命的危險救她，使她免於淹死。

n. 冒險的事業

v. 冒～之險
同 risk

> ---【記憶技巧】---
> ***vent*** (come) + ***ure*** (*n.*)（讓危險迎面而來，就是在冒險）

wealthy
〔ˈwɛlθɪ〕

Mr. Johnson is a very ***wealthy*** man.
強生先生是個非常富有的人。

adj. 有錢的；
富有的

wrist
〔rɪst〕

He took the girl by the ***wrist***.
他抓住那女孩的手腕。

n. 手腕

Exercise 10.5 從第五部分中選出最適當的一個英文字，填入空格內。

1. The carpenter _____ the lumber with a plane.

2. This can is made of steel protected by a coating of _____.

3. She is in a bad _____ because she missed the bus and had to walk to work.

4. Dr. White is a(n) _____ in diseases of the nose and throat.

5. The buyers _____ the goods offered for sale.

> ----【解答】----
> 1. trimmed　2. tin　3. temper　4. specialist　5. surveyed

成果測驗

I. 找出一個與斜體字的意義最接近的單字：

(　) 1. *bold* behavior
  (A) common
  (C) lazy
  (B) brave
  (D) military

(　) 2. in a good *temper*
  (A) speed
  (C) disposition
  (B) stake
  (D) temperature

(　) 3. to *repair* shoes
  (A) stretch　(B) accord　(C) mend　(D) make

(　) 4. to *inquire* something
  (A) ask　(B) identify　(C) require　(D) protest

(　) 5. to *expose* one's secret
  (A) forgive　(B) conceal　(C) object　(D) disclose

(　) 6. *reckless* behavior
  (A) safe
  (C) innocent
  (B) careless
  (D) earnest

(　) 7. a *farewell* speech
  (A) goodbye
  (C) powerful
  (B) competent
  (D) honorable

(　) 8. to get treated without *distinction* of rank
  (A) consolation
  (C) function
  (B) discrimination
  (D) disposition

Lesson 10

(　) 9. the *decayed* teeth

    (A) repaired　　　　　　　(B) golden

    (C) rotten　　　　　　　　(D) shaking

(　) 10. to *applaud* the singer

    (A) account　　　　　　　(B) complain

    (C) accord　　　　　　　　(D) cheer

II. 找出一個與題前中文意思相同的英文字：

(　) 1. 專家

    (A) literature　　　　　　(B) saint

    (C) host　　　　　　　　　(D) specialist

(　) 2. 謀殺

    (A) liver　　　　　　　　(B) destruction

    (C) murder　　　　　　　(D) stalk

(　) 3. 抱怨

    (A) complain　　　　　　(B) deteriorate

    (C) acclaim　　　　　　　(D) furnish

(　) 4. 整齊的

    (A) swift　　　(B) trim　　　(C) trivial　　　(D) mild

(　) 5. 墜毀

    (A) rent　　　(B) crack　　　(C) crash　　　(D) stake

III. 找出一個與斜體字意義相反的單字：

(　) 1. *swift*

    (A) huge　　　(B) strict　　　(C) gradual　　　(D) trivial

Lesson 10

(   ) 2. *cowardly*

    (A) average   (B) miserable   (C) innocent   (D) bold

(   ) 3. *reply*

    (A) inquire   (B) award   (C) deserve   (D) uncover

(   ) 4. *violate*

    (A) provide   (B) obey   (C) search   (D) expose

(   ) 5. *educated*

    (A) enormous (B) ignorant (C) wealthy (D) reckless

IV. 完整拼出下列各句中所欠缺的單字，每一格代表一個字母：

1. I remember that our English teacher was very s_ _ _ _t.（嚴格的）

2. The author's m_ _ _ _ _ _ _ _t was accepted for publication.
（原稿）

3. You work very hard; you d_ _ _ _ _e good pay.（應得）

4. She broke her right w_ _ _t by falling on the ice.（手腕）

5. A father must p_ _ _ _ _e food and clothes for his children.
（提供）

V. 選出最適合句意的一個單字：

(   ) 1. Your presence was a _____ to me at such a sad time.

    (A) discrimination   (B) consolation

    (C) crash   (D) stalk

(   ) 2. The lightning was followed by a(n) _____ of thunder.

    (A) crash   (B) echo   (C) stake   (D) trick

Lesson 10

(   ) 3. The film which has been _____ to light is no longer usable.
      (A) provided   (B) decayed
      (C) expressed   (D) exposed

(   ) 4. A person who is _____ does not have much knowledge.
      (A) lame   (B) ignorant   (C) idle   (D) innocent

(   ) 5. The gardener _____ the dead branches from the trees.
      (A) deserved (B) protected (C) trimmed   (D) repaired

VI. 將題前的斜體字轉換為適當詞性，填入空格中：

1. *inquire*   My _____ about his health was never answered.

2. *complain*   The children were full of _____ about their food.

3. *obey*   Soldiers act in _____ to the orders of their
               superior officers.

4. *distinction* The twins were so much alike that it was impossible
               to _____ one from the other.

5. *expose*   _____ of the body to strong sunlight may be
               harmful.

【解答】

I. 1. B 2. C 3. C 4. A 5. D 6. B 7. A 8. B 9. C 10. D
II. 1. D 2. C 3. A 4. B 5. C
III. 1. C 2. D 3. A 4. B 5. B
IV. 1. strict 2. manuscript 3. deserve 4. wrist 5. provide
V. 1. B 2. A 3. D 4. B 5. C
VI. 1. inquiry 2. complaints 3. obedience 4. distinguish
    5. Exposure

Lesson 11

✦ 第一部分

accustom
〔 ə'kʌstəm 〕

She could not ***accustom*** herself to the hot climate in Africa.
她無法習慣非洲炎熱的氣候。

【記憶技巧】
ac + custom（習俗）

v. 使習慣
同 habituate

ankle
〔'æŋkḷ 〕

Human beings and all other animals that have feet and legs have ***ankles***.
人類和其他所有有腳和腿的動物都有腳踝。

【記憶技巧】
想到 ankle（腳踝）和地面有 angle（角度）。

n. 腳踝

bachelor
〔'bætʃələ 〕

The young ***bachelor*** will soon be taking a wife.
那年輕的單身漢不久就要娶太太。

n. 單身漢
反 spinster

border
〔'bɔrdə 〕

When we went camping, we put up our tents on the ***border*** of the lake.
露營時，我們在湖邊紮營。

n. 邊界
同 frontier

calm
〔 kɑm 〕

Mother's ***calm*** behavior made the frightened child quiet. 母親冷靜的態度使那受驚的孩子安靜下來。

adj. 冷靜的
同 quiet

chew
〔 tʃu 〕

You should ***chew*** your food well before you swallow it.
你應該先細嚼食物後，再吞下去。

v. 咀嚼

complex
〔'kɑmplɛks 〕

The instructions for building the radio were so ***complex*** that we could not follow them. 組合收音機的說明太複雜了，我們看不懂。

adj. 複雜的
同 complicated
名 complexity

consolidate
〔 kən'salə,det 〕

Britain is trying to **consolidate** her position in the North Atlantic.
英國試圖鞏固她在北大西洋的地位。

v. 鞏固
同 solidify

crawl
〔 krɔl 〕

The wounded soldier tried to **crawl** back to the tent.
那傷兵試圖爬回帳篷。

v. 爬
同 creep

decent
〔'disṇt 〕

You need **decent** clothes when you go to church.
你去教堂時需著端莊的衣服。

adj. 高尚的；
端莊的；
不錯的

【記憶技巧】
de + **cent** (一分錢)

Exercise 11.1　從第一部分中選出最適當的一個英文字，填入空格內。

1. You can get quite a(n) _____ meal there without spending too much money.

2. The presidential candidate _____ his reputation by winning several primary elections.

3. He _____ a mouthful of meat but it was too much to swallow.

4. The Rio Grande River is the _____ between the United States and Mexico.

5. Hunting dogs are _____ to the noise of a gun.

【解答】
1. decent　2. consolidated　3. chewed　4. border　5. accustomed

✦ 第二部分

despair
〔 dɪ'spɛr 〕

A feeling of *despair* came over him as the boat sank deeper in the water.
當船在水中沉得更深時，他感到絕望。

n. 絕望
同 desperation
反 hope

> 【記憶技巧】
> *de* (away) + *spair* (hope)（失去希望，也就是「絕望」）

distress
〔 dɪ'strɛs 〕

Her husband has just died and she is in great *distress*.
她的丈夫剛死，所以她非常悲痛。

n. 痛苦；悲痛
同 worry
反 comfort; relief

> 【記憶技巧】
> *di*（加重語氣的字首）+ *stress*（壓力）（壓力會帶來「痛苦」）

edge
〔 ɛdʒ 〕

Don't put the glass on the *edge* of the table; it may get knocked off.
不要將杯子放在桌邊；它可能會被打落。

n. 邊緣
同 margin; border
反 center

enterprise
〔 'ɛntɚ‚praɪz 〕

Building the steel manufacturing company is a great *enterprise*.
成立鋼鐵廠是項大企業。

n. 企業
同 business

> 【記憶技巧】
> *enter* (among) + *prise* (take in hand)

export
〔 'ɛksport 〕

Last year our *exports* exceeded our imports in value.
去年我們的出口貨物的價值超過進口。

n. 出口
反 import

Lesson 11

fasten
〔'fæsn̩〕

He *fastened* the pages together with a pin. 他用大頭針將文件固定在一起。

v. 繫上；固定

【記憶技巧】
fast（牢固的）+ *en* (v.)

flesh
〔flɛʃ〕

A fat man has much more *flesh* than a thin man.
胖子的肉比瘦子的肉要多得多。

n. 肉

fund
〔fʌnd〕

That *fund* will be used for the expenses of the poor people.
那份基金將用來作爲窮人的津貼。

n. 基金
同 capital

graduate
〔'grædʒʊ,et〕

Her brother *graduated* from Harvard University last year.
她兄弟去年畢業於哈佛大學。

v. 畢業
名 graduation

【記憶技巧】
gradu (grade) + *ate* (v.)（不斷升級，最後「畢業」）

heal
〔hil〕

The medicine and rest will soon *heal* your wound.
藥物和休息很快就能治癒你的傷口。

v. 治癒
同 cure

Exercise 11.2 從第二部分中選出最適當的一個英文字，填入空格內。

1. He was filled with _____ as his enemies crowded around him.

2. The high cost of living is a(n) cause of _____ to most people.

3. Shipbuilding is one of the biggest _____ in this country.

4. Wood is one of the chief _____ of Australia.

5. The sharp knife cut into the _____ of his arm.

┌─ 【解答】 ──────────────────────────────────────┐
│ 1. despair   2. distress   3. enterprises   4. exports   5. flesh │
└──┘

✦ 第三部分

illustrate
〔'ɪləstret ,
ɪ'lʌstret 〕

The teacher compared the heart to a pump to **illustrate** its function. 老師將心臟比喻成幫浦，以說明心臟的功能。

v. 圖解說明；
　　說明
同 complain
名 illustration

┌─ 【記憶技巧】 ─────────────────────────┐
│ **il** (in) + **lustr** (bright) + **ate** (v.)（使變亮， │
│ 就是用圖解「說明」，使讀者一目了然） │
└──────────────────────────────────┘

insist
〔 ɪn'sɪst 〕

She **insisted** that she was right.
她堅持她是對的。

v. 堅持

┌─ 【記憶技巧】 ─────────────────────────┐
│ **in** (on) + **sist** (stand)（一直站在自己的立 │
│ 場，就是「堅持」自己的想法） │
└──────────────────────────────────┘

jar
〔 dʒɑr 〕

A **jar** has a wide mouth and sometimes has two handles.
廣口瓶有個大口，有時候還有兩個把手。

n. 廣口瓶

lane
〔 len 〕

He was driving his car down a narrow **lane** in a town.
他正沿著城中的窄巷開車。

n. 巷子；通道
同 passage

loan
〔 lon 〕

He asked his brother for a small *loan* to buy a house.
他向他兄弟借一點錢買房子。

n. 債款;貸款

maple
〔'mepḷ 〕

We have a *maple* in our yard.
我們院內有棵楓樹。

n. 楓樹

mingle
〔'mɪŋgḷ 〕

It is not easy for him to *mingle* with people because he is very shy.
由於他非常害羞,因此和別人交往,對他來說不是一件簡單的事。

v. 混合;交往
同 mix; blend

【記憶技巧】
用 mix (混合) + single (單一) = mingle
聯想

muscle
〔'mʌsḷ 〕

You can develop your arm *muscles* by playing tennis.
你可以藉打網球來使你的臂肌發達。

n. 肌肉

object
〔'ɑbdʒɪkt 〕

A dark *object* moved between me and the door.
一個黑色物體在我和門之間移動著。

n. 物體

〔 əb'dʒɛkt 〕

He stood up and *objected* in strong language.　他站起來以激烈的言詞反對。

v. 反對
名 objection

【記憶技巧】
ob (against) + *ject* (throw) (把東西丟向某人,就是「反對」)

origin
〔'ɔrədʒɪn 〕

Ancient Greece is often called the *origin* of Western civilization.
古希臘常被稱為西方文明的起源。

n. 起源
同 source

Exercise 11.3 從第三部分中選出最適當的一個英文字，填入空格內。

1. I _____ to being treated like a child.

2. He injured the _____ of his arm by throwing the heavy weight.

3. The king often left his palace at night and _____ with the people in the streets.

4. He asked me for a(n) _____ of five hundred dollars.

5. The _____ of this river is a stream in the mountains.

【解答】

1. object   2. muscles   3. mingled   4. loan   5. origin

✦ 第四部分

parlor 〔'parlɚ〕	The *parlor* was crowded with many people during the party. 在宴會中，客廳擠滿了許多人。	*n.* 店；客廳
perceive 〔pɚ'siv〕	I soon *perceived* that I could not change his mind. 我很快發覺我不能使他改變想法。	*v.* 察覺 名 perception

【記憶技巧】
per (through) + *ceive* (take) (憑感覺取得，就是「察覺」)

poisonous 〔'pɔɪznəs〕	Some plants have *poisonous* roots or fruits. 有些植物的根或果實有毒。	*adj.* 有毒的 名 poison

Lesson 11

previous
〔'priviəs 〕

I can't go, for I have a *previous* engagement.
我不能去，因為我有先約。

adj. 先前的
同 earlier

province
〔'pravıns 〕

Most countries are divided into several *provinces*.
大多數的國家被分成好幾省。

n. 省

recommend
〔,rɛkə'mɛnd 〕

The doctor *recommended* that she should stay in bed for a week.
醫生勸她應該在床上躺一星期。

v. 推薦；勸告
名 recommendation

---【記憶技巧】---
re（加強語氣的字首）+ *commend*（稱讚）（「推薦」是最由衷的讚美）

replace
〔 rı'ples 〕

Most telephone operators have been *replaced* by dial telephones. 大多數的電話接線生已被自動電話取代。

v. 取代；代替
名 replacement

ridiculous
〔 rı'dıkjələs 〕

It would be *ridiculous* to speak ill of one's parents in public. 公開說自己父母親的壞話是荒謬的。

adj. 荒謬的；可笑的

shift
〔 ʃıft 〕

The wind *shifted* from east to west. 風向由東轉西。

v. 轉移
同 change

slip
〔 slıp 〕

She *slipped* on the ice and hurt her hand.
她在冰上滑倒傷了手。
He inserted a *slip* marking his place in the book. 他在書中插入一紙片，以標示他讀到的地方。

v. 滑倒
同 slide

n. 紙片

Exercise 11.4 從第四部分中選出最適當的一個英文字，填入空格內。

1. He _____ on the icy road and broke his leg.

2. You look _____ in that old hat.

3. Her former employer _____ Miss Kim as a good typist.

4. Have you had any _____ experience, or is this kind of work new to you?

5. The _____ of their house is nicely decorated.

【解答】

1. slipped　2. ridiculous　3. recommended　4. previous　5. parlor

✦ 第五部分

sphere 〔sfɪr〕	All points on the surface of a *sphere* are equally distant from the center. 球心到球面上任何一點的距離都一樣。 【記憶技巧】 *sphere* (ball)	*n.* 球體；球
startle 〔'stɑrtḷ〕	I was *startled* at the news of his death. 他死亡的消息使我大吃一驚。 【記憶技巧】 *start*（開始）+ *le*	*v.* 使嚇一跳；使吃驚 同 frighten
stroke 〔strok〕	The *strokes* of the church bell awakened us. 教堂的鐘聲敲醒了我們。	*n.* 打擊；敲打聲 同 blow
suspicion 〔sə'spɪʃən〕	The young man is under *suspicion* of murder. 那年輕人有謀殺的嫌疑。	*n.* 嫌疑；懷疑

Lesson 11

temple
〔'tɛmpḷ〕

The people went to the ***temple*** to pray. 人們到寺廟裏祈禱。
He had a cut on his right ***temple***.
他右邊太陽穴上有道傷痕。

n. 1. 寺廟；
　　 神殿
　 2. 太陽穴

toad
〔 tod 〕

Toads have shorter legs and are generally clumsier than frogs. 蟾蜍的腿比青蛙短，而且通常比青蛙醜。

n. 蟾蜍

【記憶技巧】
想到 road（路）有 toad（蟾蜍）。

troublesome
〔'trʌbḷsəm〕

He is the most ***troublesome*** person in our class. 他是我們班上最討厭的人。

adj. 麻煩的；
　　 討厭的

【記憶技巧】
-some 表「引起…的」的字尾。

vessel
〔'vɛsḷ〕

Empty ***vessels*** make the most sound.
空的容器最響；滿瓶不響，半瓶響叮噹。
The mark on her skin was caused by broken blood ***vessels***.
她皮膚上的傷疤是因血管破裂所造成。
The port of London is filled with ***vessels*** of all kinds.
倫敦港口停滿了各式各樣的船隻。

n. 1. 容器

2. （血）管

3. 船隻
同 ship;
　 boat

web
〔 wɛb 〕

A spider captures small insects with its ***web***. 蜘蛛用網捕捉小昆蟲。

n. 網

yell
〔 jɛl 〕

His ***yell*** of anger could be heard in the next room.
隔壁房間都聽得見他生氣的叫喊聲。
During the game the students often ***yelled*** with cheers.
比賽中，學生們經常大聲歡呼。

n. 大叫;喊叫
同 shout

v. 呼喊

Lesson 11

Exercise 11.5 從第五部分中選出最適當的一個英文字，填入空格內。

1. Bowls and cups were among the ancient _____ they found.

2. She was _____ to see him looking so ill.

3. She can't swim yet, but has made a few _____ with her arms.

4. The real thief tried to turn _____ toward others.

5. Ancient Greek _____ were beautifully built.

【解答】
1. vessels 2. startled 3. strokes 4. suspicion 5. temples

成果測驗

I. 找出一個與其他三個不相關的字：

( ) 1. (A) surprise　(B) frighten　(C) flee　(D) startle

( ) 2. (A) province　(B) margin　(C) edge　(D) border

( ) 3. (A) ridiculous　(B) absurd　(C) silly　(D) reckless

( ) 4. (A) blend　(B) replace　(C) mingle　(D) mix

( ) 5. (A) vessel　(B) ship　(C) boat　(D) cabin

( ) 6. (A) accustom　(B) consolidate
　　　 (C) habituate　(D) familiarize

( ) 7. (A) margin　(B) source
　　　 (C) beginning　(D) origin

II. 找出一個與題前中文意思相同的英文字：

( ) 1. 嫌疑
 (A) disposition (B) suspicion
 (C) venture (D) province

( ) 2. 畢業
 (A) graduate (B) illuminate (C) perceive (D) shift

( ) 3. 爬
 (A) heal (B) slip (C) stalk (D) crawl

( ) 4. 咀嚼
 (A) shift (B) slip (C) chew (D) creep

( ) 5. 堅持
 (A) perceive (B) insist
 (C) object (D) consolidate

III. 找出一個與斜體字意義相反的單字：

( ) 1. *loosen*
 (A) enrich (B) fasten (C) fold (D) untie

( ) 2. *relief*
 (A) suspicion (B) border (C) operation (D) distress

( ) 3. *import*
 (A) edge (B) object (C) export (D) report

( ) 4. *spinster*
 (A) bachelor (B) toad (C) parlor (D) border

( ) 5. *edge*
 (A) margin (B) center (C) sphere (D) temple

IV. 完整拼出下列各句中所欠缺的單字，每一格代表一個字母：

1. I tell you that d_ _ _ _t people just don't do things like that.
   （高尚的）

2. Some people believe in private e_ _ _ _ _ _ _ _e, while others
   believe in government ownership of industry. （企業）

3. His political ideas were too c_ _ _ _ _x to get support from
   ordinary people. （複雜的）

4. A good traveler can a_ _ _ _ _ _m himself to almost any kind
   of food. （使習慣）

5. He could not p_ _ _ _ _ _e any difference between the twins.
   （察覺）

V. 找出一個與句中斜體字意義最接近的單字：

(   ) 1. His cut finger *healed* in a few days.
   (A) cured   (B) decayed
   (C) weakened   (D) deteriorated

(   ) 2. The teacher cut an apple into four equal pieces to *illustrate*
   what 1/4 means.
   (A) familiarize   (B) replace
   (C) perceive   (D) explain

(   ) 3. Although she was frightened, she answered with a *calm*
   voice.
   (A) silly   (B) simple   (C) quiet   (D) humble

(   ) 4. She did better in the *previous* lesson.
   (A) troublesome (B) earlier   (C) following (D) gradual

( ) 5. The unexpected noise *startled* the audience.

(A) mingled (B) frightened

(C) started (D) exposed

( ) 6. He broke the lock with one *stroke* of the hammer.

(A) crack (B) crash (C) wrist (D) blow

( ) 7. He *shifted* the suitcase from one hand to another.

(A) changed (B) replaced

(C) mended (D) stalked

( ) 8. The President walked down a *lane* formed by two lines of soldiers.

(A) edge (B) passage (C) loan (D) sphere

( ) 9. Part of the school sports *fund* will be used to improve the condition of the football field.

(A) capital (B) loan

(C) ground (D) equipment

( ) 10. The failure of the rice harvest will cause great *distress* among the farmers.

(A) worry (B) debt

(C) yell (D) damage

【解答】

I. 1. C 2. A 3. D 4. B 5. D 6. B 7. A

II. 1. B 2. A 3. D 4. C 5. B

III. 1. B 2. D 3. C 4. A 5. B

IV. 1. decent 2. enterprise 3. complex 4. accustom
    5. perceive

V. 1. A 2. D 3. C 4. B 5. B 6. D 7. A 8. B 9. A 10. A

Lesson 12

✦ 第一部分

ache 〔ek〕	The boy is trying to forget the *ache* in his back. 那男孩試圖忘掉背部的疼痛。	*n.* 疼痛 同 pain
apparent 〔ə'pærənt〕	It is *apparent* that you dislike your job. 顯然你不喜歡你的工作。 【記憶技巧】 *ap* (to) + *par* (appear) + *ent* (*adj.*) (讓東西顯現出來，就是變得「明顯的」)	*adj.* 明顯的 同 obvious 反 unclear
barn 〔bɑrn〕	A farmer keeps his crops in the *barn*. 農夫將穀物收藏在穀倉中。	*n.* 穀倉
bore 〔bɔr〕	The man *bores* me; I've heard all his stories before. 那男人使我厭煩；我早就聽說過他的所有故事了。	*v.* 使無聊； 使厭煩 名 boredom
canal 〔kə'næl〕	*Canals* have been built to take water to the desert. 建造運河是用來將水運送至沙漠。	*n.* 運河
chilly 〔'tʃɪlɪ〕	You will feel *chilly* if you don't wear a coat on a cold day. 如果你在冷天不穿上外套，將會感覺寒冷。	*adj.* 寒冷的 名 chill
compose 〔kəm'poz〕	The chemistry teacher asked the students what water is *composed* of. 化學老師問學生，水是由什麼組成的。 【記憶技巧】 *com* (together) + *pose* (put) (放在一起，就是「組成」)	*v.* 組成 名 composition

Lesson 12

constant
〔'kɑnstənt 〕

He was tired of his wife's ***constant*** complaint.
他厭倦他太太不停的抱怨。

adj. 不斷的
同 continual; unceasing

create
〔 krɪ'et 〕

The Bible says that God ***created*** this world in seven days.
聖經上說，上帝在七天內創造了這個世界。

v. 創造
名 creation

--- 【記憶技巧】---
cre (make) + *ate* (*v.*)

decisive
〔 dɪ'saɪsɪv 〕

Our air force was ***decisive*** in winning the war.
我們的空軍是打贏這場戰爭的關鍵。

adj. 決定性的
名 decide

Exercise 12.1 從第一部分中選出最適當的一個英文字，填入空格內。

1. Crops and food for animals are usually stored in the _____.

2. _____ are used for ships or for carrying water to places that need it.

3. I hope you are not getting _____ listening to me.

4. The king was given a(n) _____ welcome when he arrived on the island.

5. Three days of _____ rain made the river overflow its banks.

--- 【解答】---
1. barn   2. Canals   3. bored   4. chilly   5. constant

✦ 第二部分

desperate
〔'dɛspərɪt 〕

She became so *desperate* that we feared for her sanity. 她變得如此自暴自棄，使我們擔心她的神智。
The prisoners became *desperate* in their attempts to get free.
那些囚犯拼命想要逃脫。

adj. 1. 絕望的；
　　　　自暴自棄的
　　　同 hopeless
　　　2. 不顧一切的；
　　　　拼命的

---

district
〔'dɪstrɪkt 〕

The farming *district* of the United States is in the Midwest.
美國的農業區在中西部。

n. 區域
同 region; area

　【記憶技巧】
　di + *strict*（嚴格的）

---

edible
〔'ɛdəbl̩ 〕

This apple is rotten and no longer *edible*. 這個蘋果已腐爛，不能吃了。

adj. 可吃的；
　　　　可食用的
同 eatable

　【記憶技巧】
　ed（eat）+ *ible*（*adj.*）

---

entertain
〔,ɛntɚ'ten 〕

The circus *entertained* the children. 馬戲團娛樂了孩子。

v. 娛樂
名 entertainment

　【記憶技巧】
　enter（進入）+ *tain*（進入人心才能「娛樂」）

---

explore
〔 ɪk'splor 〕

Columbus discovered America but did not *explore* the new continent.
哥倫布發現美洲，可是並沒有到那個新大陸上去探險。

v. 探險
同 search

---

fate
〔 fet 〕

It was their *fate* to meet and marry.
他們的相識和結合是天意。

n. 命運

---

float
〔 flot 〕

Wood *floats* on water and dust *floats* in the air.
木頭浮於水上，灰塵則飄於空中。

v. 漂浮；飄浮

fundamental
(ˌfʌndəˈmɛntḷ)

Freedom of speech is one of the *fundamental* human rights.
言論自由是基本人權之一。

adj. 基本的

----【記憶技巧】-----
funda (base) + *ment* (n.) + *al* (adj.)

grand
(grænd)

The *grand* sight of the Niagara Falls cannot be forgotten for a long time. 尼加拉瀑布的雄偉景象使人久久無法忘懷。

adj. 雄偉的；
華麗的
同 magnificent;
splendid

healthy
(ˈhɛlθɪ)

The children are quite *healthy* although they have slight colds at the moment. 孩子們此時雖然都有輕微的感冒，可是仍相當健康。

adj. 健康的
同 wholesome

Exercise 12.2 從第二部分中選出最適當的一個英文字，填入空格內。

1. There is a(n) _____ difference between your proposal and mine.

2. The boat was _____ down the river when I saw it.

3. Many people blame _____ for their failure in life.

4. Can you distinguish the _____ and the poisonous mushrooms?

5. His failure made him _____ and he resolved to succeed next time or die in the attempt.

----【解答】----
1. fundamental　　2. floating　　3. fate　　4. edible　　5. desperate

Lesson 12

✦ 第三部分

imagine
〔 ɪ'mædʒɪn 〕

I can ***imagine*** the scene clearly in my mind.
我能在腦中清晰地想像出那情景。

v. 想像
名 imagination

inspire
〔 ɪn'spaɪr 〕

His brother's success ***inspired*** the boy to work harder.　他兄弟的成功激勵了那男孩更努力工作。

v. 激勵
名 inspiration

> 【記憶技巧】
> ***in*** + ***spire*** (breathe) (吹入生氣)

jealous
〔'dʒɛləs 〕

He was very ***jealous*** when he discovered that she loved someone else.　當他發現她愛上別人時，非常嫉妒。

adj. 嫉妒的
名 jealousy

lantern
〔'læntən 〕

My wife bought a beautiful Chinese ***lantern*** for the living room.　我太太買了一個漂亮的中國式燈籠來裝飾客廳。

n. 燈籠

local
〔'lokl̩ 〕

We have a small ***local*** broadcasting station in our town.
我們鎮上有個小規模的地方廣播電台。

adj. 當地的；
　　　 地方的
同 provincial

> 【記憶技巧】
> ***loc*** (place) + ***al*** (*adj.*) (地方性的，也就是「當地的」)

marble
〔'marbl̩ 〕

He was buried in a ***marble*** tomb.
他被葬於大理石的墳墓裏。

n. 大理石

minor
〔'maɪnɚ 〕

The young actress was given a ***minor*** part in the new play.　那年輕的女演員在新劇中被分到一個配角。

adj. 次要的；較小
　　　 的；較少的
名 minority

Lesson 12

mutual
〔ˈmjutʃʊəl〕

We were happy to have him as our ***mutual*** friend.
我們很高興讓他成爲我們共同的朋友。

adj. 互相的；
　　　共同的
同 reciprocal

> 【記憶技巧】
> ***mut*** (change) + ***ual*** (*adj.*)

objective
〔 əbˈdʒɛktɪv 〕

She always wanted to own her own house, and now she had obtained her ***objective***. 她一直想擁有一棟屬於自己的房子，現在她已達成目標。

adj. 客觀的
n. 目標
同 goal; aim

ornament
〔ˈɔrnəmənt 〕

There were carved ***ornaments*** on the cabinet door.
櫥櫃的門上有雕刻的裝飾。

n. 裝飾（品）
同 decoration
形 ornamental

> 【記憶技巧】
> ***orna*** (decorate) + ***ment*** (*n.*) （用來裝飾的東西，就是「裝飾品」）

Exercise 12.3 從第三部分中選出最適當的一個英文字，填入空格內。

1. When my little brother sees Mother holding the new baby, he becomes _____.

2. The front of the building was covered with _____.

3. He left most of his money to his sons; his daughter received only a(n) _____ part of his wealth.

4. Can you _____ life without gas, electricity, radio, and other modern conveniences?

5. We must bring a(n) _____ to stay overnight on the mountain.

【解答】
1. jealous   2. marble   3. minor   4. imagine   5. lantern

✦ 第四部分

partial
〔ˈpɑrʃəl〕
The play was only a *partial* success.
那齣戲只成功一部份。
A parent should not be *partial* to any one of his children.
做父母的不應該偏袒任何一個孩子。
【記憶技巧】
part (部分) + *ial* (*adj.*)

adj. 1. 部分的
2. 偏袒的
同 biased
反 fair

perform
〔pəˈfɔrm〕
What kind of play will be *performed* in the theater tonight?
今晚戲院將演出何種戲劇？
He always *performs* his work with great care. 他一向很謹慎地執行工作。

v. 1. 表演
2. 做；執行

polish
〔ˈpɑlɪʃ〕
We *polished* the furniture on the day the guest arrived.
我們在客人到達的那一天，把家具擦亮。

v. 擦亮

priceless
〔ˈpraɪslɪs〕
Only a very rich man could afford to buy these *priceless* paintings.
只有非常有錢的人才買得起這些貴重的畫。

adj. 無價的；貴重的

publish
〔ˈpʌblɪʃ〕
It is a good story, but we can't *publish* it; it would offend too many people. 這是一個好故事，可是我們不能發表，因為它會冒犯許多人。
【記憶技巧】
publ (out) + *ish* (*v.*) (「出版」就是把文章公開)

v. 出版；發表
名 publication

recognize
(ˈrɛkəɡˌnaɪz)

Honesty and sincerity in students are easily ***recognized*** by teachers.
老師很容易就看出學生的誠實和真摯。

v. 認得;認出
名 recognition

> 【記憶技巧】
> ***re*** (again) + ***cogn*** (know) + ***ize*** (*v.*)(再看一次仍知道,表示「認得;認出」)

repeat
(rɪˈpit)

If you ***repeat*** that mistake, you will be punished.
如果你再犯那個錯誤,將會受罰。

v. 重覆
同 repetition

reward
(rɪˈwɔrd)

As a ***reward*** for his bravery, the soldier was given a gold medal. 為獎賞他的勇敢,該士兵被授與一面金牌。

n. 報酬;獎賞

sake
(sek)

If you won't do it for your own ***sake***, then do it for my ***sake***. 如果你不是為了自己做這件事,那麼就算是為了我吧。

n. 緣故
同 benefit

secret
(ˈsikrɪt)

The old man had learned many of the ***secrets*** of nature.
那老人知道許多大自然的奧祕。
He kept some money in a ***secret*** place.
他將一些錢存放在一個隱密的地方。

n. 祕密

adj. 祕密的

> 【記憶技巧】
> ***se*** (apart) + ***cret*** (separate)(與平常能講的話區隔開來,也就是不能說的「祕密」)

Exercise 12.4 從第四部分中選出最適當的一個英文字,填入空格內。

1. You can easily _____ silverware with this special cloth.

2. These plans must be kept _____ from the enemy.

3. He fought the war for the _____ of his country's freedom.

4. To buy books for your children is a _____ investment.

5. He received a title as a _____ for his services.

┌─【解答】─────────────────────────────────────┐
│ 1. polish 2. secret 3. sake 4. priceless 5. reward │
└──┘

✦ 第五部分

shield
〔 ʃild 〕

The *shield* protected him from the blows of his enemy.
這面盾保護他免受敵人的打擊。
Her wide hat *shielded* her eyes from the sun. 寬帽保護她的眼睛以防日曬。

n. 盾
反 spear
v. 保護
同 protect

slight
〔 slaɪt 〕

He stayed home for a day because of a *slight* illness. 他因為小病，留在家一天。

┌─【記憶技巧】────────────┐
│ *s* + *light*（光） │
└────────────────────────┘

adj. 輕微的

spell
〔 spɛl 〕

He is under my *spell* and will do as I say.
他被我的符咒鎮住，會照著我說的話去做。
We had a long *spell* of hot weather last summer. 去年夏天有一段很長的熱天。

v. 拼字
n. 1. 符咒；吸引力
　　同 enchantment
　　2. 一段時間

stare
〔 stɛr 〕

The little girl *stared* at the strange man at the store.
小女孩凝視著在商店裏的那個陌生人。

v. 凝視；瞪視
同 gaze

string
〔 strɪŋ 〕

The package was tied with red *strings*. 那包裹用紅繩綁著。

n. 細繩；一串

同 thread; cord

suspect
〔 sə'spɛkt 〕

The mouse *suspected* danger and did not touch the trap. 老鼠懷疑有危險，沒有去觸碰那陷阱。

v. 懷疑

〔'sʌspɛkt 〕

The police have arrested two *suspects* in connection with the bank robbery. 警方逮捕兩名與銀行搶案有關的嫌疑犯。

n. 嫌疑犯

【記憶技巧】
su (under) + *spect* (see) (私底下觀察別人的行為，表示「懷疑」)

temperature
〔'tɛmprətʃɚ 〕

What's the average *temperature* in Taipei on a summer day? 台北夏天的平均溫度是多少？

n. 溫度

tissue
〔'tɪʃʊ 〕

The teacher showed pictures of muscle *tissues* and brain *tissue*. 老師展示肌肉組織和腦部組織的圖片。

n. 面紙；組織

【記憶技巧】
先背 issue (議題)。

troop
〔 trup 〕

The soldiers are preparing to attack enemy *troops*. 士兵們正準備攻擊敵軍。

n. 1. 軍隊

同 forces

A *troop* of children gathered around the teacher. 一群孩童聚集在老師周圍。

2. 群；組

Lesson 12

verse 〔 vɝs 〕	A collection of his ***verse*** has just been published. 他的一套詩集才剛出版。	*n.* 詩;韻文 反 prose
weary 〔'wɪrɪ〕	He felt ***weary*** after playing tennis for two hours. 打了兩個小時的網球後,他感到疲倦。 The boy ***wearies*** me with constant questions. 那男孩不斷地問問題,使我厭煩。	*adj.* 疲倦的 同 tired *v.* 使厭煩

Exercise 12.5 從第五部分中選出最適當的一個英文字,填入空格內。

1. We were under the _____ of the beautiful music.

2. He got a _____ wound on his back but is all right now.

3. She often wears a _____ of pearls around her neck.

4. The nurse took the _____ of the patient — it was 38.5℃.

5. The long hours of work have _____ me a lot.

【解答】
1. spell   2. slight   3. string   4. temperature   5. wearied

成果測驗

I. 找出一個與斜體字的意義最接近的單字:

( ) 1. *weary* in mind and body
　　　 (A) healthy　　　　　(B) sound
　　　 (C) tired　　　　　　(D) warm

(   ) 2. to cast a *spell* over someone
- (A) marble
- (B) enchantment
- (C) stroke
- (D) spear

(   ) 3. to *stare* at someone
- (A) gaze
- (B) yell
- (C) inspire
- (D) surmise

(   ) 4. *constant* practice
- (A) apparent
- (B) hard
- (C) decisive
- (D) unceasing

(   ) 5. the outlook was *desperate*
- (A) careless
- (B) decisive
- (C) hopeless
- (D) fundamental

(   ) 6. *edible* fish
- (A) trivial   (B) audible   (C) eatable   (D) tiny

(   ) 7. to *entertain* someone
- (A) amuse   (B) frighten   (C) encourage   (D) suspect

(   ) 8. to *explore* an unknown world
- (A) destroy   (B) search   (C) perceive   (D) inquire

(   ) 9. wonderful *ornament*
- (A) decoration
- (B) enchantment
- (C) string
- (D) organization

(   ) 10. living in a *grand* style
- (A) splendid
- (B) huge
- (C) gradual
- (D) miserable

II. 找出一個與題前中文意思相同的英文字：

( ) 1. 絕望的
    (A) desperate   (B) sake
    (C) saint   (D) marble

( ) 2. 嫉妒的
    (A) wholesome   (B) obvious
    (C) conclusive   (D) jealous

( ) 3. 大理石
    (A) tissue   (B) canal   (C) marble   (D) tin

( ) 4. 目標
    (A) operation   (B) objective
    (C) item   (D) protection

( ) 5. 報酬
    (A) reward   (B) verse   (C) benefit   (D) spear

III. 找出一個與斜體字意義相反的單字：

( ) 1. *major*
    (A) healthy   (B) vigorous
    (C) jealous   (D) minor

( ) 2. *biased*
    (A) reciprocal   (B) partial
    (C) fair   (D) wholesome

( ) 3. *verse*
    (A) tired   (B) prose   (C) plain   (D) chilly

( ) 4. *apparent*

    (A) unclear   (B) constant   (C) calm   (D) local

( ) 5. *sink*

    (A) bore   (B) float   (C) compose   (D) publish

IV. 完整拼出下列各句中所欠缺的單字，每一格代表一個字母：

1. Doctors should p_ _ _ _ _m their operations with great care.
（執行）

2. P_ _ _ _h your shoes with a brush.（擦亮）

3. Dogs r_ _ _ _ _ _ _e people by their smell.（認出）

4. The continuous a_ _e in his head worried him.（疼痛）

5. It is a_ _ _ _ _ _t that the days become longer in June and July.
（明顯的）

V. 選出最適合句意的一個單字：

( ) 1. It is not polite to _____ at other people.

    (A) nod   (B) stare   (C) look   (D) inspire

( ) 2. You have to present _____ evidence in the court.

    (A) decisive   (B) weary

    (C) silly   (D) decent

( ) 3. We were all anxious about the _____ of the missing
fisherman.

    (A) secret   (B) ache   (C) fate   (D) reward

(   ) 4. He has a _____ appearance even though he is not well.
        (A) weary   (B) apparent
        (C) grand   (D) wholesome

(   ) 5. A family has _____ affection when each person likes the others and is liked by them.
        (A) mutual   (B) provincial
        (C) slight   (D) desperate

VI. 將題前的斜體字轉換為適當詞性，填入空格中：

1. *bore*   The patient spent long days of _____ in the hospital.

2. *entertain*   The city offers all kinds of _____ for young and old.

3. *repeat*   The play was a _____ of a theme used twenty years ago.

4. *minor*   The nation wants peace; only a _____ want the war to continue.

5. *chilly*   There is a _____ in the air this morning.

【解答】

  I. 1. C   2. B   3. A   4. D   5. C   6. C   7. A   8. B   9. A   10. A
 II. 1. A   2. D   3. C   4. B   5. A
III. 1. D   2. C   3. B   4. A   5. B
IV. 1. perform   2. Polish   3. recognize   4. ache   5. apparent
 V. 1. B   2. A   3. C   4. D   5. A
VI. 1. boredom   2. entertainment   3. repetition   4. minority
     5. chill

Lesson 13

Lesson 13

✦ 第一部分

achieve
〔 ə'tʃiv 〕

The soldiers fought bravely and finally ***achieved*** victory.
士兵們勇敢地作戰，終於獲得勝利。

v. 達成；獲得

---

appreciate
〔 ə'priʃɪˌet 〕

You can't ***appreciate*** English poetry unless you have a good knowledge of how English is spoken. 除非你精通如何說英文，否則無法欣賞英詩。

v. 1. 欣賞

Thank you very much for your help; I ***appreciate*** it.
非常謝謝你的幫忙；我很感激。

2. 感激

---

basis
〔 'besɪs 〕

We judge a worker on the ***basis*** of his performance.
我們根據工作表現來評估一個員工。

n. 基礎；根據

---

bother
〔 'baðɚ 〕

Don't ***bother*** me with such foolish questions.
不要用如此愚蠢的問題來煩我。

v. 打擾；煩擾

同 annoy

【記憶技巧】
想到 brother（弟弟）會 bother（煩擾）你。

---

candle
〔 'kændl̩ 〕

There are ten ***candles*** on his birthday cake. 他的生日蛋糕上有十枝蠟燭。

n. 蠟燭

【記憶技巧】
cand (bright) + ***le*** (small thing)（會發光的小東西，就是「蠟燭」）

choice
〔 tʃɔɪs 〕
I don't like her, but if she's the people's *choice*, I will obey her.
我不喜歡她，可是如果她是大家選上的，我會服從她。
n. 選擇

compound
〔 kɑm'paʊnd 〕
He *compounded* various substances into an effective medicine.
他把不同的物質調配成特效藥。
n. 化合物
v. 調配

> 【記憶技巧】
> *com* (together) + *pound* (put) (把許多元素放在一起，就是「化合物」)

constitute
〔 'kɑnstə‚tjut 〕
Government should be *constituted* by the will of the people.
政府應由人們的意願所組成。
v. 組成

> 【記憶技巧】
> *con* (together) + *stitute* (stand) (站在一起，就是「組成」)

deck
〔 dɛk 〕
It's very hot in the cabin; let's go on the *deck*.
船艙內很熱；我們到甲板上去吧。
n. 甲板

despise
〔 dɪ'spaɪz 〕
Fools *despise* wisdom and instruction. 傻子輕視智慧和教育。
v. 輕視
反 esteem

> 【記憶技巧】
> *de* (down) + *spise* (see) (把別人看得很低，即「輕視」)

Exercise 13.1 從第一部分中選出最適當的一個英文字，填入空格內。

1. Einstein's knowledge is so specialized that I cannot _____ it.

2. I am sorry to _____ you, but can you tell me the time?

3. The light from the _____ is not as strong as the sunlight.

4. Boys who tell lies and cheat on examinations are _____ by their classmates.

5. Seven specialists _____ the committee to investigate the accident.

【解答】

1. appreciate　2. bother　3. candle　4. despised　5. constituted

✦ 第二部分

distribute 〔 dɪ'strɪbjʊt 〕	The teacher ***distributed*** the examination papers to each student of the class. 老師分發考卷給班上每一位同學。	*v.* 分發

【記憶技巧】

dis (apart) + ***tribute*** (give) (將東西分送給出去，表示「分發」)

educate 〔'ɛdʒə,ket 〕	He was ***educated*** at a very good school when he was young. 他年輕時在一所非常好的學校受教育。	*v.* 教育

【記憶技巧】

e (out) + ***ducate*** (lead) (引導出才能，也就是「教育」)

enthusiastic 〔 ɪn,θjuzɪ'æstɪk 〕	My little brother is very ***enthusiastic*** about going to kindergarten. 我小弟非常熱衷於上幼稚園。	*adj.* 熱心的

explode
〔 ɪk'splod 〕

The bomb fell on a field and *exploded* harmlessly.
炸彈落在田野中爆炸，沒有造成損傷。

v. 爆炸

fault
〔 fɔlt 〕

She loves him in spite of his *faults*.
他雖有缺點，她仍然愛他。

n. 過錯；缺點

flood
〔 flʌd 〕

The rainstorms caused *floods* in the low-lying parts of the town.
暴風雨在此鎮的低窪處造成水災。

n. 水災
反 draught

funeral
〔'fjunərəl 〕

Many friends attended the old lady's *funeral*.
很多朋友參加那位老太太的葬禮。

n. 葬禮

【記憶技巧】
諧音：夫難落，丈夫遇難掉落，要辦「葬禮」。

grant
〔 grænt 〕

He was *granted* admission to Harvard University for the next fall semester.
哈佛大學准許他明年秋季入學。

v. 准許；給予
同 allow; give

heap
〔 hip 〕

The mother *heaped* the child's plate with food.
母親將孩子的盤子裝滿食物。

n. 一堆
v. 堆積；裝滿
同 pile

immediate
〔 ɪ'midɪɪt 〕

When there is a fire, it is necessary to take *immediate* action.
發生火災時，必須採取立即的行動。

adj. 立即的

【記憶技巧】
im (not) + *medi* (middle) + *ate* (*adj.*) (事情立刻做完，不中斷)

Lesson 13

Exercise 13.2 從第二部分中選出最適當的一個英文字，填入空格內。

1. Our requests for financial assistance were _____ by the committee.

2. Please send a(n) _____ reply to my letter.

3. He is always finding _____ with the way I do my hair.

4. The boiler _____ and many people were injured by the hot steam.

5. The postman had thirty letters to be _____ at houses all over the town.

> 【解答】
>
> 1. granted   2. immediate   3. fault   4. exploded   5. distributed

✦ 第三部分

instance
〔'ɪnstəns 〕

Lincoln is an ***instance*** of a poor boy who became famous.
林肯是一個由窮孩子變成名人的例子。

n. 例子

jewel
〔'dʒuəl 〕

The ***jewel*** in her ring is a diamond.
她戒指上的珠寶是顆鑽石。

n. 珠寶

同 gem

> 【記憶技巧】
> ***jew*** (Jew 是猶太人) + ***el*** (猶太人很會賺錢，身上總有「珠寶」)

lap
〔 læp 〕

Mother holds the baby on her ***lap***.
母親把嬰兒抱在膝上。

n. 膝上；膝部

locate 〔 lo'kæt 〕	Where shall we ***locate*** our new office? 我們的新辦公室將設於何處？	*v.* 使位於 同 situate
marvel 〔'mɑrvḷ 〕	Space travel is one of the ***marvels*** of our time. 太空旅行是我們這個時代的奇蹟之一。	*n.* 奇蹟 同 wonder

minute
〔*adj.* mə'njut ,
  maɪ- 〕
〔*n.* 'mɪnɪt 〕
	He gave me a ***minute*** description of the structure of the building.
	他給我這棟建築物構造的詳細說明書。
		adj. 微小的；
		  詳細的
		同 precise
		n. 分鐘

mysterious 〔 mɪs'tɪrɪəs 〕	She had a ***mysterious*** telephone call last night. 她昨晚接到一通神秘電話。	*adj.* 神秘的
oblige 〔 ə'blaɪdʒ 〕	The students were ***obliged*** to do what the teacher had asked. 學生必須做老師所要求的事。	*v.* 使感激； 使不得不

【記憶技巧】
ob (to) + ***lige*** (bind) (綁住你，使你「不得不」去做)

outbreak 〔'aʊt͵brek 〕	The ***outbreak*** of disorder was put down by the police in two hours. 警察在兩小時內鎮壓了紊亂的暴動。	*n.* 爆發；暴動
participate 〔 pɑr'tɪsə͵pet 〕	Most of the students ***participated*** in the discussion. 大部分學生都參與討論。	*v.* 參加 同 take part

【記憶技巧】
parti (part) + ***cip*** (take) + ***ate*** (*v.*) (take part in，就是「參加」)

Exercise 13.3 從第三部分中選出最適當的一個英文字，填入空格內。

1. He gave me _____ instructions about how to do my work.

2. The airplane and television are among the _____ of science.

3. Television is a(n) _____ of improved communication facilities.

4. They were _____ to sell their house in order to pay their debts.

5. The disappearance of the ship still remains _____.

【解答】
1. minute   2. marvels   3. instance   4. obliged   5. mysterious

✦ 第四部分

perilous
〔ˈpɛrələs 〕

It is always *perilous* to neglect our national defense.
忽視國防始終都是危險的。

【記憶技巧】
諧音：怕了冷死，到了「危險的」地方。

adj. 危險的
同 dangerous
反 safe
名 peril

polite
〔 pəˈlaɪt 〕

He was *polite* to everyone he met at the party.
他對每一個在宴會上遇到的人都很客氣。

adj. 有禮貌的；
客氣的
同 courteous

priest
〔 prist 〕

The *priest* will lead the church ceremony. 牧師將帶領做禮拜儀式。

n. 牧師

purchase
〔ˈpɝtʃəs 〕

They've just *purchased* a new house near Keelung.
他們剛在基隆附近買了一棟房子。

v. 購買
同 buy

They saved their money for the *purchase* of a house. 他們存錢買房子。

n. 購買

【記憶技巧】
pur (for) + *chase* (追求) (人常常花錢「購買」自己追求的東西)

reference (ˈrɛfərəns)	The journalist kept a card file of information on his desk for easy *reference*. 新聞記者為方便參考，將資料的目錄卡放在桌上。	*n.* 參考 動 refer
request (rɪˈkwɛst)	Your *request* for a ticket was made too late. 你太晚來索取入場券了。 He *requested* that she go fishing with him. 他邀她一起去釣魚。	*n.* 要求；請求 同 ask; beg *v.* 請求

【記憶技巧】
想到 re + question（問題）– ion，有問題要「請求」。

ripe (raɪp)	*Ripe* fruits taste good; unripe fruits usually taste bad. 成熟的水果味道不錯；不熟的水果通常不好吃。	*adj.* 成熟的 反 unripe; 　　 raw
satisfy (ˈsætɪsˌfaɪ)	Nothing *satisfies* him; he is always complaining. 沒有東西能讓他滿意；他總是在抱怨。	*v.* 使滿意； 　　 使滿足
security (sɪˈkjʊrətɪ)	I helped the old lady cross the street in *security*. 我幫助那老太太安全過街。	*n.* 安全
shortcoming (ˈʃɔrtˌkʌmɪŋ)	He is a good man, but he has many *shortcomings*. 他是一個好人，可是仍有許多缺點。	*n.* 缺點 同 defect 反 merit

【記憶技巧】
short + *coming*（短處就是「缺點」）

Exercise 13.4 從第四部分中選出最適當的一個英文字，填入空格內。

1. Keep the dictionary on your desk for easy _____.

2. We _____ a loan from the City Bank.

3. The apples are not _____ enough to eat.

4. In spite of all my friend's _____, I still like him.

5. He _____ his hunger with bread and milk.

【解答】

1. reference　2. requested　3. ripe　4. shortcomings　5. satisfied

✦ 第五部分

smash 〔 smæʃ 〕	We heard a **smash** in the kitchen. 我們聽到廚房嘩啦的破碎聲。 The cup **smashed** when the girl dropped it. 女孩掉落了杯子，打得粉碎。	【記憶技巧】 s + **mash**（搗碎）	*n.* 粉碎；破碎聲 *v.* 打成粉碎 同 crush
spin 〔 spɪn 〕	The earth **spins** as it moves around the sun. 地球在繞著太陽公轉時也自轉。 There were hundreds of machines **spinning** cotton into thread. 有幾百部的機器將棉紡成紗。		*v.* 1. 旋轉 　同 rotate 　2. 紡（紗）
steady 〔'stɛdɪ 〕	He is making **steady** progress at school. 他在校的功課正穩定進步中。		*adj.* 穩定的
stuff 〔 stʌf 〕	The shoes were made of some **stuff** that looked like leather. 那鞋子是用一些像皮革的材料製成的。 She **stuffed** the pillow with feathers. 她將羽毛塞入枕頭裏。		*n.* 東西；材料 同 substance *v.* 塞入；塞滿 同 fill 反 empty
sweat 〔 swɛt 〕	We **sweat** when it is very hot. 天氣很熱時，我們會流汗。 The old farmer wiped the **sweat** off his brow. 那老農夫擦去額頭上的汗水。		*v.* 流汗 *n.* 汗

terrible
('tɛrəbḷ)

The ***terrible*** storm destroyed many houses in the town.

可怕的暴風雨摧毀了鎮上許多房子。

adj. 可怕的

> 【記憶技巧】
> ***terr*** (frighten) + ***ible*** (*adj.*) (讓人害怕的，表示「可怕的」)

torch
(tɔrtʃ)

The Statue of Liberty holds a ***torch*** in her right hand.

自由女神像的右手握了一支火把。

n. 火把

turtle
('tɝtḷ)

Turtles live in fresh or salt water or on land. 龜生活在淡水、海水，或陸地上。

n. 海龜；龜

victim
('vɪktɪm)

They were the ***victims*** of a dishonest merchant. 他們是一個不誠實商人的受害者。

n. 受害者

welfare
('wɛl,fɛr)

They did everything for the ***welfare*** of their children.

他們願為孩子的幸福做每一件事。

n. 福利；幸福
[同] well-being

> 【記憶技巧】
> ***wel*** (good) + ***fare*** (go) (「福利」是對人有益的東西)

Exercise 13.5　從第五部分中選出最適當的一個英文字，填入空格內。

1. She _____ the trunk with old clothing.

2. He kept up a _____ speed on the road.

3. Climbing up the hill made us _____.

4. The _____ fire filled the sky with flames.

5. He fell a _____ to the dagger of an assassin.

【解答】

1. stuffed　　2. steady　　3. sweat　　4. terrible　　5. victim

成果測驗

I. 找出一個與其他三個不相關的字：

(　　) 1. (A) safety　　　(B) protection　　(C) security　　(D) victim

(　　) 2. (A) shortcoming　　　　　(B) defect
　　　　(C) advantage　　　　　　(D) weakness

(　　) 3. (A) perilous　　　　　　(B) risky
　　　　(C) dangerous　　　　　　(D) steep

(　　) 4. (A) ripe　　　　　　　　(B) enthusiastic
　　　　(C) eager　　　　　　　　(D) anxious

(　　) 5. (A) instance　　(B) fault　　(C) example　　(D) case

(　　) 6. (A) grant　　(B) grand　　(C) allow　　(D) give

(　　) 7. (A) study　　(B) teach　　(C) instruct　　(D) educate

(　　) 8. (A) assemble　　　　　　(B) gather
　　　　(C) participate　　　　　(D) accumulate

(　　) 9. (A) achieve　　　　　　(B) participate
　　　　(C) succeed　　　　　　(D) accomplish

( ) 10. (A) welfare （B) well-being
(C) happiness （D) outbreak

II. 找出一個與題前中文意思相同的英文字：

( ) 1. 安全
(A) decoration （B) foundation
(C) substance （D) security

( ) 2. 汗
(A) instance （B) sweat （C) spell （D) flood

( ) 3. 分發
(A) distribute （B) participate
(C) smash （D) accumulate

( ) 4. 打成粉碎
(A) explode （B) spin （C) smash （D) heap

( ) 5. 火把
(A) marvel （B) torch （C) stuff （D) turtle

III. 找出一個與斜體字意義相反的單字：

( ) 1. *esteem*
(A) admire （B) comprise （C) despise （D) annoy

( ) 2. *merit*
(A) benefit （B) shortcoming
(C) wonder （D) victim

( ) 3. *ripe*
(A) safe （B) fault
(C) direct （D) immature

(   ) 4. *drought*

      (A) flood   (B) outbreak   (C) sweat   (D) well-being

(   ) 5. *perilous*

      (A) dull   (B) safe   (C) terrible   (D) changing

IV. 完整拼出下列各句中所欠缺的單字，每一格代表一個字母：

1. We took the v_ _ _ _ms of the storm into our house for the night. (受害者)

2. He has worked for the w_ _ _ _ _e of the nation throughout his life. (幸福)

3. The band is playing this song at the r_ _ _ _ _t of the Queen. (請求)

4. You will never a_ _ _ _ _e anything if you don't work hard. (獲得)

5. She was very careful in her c_ _ _ _e of friends. (選擇)

V. 找出一個與句中斜體字意義最接近的單字：

(   ) 1. The problem *bothered* the scientists for many years.

      (A) annoyed   (B) bored

      (C) amused   (D) consolidated

(   ) 2. He gave me a *minute* description of the inside of his house.

      (A) important   (B) precise

      (C) splendid   (D) fundamental

(   ) 3. The operation was a *marvel* of medical skill.

      (A) success   (B) jewel   (C) merit   (D) wonder

Lesson 13

(   ) 4. He has many *shortcomings*, but I still love him.
    (A) pains   (B) destiny
    (C) defects   (D) outbreaks

(   ) 5. His office is *located* on the ground floor.
    (A) compounded   (B) situated
    (C) floated   (D) constituted

(   ) 6. She *heaped* the dirty clothes next to the washing machine.
    (A) placed   (B) smashed
    (C) piled   (D) achieved

(   ) 7. All the teachers *took part* in the children's game.
    (A) participated   (B) discussed
    (C) requested   (D) wanted

(   ) 8. A *gem* is a precious stone.
    (A) spell   (B) marble   (C) stuff   (D) jewel

(   ) 9. She *purchased* a new dress in her friend's shop.
    (A) ordered   (B) bought
    (C) sold   (D) requested

(   ) 10. The *courteous* boy gave the lady his seat on the bus.
    (A) tired   (B) polite
    (C) wholesome   (D) jealous

【解答】

I. 1. D   2. C   3. D   4. A   5. B   6. B   7. A   8. C   9. B   10. D
II. 1. D   2. B   3. A   4. C   5. B
III. 1. C   2. B   3. D   4. A   5. B
IV. 1. victims   2. welfare   3. request   4. achieve   5. choice
V. 1. A   2. B   3. D   4. C   5. B   6. C   7. A   8. D   9. B   10. B

Lesson 14

✦ 第一部分

actual 〔ˈæktʃuəl〕	The *actual* amount of money was not known although they knew it was large. 雖然他們知道金額很龐大，但並不知道實際的數目。	*adj.* 實際的 同 true; real
ash 〔æʃ〕	Don't drop your cigarette *ash* on the carpet; use an ashtray. 不要把煙灰抖落在地毯上；要用煙灰缸。	*n.* 灰
beat 〔bit〕	The rain was *beating* against the windows. 雨正打落在窗上。	*v.* 打 同 strike; hit
bowl 〔bol〕	He ate only one *bowl* of rice and drank a glass of milk. 他只吃了一碗飯，喝了一杯牛奶。	*n.* 碗

carpenter
〔ˈkɑrpəntɚ〕

A *carpenter* builds and repairs the wooden parts of houses, barns, or ships. 木匠建造和修補房屋、穀倉，或船的木製部分。

n. 木匠

【記憶技巧】
car（車）+ *p* + *enter*（進入）

circumstance
〔ˈsɝkəmˌstæns〕

Under no *circumstances* must a soldier leave his post without permission. 不論在何種情況，士兵沒有得到許可，絕不能離開崗位。

n. 情況

【記憶技巧】
circum (around) + *stan* (stand) + *ce*
(*n.*)（關於某人或某事周圍的「情況」）

conceive 〔 kən'siv 〕	Young children like to watch television; they cannot *conceive* of life without it. 小孩子喜歡看電視；他們無法想像沒有電視的生活。	*v.* 想像 名 conception 同 think; imagine
contain 〔 kən'ten 〕	The book *contains* all the information you need. 本書包含你需要的所有資訊。	*v.* 包含 同 exclude

【記憶技巧】
con (with) + *tain* (hold)

crime 〔 kraɪm 〕	He was found guilty of committing a serious *crime*. 他被判定犯了重大的罪。	*n.* 罪 同 offense
decorate 〔'dɛkə,ret 〕	The streets were *decorated* with flags for the King's visit. 由於國王來訪，街上懸掛旗幟作為裝飾。	*v.* 裝飾 同 adorn 名 decoration

【記憶技巧】
decor (ornament) + *ate* (*v.*)

Lesson 14

Exercise 14.1　從第一部分中選出最適當的一個英文字，填入空格內。

1. The boy _____ the girl with a stick.

2. The book _____ a good deal of useful information.

3. I can't _____ of your allowing a child of five to go on such a long journey alone.

4. We _____ the Christmas tree with shining balls and bells last year.

5. If you commit a _____ you must expect to be punished.

【解答】
1. beat　2. contains　3. conceive　4. decorated　5. crime

✦ 第二部分

determine
〔 dɪ'tɝmɪn 〕

The size of your shoes is ***determined*** by the size of your feet. 你腳的大小決定鞋的尺寸。

v. 決定；決心
名 determination

divide
〔 də'vaɪd 〕

The small river ***divides*** my land from his. 這條小河隔開我和他的地。

v. 劃分；隔開；分割

> 【記憶技巧】
> ***di*** (apart) + ***vide*** (separate) (把東西分開，就是「分割」)

elbow
〔'ɛl,bo 〕

He was watching television with his ***elbows*** bent, his chin in his hands. 他正彎著手肘，用手托著下巴看電視。

n. 手肘

> 【記憶技巧】
> ***el*** (forearm) + ***bow*** (弓)(前臂可以弓起來的部分，就是「手肘」)

entrance
〔'ɛntrəns 〕

The ***entrance*** to the cave had been blocked up.
洞穴的入口已被堵塞。

n. 入口
動 enter
反 exit

expense
〔 ɪk'spɛns 〕

Most children are educated at public ***expense***.
大多數的兒童靠公費受教育。

n. 費用
形 expensive

feast
〔 fist 〕

The king invited them to a ***feast*** last night.
國王昨晚邀請他們參加盛宴。

n. 盛宴
同 banquet

> 【記憶技巧】
> ***f*** + ***east*** (東方)

fog
〔fɑg , fɔg 〕

We often have bad *fogs* on the southern coast during winter.
冬天在南海岸經常有大霧。

n. 霧
形 foggy
同 mist

furnish
〔ˈfɜnɪʃ 〕

The new hotel is finished, but it is not yet *furnished*.
新旅館已完工，可是尚未裝修。
No one in the class could *furnish* the right answer to the question.
班上沒有人能對此問題提供正確的答案。

v. 1. 裝置家具；
裝修
同 equip
2. 供給
同 supply; give

---【記憶技巧】---
furn（備有）+ *ish* (*v.*)（家裡擁有所需的裝備，就是「裝置家具」）

greedy
〔ˈgridɪ 〕

Don't be so *greedy*! There is enough for everyone.
不要如此貪心！足夠分給每個人。

adj. 貪心的
名 greed

hesitate
〔ˈhɛzəˌtet 〕

He *hesitated* to take such a big risk in his business.
他不願在事業上冒如此大的風險。

v. 猶豫；不願

---【記憶技巧】---
hesit（stick 黏住）+ *ate* (*v.*)（「猶豫」就像被黏住）

Lesson 14

Exercise 14.2 從第二部分中選出最適當的一個英文字，填入空格內。

1. He got a deep wound on his right _____.

2. The _____ is the sailor's greatest enemy.

3. The _____ to the hotel was blocked with baggage so that no one could enter or leave.

4. I _____ to take his side until I knew the whole story.

5. This hotel _____ clean sheets and towels every day.

【解答】

1. elbow　2. fog　3. entrance　4. hesitated　5. furnishes

✦ 第三部分

impossible 〔ɪmˋpɑsəb!〕	Today it is ***impossible*** to cure cancer completely. 現在要完全治好癌症是不可能的。	*adj.* 不可能的
institution 〔͵ɪnstəˋtjuʃən〕	Colleges and universities are educational ***institutions***. 學院和大學都是教育機構。	*n.* 機構

journal
〔ˋdʒɝn!〕

Both he and his wife write for a business ***journal***.
他和他太太都為商業雜誌執筆。

n. 期刊；雜誌

【記憶技巧】
想到 journey（旅行）要發表成 journal（期刊）。

launch
〔lɔntʃ〕

The United States ***launched*** a new spaceship yesterday.
美國昨天發射了一艘新的太空船。

v. 發射；使（新建造的船）下水

【記憶技巧】
lunch（午餐）+ ***a***

loss
〔 lɔs 〕

Loss of health is more serious than *loss* of wealth.
喪失健康比損失財富更嚴重。

n. 損失；喪失
動 lose
反 gain

match
〔 mætʃ 〕

The drapes of the room *match* the rug on the floor.
房間的窗簾和地上的地毯很相配。
You can't *match* him in knowledge of wild plants.
在野生植物方面的知識，你無法和他相比。

v. 1. 相配
同 become

2. 與…匹敵

misfortune
〔 mɪs'fɔrtʃən 〕

His failure in business was due not to *misfortune*, but to his mistakes. 他生意上的失敗不是因為運氣差，而是因為他犯的錯誤。

n. 不幸；壞運氣
反 luck

--- 【記憶技巧】---
mis (badly) + *fortune*（運氣）（運氣不好就會「不幸」）

native
〔'netɪv 〕

The politician was never popular in his *native* country.
那政客在本國從不受歡迎。

adj. 本國的；原產的

obvious
〔'ɑbvɪəs 〕

It is *obvious* that two and two makes four.
二加二等於四是很明顯的。

adj. 明顯的
同 evident

--- 【記憶技巧】---
ob (near) + *vi* (way) + *ous* (*adj.*)（擋在路中央的東西，看起來是非常「明顯的」）

outstanding
〔'aʊt'stændɪŋ 〕

He is an *outstanding* pitcher because of his ball control.
他因控球好而是個傑出的投手。

adj. 傑出的
同 prominent

Exercise 14.3 從第三部分中選出最適當的一個英文字，填入空格內。

1. One of the _____ animals of India is the tiger.

2. She always thought that the greatest of her _____ was that she'd never had any children.

3. The carpets should _____ the wallpaper.

4. The _____ of so many ships worried the admiral.

5. The new ship was _____ as the crowd cheered.

【解答】
1. native   2. misfortunes   3. match   4. loss   5. launched

✦ 第四部分

pasture 〔'pæstʃɚ〕	I saw many horses grazing in the ***pasture***. 我看見許多馬在草地上吃草。	*n.* 草地
personality 〔ˌpɝsṇ'ælətɪ〕	She was elected class president because of her good ***personality***. 她因品格好而被選爲班長。	*n.* 人格

【記憶技巧】
person（人）+ ***al***（*adj.*）+ ***ity***（*n.*）

port 〔pɔrt〕	New York and San Francisco are important ***ports*** of the United States. 紐約和舊金山都是美國重要的港口。	*n.* 港口 同 harbor

Lesson 14

privilege
〔'prɪvḷɪdʒ〕

The members of the club have the *privilege* of buying the football tickets at special rates. 此俱樂部的會員有特權能以特價買到足球入場券。

n. 特權

【記憶技巧】
privi (private) + *lege* (law) (限於一個人的法律，表示「特權」)

puzzle
〔'pʌzḷ〕

No one has yet succeeded in explaining the *puzzle* of how life first began. 至今尚無人能圓滿地解釋生命最初是如何開始的謎。

v. 使困惑
n. 謎
同 riddle

region
〔'ridʒən〕

New England is one of the *regions* of the United States. 新英格蘭是美國的一區。

n. 地區
同 area

【記憶技巧】
reg (rule) + *ion* (*n.*) (統治的地方，就是「地區」)

resemble
〔 rɪ'zɛmbḷ 〕

They *resemble* each other in shape but not in color.
它們的形狀很像，可是顏色不同。

v. 相像

【記憶技巧】
re (again) + *semble* (same) (再次出現相同的東西)

roast
〔 rost 〕

We need an oven to *roast* meat and potatoes.
我們需要一個烤箱來烤肉和馬鈴薯。

v. 烤

savage
〔'sævɪdʒ〕

They carried guns to protect themselves from the *savage* tribes. 他們帶槍以保護自己，防備野蠻部落的攻擊。

adj. 野蠻的
同 barbarous; wild

sentiment
('sɛntəmənt)

The young girls preferred stories full of *sentiment*.
年輕女孩較喜歡充滿感情的故事。

n. 感情
同 feeling

> 【記憶技巧】
> *sent* (sense) + *i* + *ment* (*n.*) (感覺就是「感情」)

Exercise 14.4 從第四部分中選出最適當的一個英文字，填入空格內。

1. In modern times there is less _____ and more of an equal chance in life for everyone.

2. There is only one _____ along this rocky coast.

3. She _____ her sister in appearance but not in character.

4. Instead of frying, she likes to _____ the meat.

5. How to get all my clothes into one suitcase was a _____.

> 【解答】
> 1. privilege 2. port 3. resembles 4. roast 5. puzzle

✦ 第五部分

silence
('saɪləns)

Students are required to maintain *silence* in the library.
學生在圖書館中被要求保持安靜。

n. 沉默；安靜
同 quietness
反 noise

sob
(sab)

She *sobbed* when she heard the bad news. 她聽到壞消息時哭了。

v. 啜泣
同 weep

spit
(spɪt)

Please *spit* out your gum before you come into the classroom.
進入教室前，請把你的口香糖吐掉。

v. 吐出；吐痰

steep
〔 stip 〕

The hill was too *steep* for them to climb. 那座山丘太陡，他們不能爬。

adj. 陡峭的；
（上升或下降）急劇的

【記憶技巧】
用 deep（深的）聯想 steep（陡峭的）。

substantial
〔 səb'stænʃəl 〕

John has made a *substantial* improvement in his health. 約翰在健康方面已有了相當大的改善。

adj. 實質的；
相當大的
同 great

swift
〔 swɪft 〕

Be careful not to fall down; the current of the river is *swift*.
當心別掉下去；河流很急。

adj. 快速的
同 quick

thermometer
〔 θə'mɑmətɚ 〕

The doctor used a clinical *thermometer* to measure the patient's temperature.
醫生用體溫計測量病人的溫度。

n. 溫度計

【記憶技巧】
thermo (heat) + *meter* (measure)（測量溫度的，就是「溫度計」）

tower
〔'tauɚ 〕

You should visit the *Tower* of London when you have a chance to visit England. 當你有機會到英國時，應該遊覽一下倫敦塔。

n. 塔

typical
〔'tɪpɪkḷ 〕

Turkey is a *typical* food for the Thanksgiving Day dinner.
火雞是感恩節晚餐的代表性食物。

adj. 典型的；
代表性的
動 typify

virgin
〔'vɝdʒɪn 〕

The man decided to marry a *virgin* who lives in the house next to his uncle. 那人決定娶一位住在他叔叔隔壁的少女。

n. 處女；少女

whisper
〔'hwɪspɚ 〕

She *whispered* a few words at the corner. 她在角落低聲說了一些話。

v. 小聲說；
低聲地說

Lesson 14

Exercise 14.5 從第五部分中選出最適當的一個英文字，填入空格內。

1. If you _____ in the classroom, you may be punished by the teacher.

2. A _____ rise in cost of living makes our life hard.

3. The building is a _____ 18th-century church.

4. What the _____ is to temperature, the speedometer is to speed.

5. He has _____ evidence for his claim.

【解答】
1. spit　2. steep　3. typical　4. thermometer　5. substantial

成果測驗

I. 找出一個與斜體字的意義最接近的單字：

( ) 1. to *decorate* the wall with paintings
　　　(A) furnish　(B) adorn　(C) match　(D) describe

( ) 2. a serious *offense*
　　　(A) crime　(B) attack　(C) expense　(D) misfortune

( ) 3. a *port* in the southern coast
　　　(A) island　(B) city　(C) tower　(D) harbor

( ) 4. an *outstanding* achievement
　　　(A) unknown　(B) impossible
　　　(C) prominent　(D) evident

(   ) 5. a *swift* glance

    (A) secret   (B) wild   (C) slight   (D) quick

(   ) 6. to *furnish* a new building

    (A) decorate   (B) equip   (C) finish   (D) purchase

(   ) 7. to get invited to a *feast*

    (A) parlor   (B) funeral   (C) banquet   (D) wedding

(   ) 8. a *substantial* improvement

    (A) great   (B) false   (C) surprising   (D) unexpected

(   ) 9. an *obvious* mistake

    (A) insignificant   (B) serious

    (C) evident   (D) real

(   ) 10. a difficult *puzzle*

    (A) riddle   (B) work   (C) language   (D) battle

II. 找出一個與題前中文意思相同的英文字：

(   ) 1. 特權

    (A) priest   (B) character   (C) privilege   (D) journal

(   ) 2. 相像

    (A) waver   (B) resemble   (C) assume   (D) match

(   ) 3. 野蠻的

    (A) savage   (B) flat

    (C) native   (D) impossible

(   ) 4. 代表性的

    (A) substantial   (B) outstanding

    (C) genuine   (D) typical

Lesson 14

( ) 5. 費用

    (A) instance   (B) loss   (C) expense   (D) reference

Ⅲ. 找出一個與斜體字意義相反的單字：

( ) 1. *noise*

    (A) well-being (B) merit   (C) luck   (D) silence

( ) 2. *gain*

    (A) crime   (B) loss

    (C) virgin   (D) misfortune

( ) 3. *contain*

    (A) divide   (B) conceive (C) spit   (D) exclude

( ) 4. *misfortune*

    (A) offense   (B) feast   (C) luck   (D) welfare

( ) 5. *exit*

    (A) entrance   (B) ash   (C) fog   (D) journal

Ⅳ. 完整拼出下列各句中所欠缺的單字，每一格代表一個字母：

1. It is o_ _ _ _ _s that a blind man ought not to drive a car.
（明顯的）

2. The wooded r_ _ _ _n will be transformed into a park. （區域）

3. There is no place for s_ _ _ _ _ _ _t in business affairs. （感情）

4. Tomorrow's weather will d_ _ _ _ _ _ _e whether we are to go
or stay. （決定）

5. I h_ _ _ _ _ _e to ask you, but will you lend me some money?
（不願）

V. 選出最適合句意的一個單字：

(   ) 1. Scientists first _____ the idea of the atomic bomb in the 1930s.
    (A) contained   (B) purchased
    (C) compounded   (D) conceived

(   ) 2. It is the business of the police to detect _____ and of the law courts to punish criminals.
    (A) crimes   (B) puzzles   (C) losses   (D) faults

(   ) 3. The ribbon does not _____ the hat.
    (A) resemble   (B) match
    (C) appreciate   (D) allow

(   ) 4. The cruel rider _____ his horse with a stick.
    (A) roasted   (B) heaped   (C) whispered   (D) beat

(   ) 5. A large number of houses were burnt to _____.
    (A) victims   (B) misfortune   (C) ashes   (D) noises

(   ) 6. Before we judge a person's acts, we must know all the _____.
    (A) circumstances   (B) expenses
    (C) puzzles   (D) faults

(   ) 7. The king and his nobles celebrated the birth of his heir with a _____.
    (A) bowl   (B) benefit   (C) sob   (D) feast

(   ) 8. It is _____ to grow rice in the desert.
    (A) genuine   (B) impossible
    (C) perilous   (D) partial

(   ) 9. There are many _____ in our society such as churches, schools, hospitals, and prisons.

    (A) institutions   (B) foundations

    (C) journals   (D) regions

(   ) 10. He gave his friend the _____ of using his private library.

    (A) reference   (B) security

    (C) privilege   (D) expense

VI. 將題前的斜體字轉換爲適當詞性，填入空格中：

1. *decorate*   The _____ at the party were bright and cheery.

2. *determine*   He has a firm _____ to do his best in the final examination.

3. *entrance*   The thief _____ through a rear window last night.

4. *expense*   This radio is very _____.

5. *greedy*   His _____ for money led him to steal a painting from the museum.

【解答】

I. 1. B   2. A   3. D   4. C   5. D   6. B   7. C   8. A   9. C   10. A

II. 1. C   2. B   3. A   4. D   5. C

III. 1. D   2. B   3. D   4. C   5. A

IV. 1. obvious   2. region   3. sentiment   4. determine
     5. hesitate

V. 1. D   2. A   3. B   4. D   5. C   6. A   7. D   8. B   9. A   10. C

VI. 1. decorations   2. determination   3. entered   4. expensive
     5. greed

Lesson 14

Lesson 15

✦ 第一部分

additional
〔 ə'dɪʃənḷ 〕

Mother needs ***additional*** help in the kitchen when we have guests for dinner. 晚餐有客人時，母親在廚房需要額外的幫忙。

adj. 額外的
名 addition

---

aspect
〔 'æspɛkt 〕

You must consider all ***aspects*** of this plan before we decide. 在我們決定前，你必須把這計畫的各個方面都考慮到。

n. 方面

【記憶技巧】
a (to) + ***spect*** (see) (看事情，可從各「方面」去看)

---

beard
〔 bɪrd 〕

My grandfather has a long ***beard*** on his chin and cheeks.
祖父的下巴和臉頰上留著很長的鬍子。

n. 鬍子

---

brass
〔 bræs 〕

He has ***brass*** buttons on his jackets. 他的夾克上有黃銅扣子。

【記憶技巧】
br + ***ass*** (屁股)

n. 黃銅

---

carve
〔 kɑrv 〕

The picture was ***carved*** on the surface of a piece of wood.
那幅畫被刻在一塊木頭的表面上。

v. 雕刻
同 inscribe

---

civil
〔 'sɪvḷ 〕

The judge ordered that the prisoner should lose his ***civil*** rights.
法官判定這犯人應喪失公民權。
The soldiers thought it would be a long time before ***civil*** government would be reestablished. 士兵們認爲要在很久以後才能重建平民政府。

adj. 1. 公民的

2. 平民的
名 civilian

Lesson 15

concern
〔 kən'sɝn 〕

Don't trouble about things that don't *concern* you.
不要為和你無關的事煩惱。
I am very much *concerned* about the future of this country.
我非常擔心這個國家的前途。

v. 1. 與…有關
同 relate to

2. 使擔心
同 worry

contest
〔 'kɑntɛst 〕

The *contest* between France and England for North America ended in victory for England. 法國和英國爭取北美的競賽，結果英國勝利。

n. 比賽
同 competition;
struggle;
conflict

〔 kən'tɛst 〕

The blackbirds *contested* with one another for nesting territory.
山鳥鳥為築巢的地點互相競爭。

v. 競爭
同 compete

【記憶技巧】
con (together) + *test* (考試) (一起考試，就是「比賽」)

critical
〔 'krɪtɪk!〕

I don't like people who are too *critical* about everything.
我不喜歡對每件事都太吹毛求疵的人。
His condition is reported as being very *critical*.
有人報導他的情況非常危急。

adj. 1. 批評的；
吹毛求疵的
同 faultfinding
2. 危急的

decrease
〔 dɪ'kris 〕

The workmen want to *decrease* the number of working hours and to increase pay.
工人們要減少工作時間，增加工資。

v. 減少
反 increase

【記憶技巧】
de (down) + *crease* (grow) (向下成長，就是「減少」)

Exercise 15.1 從第一部分中選出最適當的一個英文字，填入空格內。

1. The doctor was _____ about the health of his aged patient.

Lesson 15

2. Government must protect the _____ rights of its citizens.

3. If you really understood the difficulties of the government, you wouldn't be so _____ of its policy.

4. John no longer wears a(n) _____.

5. _____ is made by mixing copper and zinc.

【解答】

1. concerned　2. civil　3. critical　4. beard　5. Brass

✦ 第二部分

device
〔 dɪ'vaɪs 〕

He invented a *device* for automatically lighting a gas stove.
他發明一種自動點燃煤氣爐的裝置。
The child's tears were a *device* to get attention.
孩子的眼淚是引起注意的一種策略。

n. 1. 裝置
　同 design
2. 策略
　同 method

【記憶技巧】
用 advice（建議）想到 device（裝置）。

divine
〔 də'vaɪn 〕

To err is human, to forgive *divine*.
【諺】犯錯是人，寬恕是神。

adj. 神聖的；神的

election
〔 ɪ'lɛkʃən 〕

The *election* results will be broadcast tonight.
今晚將會廣播選舉的結果。

n. 選舉
　動 elect
　形 elective

envy
〔'ɛnvɪ 〕

The boy's new bicycle was an object of *envy* to all his friends. 那男孩的新腳踏車是他所有朋友羨慕的東西。

n. 羨慕；嫉妒
　形 envious
v. 羨慕；嫉妒

Lesson 15

expedition
〔͵ɛkspɪˈdɪʃən〕

He was a member of the Everest *expedition*.
他是埃弗勒斯峯探險隊的隊員。

【記憶技巧】
ex (out) + *pedi* (foot) + *tion* (走出戶外，尋求「探險」的感覺)

n. 探險；探險隊

feature
〔ˈfitʃɚ〕

The main *features* of southern California are the warm climate and the beautiful scenery.
南加州的主要特色是溫暖的氣候及美麗的風景。

n. 特色
同 characteristic

folly
〔ˈfɑlɪ〕

After one year at the university he gave up his studies; it was an act of the greatest *folly*.
他在那所大學一年後，放棄求學；這是最愚蠢的行爲。

n. 愚蠢；愚行
同 foolishness
反 sagacity

fury
〔ˈfjʊrɪ〕

In his *fury* at being punished, he broke the teacher's favorite vase.
他受懲罰，一時憤怒而將老師最心愛的花瓶打破。

n. 憤怒
同 anger; rage

grief
〔 grif 〕

She nearly went mad with *grief* after the child died.
孩子死後，她悲傷得幾乎瘋狂。

【記憶技巧】
gr (gravity) + *ief* (心中有沈重的事，即「悲傷」)

n. 悲傷
同 sorrow
反 pleasure

hide
〔 haɪd 〕

Hide it where no one else can find it.
把它藏在沒有人找得到的地方。

v. 隱藏
同 conceal
反 reveal

Exercise 15.2 從第二部分中選出最適當的一個英文字，填入空格內。

1. The old man smiled sadly as he remembered the _____ of his youth.

2. He used a strange _____ to pick up the paper.

3. Some boys were full of _____ when they saw my new bicycle.

4. I _____ the broken dish behind the table yesterday.

5. His failure to live a good life was a(n) _____ to his parents.

> 【解答】
> 1. follies   2. device   3. envy   4. hid   5. grief

✦ 第三部分

impression
〔ɪmˈprɛʃən〕

His speech made a strong ***impression*** on the audience.
他的演說給聽眾很深刻的印象。

n. 印象
動 impress

instruct
〔ɪnˈstrʌkt〕

We have one teacher who ***instructs*** us in geography, English, and history. 我們有一位老師教我們地理、英文，還有歷史。

v. 教導
名 instruction

> 【記憶技巧】
> ***in*** (in) + ***struct*** (build)（透過「教導」把所學的內容建構在心中）

journey
〔ˈdʒɝnɪ〕

Life is a long ***journey*** from birth to death.
人生是個從出生至死亡的漫長旅程。

n. 旅程

lawn
〔 lɔn 〕
I spent the whole afternoon mowing the *lawn* in the backyard.
我花了整個下午在後院修剪草坪。
n. 草地

lovely
〔 'lʌvlɪ 〕
She was wearing a *lovely* dress at the party.
她在宴會中穿了一件非常可愛的洋裝。
adj. 可愛的

material
〔 mə'tɪrɪəl 〕
When building *materials* cost more, the price of houses increases.
當建築材料漲價時，房屋價格也會提高。
n. 物質；材料
同 substance

mislead
〔 mɪs'lid 〕
Her appearance *misled* him; he thought she was young, but she wasn't. 她的容貌誤導他；他以爲她年輕，其實不然。
v. 誤導
pp. misled
同 misguide

【記憶技巧】
mis (wrong) + *lead* (引導)

navy
〔 'nevɪ 〕
The *navy* defends the country's shores and seas. 海軍保衛國家的海岸和海域。
n. 海軍

occasion
〔 ə'keʒən 〕
I wish to express my sorrow on this *occasion*.
我希望能在此場合表達我的哀傷。
n. 場合；特別的大事

【記憶技巧】
oc (before) + *cas* (fall) + *ion* (*n.*) (掉到你面前的事，就是「特別的大事」)

overcome
〔 ˌovɚ'kʌm 〕
In order to succeed, you must *overcome* any hardships.
爲了成功，你必須克服任何困難。
v. 克服；打敗
同 conquer;
vanquish

Lesson 15

Exercise 15.3 從第三部分中選出最適當的一個英文字，填入空格內。

1. Our guide _____ us in the woods, and we got lost.

2. He is going to make a(n) _____ around the world.

3. Rubber is a widely used _____.

4. A birthday is not a(n) _____ for tears.

5. The child was _____ by weariness and slept deeply.

> 【解答】
> 1. misled 2. journey 3. material 4. occasion 5. overcome

✦ 第四部分

pat 〔 pæt 〕	The child gave the dog a ***pat*** on the head. 那孩子輕拍狗的頭。 She ***patted*** her hair to be sure that it was neat. 她撫平頭髮，以確定整齊。	*n.* 輕拍 *v.* 輕拍；撫平 同 tap
persuade 〔 pɚˋswed 〕	I know I should study, but he ***persuaded*** me to go to the movies. 我知道我應該唸書，可是他說服我去看電影。	*v.* 說服 名 persuasion 反 dissuade

> 【記憶技巧】
> ***per*** (thoroughly) + ***suade*** (advise) (徹底地勸告，就是「說服」)

portable 〔ˋpɔrtəbḷ〕	A ***portable*** computer can be easily moved from place to place. 手提電腦可輕便地到處攜帶。	*adj.* 手提的

procedure
〔 prə'sidʒɚ 〕

The new secretary learned the ***procedure*** in the office.
新來的秘書學習辦公室內的程序。

n. 程序

quality
〔'kwɑlətɪ 〕

Quality is more important than quantity. 質比量更重要。

n. 品質；特質

register
〔'rɛdʒɪstɚ 〕

You are required to ***register*** before the election. 選舉前，你必須先登記。

v. 登記；註冊

> 【記憶技巧】
> ***re*** (back) + ***gister*** (carry) (「登記」時，把資料帶過去)

resent
〔 rɪ'zɛnt 〕

He strongly ***resents*** being called a fool. 他非常憎恨被人叫作傻瓜。

v. 憎恨

> 【記憶技巧】
> ***re*** (加強語氣的字首) + ***sent*** (feel) (「憎恨」是很強烈的情緒)

rod
〔 rɑd 〕

She hung curtains on a ***rod***.
她把窗簾掛在竿子上。

n. 竿子

scarcity
〔'skɛrsətɪ 〕

The ***scarcity*** of fruit was caused by the drought.
由於乾旱，造成水果不足。

n. 不足
反 abundance
形 scarce

series
〔'sɪrɪz,
'siriz 〕

A ***series*** of rainy days spoiled their vacation.
連日的雨天，破壞了他們的假期。

n. 一連串；連續

Lesson 15

Exercise 15.4 從第四部分中選出最適當的一個英文字，填入空格內。

1. He _____ the promotion of his younger colleague to a rank above his own.

2. It took the whole afternoon to _____ his new car.

3. She wanted to buy an orange dress, but we _____ her that the blue one was more attractive.

4. He bought a _____ television for the trip.

5. An important _____ of steel is its strength.

【解答】
1. resented   2. register   3. persuaded   4. portable   5. quality

✦ 第五部分

silly (ˈsɪlɪ)	It's **silly** of you to trust him. 你會信任他，真是愚蠢。	*adj.* 愚蠢的 反 sensible
social (ˈsoʃəl)	Juvenile delinquency is a serious **social** problem in this country. 青少年犯罪是這個國家嚴重的社會問題。 It was a **social** meeting, and no one discussed business. 這是社交聚會，沒有人討論生意。	*adj.* 1. 社會的 2. 社交的 名 society
splendid (ˈsplɛndɪd)	The rich man lives in a **splendid** house over there. 那有錢人住在那邊一棟華麗的房屋內。	*adj.* 壯麗的； 華麗的

【記憶技巧】
splend (shine) + **id** (*adj.*) (閃耀著光輝的，就是「壯麗的」)

steer
〔stɪr〕

We ***steered*** the boat toward land.
我們將船駛向陸地。
The ***steers*** were fattened for market. 養肥公牛是為了銷售。

v. 駕駛
同 guide; navigate
n. 公牛
同 ox

【記憶技巧】
seer (觀看者) + ***t*** (「駕駛」車要觀看路況)

substitute
〔'sʌbstəˌtjut〕

We often ***substitute*** margarine for butter. 我們經常以人造奶油代替奶油。

v. 用⋯代替

【記憶技巧】
sub (under) + ***stitute*** (stand) (站在下面準備「代替」別人)

swing
〔swɪŋ〕

The big ape ***swung*** itself from branch to branch.
那大猩猩在樹枝間盪來盪去。

v. 搖擺

thirst
〔θɝst〕

The horse satisfied its ***thirst*** at the river. 那匹馬在河邊喝水解渴。

n. 口渴
形 thirsty

trace
〔tres〕

His family can ***trace*** its history back to the 10th century.
他的家族史可追溯至第十世紀。
The police were unable to find any ***trace*** of the thief.
警察找不到小偷的任何踪跡。

v. 追溯
同 track

n. 踪跡；痕跡

union
〔'junjən〕

The United States of America is a federal ***union*** of fifty states.
美國是有五十州的聯邦。

n. 聯合；聯邦
同 combination

Lesson 15

visible
〔'vɪzəbl̩〕

The shore was barely ***visible*** through the fog. 從霧中幾乎看不見海岸。

adj. 看得見的
反 hidden

------【記憶技巧】------
vis (see) + ***ible*** (*adj.*)

whistle
〔'hwɪsl̩〕

The policeman ***whistled*** for the automobile to stop. 警察吹哨子要汽車停下來。

v. 吹哨子

Exercise 15.5 從第五部分中選出最適當的一個英文字，填入空格內。

1. Sorrow had left its _____ on his face.

2. The pilot _____ the ship for the harbor in the morning.

3. We _____ red balls for blue ones to see if the baby would notice.

4. After running 5 miles we really had a _____.

5. He was _____ his arms as he walked.

------【解答】------
1. traces   2. steered   3. substituted   4. thirst   5. swinging

成果測驗

I. 找出一個與其他三個不相關的字：

(　) 1. (A) overcome　(B) contest　(C) conquer　(D) vanquish

(　) 2. (A) fury　(B) anger　(C) rage　(D) folly

(　) 3. (A) loss　(B) lack　(C) rarity　(D) scarcity

Lesson 15

(　　) 4. (A) foolish　　(B) stupid　　(C) ugly　　(D) silly

(　　) 5. (A) lovely　　(B) attractive　　(C) divine　　(D) beautiful

(　　) 6. (A) procedure (B) journey　　(C) excursion　　(D) travel

(　　) 7. (A) mislead　　(B) mistake　　(C) misdirect　　(D) misguide

(　　) 8. (A) splendid　　　　　　(B) brilliant
　　　　　(C) magnificent　　　　　(D) substantial

(　　) 9. (A) suffering　(B) grief　　(C) offense　　(D) sorrow

(　　) 10. (A) contest　　(B) competition　(C) struggle　　(D) device

II. 找出一個與題前中文意思相同的英文字：

(　　) 1. 手提的
　　　　　(A) portable　　(B) divine　　(C) actual　　(D) native

(　　) 2. 登記
　　　　　(A) contain　　(B) furnish　　(C) register　　(D) determine

(　　) 3. 憎恨
　　　　　(A) contest　　(B) resent　　(C) steer　　(D) resign

(　　) 4. 鬍子
　　　　　(A) fury　　(B) lawn　　(C) series　　(D) beard

(　　) 5. 印象
　　　　　(A) impression　(B) feature　　(C) device　　(D) quality

III. 找出一個與斜體字意義相反的單字：

(　　) 1. *sensible*
　　　　　(A) civil　　(B) wise　　(C) critical　　(D) silly

Lesson 15

(　) 2. *abundance*

    (A) fury   (B) scarcity   (C) quantity   (D) quality

(　) 3. *grief*

    (A) pleasure   (B) journey   (C) folly   (D) competition

(　) 4. *dissuade*

    (A) persuade   (B) conquer   (C) conceal   (D) concern

(　) 5. *hidden*

    (A) divine   (B) visible   (C) social   (D) additional

IV. 完整拼出下列各句中所欠缺的單字，每一格代表一個字母：

1. You have only considered one a_ _ _ _t of the difficulty, but there are many. （方面）

2. The furniture that the store sells is known for its good q_ _ _ _ _y. （品質）

3. D_ _ _ _ _ _c the dose of medicine when you feel better. （減少）

4. In our city we have an e_ _ _ _ _ _n for mayor every two years. （選舉）

5. They lost their way in the desert and died of t_ _ _ _t. （口渴）

V. 找出一個與句中斜體字意義最接近的單字：

(　) 1. He *patted* me on the shoulder.

    (A) persuaded (B) trimmed   (C) tapped   (D) spat

(　) 2. The early settlers had many difficulties to *overcome*.

    (A) perform   (B) decrease

    (C) conquer   (D) understand

Lesson 15

(   ) 3. The police *traced* the thief to his hiding place.

    (A) searched   (B) tracked   (C) vanquished (D) located

(   ) 4. They *carved* their names on the tree.

    (A) inscribed   (B) described   (C) inspired   (D) wrote

(   ) 5. We *steered* the boat toward the port in the south.

    (A) hid   (B) swung   (C) spied   (D) guided

(   ) 6. It is a *folly* to drink too much during the picnic.

    (A) puzzle   (B) danger   (C) foolishness (D) feast

(   ) 7. Janet is only too *critical* of Alice because she doesn't like her.

    (A) faultfinding   (B) substantial

    (C) jealous   (D) negligent

(   ) 8. She *hid* the toy in the drawer.

    (A) hit   (B) concealed (C) disclosed   (D) put

(   ) 9. Wet weather is a *feature* of life in Scotland.

    (A) characteristic   (B) quantity

    (C) occasion   (D) device

(   ) 10. It is no use trying to argue with you when you fly into a *fury* over the slightest thing.

    (A) privilege   (B) journey   (C) rage   (D) rarity

Lesson 15

【解答】

  I. 1. B   2. D   3. A   4. C   5. C   6. A   7. B   8. D   9. C   10. D

 II. 1. A   2. C   3. B   4. D   5. A

III. 1. D   2. B   3. A   4. A   5. B

IV. 1. aspect   2. quality   3. Decrease   4. election   5. thirst

 V. 1. C   2. C   3. B   4. A   5. D   6. C   7. A   8. B   9. A   10. C

Lesson 16

✦ 第一部分

admire 〔 əd'maɪr 〕	We all ***admire*** a brave boy, a beautiful picture, or a fine piece of work. 我們都會讚賞勇敢的孩子、美麗的圖畫，或很好的作品。	*v.* 欽佩；讚賞 同 esteem 名 admiration

assemble 〔 ə'sɛmbḷ 〕	The students were ***assembled*** in the school hall. 學生們在學校禮堂內集合。	*v.* 集合；裝配

【記憶技巧】
as (to) + ***semble*** (same)（到相同地點，就是「集合」）

beast 〔 bist 〕	Lions, bears, cows, and horses are ***beasts***. 獅子、熊、牛和馬都是獸類。	*n.* 野獸

bravery 〔'brevərɪ 〕	A young man of ***bravery*** saved the child from the burning house. 一個勇敢的年輕人將那孩子從著火的房子中救出。	*n.* 勇敢 同 courage 反 cowardice 形 brave

【記憶技巧】
brave（勇敢的）+ ***ry*** (*n.*)

castle 〔'kæsḷ 〕	A king once lived in the mountain ***castle***. 從前有一位國王住在山上的城堡中。	*n.* 城堡

claim 〔 klem 〕	Every citizen may ***claim*** the protection of the law. 每一位公民都可要求法律保護。	*v.* 宣稱；要求 同 demand

Lesson 16

conclude
〔kən'klud〕

As he didn't get here at six, I *concluded* that he had been delayed.
由於他六點還沒到，我斷定他被耽擱了。

v. 下結論；
斷定；結束
图 conclusion

【記憶技巧】
con (together) + *clude* (shut)（做關上的動作，表示「結束」）

contract
〔*n.* 'kɑntrækt〕
〔*v.* kən'trækt〕

Our shop *contracted* with a local clothing firm for 100 coats a week.
本店和當地的服飾公司簽約，每星期購買一百件外套。
Most metals *contract* when they cool. 大部分的金屬在冷卻時會收縮。

n. 合約
v. 1. 簽約

2. 收縮
同 diminish

【記憶技巧】
con (together) + *tract* (draw)（「合約」是雙方簽訂的文件）

crop
〔krɑp〕

Wheat, corn and cotton are the three main *crops* of the United States. 小麥、玉米和棉花是美國三種主要的農作物。
The drought made the potato *crop* very small this year.
乾旱使今年馬鈴薯的收穫量很少。

n. 1. 農作物

2. 收穫量

deed
〔did〕

Good *deeds* should be rewarded and evil *deeds* should be punished.
好的行為應受獎賞，壞的行為應受懲罰。

n. 行為
同 behavior;
act

Exercise 16.1 從第一部分中選出最適當的一個英文字，填入空格內。

1. The grandfather _____ all the members of his family for the annual meeting last week.

2. We _____ people who succeed in spite of difficulties.

3. They _____ to pay cash for the house just yesterday.

4. The injured man _____ compensation for damages at the trial yesterday.

5. His _____ do not always agree with his words.

【解答】
1. assembled 2. admire 3. contracted 4. claimed 5. deeds

✦ 第二部分

devote
〔 dɪ'vot 〕

He *devoted* his efforts to the improvement of the parks in the city.
他致力於市區公園的改善。

【記憶技巧】
de (from) + *vote* (vow) (發誓要做某件事,就是「致力於」)

v. 奉獻;
致力於
名 devotion
同 dedicate

divorce
〔 də'vɔrs 〕

He has been *divorced* for a year.
他已離婚一年。
His wife asked him for a *divorce*.
他的太太要求離婚。

v. 離婚;分離

n. 離婚
同 separate

elegant
〔 'ɛləgənt 〕

The furnishings of the palace were *elegant*.
這皇宮的裝飾很高雅。

adj. 優雅的
同 graceful
反 vulgar

equator
〔 ɪ'kwetɚ 〕

The United States is north of the *equator*. 美國在赤道的北邊。

n. 赤道

Lesson 16

exist
〔 ɪg'zɪst 〕

We cannot *exist* without air, food, and water.
我們沒有空氣、食物和水，就不能生存。

v. 存在

【記憶技巧】
ex (forth) + *ist* (stand)（繼續站在世界上，表示「存在」）

federal
〔'fɛdərəl 〕

The United States has a *federal* government. 美國有一個聯邦政府。

adj. 聯邦的

【記憶技巧】
feder (treaty) + *al* (*adj.*)（由條約束縛的，就是「聯邦的」）

forbid
〔 fɚ'bɪd 〕

Smoking is *forbidden* in the crowded bus.
在擁擠的公車上禁止吸煙。

v. 禁止
同 prohibit
反 permit; allow

gallery
〔'gælərɪ 〕

Many pictures were hung on the walls of the *gallery*. 畫廊牆上掛著許多畫。

n. 畫廊；美術品陳列室

grind
〔 graɪnd 〕

That mill *grinds* corn into meal, and wheat into flour. 那家製粉廠將玉米磨成玉米粉，小麥磨成麵粉。

v. 磨

improve
〔 ɪm'pruv 〕

She *improved* her handwriting by constant practice. 她藉著不斷的練習，來改進她的筆跡。

v. 改善
名 improvement

【記憶技巧】
im（表「引起」的字首）+ *prove* (profit)（「改善」會帶來好處）

Exercise 16.2 從第二部分中選出最適當的一個英文字，填入空格內。

1. The mother _____ herself to caring for her sick child last week.

2. The _____ is an imaginary circle around the middle of the earth at an equal distance from the North and South poles.

3. What happens to the soul when it is _____ from the body?

4. In the United States, foreign policy is decided by the _____ government.

5. If her father had known it, he would have _____ the marriage.

> 【解答】
> 1. devoted   2. equator   3. divorced   4. federal   5. forbidden

✦ 第三部分

instrument 〔'ɪnstrəmənt 〕	A doctor's ***instruments*** must be kept clean. 醫生的用具必須保持清潔。	*n.* 儀器；用具；樂器
junior 〔'dʒunjɚ 〕	This teaching course is for ***junior*** officers. 這門教學課程是爲下級軍官設的。	*adj.* 年少的；下級的；資淺的 反 senior
leak 〔 lik 〕	There is a ***leak*** in the roof. 屋頂上有個漏洞。 The rain is ***leaking*** in through a crack in the roof. 雨正從屋頂上的縫隙漏進來。	*n.* 漏洞 *v.* 漏；漏水

Lesson 16

Lesson 16

lower 〔'loɚ 〕	We usually *lower* our flag at six o'clock. 我們通常在六點降旗。	*v.* 降低；降下
mayor 〔'meɚ 〕	A *mayor* is the chief government official of a city or town. 市長是一市或一鎮的主要政府官員。	*n.* 市長

【記憶技巧】
想到 <u>major</u>（主要的；重大的）<u>mayor</u>（市長）

mistrust 〔 mɪs'trʌst 〕	He keeps his money at home because he *mistrusts* banks. 他把錢放在家裏，因為他不信任銀行。	*v.* 不信任 反 believe; trust
neat 〔 nit 〕	The girl was taught to put away her toys and clothes to keep her room *neat*. 那女孩被教導要將玩具和衣服收拾好，以維持房間的整潔。	*adj.* 整潔的； 工整的
occupy 〔'ɑkjə,paɪ 〕	Mr. Smith *occupies* an important position in the Ministry of Education. 史密斯先生在教育部擔任要職。	*v.* 佔據；充任 名 occupation

【記憶技巧】
oc (over) + *cupy* (seize)（奪取，也就是「佔據」）

overall 〔'ovɚ,ɔl 〕	The *overall* length of the table is six feet. 那桌子全長六呎。	*adj.* 全面的； 全部的
patch 〔 pætʃ 〕	She sewed *patches* on the elbows of his jacket. 她將補丁縫在他夾克的肘彎處。	*n.* 補丁
	The mother *patched* the boy's trousers. 母親縫補那男孩的褲子。	*v.* 縫補

Exercise 16.3 從第三部分中選出最適當的一個英文字，填入空格內。

1. A drill is one of the important _____ used by dentists.

2. There is a(n) _____ in the paper bag that lets sugar run out.

3. He has thousands of books, and they _____ a lot of space.

4. The _____ will lead the town meeting about taxes.

5. Her _____ handwriting is easy to read.

【解答】
1. instruments　2. leak　3. occupy　4. mayor　5. neat

✦ 第四部分

phrase
〔 frez 〕

He spoke in simple *phrases* so that the children understood him.
他用簡單的語句說，使孩子聽得懂。

n. 片語；措辭；說法

portion
〔'pɔrʃən 〕

His *portion* of the family property was the largest. 他分得的家產最多。

n. 部份；分得的財產

【記憶技巧】
por (part) + *tion* (*n.*)

procession
〔 prə'sɛʃən 〕

A funeral *procession* moved along the main street.
送葬行列沿著大街走。

n. 行列

quarrel
〔'kwɔrəl 〕

We have had a *quarrel* and don't speak to each other.
我們爭吵過後，就不再和對方說話了。

n. 爭吵

Lesson 16

regret
〔 rɪˈgrɛt 〕

They said goodbye with great *regret*. 他們非常遺憾地說再見。
n. 後悔；遺憾

I *regret* to say that I cannot help you this time.
我很遺憾地說，這次我幫不上你的忙。
v. 後悔；遺憾

reserve
〔 rɪˈzɝv 〕

The seats are *reserved* for old and sick people.
這些座位是保留給老人和病人們坐的。
v. 預訂；保留

> 【記憶技巧】
> *re* (back) + *serve* (keep) (「預訂」就是先把東西保留在後面)

role
〔 rol 〕

His *role* in that movie proved his acting ability. 他在那部電影中的角色證明了他的表演能力。
n. 角色
同 part

scare
〔 skɛr 〕

The sudden noise *scared* her.
突然的聲音嚇了她一跳。
v. 驚嚇

serious
〔ˈsɪrɪəs 〕

He spoke about the problem in a *serious* way.
他嚴肅地談論那個問題。
adj. 嚴重的；認眞的；嚴肅的
同 thoughtful

silverware
〔ˈsɪlvɚˌwɛr 〕

Her *silverware* consists of knives, forks, spoons, a water pitcher, and candlesticks. 她的銀器包括刀、叉、湯匙、一個水壺，還有燭台。
n. 銀器

> 【記憶技巧】
> *silver* (銀) + *ware* (製品)

Lesson 16

Exercise 16.4 從第四部分中選出最適當的一個英文字，填入空格內。

1. They were _____ by the strange sound.

2. Raising money for our club is a _____ matter.

3. The first three rows of the hall are _____ for special guests.

4. The children had a _____ about the division of the candy.

5. The workers marched in _____ to the minister's office.

【解答】

1. scared 2. serious 3. reserved 4. quarrel 5. procession

✦ 第五部分

sole 〔 sol 〕	He was the *sole* heir to the fortune when his rich aunt died. 當他有錢的姑姑去世時，他是唯一的財產繼承人。 The stone cut the *sole* of his foot. 石頭割傷了他的腳底。	*adj.* 唯一的 同 single 反 multiple *n.* 腳底；(鞋)底
split 〔 splɪt 〕	The boys *split* the money into four shares. 男孩們將錢分成四份。	*v.* 使分裂；分配 反 combine
stern 〔 stɜn 〕	He is very *stern* in his students' discipline. 他對學生的紀律非常嚴格。	*adj.* 嚴格的 同 strict 反 mild
subtract 〔 səb'trækt 〕	*Subtract* 2 from 4, and the remainder is 2. 四減二得二。	*v.* 減去

【記憶技巧】

sub (under) + *tract* (draw)（從底下抽出來，也就是「減去」）

sword 〔 sord 〕	Those who live by the *sword* shall perish by the *sword*. 那些靠刀劍吃飯的人，終將死於刀劍之下。	*n.* 劍；刀

Lesson 16

thorough
〔'θɝo 〕

You must give the horse a ***thorough*** cleaning every day.
你必須每天替馬徹底清洗。

adj. 徹底的
同 complete

tradition
〔 trə'dɪʃən 〕

It is a ***tradition*** that women get married in long white dresses.
女人結婚時穿白色長禮服是一種傳統。

n. 傳統；傳說
同 custom

> 【記憶技巧】
> ***tra*** (over) + ***dit*** (give) + ***ion*** (*n.*) (「傳統」是要一代傳一代的)

unite
〔 ju'naɪt 〕

The common interests made the countries ***unite***.
共同的利益使這些國家聯合起來。

v. 聯合

vision
〔'vɪʒən 〕

The old man wears glasses because his ***vision*** is very poor.
那老人因為視力太差而戴眼鏡。
We need a man of ***vision*** as president.
我們需要一個有洞察力的人做董事長。

n. 1. 視力
同 sight

2. 洞察力

> 【記憶技巧】
> 想到 tele<u>vision</u>（電視）。

widow
〔'wɪdo 〕

A ***widow*** is a woman whose husband has died, and who has not married again. 寡婦就是一個死了丈夫，而未再嫁的女人。

n. 寡婦
反 widower

Lesson 16

Exercise 16.5 從第五部分中選出最適當的一個英文字，填入空格內。

1. According to the old _____, Romulus was the founder of Rome.

2. Our club was _____ by the argument.

3. He is a _____ scoundrel.

4. The pen is mightier than the _____.

5. Several firms were _____ to form one company.

> 【解答】
>
> 1. tradition   2. split   3. thorough   4. sword   5. united

成果測驗

I. 找出一個與斜體字的意義最接近的單字：

(   ) 1. a *thorough* defeat
     (A) severe   (B) complete   (C) critical   (D) hidden

(   ) 2. *elegant* behavior
     (A) prompt   (B) greedy   (C) typical   (D) graceful

(   ) 3. to *forbid* something
     (A) order   (B) allow   (C) prohibit   (D) mistrust

(   ) 4. to *devote* one's life
     (A) admire   (B) reserve   (C) bother   (D) dedicate

(   ) 5. a good *deed*
     (A) contest   (B) impression   (C) act   (D) feature

(   ) 6. a medal for *bravery*
     (A) gallery   (B) quarrel   (C) courage   (D) fighting

(   ) 7. a *serious* person
     (A) thoughtful   (B) attractive
     (C) silly   (D) thorough

(   ) 8. a *stern* parent

    (A) stupid   (B) unique   (C) chilly   (D) strict

(   ) 9. to *esteem* someone

    (A) envy   (B) admire   (C) permit   (D) despise

(   ) 10. to *claim* something

    (A) demand   (B) assemble   (C) occupy   (D) contract

Ⅱ. 找出一個與題前中文意思相同的英文字：

(   ) 1. 寡婦

    (A) bachelor   (B) widow   (C) widower   (D) virgin

(   ) 2. 傳統

    (A) impression   (B) procession

    (C) expedition   (D) tradition

(   ) 3. 用具

    (A) instrument   (B) deed   (C) patch   (D) sword

(   ) 4. 整潔的

    (A) neat   (B) stern   (C) sole   (D) obvious

(   ) 5. 降低

    (A) subtract   (B) leak   (C) lower   (D) fall

Ⅲ. 找出一個與斜體字意義相反的單字：

(   ) 1. *vulgar*

    (A) ugly   (B) single   (C) elegant   (D) swift

(   ) 2. *cowardice*

    (A) well-being   (B) courage   (C) scarcity   (D) grief

Lesson 16

(   ) 3. *permit*

       (A) discourage   (B) lower   (C) reserve   (D) forbid

(   ) 4. *combine*

       (A) split   (B) scare

       (C) consolidate   (D) prohibit

(   ) 5. *stern*

       (A) abundant   (B) mild   (C) severe   (D) thorough

IV. 完整拼出下列各句中所欠缺的單字，每一格代表一個字母：

1. I shouted suddenly to s_ _ _e her. (驚嚇)

2. How do the very poor e_ _ _t on such low wages? (生存)

3. Practice will i_ _ _ _ _e your handwriting. (改善)

4. We heard with r_ _ _ _t that you had failed the examination.
   (遺憾)

5. If you saw a man dressed in poor clothes, you might c_ _ _ _ _ _e
   that he had little money. (斷定)

V. 選出最適合句意的一個單字：

(   ) 1. A foreign firm has _____ to build a new railway across
       Africa.

       (A) contracted   (B) assembled

       (C) subtracted   (D) occupied

(   ) 2. He hits his gentle wife like a _____.

       (A) feast   (B) victim   (C) beast   (D) beard

( ) 3. _____ are better than words when people are in trouble.

    (A) Defects   (B) Visions   (C) Phrases   (D) Deeds

( ) 4. It is wrong to _____ yourself only to amusement.

    (A) divorce   (B) devote   (C) claim   (D) esteem

( ) 5. He did not like his daughter's boyfriend, and _____ her to meet him.

    (A) split   (B) deducted

    (C) forbade   (D) mistrusted

( ) 6. _____ is needed to try again after a defeat.

    (A) Quarrel   (B) Folly   (C) Bravery   (D) Gallery

( ) 7. The wheat has been _____ down to good white flour.

    (A) assembled   (B) forbidden   (C) devoted   (D) ground

( ) 8. The air conditioner soon _____ the temperature of the room.

    (A) lowered   (B) improved

    (C) reserved   (D) contracted

( ) 9. They _____ some of the corn to use as seed.

    (A) occupied   (B) scared   (C) reserved   (D) sucked

( ) 10. She did her best to fulfil her _____ as a mother.

    (A) patience   (B) role   (C) tradition   (D) crop

Lesson 16

------【解答】------------------------------

I. 1. B   2. D   3. C   4. D   5. C   6. C   7. A   8. D   9. B   10. A

II. 1. B   2. D   3. A   4. A   5. C

III. 1. C   2. B   3. D   4. A   5. B

IV. 1. scare   2. exist   3. improve   4. regret   5. conclude

V. 1. A   2. C   3. D   4. B   5. C   6. C   7. D   8. A   9. C   10. B

Lesson 17

✦ 第一部分

admit 〔əd'mɪt〕	The servant opened the door and ***admitted*** me into the house. 佣人開門，准許我進入屋內。	*v.* 承認；准許 （進入） 名 admittance
assist 〔ə'sɪst〕	She ***assisted*** her mother with the housework. 她幫忙母親做家事。 ┈【記憶技巧】┈ ***as*** (to) + ***sist*** (stand)（站在旁邊，給予「幫助」）	*v.* 幫助 同 help 名 assistance
behave 〔bɪ'hev〕	He has ***behaved*** well to his wife and children as well. 他對妻兒的態度都很好。	*v.* 行為舉止
cattle 〔'kætl̩〕	The rancher raises 1,000 head of ***cattle*** on his ranch. 那牧場主人在他的牧場上養了一千頭牛。	*n.* 牛【集合名詞】
clay 〔kle〕	***Clay*** is used for making pots, dishes, and bricks. 黏土被用來製造花盆、盤子，和磚頭。	*n.* 黏土
condemn 〔kən'dɛm〕	All the newspapers ***condemned*** the general for his speech attacking a friendly nation. 將軍攻擊友邦國家的演說，受到所有報紙的譴責。 ┈【記憶技巧】┈ ***con***（加強語氣的字首）+ ***demn*** (harm)	*v.* 譴責 同 censure; blame

contrary
〔'kɑntrɛrɪ〕

If you act **contrary** to the doctor's advice, you won't get well again. 如果你違反醫生的勸告，就無法再康復了。

adj. 相反的
adv. 相反地
同 opposite

crude
〔krud〕

Oil and sugar are **crude** before being prepared for use. 油和糖在尚未備妥使用前都是未經提煉的。

His manners were **crude** at the party. 他在宴會上的態度很粗魯。

adj. 1. 未經加工的；
　　　　未提煉的

　　　 2. 粗魯的
　　　 同 impolite

defeat
〔dɪ'fit〕

We **defeated** Lincoln High School in the baseball game yesterday. 昨天的棒球比賽，我們打敗了林肯中學。

v. 打敗
同 conquer

> 【記憶技巧】
> **de** (away) + **feat** (功績)（把別人的功績拿走，就是「打敗」）

differ
〔'dɪfɚ〕

The two brothers are like each other in appearance but **differ** widely in their tastes. 這兩兄弟的外貌相像，可是嗜好卻大不相同。

v. 不同
同 disagree
名 difference

> 【記憶技巧】
> **dif** (apart) + **fer** (carry)

Exercise 17.1 從第一部分中選出最適當的一個英文字，填入空格內。

1. The children _____ badly; their manners were bad.

2. Only 100 boys are _____ to the school every year.

3. If we had snow in summer, it would be _____ to all experience.

4. In the last class, my answer to the arithmetic problem _____ from hers.

5. He _____ the enemy and was raised to the rank of general as a reward.

【解答】

1. behaved　2. admitted　3. contrary　4. differed　5. defeated

✦ 第二部分

doll
〔 dɑl 〕

My granddaughter is as pretty as a little *doll*. 我的孫女像小洋娃娃一樣美。

n. 洋娃娃；
玩偶

elementary
〔 ͵ɛlə'mɛntərɪ 〕

The *elementary* principles of mathematics are taught in the lower grades at school.
學校低年級會教數學的基本原理。

adj. 基本的
字 element

equip
〔 ɪ'kwɪp 〕

Is the ship fully *equipped* for its voyage? 這艘船已為出航裝備好了嗎？

v. 裝備；
使配備

exhibit
〔 ɪg'zɪbɪt 〕

Our men *exhibited* great bravery in the battle.
在那場戰役中，我方表現得非常英勇。

v. 展示；
展現
同 show
反 conceal

【記憶技巧】
ex (out) + *hibit* (hold) (把東西拿出來，就是「展示」)

feed
〔 fid 〕

She always *feeds* the baby with a spoon. 她一向用湯匙餵嬰兒。

v. 餵；餵食
pp. fed

force
〔 fors 〕

The thief took the money from the old man by *force*.
小偷用暴力從老人身上搶走錢。

n. 力量；暴力
v. 強迫

gallop
〔'gæləp 〕

The wild horse *galloped* down the hill.
野馬奔馳下山。
She went through the work at a *gallop*, so it couldn't have been done very well.
她匆促地做完工作，因而沒有做得很好。

v. 奔馳

n. 匆促地進行

---【記憶技巧】---
諧音：趕老婆，要「奔馳」。

grip
〔 grɪp 〕

He *gripped* the boy by the arm.
他抓住男孩的手臂。

v. 緊抓；抓住
同 seize

hind
〔 haɪnd 〕

The *hind* wings of some insects are shorter than the fore wings.
有些昆蟲的後翼比前翼短。

adj. 後部的

impulse
〔'ɪmpʌls 〕

A sudden *impulse* of anger arose in him when he was insulted.
當他受到侮辱時，突然湧起一股憤怒的衝動。

n. 衝動

---【記憶技巧】---
im (in) + *pulse* (push)（被心裡的想法驅使，因而產生「衝動」）

Exercise 17.2 從第二部分中選出最適當的一個英文字，填入空格內。

1. He _____ interest whenever you talk about dogs.

2. He _____ the nail and pulled it out.

3. The horse rose on its _____ legs.

4. The boy found a cave and stepped in it under the _____ of curiosity.

5. The expedition was fully _____ with food, tents, medicine, and other supplies.

【解答】
1. exhibits   2. gripped   3. hind   4. impulse   5. equipped

✦ 第三部分

insult
〔*n.* ′ɪnsʌlt 〕
〔*v.* ɪn′sʌlt 〕

To call a brave man a coward is an *insult*.
叫一個勇敢的人懦夫是一種侮辱。
The man *insulted* me by calling me a liar.
那男人叫我騙子來侮辱我。

n. 侮辱
反 respect
v. 侮辱
同 offend

【記憶技巧】
in (on) + *sult* (leap)（跳到別人的身上，表示「侮辱」）

jury
〔′dʒʊrɪ 〕

The *jury* decided the man was guilty.
陪審團判定這人有罪。

n. 陪審團

lean
〔 lin 〕

He *leaned* forward to hear what she said to him. 他傾身向前聽她說話。
Do you see a *lean* lady walking across the street?
你有看到一位瘦瘦的小姐走過這條街嗎？

v. 傾身；傾斜
adj. 瘦的
同 slender

loyal
〔′lɔɪəl 〕

As a *loyal* citizen, he supported his government.
身為一個忠貞的國民，他支持政府。

adj. 忠實的
同 faithful

meantime
('min,taɪm)

Her husband left at four and returned at seven, and in the *meantime* she wrote three letters. 她的丈夫四點離開，七點回來，在此期間她寫了三封信。

n. 其間；當中時間
同 meanwhile

mixture
('mɪkstʃə)

Green is a *mixture* of yellow and blue. 綠色是黃色和藍色的混合。

n. 混合

needle
('nidḷ)

Mother sewed the button on my coat with *needle* and thread. 母親用針線將扣子縫在我的外套上。

n. 針

occur
(ə'kɝ)

The terrible car accident *occurred* last Friday. 那場可怕的車禍發生在上星期五。
Just then a bright idea *occurred to* me. 就在那時，我想到了一個很妙的主意。

v. 1. 發生
同 happen

2. 使想到 < *to* >
同 strike

overlook
(,ovə'lʊk)

Our garden is *overlooked* by the neighbor's window. 鄰居的窗口可俯視我們的花園。

v. 忽視；俯視

┌─【記憶技巧】─────────────┐
over (上面) + *look* (看) (在上面看，就是「俯視」，容易「忽視」)
└────────────────────────┘

path
(pæθ)

The moon has a regular *path* through the sky. 月球在天空中有固定的軌道。

n. 小徑；軌道；路線
同 route

Exercise 17.3 從第三部分中選出最適當的一個英文字，填入空格內。

1. Your refusal to believe my story is a(n) _____ to me.

Lesson 17

2. This tobacco is a(n) _____ of three different sorts.

3. It had never _____ to me to say "thanks."

4. From our house on the hillside, we can _____ the whole city.

5. Grass has grown over the _____ through the woods.

【解答】

1. insult   2. mixture   3. occurred   4. overlook   5. path

✦ 第四部分

physical 〔'fɪzɪkḷ〕	The doctor's examination showed that he was in excellent ***physical*** condition. 醫生的檢查顯示,他的身體狀況良好。 They study the ***physical*** features of the earth in the science class. 他們在科學課研究地球的自然特徵。 【記憶技巧】 *phys-*表「身體」的字首。	*adj.* 1. 身體的 　　 反 spiritual; 　　　 mental 　　 2. 自然的; 　　　 物質的
positive 〔'pɑzətɪv〕	We have ***positive*** proof that the earth moves around the sun. 我們有確實的證據顯示地球繞著太陽運轉。	*adj.* 肯定的; 　　 確實的 　 同 unquestionable
proclaim 〔pro'klem〕	Many former colonies have ***proclaimed*** their independence. 許多昔日的殖民地已宣布獨立。	*v.* 宣布 　 同 announce
queer 〔kwɪr〕	There was something ***queer*** about the way he walked. 他走路的方式有點奇怪。	*adj.* 奇怪的 　 同 unusual 　 反 ordinary

Lesson 17

reign
〔 ren 〕

The queen's ***reign*** lasted more than fifty years. 女王的統治持續了五十多年。　*n.* 統治
He ***reigned*** over the small country for ten years. 他統治那小國十年。　*v.* 統治　同 rule

---【記憶技巧】---
用 fo<u>reign</u>（外國的）來記憶。

reside
〔 rɪ'zaɪd 〕

He has ***resided*** abroad for over ten years. 他住在國外已十年多了。　*v.* 1. 居住　同 live
Her charm ***resides*** in her happy smile. 她的魅力在於她快樂的微笑。　2. 存在

rooster
〔'rustɚ 〕

A ***rooster*** was leading many hens. 一隻公雞正帶領著許多母雞。　*n.* 公雞

scarf
〔 skɑrf 〕

The girl wore a green ***scarf*** over her shoulders.
那女孩披了一條綠色的圍巾在肩上。　*n.* 圍巾

---【記憶技巧】---
car-scar（疤痕）-scarf（圍巾）

servant
〔'sɝvənt 〕

They have two ***servants***, a cook and a maid. 他們有兩個僕人、一個廚師，和一個女佣。　*n.* 僕人　反 master

similarity
〔 ˌsɪmə'lærətɪ 〕

Their differences are more noticeable than their ***similarities***.
他們的不同點比相似之處要明顯得多。　*n.* 相似之處　反 difference

Exercise 17.4 從第四部分中選出最適當的一個英文字，填入空格內。

1. How much _____ is there between the two religions?

2. The ringing bells _____ the news of the birth of the prince.

3. The power to legislate _____ in the legislature.

4. A politician should be a _____ of the people.

5. The guard has _____ instructions not to admit anyone.

【解答】
1. similarity　2. proclaimed　3. resides　4. servant　5. positive

✦ 第五部分

solemn 〔'saləm 〕	We watched the ***solemn*** ceremony in the church. 我們在教堂裏觀看隆重的儀式。	*adj.* 嚴肅的； 　　　 隆重的
spoil 〔 spɔɪl 〕	She ***spoiled*** the meat by burning it. 她把肉燒壞了。	*v.* 破壞 同 ruin
stiff 〔 stɪf 〕	Leather shoes are usually ***stiff*** when they are new. 新的皮鞋通常很硬。	*adj.* 僵硬的； 　　　 硬的 同 rigid
subway 〔'sʌb,we 〕	He always goes to work by ***subway***. 他總是搭地鐵上班。	*n.* 地鐵
syllable 〔'sɪləbḷ 〕	There are two ***syllables*** in the word "button." button 這個字有兩個音節。	*n.* 音節

【記憶技巧】
syl (together) + ***lable*** (hold)（把幾個音放在一起唸，就是「音節」）

Lesson 17

thread
〔 θrɛd 〕

Nylon *thread* is stronger than cotton *thread*. 尼龍線比棉線堅韌。

n. 線

trademark
〔'tred,mɑrk 〕

The registration and protection of *trademarks* are now provided for by law.

現在商標的註冊和保護已有法律規定。

n. 商標

【記憶技巧】
「交易」(trade) 時，代表公司的「記號」
(mark)，就是「商標」(trademark)。
---

university
〔,junə'vɝsətɪ 〕

Several new *universities* have been built in the last ten years.

過去十年內建了幾所新大學。

n. 大學

vocabulary
〔 və'kæbjə,lɛrɪ 〕

A lot of reading will increase your *vocabulary*. 大量閱讀能增加你的字彙。

n. 字彙

wilderness
〔'wɪldənɪs 〕

Jesus went out into the *wilderness* alone to think.

耶穌獨自走到荒地去思考。

n. 荒野；荒地

Exercise 17.5 從第五部分中選出最適當的一個英文字，填入空格內。

1. She used silk _____ in sewing her dress.

2. He gave his _____ promise to defend his country.

3. A group of travelers were lost in the _____.

4. The _____ of science has grown tremendously in the past 20 years.

5. A(n) _____ consists of several colleges, such as liberal arts, law, medicine, etc.

【解答】
1. thread　2. solemn　3. wilderness　4. vocabulary　5. university
---

成果測驗

I. 找出一個與其他三個不相關的字：

(　) 1. (A) prohibit　　　　　　(B) declare
　　　　(C) announce　　　　　(D) proclaim

(　) 2. (A) likeness　　　　　　(B) similarity
　　　　(C) resemblance　　　　(D) mixture

(　) 3. (A) hind　(B) fore　　(C) back　　(D) rear

(　) 4. (A) power　(B) strength　(C) bravery　(D) force

(　) 5. (A) admit　(B) blame　(C) condemn　(D) censure

(　) 6. (A) queer　(B) lean　　(C) unusual　(D) strange

(　) 7. (A) grave　(B) solemn　(C) contrary　(D) serious

(　) 8. (A) vanish　　　　　　(B) defeat
　　　　(C) conquer　　　　　(D) overcome

(　) 9. (A) untreated　　　　　(B) raw
　　　　(C) crude　　　　　　(D) stern

(　) 10. (A) exhibit　(B) differ　(C) display　(D) show

II. 找出一個與題前中文意思相同的英文字：

( ) 1. 侮辱
(A) defeat　　(B) condemn　　(C) proclaim　　(D) insult

( ) 2. 大學
(A) servant　　　　　　(B) university
(C) vocabulary　　　　(D) mixture

( ) 3. 相反的
(A) contrary　　(B) crude　　(C) positive　　(D) loyal

( ) 4. 陪審團
(A) gallop　　(B) clay　　(C) jury　　(D) mayor

( ) 5. 俯視
(A) spoil　　(B) mistrust　　(C) overlook　　(D) regret

III. 找出一個與斜體字意義相反的單字：

( ) 1. *conceal*
(A) offend　　(B) exhibit　　(C) reside　　(D) disagree

( ) 2. *difference*
(A) path　　(B) esteem　　(C) similarity　　(D) courage

( ) 3. *physical*
(A) raw　　(B) stiff　　(C) elementary　　(D) mental

( ) 4. *respect*
(A) behavior　　(B) insult　　(C) proclaim　　(D) differ

( ) 5. *ordinary*
(A) queer　　(B) physical　　(C) positive　　(D) grave

(　　) 6. *servant*

      (A) regret　　(B) master　　(C) negative　　(D) impulse

IV. 完整拼出下列各句中所欠缺的單字，每一格代表一個字母：

1. The i_ _ _ _ _e of hunger compelled the proud man to go begging for bread. (衝動)

2. Cows, bulls, steers, and oxen are c_ _ _ _e. (牛)

3. Will you please f_ _d my cat for me? (餵食)

4. You must b_ _ _ _e well to your seniors. (舉止)

5. The n_ _ _ _e of the compass shows we are facing north. (針)

V. 找出一個與句中斜體字意義最接近的單字：

(　　) 1. Where do you *reside* now?

      (A) reserve　　　　　　(B) live

      (C) reign　　　　　　　(D) exist

(　　) 2. It had never *occurred to* me to think she was a widow.

      (A) existed　　　　　　(B) behaved

      (C) expressed　　　　　(D) struck

(　　) 3. He had a choice between the shorter or the better *path*.

      (A) route　　　　　　　(B) cock

      (C) subway　　　　　　(D) role

(　　) 4. He wanted to be *loyal* to his firm as well as to his family.

      (A) solemn　　　　　　(B) thorough

      (C) faithful　　　　　　(D) positive

(   ) 5. The frightened boy *gripped* his mother's hand.
    (A) contracted   (B) ground
    (C) spoiled   (D) seized

(   ) 6. She *assisted* him in building the house.
    (A) behaved   (B) occupied
    (C) forbade   (D) helped

(   ) 7. What a *queer* story it is!
    (A) unusual   (B) interesting
    (C) old   (D) silly

(   ) 8. The heavy rain *spoiled* the crops.
    (A) subtracted   (B) ruined
    (C) improved   (D) lowered

(   ) 9. This paint brush is too *stiff* to use.
    (A) lean   (B) solemn
    (C) rigid   (D) good

(   ) 10. The child *exhibited* a bad temper at an early age.
    (A) concealed   (B) showed
    (C) spoiled   (D) conquered

【解答】

I. 1. A   2. D   3. B   4. C   5. A   6. B   7. C   8. A   9. D   10. B
II. 1. D   2. B   3. A   4. C   5. C
III. 1. B   2. C   3. D   4. B   5. A   6. B
IV. 1. impulse   2. cattle   3. feed   4. behave   5. needle
V. 1. B   2. D   3. A   4. C   5. D   6. D   7. A   8. B   9. C   10. B

Lesson 18

✦ 第一部分

---

advance
〔 əd'væns 〕

There were so many people that our *advance* was slow.
人太多，因此我們的前進速度很慢。
We had made great *advances* in airplane design.
我們在飛機的設計上進步很大。

【記憶技巧】
adv (from) + *ance* (before)（從「以前」來到「現在」，就是「前進」）

n. 1. 前進
反 withdrawal

2. 進步
同 progress

---

assure
〔 ə'ʃur 〕

The captain *assured* the passengers that there was no danger.
機長向乘客保證沒有危險。

【記憶技巧】
as + *sure*（確定的）

v. 向…保證
名 assurance
同 guarantee;
　 convince

---

biology
〔 baɪ'ɑlədʒɪ 〕

Specialists in *biology* study the origin and structure of plant and animal life. 生物學專家研究動植物生命的起源和構造。

【記憶技巧】
bio (life) + *logy* (study)（研究生命，就是「生物學」）

n. 生物學

---

brilliant
〔 'brɪljənt 〕

We have had a week of *brilliant* sunshine.
我們有一星期陽光普照的好天氣。
Everyone likes to hear him; he is a *brilliant* speaker. 每個人都喜歡聽他說話；他是個出色的演說家。

adj. 1. 燦爛的；
　　　 亮麗的

2. 出色的；
　 有才氣的
名 brilliance

cause
〔 kɔz 〕

The flood last month was the *cause* of much damage.
上個月的水災是造成許多損害的原因。

n. 原因
同 reason
v. 造成

colony
〔'kɑlənɪ 〕

Canada and Australia used to be British *colonies*; now they are self-governing. 加拿大和澳洲以前是英國的殖民地；現在已自治了。

n. 殖民地

conduct
〔*n.* 'kɑndʌkt 〕
〔*v.* kən'dʌkt 〕

The children were rewarded for good *conduct* and punished for bad *conduct*. 孩子們因良好的行為而受獎勵；因不良的行為而受懲罰。

n. 行為
同 behavior
v. 做；進行

【記憶技巧】
con (together) + *duct* (lead)

contrast
〔*n.* 'kɑntræst 〕
〔*v.* kən'træst 〕

Contrast these foreign goods with the domestic products.
把這些外國商品和本國產品比較一下。

n. 對比
v. 比較

CONTRAST

【記憶技巧】
contra (against) + *st* (stand) (站在相反的立場，形成「對比」)

cruel
〔'kruəl 〕

The *cruel* master beat his slaves mercilessly with a whip.
殘忍的主人用鞭子無情地鞭打奴隸。

adj. 殘忍的
同 merciless
反 merciful

defect
〔'difɛkt ,
dɪ'fɛkt 〕

The car was unsafe because of a *defect* in its construction.
這部車不安全，因為構造上有瑕疵。

n. 瑕疵；缺點
形 defective
同 shortcoming

【記憶技巧】
de (down) + *fect* (make) (沒有把事做好，顯露自己的「缺點」)

Exercise 18.1 從第一部分中選出最適當的一個英文字，填入空格內。

1. The teacher _____ the hot climate of our country with the cold climate of another in the last class.

2. He is very interested in plant and animal life; he will study _____ in the university.

3. A(n) _____ is a country or area under the control of a distant country and settled by people from that country.

4. We tried to _____ the nervous old lady that flying in an airplane was quite safe.

5. You are old enough to know the rules of _____.

【解答】
1. contrasted 2. biology 3. colony 4. assure 5. conduct

✦ 第二部分

differentiate
〔͵dɪfəˈrɛnʃɪ͵et〕
Can you *differentiate* this kind of rose from the others?
你能區分這種玫瑰和其他種類的不同嗎？
v. 區別；區分

domestic
〔dəˈmɛstɪk〕
Most newspapers publish both *domestic* and foreign news.
大部分的報紙都會刊登國內外的消息。
adj. 國內的
反 foreign

embrace
〔ɪmˈbres〕
She *embraced* the pretty baby with great affection.
她深情地抱著那個漂亮的嬰兒。
v. 擁抱
同 hug

【記憶技巧】
em (in) + *brace* (two arms)（在雙臂之中，也就是「擁抱」）

Lesson 18

error
〔ˈɛrɚ 〕

I failed my test because of ***errors*** in spelling.
我因拼字錯誤而未通過考試。

n. 錯誤
形 erroneous
同 mistake

exhaust
〔 ɪgˈzɔst 〕

They were almost ***exhausted*** when they reached the top of the mountain.
他們到達山頂時，幾乎筋疲力盡。

v. 使筋疲力盡
n. 廢氣

---【記憶技巧】---
ex (out) + ***haust*** (draw)（從排氣管抽出來的東西，就是「廢氣」）

festival
〔ˈfɛstəvḷ 〕

Every year the city has a summer music ***festival*** in August.
每年八月該市皆舉辦夏季音樂節。

n. 節日
同 celebration

formation
〔 fɔrˈmeʃən 〕

School life has a great influence on the ***formation*** of a child's character.
學校生活對孩子的個性形成有很大影響。

n. 形成
同 structure
動 form

garment
〔ˈgɑrmənt 〕

A new ***garment*** should be washed carefully. 新衣服應該小心清洗。

n. 衣服
同 costume

groan
〔 gron 〕

The wounded man lay there ***groaning***, with no one to help him.
傷患躺在那裏呻吟著，無人救助。
We heard the ***groans*** of the man who had fallen off the cliff.
我們聽到那跌落懸崖者的呻吟聲。

v. 呻吟
同 moan

n. 呻吟

---【記憶技巧】---
想到 <u>loan</u>（貸款）會使人 <u>groan</u>（呻吟）。

hire
〔 haɪr 〕

The storekeeper ***hired*** a boy to deliver groceries. 店主雇用一名男孩送雜貨。
He ***hired*** a car and a man to drive it.
他租一輛車並雇一個人來駕駛。

v. 1. 雇用
同 employ
反 fire
2. 租

Exercise 18.2 從第二部分中選出最適當的一個英文字，填入空格內。

1. The nation is going to have a week of _____ in honor of the king's marriage.

2. The tired horse _____ under the heavy load.

3. The government urged the people to buy _____ goods, not foreign goods.

4. The two sisters met and _____ each other.

5. Climbing up the hill in an hour completely _____ us.

【解答】
1. festival　2. groaned　3. domestic　4. embraced　5. exhausted

✦ 第三部分

incidental 〔͵ɪnsə'dɛntḷ 〕	Certain discomforts are *incidental* to the joys of camping out. 享受露營的歡樂時，難免也會有些不便之處。	*adj.* 附帶的 同 incident

【記憶技巧】
用 ac**cident**al（意外的）來背。

intelligent 〔 ɪn'tɛlədʒənt 〕	All human beings are more *intelligent* than animals. 所有的人類都比動物聰明。	*adj.* 聰明的
justice 〔'dʒʌstɪs 〕	Judges should have a sense of *justice*. 法官應該要有正義感。	*n.* 正義；公正
leap 〔 lip 〕	He *leaped* with joy at the good news. 聽到好消息，他高興地跳了起來。	*v.* 跳 同 jump

Lesson 18

luck 〔lʌk〕	She had the ***luck*** to win first prize. 她很幸運，贏得了頭獎。	*n.* 運氣；幸運 形 lucky
measure 〔ˈmɛʒɚ〕	The tailor ***measured*** me for a new suit of clothes. 裁縫師為 我量身做一套新衣服。	*v.* 測量 名 measurement
mock 〔mɑk〕	The naughty boys ***mocked*** the blind beggar. 頑皮的孩童嘲笑瞎眼的乞丐。	*v.* 嘲笑 同 laugh at
negative 〔ˈnɛgətɪv〕	The unhappy man has a ***negative*** attitude toward life. 那個不快樂的人 對人生抱持消極的態度。	*adj.* 負面的；消極 　　的；否定的 反 positive

> 【記憶技巧】
> ***neg*** (deny) + ***ative*** (*adj.*) (對任何事情都
> 抱持否定的態度)

odd 〔ɑd〕	Life would be very dull without the ***odd*** adventure now and then. 生活中 若缺乏偶爾的奇遇，將會變得非常無聊。	*adj.* 古怪的；奇特的 同 strange; 　　unusual
owe 〔o〕	He ***owes*** his success to good luck more than to his ability. 他將自己的成功歸功於運氣而非能力。	*v.* 欠；歸功於

> 【記憶技巧】
> 不要和 own (擁有) 及 awe (敬畏) 搞混。

Exercise 18.3　從第三部分中選出最適當的一個英文字，填入空格內。

1. All men should be treated with _____.

2. We _____ the room and found it was 20 feet long and 15 feet
　 wide.

3. We must know that we _____ a great deal to our parents and teachers.

4. We must take precautions against dangers _____ to a soldier's life.

5. The sounds of a foreign language are always _____ to non-natives.

【解答】

1. justice   2. measured   3. owe   4. incidental   5. odd

✦ 第四部分

patience
〔'peʃəns 〕

It needs great *patience* to teach little children. 教導小孩需要很大的耐心。

【記憶技】
pati (endure) + *ence* (n.)

n. 耐心
同 forbearance
形 patient

physician
〔 fə'zɪʃən 〕

The *physician* gave his sick patient some strong medicine.
內科醫生給病人一些強烈的藥。

n. 內科醫生
反 surgeon

possess
〔 pə'zɛs 〕

He didn't have much money, but he always *possessed* good health.
他沒有很多錢，可是他身體一向很好。

【記憶技巧】
pos (toward) + *sess* (sit) (向有～的方向坐著，就能「擁有」)

v. 擁有
同 own

profession
〔 prə'fɛʃən 〕

He is preparing for the teaching *profession*. 他準備從事教書的職業。

n. 職業

quit
〔 kwɪt 〕

The doctor told his patient to *quit* smoking and drinking.
醫生叫病人戒除煙酒。

v. 停止；辭職
同 cease; stop

reject
〔 rɪˈdʒɛkt 〕

He tried to join the army but was *rejected* because of his poor health.
他想從軍，可是因健康不好而被拒絕。

v. 拒絕
同 refuse

> 【記憶技巧】
> *re* (back) + *ject* (throw) (將別人的請求丟回去，表示「拒絕」)

resign
〔 rɪˈzaɪn 〕

The man *resigned* from his job because of illness. 那人因病辭職。

v. 辭職

> 【記憶技巧】
> *re* (again) + *sign* (簽名)(離開公司要再次簽名，表示「辭職」)

rotten
〔ˈrɑtn̩ 〕

The apples fallen on the ground will soon become *rotten*.
掉到地上的蘋果很快就會腐爛。

adj. 腐爛的
反 fresh

scatter
〔ˈskætɚ 〕

The farmer *scattered* seeds on the field. 農夫播種於田中。

v. 散播

severe
〔 səˈvɪr 〕

The man was given a *severe* punishment for stealing.
那人因偷竊而受到嚴厲的處罰。

adj. 嚴格的；
嚴厲的
同 strict; cruel

Exercise 18.4　從第四部分中選出最適當的一個英文字，填入空格內。

1. The cat watched the mouse hole with great _____.

2. He was _____ from the army because of his bad eyes.

3. Having a long summer vacation is one of the benefits of the teaching _____.

4. He was told to _____ ashes on the icy sidewalk.

5. She was forced to _____ her position as secretary of the club.

> 【解答】
> 1. patience　2. rejected　3. profession　4. scatter　5. resign

✦ 第五部分

sin
〔 sɪn 〕

Lying, stealing, dishonesty, and cruelty are *sins*.
撒謊、偷竊、不誠實，和殘忍都是罪惡。

n. 罪；罪惡
cf. crime

solid
〔'sɑlɪd 〕

When water freezes and becomes *solid*, we call it ice.
水凍結變成固體時，我們稱之為冰。
At what temperature does water become a *solid*?
水在多少溫度會變成固體？

adj. 固體的；
　　　堅固的
 firm
n. 固體

> 【記憶技巧】
> *sol* (sole) + *id* (*adj.*)（結合成一體，表示堅固的）

spokesman
〔'spoksmən 〕

At the meeting, the *spokesman* for the government gave us the President's views. 政府發言人在會議上告訴我們總統的意見。

n. 發言人

still
〔 stɪl 〕

The room was *still* at the end of his speech.
他的演說結束時，整個房間安靜無聲。

adv. 仍然
adj. 靜止的；安靜的

suck
〔 sʌk 〕

The baby *sucked* milk from its mother's breast. 嬰兒吸食母乳。

v. 吸

symbolize
〔 'sɪmbḷ͵aɪz 〕

The red color *symbolizes* danger in many countries.
紅色在許多國家代表危險。

v. 象徵；代表

【記憶技巧】
symbol (象徵) + *ize* (*v.*)

threat
〔 θrɛt 〕

Your *threats* will not stop me from going. 你的威脅阻止不了我走。

n. 威脅

traffic
〔 'træfɪk 〕

The police control the *traffic* in large cities. 警察在大城市中管制交通。

n. 交通

volcano
〔 vɑl'keno 〕

A dormant *volcano* may explode at any time. 休火山可能在任何時間爆發。

n. 火山

wipe
〔 waɪp 〕

She *wiped* the dishes with a paper towel. 她用紙巾擦盤子。

v. 擦

Exercise 18.5 從第五部分中選出最適當的一個英文字，填入空格內。

1. The baby tried to _____ the orange juice through a straw.

2. That door is made of a _____ piece of wood.

3. He was the _____ for the workers in the strike against the factory owner.

4. An extinct _____ has ceased to be able to explode.

5. He asked the noisy children to be _____.

【解答】

1. suck   2. solid   3. spokesman   4. volcano   5. still

成果測驗

I. 找出一個與斜體字的意義最接近的單字：

(   ) 1. to *reject* one's suggestion
     (A) proclaim   (B) resign
     (C) refuse   (D) overlook

(   ) 2. an old *garment*
     (A) thread   (B) costume   (C) patch   (D) gallop

(   ) 3. *groan* of a sick man
     (A) profession   (B) regret
     (C) outbreak   (D) moan

(   ) 4. *merciless* punishment
     (A) cruel   (B) odd   (C) crude   (D) unusual

(   ) 5. *odd* behavior
     (A) dangerous   (B) contrary
     (C) lean   (D) strange

(   ) 6. my friend's *defects*
     (A) errors   (B) insults
     (C) shortcomings   (D) regrets

( ) 7. to lose one's *patience*

    (A) justice   (B) forbearance

    (C) courage   (D) strength

( ) 8. to *hire* someone

    (A) reject   (B) admire   (C) employ   (D) hide

( ) 9. to *laugh at* one's behavior

    (A) encourage   (B) mock

    (C) mistrust   (D) assist

( ) 10. to *own* a house

    (A) possess   (B) owe   (C) hire   (D) equip

II. 找出一個與題前中文意思相同的英文字：

( ) 1. 行為

    (A) threat   (B) conduct   (C) cause   (D) error

( ) 2. 生物學

    (A) biology   (B) colony

    (C) surgeon   (D) vocabulary

( ) 3. 擁抱

    (A) owe   (B) possess   (C) assure   (D) embrace

( ) 4. 節日

    (A) profession   (B) volcano

    (C) festival   (D) gallery

( ) 5. 耐心

    (A) error   (B) patience

    (C) bravery   (D) justice

III. 找出一個與斜體字意義相反的單字：

( ) 1. *merciful*
    (A) stiff   (B) incidental
    (C) cruel   (D) motionless

( ) 2. *foreign*
    (A) dangerous   (B) strange
    (C) federal   (D) domestic

( ) 3. *rotten*
    (A) fresh   (B) queer   (C) neat   (D) mild

( ) 4. *hire*
    (A) quit   (B) fire   (C) scatter   (D) continue

( ) 5. *withdrawal*
    (A) advance   (B) possess   (C) exhaust   (D) leap

IV. 完整拼出下列各句中所欠缺的單字，每一格代表一個字母：

1. I obeyed her order but only under the t_ _ _ _t of punishment.
（威脅）

2. I don't have the p_ _ _ _ _ _e to hear your complaints again.
（耐心）

3. The j_ _ _ _ _e of these remarks was clear to everyone. （公正）

4. If you don't like your job, you may q_ _t. （辭職）

5. There is heavy t_ _ _ _ _c on the street during the rush hours.
（交通）

V. 選出最適合句意的一個單字：

(   ) 1. Carelessness is often the _____ of fires.
    (A) errors   (B) cause
    (C) threat   (D) consequence

(   ) 2. In the elementary school there is often a prize for good
    _____.
    (A) conduct   (B) defect
    (C) servant   (D) threat

(   ) 3. He could not _____ green from red.
    (A) measure   (B) symbolize
    (C) exhibit   (D) differentiate

(   ) 4. The doctor _____ him that his child would recover from
    the illness.
    (A) refused   (B) assisted
    (C) contrasted   (D) assured

(   ) 5. _____ was with us and we won the baseball game easily.
    (A) Defect   (B) Luck
    (C) Vision   (D) Justice

(   ) 6. Heat causes the _____ of steam from water.
    (A) mixture   (B) scarcity
    (C) formation   (D) profession

(   ) 7. The thoughtless children _____ the speech of the new
    boy.
    (A) mocked   (B) sucked
    (C) owned   (D) owed

(   ) 8. A dog _____ a keen sense of smell.
        (A) embraces   (B) symbolizes
        (C) behaves   (D) possesses

(   ) 9. I _____ it to you that I am still alive.
        (A) reign   (B) hire   (C) owe   (D) own

(   ) 10. A dove _____ peace, whereas a hawk _____ war.
        (A) symbolizes   (B) contrasts
        (C) assures   (D) differentiates

VI. 將題前的斜體字轉換爲適當詞性，填入空格中：

1. *error*   The facts are correct, but your conclusion is _____.

2. *brilliant*   The diamond glowed with a pure white _____.

3. *measure*   The _____ of individual intelligence is very difficult.

4. *incidental* The _____ has been forgotten for a long time.

5. *assure*   The plumber gave us his _____ that he would fix the pipes tomorrow.

【解答】

  I. 1. C 2. B 3. D 4. A 5. D 6. C 7. B 8. C 9. B 10. A
 II. 1. B 2. A 3. D 4. C 5. B
III. 1. C 2. D 3. A 4. B 5. A
IV. 1. threat 2. patience 3. justice 4. quit 5. traffic
 V. 1. B 2. A 3. D 4. D 5. B 6. C 7. A 8. D 9. C 10. A
VI. 1. erroneous 2. brilliance 3. measurement 4. incident
    5. assurance

Lesson 19

✦ 第一部分

advantage
〔əd'væntɪdʒ〕

He had the *advantage* of being born into a rich family.
他有出生富裕之家的優勢。

n. 優點；優勢

---

atmosphere
〔'ætməsˌfɪr〕

Most cities no longer have a clear *atmosphere*.
大部分的都市不再有清新的空氣。
There is an *atmosphere* of calm and peace in the country that is quite different from the *atmosphere* of a big city. 鄉間的氣氛是平靜而安詳的，與大都市截然不同。

n. 1. 大氣層；空氣
同 air
2. 氣氛

> 【記憶技巧】
> *atmo* (vapor) + *sphere* (ball)（地球四周的氣體，就是「大氣層」）

---

broad
〔brɔd〕

Miss Smith, our English teacher, has *broad* experience with children.
我們的英文老師史密斯小姐，對兒童有豐富的經驗。

adj. 寬的；廣大的；豐富的
同 wide

> 【記憶技巧】
> *b* + *road*（路）

---

cautious
〔'kɔʃəs〕

A *cautious* thinker does not believe things without proof.
謹慎的思想家不相信沒有證據的事。

adj. 謹慎的
同 careful
名 caution

---

color-blind
〔'kʌləˌblaɪnd〕

A *color-blind* man can't tell red from green. 有色盲的人無法分辨紅綠。

adj. 色盲的

conference
〔'kɑnfərəns〕

Many international *conferences* have been held in Geneva.
在日內瓦已舉行過多次國際會議。

n. 會議

contribute
〔kən'trɪbjut〕

Honesty and hard work *contribute* to success and to happiness.
誠實和努力有助於成功和幸福。
Each worker *contributed* a dollar to the Red Cross.
每一個員工捐一美元給紅十字會。

v. 1. 有助於

2. 捐獻
名 contribution

crush
〔krʌʃ〕

Wine is made by *crushing* grapes.
葡萄酒是由壓榨葡萄而製成。

v. 壓碎；壓榨
同 smash; break

defend
〔dɪ'fɛnd〕

When the dog attacked me, I *defended* myself with my stick.
那隻狗攻擊我時，我用手杖保護自己。

v. 保衛；保護
名 defense
同 guard
反 attack

【記憶技巧】
de (away) + *fend* (strike) (把敵人打跑，就是「保衛」自己)

digest
〔daɪ'dʒɛst〕

If you rest for half an hour after a meal, you will *digest* your food more easily. 如果你飯後休息半小時，食物較容易消化。

v. 消化
名 digestion

【記憶技巧】
di (apart) + *gest* (carry) (吃下去的東西要分開，才能「消化」)

Exercise 19.1 從第一部分中選出最適當的一個英文字，填入空格內。

1. The director of the school is in _____ now; you can see him later.

2. It will be to your _____ to study Spanish before you visit Mexico.

3. Everyone was asked to _____ suggestions for the party.

4. His hat was _____ when the girl sat on it.

5. The fort cannot be _____ against an air attack.

【解答】

1. conference　2. advantage　3. contribute　4. crushed　5. defended

---

✦ 第二部分

dot 〔 dɑt 〕	We watched the ship until it became a mere *dot* on the horizon. 我們看著船離去，直到它在海平面成爲一個小點。	*n.* 點 同 point
emergency 〔 ɪ'mɝdʒənsɪ 〕	I keep a box of tools and a fire extinguisher in my car for use in an *emergency*. 我在車中放了工具箱和滅火器，以備緊急之需。	*n.* 緊急情況
escape 〔 ɪ'skep 〕	The soldier *escaped* from the enemy's prison. 那士兵從敵人的監獄中逃走。 --- 【記憶技巧】 *es* (out of) + *cape* (斗篷；披肩) (迅速脫掉斗篷，表示「逃走」)	*v.* 逃走 同 flee
executive 〔 ɪg'zɛkjutɪv 〕	The *executive* branch carries out the laws which have been made by the legislature. 行政部門執行由立法機關制定的法律。	*adj.* 執行的； 行政的

Lesson 19

fetch
(fɛtʃ)

Please *fetch* me the dictionary from the study room.
請替我去閱覽室將字典拿來。

v. 去拿來

fort
(fɔrt)

They decided to build a new *fort* to protect the inhabitants of that area.
他們決定建座新碉堡，以保護該區的居民。

n. 堡壘；碉堡
同 fortress
動 fortify

gasp
(gæsp)

He *gasped* for air as he ran from the smoke-filled room.
他喘著氣從煙霧瀰漫的房間裏跑出來。
The fireman heard the *gasps* of a boy in the smoky room. 救火員聽到冒煙的房間裏有男孩的喘息聲。

v. 喘氣

n. 喘息聲

【記憶技巧】
gas (氣體) + *p* (氣音 p 是呼氣的聲音)

grocery
('grosərɪ)

We buy our rice at the nearest *grocery*.
我們在最近的一家雜貨店裏買米。

n. 雜貨店；
(*pl.*) 食品雜貨

【記憶技巧】
grocer (雜貨商) + *y* (place)

hollow
('hɑlo)

A tube or pipe is *hollow*, and therefore not heavy.
管子是中空的，因而不重。
A starving person has *hollow* eyes and cheeks.
挨餓的人，其雙眼和兩頰是凹陷的。

adj. 1. 中空的

2. 凹陷的

inclination
(͵ɪnklə'neʃən)

Most boys have a strong *inclination* for sports.
大部分男孩對運動都有強烈的愛好。

n. 傾向；愛好
同 disposition

Exercise 19.2 從第二部分中選出最適當的一個英文字，填入空格內。

1. Please _____ me a clean handkerchief from my bedroom.

2. The President of the United States is the head of the _____ branch of the government.

3. This fire extinguisher is to be used only in a(n) _____.

4. He _____ the fire in the house by jumping out of the window when he smelled smoke.

5. The horse and rider moved further and further away until they became only a(n) _____ in the distance.

【解答】
1. fetch　2. executive　3. emergency　4. escaped　5. dot

✦ 第三部分

intend 〔 ɪn'tɛnd 〕	I ***intended*** to get up early, but forgot to set the alarm. 我想早起，可是忘了設鬧鐘。	*v.* 打算；想要 同 mean

【記憶技巧】
in (towards) + ***tend*** (stretch) (把手伸過去，就是「打算」做某事)

keen 〔 kin 〕	Be careful with that knife. It's got a ***keen*** edge. 小心那把刀子，它有銳利的刀刃。 Like a knife, a woman's tongue is very ***keen***. 女人的舌頭像刀子一樣，非常尖刻。	*adj.* 1. 渴望的； 　　　銳利的 同 sharp 反 dull 2. 尖刻的

Lesson 19

leather
〔'lɛðə〕

His shoes are made of *leather* imported from England.
他的鞋子是由英國進口的皮革製成。

n. 皮革

lumber
〔'lʌmbə〕

They bought some *lumber* to make their fence. 他們買了些木材造籬笆。

n. 木材

mechanic
〔mə'kænɪk〕

The automobile *mechanic* repaired my car. 汽車機械工人修理我的車。

n. 技工；
機械工人

【記憶技巧】
mechan (machine) + *ic*（人）

mode
〔mod〕

He suddenly became wealthy, which changed his *mode* of life.
突然致富改變了他的生活方式。

n. 模式；方式

neglect
〔nɪ'glɛkt〕

Don't *neglect* writing to your parents at least once a month. 不要疏忽寫信給你的父母，一個月至少一次。

v. 忽略；疏忽
同 ignore;
   disregard

【記憶技巧】
neg (deny) + *lect* (select)（不願做選擇，就是故意「忽略」）

offend
〔ə'fɛnd〕

My friend was *offended* by the reporter's questions.
我的朋友被記者的問題觸怒。

v. 冒犯；觸怒
同 insult

【記憶技巧】
of (against) + *fend* (strike)（所做的事讓人反感，表示「冒犯」到他人）

owl
〔aʊl〕

Most *owls* hunt at night and live on small animals. 大多數的貓頭鷹夜間獵食，並以小動物為食。

n. 貓頭鷹

pause
〔pɔz〕

The dog *paused* for a moment when I called him.
當我叫那隻狗時，牠停下來一會兒。

During the radio program there were several *pauses* for advertisements.
廣播節目因廣告而中斷數次。

v. 暫停；停下來

n. 暫停；中止；停頓

同 stop

Exercise 19.3 從第三部分中選出最適當的一個英文字，填入空格內。

1. A typewriter _____ is skilled in repairing typewriters.

2. After a(n) _____ for lunch, the man returned to work.

3. What I _____ is to finish this work before I go to bed.

4. She is wearing a(n) _____ belt.

5. Don't _____ cleaning your shoes before you go out.

【解答】
1. mechanic   2. pause   3. intend   4. leather   5. neglect

✦ 第四部分

pickpocket
〔'pɪk,pakɪt〕

Most *pickpockets* work in crowds of people. 大多數的扒手通常在人群中動手。

n. 扒手

【記憶技巧】
pick + *pocket*（口袋）

pot
〔pat〕

Chinese usually keep soy sauce in a *pot*.
中國人通常將醬油放在瓶中。

n. 鍋子；瓶；花盆

同 jug

Lesson 19

profit
（'prɑfɪt）

This company makes great ***profits*** from manufacturing automobiles.
這家公司從生產汽車中獲得大量利潤。

n. 利潤
形 profitable

quiver
（'kwɪvɚ）

Her lips ***quivered*** like those of a child about to cry. 她的雙唇顫抖著，就如同要哭的孩子一般。

v. 發抖；顫抖
同 shake;
vibrate

rejoice
（rɪ'dʒɔɪs）

They ***rejoiced*** when they heard she was safe. 他們聽到她安全時，非常高興。

v. 高興

【記憶技巧】
re- 表加強語氣的字首。

resist
（rɪ'zɪst）

The troops were no longer able to ***resist*** the enemy attack.
軍隊再也無法抵抗敵人的攻擊。

v. 抵抗
同 oppose
反 obey

【記憶技巧】
re (against) + *sist* (stand)（站在對立的立場，表示「抵抗」）

rough
（rʌf）

The wall was made of ***rough*** stones.
此牆為粗石所造。

adj. 粗糙的
反 smooth

scent
（sɛnt）

The hunting dogs followed the ***scent*** of the fox. 獵犬跟隨狐狸的氣味追蹤。
A dog ***scented*** along the ground.
狗聞著地上的氣味前進。

n. 氣味
同 odor
v. 聞著氣味追獵

sew
（so）

The doctor ***sewed*** up the soldier's wound. 醫生縫好那士兵的傷口。

v. 縫

sink 〔 sɪŋk 〕	The sun is *sinking* in the west. 太陽正西下。 She washed the dishes in the *sink*. 她在水槽中洗碗。	*v.* 下沉 反 float *n.* 水槽

Exercise 19.4 從第四部分中選出最適當的一個英文字，填入空格內。

1. The ship was filled with water and it _____ at last.

2. There is some water at the bottom of the _____.

3. The _____ in this business are not large.

4. The mother _____ over her son's success.

5. The _____ road made the car shake.

```
【解答】
1. sank   2. pot   3. profits   4. rejoiced   5. rough
```

✦ 第五部分

solution 〔 sə'luʃən 〕	That problem was very hard; it took many hours to find its *solution*. 那個問題非常難；要許多小時才能得到解答。	*n.* 解決之道； 解答 同 answer
spot 〔 spɑt 〕	They are building their house at a beautiful *spot*. 他們在一個優美的地點建造他們的房子。 She has a paint *spot* on her white dress. 她的白洋裝上有個油漆污點。	*n.* 1. 地點 2. 污點 同 stain

Lesson 19

sting 〔 stɪŋ 〕	Be careful, or the bee will ***sting*** you. 要小心，否則蜜蜂會螫你。 A bee has its ***sting*** in the tail. 蜜蜂尾上有刺。	*v.* 叮咬；螫； 刺 *n.* 刺；螫

【記憶技巧】
諧音：死叮，叮就是「螫；刺」(sting)。

suffer 〔'sʌfɚ 〕	During the war, many people ***suffered*** from hunger. 在戰爭期間，許多人遭受飢餓之苦。	*v.* 遭受；受苦

sympathy 〔'sɪmpəθɪ 〕	We feel ***sympathy*** for a person who is ill. 我們同情生病的人。	*n.* 同情

【記憶技巧】
sym (together) + ***pathy*** (feeling) (跟別人
有同樣的感覺，就是「同情」)

thrill 〔 θrɪl 〕	She felt a ***thrill*** when she was kissed by a handsome pop star. 當一個英俊的流行音樂歌手親吻她時， 她感到一陣興奮。 She was ***thrilled*** when the actor winked at her. 當男演員向她眨眼時，她非常興奮。	*n.* 興奮 *v.* 使興奮

tragic 〔'trædʒɪk 〕	There was a ***tragic*** accident on the highway yesterday. 昨天公路上發生了一件悲慘的車禍。	*adj.* 悲劇的； 悲慘的 名 tragedy

up-to-date 〔'ʌptə'det 〕	The hotel is furnished with ***up-to-date*** furniture. 這家旅館備有最新的家具。	*adj.* 最新的 同 modern

volume
〔ˈvaljəm 〕

Our school has a library of 100,000 *volumes*.
我們學校擁有一所藏書十萬冊的圖書館。
The storeroom has a *volume* of 4,000 cubic feet.
這儲藏室的容積是四千立方呎。

n. 1. 音量;書籍;
冊

2. 體積;容積

willful
〔ˈwɪlfəl 〕

The *willful* child will not listen to whatever you say.
任性的孩子不管你說什麼,他都不聽。
The police think that it was a *willful* murder. 警方認為那是蓄意謀殺。

adj. 1. 任性的
同 stubborn

2. 故意的
同 intended

【記憶技巧】
will (意志) + *ful* (*adj.*)

Exercise 19.5 從第五部分中選出最適當的一個英文字,填入空格內。

1. We arrived at the very _____ where he was killed.

2. A bee _____ me on the neck when I was walking along the country road.

3. She was very generous to him, but she _____ for it when he ran away with all her money.

4. They expressed their _____ by sending flowers to her husband's funeral.

5. You can find what you want to know in the ninth _____ of the encyclopedia.

【解答】
1. spot   2. stung   3. suffered   4. sympathy   5. volume

成果測驗

I. 找出一個與其他三個不相關的字：

( ) 1. (A) ignore   (B) neglect
       (C) disregard   (D) suffer

( ) 2. (A) crush   (B) spoil   (C) smash   (D) break

( ) 3. (A) blind   (B) void   (C) hollow   (D) empty

( ) 4. (A) sharp   (B) acute   (C) narrow   (D) keen

( ) 5. (A) method   (B) fashion   (C) principle   (D) mode

( ) 6. (A) fragrance   (B) odor
       (C) scent   (D) atmosphere

( ) 7. (A) mean   (B) escape   (C) intend   (D) plan

( ) 8. (A) sting   (B) pierce   (C) resist   (D) prick

( ) 9. (A) solution   (B) advantage
       (C) gain   (D) benefit

( ) 10. (A) quiver   (B) vibrate   (C) fetch   (D) shake

II. 找出一個與題前中文意思相同的英文字：

( ) 1. 去拿來
       (A) crush   (B) pause   (C) gasp   (D) fetch

( ) 2. 同情
       (A) mode   (B) scent
       (C) sympathy   (D) atmosphere

( ) 3. 喘氣

    (A) gasp   (B) quiver   (C) rejoice   (D) suck

( ) 4. 雜貨店

    (A) garment   (B) grocery

    (C) colony   (D) conference

( ) 5. 消化

    (A) mock   (B) sew   (C) digest   (D) intend

Ⅲ. 找出一個與斜體字意義相反的單字：

( ) 1. *dull*

    (A) severe   (B) keen

    (C) solid   (D) careful

( ) 2. *obey*

    (A) defend   (B) escape   (C) rejoice   (D) resist

( ) 3. *attack*

    (A) defend   (B) contribute

    (C) scatter   (D) suffer

( ) 4. *float*

    (A) neglect   (B) oppose   (C) sink   (D) leap

( ) 5. *smooth*

    (A) stubborn   (B) rough

    (C) sharp   (D) cruel

Ⅳ. 完整拼出下列各句中所欠缺的單字，每一格代表一個字母：

  1. I should r_ _ _ _ _e to see you married to a good man. (高興)

2. Plenty of fresh air can c_ _ _ _ _ _ _ _e to good health.
（有助於）

3. It gave her quite a t_ _ _l to shake hands with the Princess.
（興奮）

4. Don't n_ _ _ _ _t to lock the door when you leave. (忽略)

5. I've made a mistake, though I didn't i_ _ _ _d to. (打算)

V. 找出一個與句中斜體字意義最接近的單字：

( ) 1. The duty of a soldier is to *defend* his country.
    (A) resist   (B) assure
    (C) guard   (D) contribute

( ) 2. He has a red *spot* on his gown.
    (A) stain   (B) belt
    (C) pot   (D) defect

( ) 3. You always follow your own *inclinations* instead of
thinking of our feelings.
    (A) conducts   (B) profits
    (C) occupations   (D) dispositions

( ) 4. Many teachers do not like to use *up-to-date* textbooks in
their classes.
    (A) odd   (B) modern
    (C) old   (D) interesting

( ) 5. We should be *cautious* in crossing a crowded street.
    (A) careful   (B) intelligent
    (C) quiet   (D) weary

Lesson 19

(   ) 6. The tree fell on the roof of a car and *crushed* it.

        (A) exploded   (B) smashed

        (C) fetched   (D) touched

(   ) 7. He *paused* for a moment, then continued speaking.

        (A) sat   (B) stood

        (C) hesitated   (D) stopped

(   ) 8. I *quivered* with fear at the strange sound.

        (A) shook   (B) escaped

        (C) stung   (D) suffered

(   ) 9. The room was filled with the *scent* of flowers.

        (A) atmosphere   (B) pot

        (C) feature   (D) odor

(   ) 10. The senator was *offended* by the reporter's silly questions.

        (A) insulted   (B) rejoiced

        (C) defended   (D) rejected

【解答】

I. 1. D   2. B   3. A   4. C   5. C   6. D   7. B   8. C   9. A   10. C

II. 1. D   2. C   3. A   4. B   5. C

III. 1. B   2. D   3. A   4. C   5. B

IV. 1. rejoice   2. contribute   3. thrill   4. neglect   5. intend

V. 1. C   2. A   3. D   4. B   5. A   6. B   7. D   8. A   9. D   10. A

Lesson 20

✦ 第一部分

adventure 〔əd'vɛntʃɚ〕	A flight in an airplane is no longer such an *adventure* as it used to be. 搭飛機不再像以前一樣是種冒險。	*n.* 冒險

【記憶技巧】
ad (to) + *vent* (come) + *ure* (*n.*) (去面臨危險，就是「冒險」)

attach 〔ə'tætʃ〕	He *attached* a stamp to the envelope. 他將郵票貼在信封上。	*v.* 附上；貼上 反 detach

【記憶技巧】
at (to) + *tach* (stake) (把東西栓上去，即「附上」)

bitter 〔'bɪtɚ〕	Good medicine tastes *bitter* to the mouth. 良藥苦口。	*adj.* 苦的； 　　痛苦的

broadcast 〔'brɔd,kæst〕	The President's speech was *broadcast* on radio and television all over the country. 總統的演說經由收音機和電視廣播到全國。	*v.* 廣播

【記憶技巧】
broad + *cast* (throw) (廣泛地投射出去，就是「廣播」)

cease 〔sis〕	They *ceased* their work for a few minutes to take a rest. 他們停止工作幾分鐘，以便休息。	*v.* 停止 同 quit; stop 反 continue

Lesson 20

combine
〔kəm'baɪn〕

The two countries ***combined*** their efforts against their enemy.
這兩國聯合力量以抵抗敵人。
Chemists ***combine*** different elements to form new compounds.
化學家將不同的元素化合成新的化合物。

v. 1. 結合
反 separate; split
2. 化合
名 combination

【記憶技巧】
com (together) + ***bine*** (two) (把兩個東西放在一起,也就是「結合」)

confess
〔kən'fɛs〕

He ***confessed*** that he had done wrong. 他承認做錯。

v. 承認;招認
名 confession

【記憶技巧】
con (fully) + ***fess*** (speak) (把實情全說出來,也就是「招認」)

converse
〔kən'vɝs〕

I like to ***converse*** with my friends about interesting subjects.
我喜歡和朋友談論有趣的話題。

v. 談話
同 talk
名 conversation

cultivate
〔'kʌltə,vet〕

The farmer ***cultivated*** his fields just before planting time.
在種植期之前,農夫先耕種田地。

v. 培養;耕種

【記憶技巧】
cultiv (耕種) + ***ate*** (*v.*)

delay
〔dɪ'le〕

The train was ***delayed*** because of heavy snow. 火車因大雪而延誤。

v. 延誤
同 postpone

【記憶技巧】
de (away) + ***lay*** (leave) (離開到較遠的地方,就會「延誤」)

Exercise 20.1 從第一部分中選出最適當的一個英文字，填入空格內。

1. The music _____ suddenly when she turned off the radio.

2. It was a(n) _____ disappointment to him when he failed his examination.

3. Jean _____ that she had eaten all the cakes.

4. The accident last night _____ the train for two hours.

5. After a year of studying at the university, I feel that I can _____ with anyone about anything.

┌─ 【解答】 ─────────────────────────────────
│ 1. ceased   2. bitter   3. confessed   4. delayed   5. converse
└──

✦ 第二部分

dignity
〔 'dɪgnətɪ 〕

A man's ***dignity*** depends not on his wealth but on what he is. 一個人高尚與否不在於他的財富，而在於他的品格。

n. 尊嚴；
人格；
高尚

┌─ 【記憶技巧】 ──────────────────────────
│ ***dign*** (worthy) + ***ity*** (*n.*) (「尊嚴」是有價值的東西)
└──────────────────────────────────────

doubt
〔 daʊt 〕

All his ***doubt*** and uncertainty made him unhappy. 所有的懷疑和不確定使他很不快樂。

n. v. 懷疑

emotion
〔 ɪ'moʃən 〕

Love, hate, joy, and fear are ***emotions***. 愛、恨、喜悅，和恐懼都是情緒。

n. 情緒

┌─ 【記憶技巧】 ──────────────────────────
│ ***e*** (out) + ***mot*** (move) + ***ion*** (*n.*) (內心釋放出的感覺，就是「情緒」)
└──────────────────────────────────────

establish
(ə'stæblɪʃ)

The university was ***established*** in 1850 by the government. 這所大學是由政府在一八五○年建立的。

【記憶技巧】
e + ***stabli*** (stable) + ***sh*** (*v.*) (使穩固，就是「建立」)

v. 建立
同 found

excuse
(*v.* ɪk'skjuz)
(*n.* ɪk'skjus)

Please ***excuse*** me for opening your letter by mistake.
請原諒我錯開了你的信。

v. 原諒
同 forgive
n. 藉口

fiber
('faɪbɚ)

Nylon is one of the most popular man-made ***fibers***.
尼龍是最受歡迎的人造纖維之一。

n. 纖維

forthright
(ˌforθ'raɪt)

His ***forthright*** behavior shows that he is honest, but he seems rude to some people. 他直率的態度說明他很誠實，但對某些人來說，他似乎是不禮貌的。

【記憶技巧】
forth (向前) + ***right*** (正確的)

adj. 直率的
同 frank;
candid

gay
(ge)

We were all ***gay*** at the thought of the coming holidays.
我們一想到即將來臨的假期，都很快樂。

adj. 快樂的
同 merry
反 gloomy;
sad
n. 同性戀者

guarantee
(ˌgærən'ti)

We have a one-year ***guarantee*** on our new car. 我們的新車有一年的保證。
The merchant ***guaranteed*** that the color of the material would not fade.
商人保證那質料不會褪色。

n. 保證

v. 保證
同 warrant

holy
('holɪ)

Jerusalem and Mecca are ***holy*** cities.
耶路撒冷和麥加是聖城。

adj. 神聖的
同 sacred

Exercise 20.2 *從第二部分中選出最適當的一個英文字，填入空格內。*

1. The speaker did not like the plan and made _____ objection to it.

2. The young people were _____ as they prepared the hall for a dance party.

3. Don't be anxious; he will come without _____.

4. I can offer my house and land as a _____.

5. The Bible and the Koran are _____ writings.

> 【解答】
> 1. forthright   2. gay   3. doubt   4. guarantee   5. holy

✦ 第三部分

income 〔'ɪnˌkʌm 〕	The government tax on *income* is called *income* tax. 政府對於收入所課的稅，稱為所得稅。	*n.* 收入 反 expenditure
interest 〔'ɪntrɪst 〕	His two great *interests* in life are music and painting. 他一生有兩大興趣：音樂和繪畫。	*n.* 興趣 反 boredom
kindle 〔'kɪndl̩ 〕	We tried to *kindle* the wood but it was wet and wouldn't *kindle* easily. 我們想點燃木頭，可是木頭太濕不容易著火。 【記憶技巧】 *kind*（善良的）+ *le*	*v.* 點燃；著火
legal 〔'ligl̩ 〕	Hunting is *legal* only in certain seasons. 打獵只有在某些季節才是合法的。	*adj.* 合法的

lung
〔 lʌŋ 〕

That opera singer has good *lungs*. 那個歌劇歌手肺活量很大。

n. 肺

medium
〔 'midɪəm 〕

Television can be a *medium* for giving information and opinions. 電視是傳播資訊和意見的媒體。

n. 媒體；
中號的衣服

moderate
〔 'mɑdərɪt 〕

It is a large house, but the garden is of *moderate* size. 那是一棟大房子，可是花園卻只有一般大小。

adj. 適度的；
一般的

反 excessive

【記憶技巧】
-ate 形容詞字尾。

neighborhood
〔 'nebɚˌhʊd 〕

She lives in the *neighborhood* of the mill.
她住在製粉廠附近。

n. 鄰近地區；
附近的鄰居

同 vicinity

odor
〔 'odɚ 〕

Water has neither *odor* nor color.
水無色無味。

n. 氣味

同 smell

pace
〔 pes 〕

The old man can walk only at a slow *pace*. 那老人只能緩步行走。

n. 步調

【記憶技巧】
p + *ace*（撲克牌的 A）

Exercise 20.3 從第三部分中選出最適當的一個英文字，填入空格內。

1. The whole _____ came to her birthday party.

2. The spark _____ the dry wood so we could make fire.

3. He has a(n) _____ in collecting stamps.

4. There was a(n) _____ of roses in the air.

5. At the time of the accident, the car was running at a(n) _____ speed.

【解答】

1. neighborhood　2. kindled　3. interest　4. odor　5. moderate

✦ 第四部分

<table>
<tr><td>

pave
〔 pev 〕

</td><td>

Today most roads are ***paved*** with asphalt. 現在大部分的道路都舖柏油。

</td><td>

v. 舖

</td></tr>
<tr><td>

picturesque
〔ˌpɪktʃəˈrɛsk 〕

</td><td>

There was a ***picturesque*** old mill at the foot of the mountain.
山腳下有個如畫般的老磨坊。

【記憶技巧】
-esque 表「似⋯般的」。

</td><td>

adj. 風景如
　　畫的；
　　如畫的

</td></tr>
<tr><td>

pour
〔 por, pɔr 〕

</td><td>

She ***poured*** milk from the bottle into the glasses.
她將牛奶從瓶子倒入玻璃杯中。

</td><td>

v. 傾倒；倒

</td></tr>
<tr><td>

progress
〔 *n.* ˈprɑgrɛs 〕
〔 *v.* prəˈgrɛs 〕

</td><td>

He is showing rapid ***progress*** in his studies. 他的學業正迅速進步中。
His work is ***progressing*** smoothly, as we expected. 正如我們所預期的，他的工作正在順利地進展。

【記憶技巧】
pro (forward) + ***gress*** (walk) (往前邁
進，表示「進步」)

</td><td>

n. 進步

v. 進展

</td></tr>
</table>

Lesson 20

quote
〔kwot〕

The judge *quoted* various cases in support of his opinion. 那法官引用許多不同的案例來支持他的意見。

v. 引用
同 cite

relate
〔rɪˈlet〕

It is difficult to *relate* these results to her mistake. 要說明這些結果和她的錯誤之間的關係是困難的。
We listened as he *related* his adventures. 我們聽他敘述他的冒險經歷。

v. 1. 使有關連；說明…之間的關係
2. 敘述
名 relation

resolve
〔rɪˈzɑlv〕

He *resolved* to do better work in the future. 他決定以後要更努力工作。

v. 決定
同 decide;
determine

【記憶技巧】
re (back) + *solve* (loosen)（把緊張情緒放鬆，表示「決定」好了）

royal
〔ˈrɔɪəl〕

The nobleman is a man of the *royal* family. 那貴族是皇室的一員。

adj. 皇家的

【記憶技巧】
不要和 loyal（忠心的）搞混。

scheme
〔skim〕

Their *scheme* of building the road has failed. 他們建造道路的計畫已經失敗了。
They *schemed* for the overthrow of the government. 他們圖謀推翻政府。

n. 計畫

v. 圖謀

situate
〔ˈsɪtʃʊˌet〕

The city is *situated* by the river. 該市位於河旁。

v. 使位於
同 locate
名 situation

Exercise 20.4　從第四部分中選出最適當的一個英文字，填入空格內。

1. The building of the new school _____ quickly during the last summer.

2. The discovery of electricity _____ the way for many inventions.

3. Many people _____ to quit smoking and never do.

4. He tried to _____ from the Bible to support his beliefs.

5. The fire station is so _____ that the firemen can easily reach all parts of the town.

【解答】
1. progressed   2. paved   3. resolve   4. quote   5. situated

✦ 第五部分

somewhat
〔'sʌmˌhwɑt〕
I was *somewhat* surprised to hear the bad news. 我聽到那壞消息，有點吃驚。
adv. 有點
同 a little

spray
〔spre〕
Jane was *spraying* green paint on the wall. 珍正在將綠漆噴在牆上。
【記憶技巧】
s + *pray*（祈禱）
v. 噴灑

stir
〔stɝ〕
She *stirred* her coffee with a teaspoon. 她用茶匙攪拌咖啡。
v. 攪動

suitable
〔'sutəbḷ〕
The park is a *suitable* place for a picnic. 這公園是個適合野餐的地方。
【記憶技巧】
suit（適合）+ *able*（能夠…的）
adj. 適合的

tale
〔tel〕
Father likes to tell us *tales* of his boyhood. 父親喜歡告訴我們他少年時期的故事。
n. 故事
同 story

throat
〔θrot〕
The murderer cut the old man's *throat*. 兇手割了老人的喉嚨。
n. 喉嚨

Lesson 20

tramp
〔 træmp 〕

The soldiers *tramped* along the street.
士兵沿著街道行走。
Someone *tramped* on my toes on the crowded bus. 在擁擠的公車上，有人踩到了我的腳趾。

v. 1. (重步) 行走
2. 踐踏

urge
〔 ɝdʒ 〕

Hunger *urged* him to steal a piece of bread.
飢餓促使他偷一片麵包。

v. 力勸；促使

┌─ 【記憶技巧】
│ 諧音：餓去，飢餓 urge（促使）慾望。
└─

vow
〔 vaʊ 〕

All the men made a *vow* of loyalty to their leader. 所有的人都發誓效忠領袖。
They *vowed* vengeance against the oppressor.
他們發誓向迫害者復仇。

n. 誓言
同 oath
v. 發誓

witch
〔 wɪtʃ 〕

It was thought that *witches* generally used their power to do evil. 一般認為，女巫通常會用她們的力量去做壞事。

n. 女巫

Exercise 20.5 從第五部分中選出最適當的一個英文字，填入空格內。

1. Choose the most _____ word for the blank in the sentence.

2. We have arrived _____ late, I'm afraid.

3. He was _____ by the doctor to rest more.

4. On returning from the war, he told us _____ of fear and sadness.

5. She felt so homesick that she _____ never to leave home again once she was back home.

┌─ 【解答】
│ 1. suitable   2. somewhat   3. urged   4. tales   5. vowed
└─

成果測驗

I. 找出一個與斜體字的意義最接近的單字：

(　　) 1. to *cite* the Bible
      (A) read   (B) attack   (C) cover   (D) quote

(　　) 2. an unpleasant *odor*
      (A) procedure (B) emotion   (C) smell   (D) stain

(　　) 3. a *vow* of loyalty
      (A) oath   (B) plan   (C) break   (D) doubt

(　　) 4. to *cease* doing something
      (A) begin   (B) quit   (C) start   (D) delay

(　　) 5. to *converse* with someone
      (A) fight   (B) talk   (C) contract   (D) rejoice

(　　) 6. to *establish* a school
      (A) found   (B) mistrust   (C) destroy   (D) guarantee

(　　) 7. to *delay* something
      (A) defend   (B) decide   (C) claim   (D) postpone

(　　) 8. *forthright* behavior
      (A) stubborn   (B) cruel   (C) candid   (D) merry

(　　) 9. a *holy* cup
      (A) strange   (B) sacred   (C) hollow   (D) solid

(　　) 10. in the *neighborhood*
      (A) place   (B) medium   (C) wood   (D) vicinity

Lesson 20

II. 找出一個與題前中文意思相同的英文字：

( ) 1. 承認
    (A) confess   (B) converse   (C) relate   (D) forgive

( ) 2. 合法的
    (A) royal   (B) executive   (C) legal   (D) incidental

( ) 3. 氣味
    (A) sorrow   (B) anger   (C) odor   (D) emotion

( ) 4. 決定
    (A) quote   (B) resolve   (C) defer   (D) resist

( ) 5. 快樂的
    (A) gay   (B) dull   (C) gloomy   (D) acute

III. 找出一個與斜體字意義相反的單字：

( ) 1. *continue*
    (A) combine   (B) pour   (C) cease   (D) contribute

( ) 2. *boredom*
    (A) reason   (B) interest   (C) progress   (D) dignity

( ) 3. *moderate*
    (A) hollow   (B) legal   (C) cautious   (D) excessive

( ) 4. *attach*
    (A) detach   (B) confess   (C) urge   (D) resolve

( ) 5. *gloomy*
    (A) extreme   (B) gay   (C) keen   (D) forthright

Lesson 20

IV. 完整拼出下列各句中所欠缺的單字，每一格代表一個字母：

1. A person's yearly i_ _ _ _e is all the money that he gets in a year. （收入）

2. He has a s_ _ _ _e for extracting gold from sea water. （計畫）

3. Will you p_ _r me a cup of tea, please? （倒）

4. The newspaper is an advertising m_ _ _ _m. （媒體）

5. I have no i_ _ _ _ _ _t in politics. （興趣）

V. 選出最適合句意的一個單字：

(　) 1. The thief _____ to the police that he had stolen the money.
(A) offended　(B) ceased　(C) confessed　(D) contributed

(　) 2. I have no _____ that you will pass the examination.
(A) fiber　　(B) doubt　　(C) mode　　　(D) sympathy

(　) 3. The trip to Alaska was quite a(n) _____ for her.
(A) spot　　(B) mode　　(C) adventure　(D) medium

(　) 4. A deaf and blind man shows _____ by facial expressions and gestures.
(A) adventure　(B) grocery　(C) profession　(D) emotions

(　) 5. Soldiers usually have to bear _____ hardship during a war.
(A) queer　　(B) royal　　(C) gay　　　(D) bitter

(　) 6. We will _____ the party for a week and hold it next Saturday.
(A) advance　(B) differ　(C) delay　　(D) forgive

( ) 7. This clock is _____ for one year.
    (A) urged   (B) situated
    (C) determined   (D) guaranteed

( ) 8. Prices in this hotel are _____, not high at all.
    (A) moderate   (B) broad   (C) excessive   (D) bitter

( ) 9. There is some beautiful scenery in our _____.
    (A) atmosphere   (B) neighborhood
    (C) fashion   (D) scheme

( ) 10. He _____ this sentence from a speech by the President.
    (A) invented   (B) attached
    (C) quoted   (D) symbolized

VI. 將題前的斜體字轉換為適當詞性，填入空格中：

1. *combine*   The _____ of yellow and blue forms green.

2. *situate*   The store is in an ideal _____ to draw tourists.

3. *confess*   The thief's _____ of guilt closed the case.

4. *relate*   There is no _____ between the nations.

5. *converse*   He had a long telephone _____.

【解答】
I. 1. D 2. C 3. A 4. B 5. B 6. A 7. D 8. C 9. B 10. D
II. 1. A 2. C 3. C 4. B 5. A
III. 1. C 2. B 3. D 4. A 5. B
IV. 1. income 2. scheme 3. pour 4. medium 5. interest
V. 1. C 2. B 3. C 4. D 5. D 6. C 7. D 8. A 9. B 10. C
VI. 1. combination 2. situation 3. confession 4. relation
    5. conversation

Lesson 20

Lesson 21

✦ 第一部分

advertise 〔ˈædvə͟ˌtaɪz〕	They *advertised* in the newspaper that they had a used car for sale. 他們在報上登廣告，說有部舊車要賣。	*v.* 登廣告
attack 〔əˈtæk〕	They *attacked* the enemy at sundown. 他們在日落時攻擊敵人。	*v.* 攻擊 同 assault
blacksmith 〔ˈblækˌsmɪθ〕	A *blacksmith* makes things with iron by heating it and hammering it into shape. 鐵匠將鐵加熱後，鎚打成形，製成物品。	*n.* 鐵匠
brook 〔brʊk〕	A *brook* is a natural waterway smaller than a river.　【記憶技巧】 *book* (書) + *r* 溪流是天然的水道，較河為小。	*n.* 小溪； 溪流
ceiling 〔ˈsilɪŋ〕	Lying on the sofa, he could see the *ceiling* of the room. 他躺在沙發上，可以看到房間的天花板。	*n.* 天花板
comfort 〔ˈkʌmfət〕	I tried to *comfort* Jean after her mother's death. 琴的母親過世後，我試著安慰她。	*v.* 安慰 *n.* 舒適

【記憶技巧】
com (wholly) + *fort* (strong) (全身強壯，就不會感到不舒服)

Lesson 21

confine
〔kən'faɪn〕

Please ***confine*** your remarks to the subject we are talking about.
請你將話題限制在我們正在談論的主題上。
John was ***confined*** to bed for a week with his cold.
約翰因感冒臥病在床一星期。

v. 1. 限制

2. 臥病

convert
〔kən'vɝt〕

Give me time and I'll ***convert*** her to our political party.
給我時間，我會使她改入我們的政黨。

v. 改變；使改
信（宗教）
同 change

cunning
〔'kʌnɪŋ〕

He is as ***cunning*** as a fox.
他像狐狸一樣狡猾。

adj. 狡猾的
同 sly

delegate
〔'dɛlə,get〕

Our club sent two ***delegates*** to attend the meeting.
我們的社團派了兩名代表去參加會議。

n. 代表

---【記憶技巧】---
de (away) + *legate* (send with a commission)（背負任務離開，就是去當「代表」）

Exercise 21.1　從第一部分中選出最適當的一個英文字，填入空格內。

1. Because of heavy rain he was _____ to his room all day.

2. We should _____ those who are in sorrow.

3. _____ can mend tools and horseshoes.

4. When people lose something valuable, they usually _____ it in the newspaper.

5. John was _____ to Buddhism by a Chinese priest.

【解答】

1. confined　2. comfort　3. Blacksmiths　4. advertise　5. converted
---

✦ 第二部分

dim 〔dɪm〕	The light is too *dim* for me to see. 燈光太暗，我看不見。	*adj.* 昏暗的； 　　微暗的
drag 〔dræg〕	The horse was *dragging* a heavy load. 馬正拖著重擔。	*v.* 拖 同 pull 反 push
emperor 〔'ɛmpərə〕	Napoleon was the *Emperor* of France. 拿破崙是法國的皇帝。	*n.* 皇帝

estate
〔ə'stet〕

The rich man left a great *estate* when he died. 那富人死時留下一大筆土地。

> 【記憶技巧】
> *e* + *state*（州）

n. 地產
同 property

exclaim
〔ɪk'sklem〕

"It's eight o'clock," his mother *exclaimed*.
「八點了，」他的母親大叫著。

> 【記憶技巧】
> *ex*（加強語氣的字首）+ *claim* (call)（用力叫，即「大叫」）

v. 大叫

fierce
〔fɪrs〕

He bought a *fierce* dog to guard his house. 他買了一隻惡犬看家。

adj. 兇猛的
同 violent

fortunate
(ˈfɔrtʃənɪt)

You are ***fortunate*** in having such a fine family.

你有一個這麼好的家庭，眞是幸運。

adj. 幸運的

反 unlucky

gaze
(gez)

For hours she sat ***gazing*** at the stars.

她坐著凝視星星好幾個小時。

v. 凝視

同 stare

habit
(ˈhæbɪt)

Some people say that smoking is a bad ***habit***. 有些人說抽煙是壞習慣。

n. 習慣

hop
(hɑp)

He had hurt his foot and had to ***hop*** along. 他的腳受傷，不得不跳著走。

v. 跳躍

Exercise 21.2　從第二部分中選出最適當的一個英文字，填入空格內。

1. Are you in the _____ of going to bed early and rising early?

2. The child had _____ at the stranger for a few minutes before answering his questions.

3. You are _____ to have such rich parents.

4. He has a beautiful _____ 40 miles from Los Angeles with a country house and a swimming pool on it.

5. He was _____ out of his hiding place.

┌─ 【解答】 ─────────────────────┐
1. habit　2. gazed　3. fortunate　4. estate　5. dragged
└───────────────────────────────┘

✦ 第三部分

independence
(ˌɪndɪ'pɛndəns)

People on these islands fought for ***independence*** and finally succeeded. 這些島上的人民爲獨立而戰，終獲勝利。

n. 獨立

international
(ˌɪntɚ'næʃənl̩)

A treaty is an ***international*** agreement. 條約是國際協定。

adj. 國際的

kite
(kaɪt)

A ***kite*** was flying in the air at the end of a long string. 風箏被綁在一根長線的尾端，飛翔在空中。

n. 風箏

leisure
('liʒɚ)

She spends at least half of her ***leisure*** in reading. 她的空閒時間至少有一半花在閱讀上。

n. 空閒

machinery
(mə'ʃɪnərɪ)

The factory has much new ***machinery***. 這家工廠有許多新機器。

n. 機器

【記憶技巧】
-ery 表「⋯類事物」的字尾。

melt
(mɛlt)

The ice will ***melt*** when the sun shines on it.
冰被太陽照射時，會融化。

v. 融化
同 dissolve
反 freeze

modest
('madɪst)

The hero was very ***modest*** about his great deeds.
那英雄對於他偉大的功績很謙虛。

adj. 謙虛的；莊重的
同 humble
反 arrogant

【記憶技巧】
mode (模式) + *st* (不超出一定的模式，就是「謙虛的」)

Lesson 21

nervous
〔'nɜvəs 〕

A person who has been overworking is likely to become **nervous**.
工作過度的人容易緊張。

adj. 緊張的

offer
〔'ɔfɚ 〕

He **offered** a few ideas to improve the plan. 他提出一些意見以改進那項計畫。

v. 提供；提
出；出（價）

【記憶技巧】
of (to) + *fer* (carry)（把東西帶來，也就是「提供」）

同 propose

pack
〔 pæk 〕

She **packed** a suitcase for the trip. 她為旅行打包了一個旅行箱。
The camper had cooking equipment in his **pack**. 那露營者的背包裏有烹飪裝備。

v. 打包

n. 背包；
包裹

Lesson 21

Exercise 21.3 從第三部分中選出最適當的一個英文字，填入空格內。

1. Six nations have signed a(n) _____ trade agreement.

2. When you begin to earn money, you can live a life of _____.

3. I like a(n) _____ girl, who is neither shy nor loud.

4. She is so _____ that she jumps at the slightest noise.

5. He _____ twenty dollars for a new stove, but the seller refused to sell it at that price.

【解答】
1. international　2. independence　3. modest　4. nervous　5. offered

✦ 第四部分

paw
〔 pɔ 〕

The dog lifted his two front *paws* before his master.
那隻狗在主人面前舉起前面兩隻腳掌。

n. 腳掌；腳爪

pigeon
〔'pɪdʒɪn 〕

Pigeons are often trained to carry messages. 鴿子常被訓練來傳送信息。

n. 鴿子
囘 dove

poverty
〔'pɑvɚtɪ 〕

His ragged clothes and broken furniture indicated his *poverty*.
他的破爛衣服和破傢俱顯示他很窮。

n. 貧窮
反 wealth
形 poor

project
〔'prɑdʒɛkt 〕

A *project* to build a new church was discussed at the meeting.
那會議討論了一個建造新教堂的計畫。

n. 計畫
囘 plan; scheme

【記憶技巧】
pro (forward) + *ject* (throw) (決定動作前，要先拿出企劃案)

reduce
〔 rɪ'djus 〕

She is now 150 pounds; she has to *reduce* her weight.
她現在一百五十磅；她必須減重。

v. 減少；降低

【記憶技巧】
re (back) + *duce* (lead) (導致數量往後退，表示「減少」)

reply
〔 rɪ'plaɪ 〕

He made no *reply* to my question.
他沒回答我的問題。
She *replied* to my letter right away.
她立刻回覆了我的信。

n. 回答

v. 回覆

Lesson 21

rifle
〔'raɪfḷ 〕

A *rifle* is usually fired from the shoulder.
步槍通常由肩上發射。

n. 步槍；
來福槍
同 musket

salary
〔'sælərɪ 〕

His *salary* will be increased next year.
他的薪水明年將會增加。

n. 薪水

【記憶技巧】
sal (salt) + *ary* (*n.*) (源於古羅馬發鹽給士兵當作「薪水」)

section
〔'sɛkʃən 〕

Mother cut the pie into eight *sections*.
母親將派切成八份。

n. 部分

The teacher *sectioned* the history class by ability ratings.
老師按能力將歷史課分班。

v. 劃分
同 divide;
classify

【記憶技巧】
sect (cut) + *ion* (*n.*) (經過切割，分成很多「部分」)

shoot
〔 ʃut 〕

He *shot* at a bird, but missed it.
他射擊一隻鳥，可是沒命中。

v. 射擊
同 fire

Exercise 21.4 從第四部分中選出最適當的一個英文字，填入空格內。

1. I asked him where to go, but he didn't _____.

2. Don't drive so fast; _____ speed, please.

3. The _____ of his family made it impossible for him to go to school.

4. Soldiers are equipped with _____ and trained to use them.

5. I _____ an arrow at the spot on the wall, but the arrow didn't even reach the wall.

> 【解答】
> 1. reply 2. reduce 3. poverty 4. rifles 5. shot

✦ 第五部分

slope
〔slop〕

We climbed the steep *slope* of the hill.
我們爬那陡峭的山坡。   *n.* 山坡

The bank *slopes* gently to the water's
edge. 堤防緩緩向水邊傾斜。   *v.* 傾斜

spider
〔'spaɪdɚ〕

A *spider* is a small animal with eight
legs. 蜘蛛是有八隻腳的小動物。   *n.* 蜘蛛

starve
〔stɑrv〕

They got lost in the desert and *starved*
to death. 他們迷失在沙漠中而餓死。   *v.* 飢餓

structure
〔'strʌktʃɚ〕

The *structure* of English is quite
different from that of Chinese.
英文的結構和中文大不相同。   *n.* 1. 結構

The city hall is a large stone *structure*.   2. 建築物
市政廳是一棟大型的石造建築物。   同 building

> 【記憶技巧】
> *struct* (build) + *ure* (*n.*)

swallow
〔'swɑlo〕

We *swallowed* all our food and drink.
我們吞嚥下所有的食物和飲料。   *v.* 吞；嚥

In the early evening, the air was
filled with graceful *swallows*.
傍晚時，空中飛滿了優雅的燕子。   *n.* 燕子

Lesson 21

tender
〔'tɛndə〕

Cook the meat a long time so that it's really *tender*. 把肉煮久一點，如此才嫩。
He *tendered* us money as payment for the book he had lost.
他給我們錢，作為他
遺失那本書的賠償。

【記憶技巧】
tend（傾向）+ *er*

adj. 嫩的
同 soft
v. 提出；支付；
償還

trust
〔trʌst〕

A child puts *trust* in his parents.
孩子信任父母親。
You shouldn't *trust* him; he is dishonest. 你不該信任他；他不誠實。

n. 信任

v. 信任
同 rely (on)

vest
〔vɛst〕

He likes to wear a *vest* under his jacket.
他喜歡在夾克裏穿件背心。

n. 背心
同 waistcoat

weed
〔wid〕

Many *weeds* are growing among the flowers. 花叢中長出許多雜草。
He spent the whole afternoon *weeding* in the garden.
他整個下午都在花園裏除草。

n. 雜草

v. 除草

yield
〔jild〕

The enemy finally *yielded* to our soldiers. 敵人終於向我們的士兵屈服。
This land *yields* good crops.
這片土地出產很好的農作物。

v. 1. 屈服 < *to* >
同 submit
2. 出產
同 produce

Exercise 21.5 從第五部分中選出最適當的一個英文字，填入空格內。

1. The man said he would _____ rather than beg for food.

2. Most _____ make webs to catch insects for food.

3. The _____ of that roof is very steep.

4. Yesterday he _____ his resignation to the Prime Minister.

5. He is not the sort of man to be _____.

【解答】
1. starve   2. spiders   3. slope   4. tendered   5. trusted

成果測驗

I. 找出一個與其他三個不相關的字：

( ) 1. (A) parcel   (B) pack   (C) part   (D) packet

( ) 2. (A) progress   (B) scheme
       (C) plan   (D) project

( ) 3. (A) cunning   (B) tender   (C) clever   (D) sly

( ) 4. (A) drag   (B) haul   (C) pull   (D) delay

( ) 5. (A) brook   (B) broom   (C) stream   (D) creek

( ) 6. (A) respond   (B) reply   (C) relate   (D) answer

( ) 7. (A) vow   (B) confidence
       (C) trust   (D) reliance

( ) 8. (A) practice   (B) custom   (C) habit   (D) comfort

( ) 9. (A) reduce   (B) yield   (C) lessen   (D) decrease

( ) 10. (A) exclaim   (B) yell   (C) proclaim   (D) shout

Lesson 21

II. 找出一個與題前中文意思相同的英文字：

( ) 1. 緊張的
    (A) tragic   (B) violent
    (C) nervous   (D) cautious

( ) 2. 空閒
    (A) patience   (B) lack
    (C) independence   (D) leisure

( ) 3. 飢餓
    (A) escape   (B) starve   (C) sting   (D) quiver

( ) 4. 登廣告
    (A) advertise   (B) broadcast
    (C) contract   (D) purchase

( ) 5. 貧窮
    (A) doubt   (B) servant
    (C) poverty   (D) cowardice

III. 找出一個與斜體字意義相反的單字：

( ) 1. *arrogant*
    (A) smooth   (B) modest   (C) soft   (D) dull

( ) 2. *grieve*
    (A) attack   (B) swallow   (C) comfort   (D) gaze

( ) 3. *push*
    (A) delay   (B) drag   (C) seize   (D) pour

( ) 4. *increase*
    (A) reduce   (B) melt   (C) reply   (D) starve

Lesson 21

( ) 5. *unlucky*

      (A) tender   (B) modest   (C) fortunate   (D) clever

IV. 完整拼出下列各句中所欠缺的單字，每一格代表一個字母：

1. I asked him, but he made no r_ _ _y. （回答）

2. Don't s_ _ _ _ _w the hot coffee; you may burn your throat.
   （吞嚥）

3. Tiberius was the e_ _ _ _ _r of Rome during the life of Jesus
   Christ. （皇帝）

4. He went hunting with a r_ _ _e in his hand. （步槍）

5. The children chose one d_ _ _ _ _ _e to buy the flowers. （代表）

V. 找出一個與句中斜體字意義最接近的單字：

( ) 1. This factory *yields* cars of good quality.

      (A) sells   (B) buys

      (C) produces   (D) offers

( ) 2. He has just bought an *estate* in the country.

      (A) pasture   (B) property

      (C) house   (D) castle

( ) 3. We *gazed* at the man, wondering who he was.

      (A) conceived   (B) conversed

      (C) mocked   (D) stared

( ) 4. The general decided to *attack* the enemy's positions.

      (A) offend   (B) oppose

      (C) guard   (D) assault

Lesson 21

( ) 5. The man was killed by a *fierce* wolf.

    (A) violent   (B) bitter

    (C) stubborn   (D) nervous

( ) 6. The rough material hurt the child's *tender* skin.

    (A) gay   (B) beautiful

    (C) soft   (D) tough

( ) 7. The snow soon *melted* away when the warm weather came.

    (A) resolved   (B) dissolved

    (C) destroyed   (D) reduced

( ) 8. Coal can be *converted* to gas by burning.

    (A) reduced   (B) yielded

    (C) changed   (D) separated

( ) 9. The young actress is very *modest* about her success.

    (A) humble   (B) proud

    (C) merry   (D) serious

( ) 10. A team of four horses *dragged* the big log out of the forest.

    (A) fetched   (B) pulled

    (C) pushed   (D) carried

Lesson 21

【解答】

I. 1. C   2. A   3. B   4. D   5. B   6. C   7. A   8. D   9. B   10. C

II. 1. C   2. D   3. B   4. A   5. C

III. 1. B   2. C   3. B   4. A   5. C

IV. 1. reply   2. swallow   3. emperor   4. rifle   5. delegate

V. 1. C   2. B   3. D   4. D   5. A   6. C   7. B   8. C   9. A   10. B

Lesson 22

✦ 第一部分

affair
〔 ə'fɛr 〕

When he asked me how much money I earned, I told him to mind his own *affairs*. 當他問我賺多少錢時，我叫他別管閒事。
She's having an *affair* with her husband's best friend.
她和丈夫最要好的朋友有外遇。

n. 1. 事情
同 business

2. 外遇

【記憶技巧】
af + *fair* (公平的)

attempt
〔 ə'tɛmpt 〕

I *attempted* to speak but was told to be quiet. 我想說話，可是有人叫我閉嘴。

v. 企圖；嘗試

【記憶技巧】
<u>tempt</u> (誘惑)；con<u>tempt</u> (輕視)

blade
〔 bled 〕

A razor should have a very sharp *blade*. 刮鬍刀應該有非常銳利的刀鋒。

n. 刀鋒

broom
〔 brum 〕

I swept the broken glass into a pile with a *broom*.
我用掃帚把碎玻璃掃成一堆。

n. 掃帚

cell
〔 sɛl 〕

All animals and plants are made of *cells*. 所有的動植物都是由細胞組成。
Bees store honey in the *cells* of a honeycomb. 蜜蜂將蜂蜜儲存在蜂巢的各個小蜂室中。

n. 1. 細胞

2. 蜂室

command
〔 kə'mænd 〕

The officer *commanded* his men to fire at the enemy.
指揮官命令部下向敵軍開火。

v. n. 命令
反 obey

Lesson 22

confirm 〔 kən'fɝm 〕	The rumor that there was flooding was ***confirmed*** by a news broadcast. 洪水的謠傳已被新聞廣播所證實。	*v.* 證實;確認 同 approve
convince 〔 kən'vɪns 〕	We are ***convinced*** that Anne went by train rather than by plane. 我們相信安是坐火車去的,不是搭飛機。	*v.* 使相信 同 persuade; assure

> 【記憶技巧】
> ***con*** (thoroughly) + ***vince*** (conquer) (完全征服對方,使對方相信)

cure 〔 kjʊr 〕	This medicine should ***cure*** you of your cold. 這種藥應該能治好你的感冒。 He has tried all sorts of ***cures*** but he is still ill. 他已嘗試過各種的治療方法,可是病還是沒好。	*v.* 治療;治癒 同 heal *n.* 治療方法 同 remedy
delicate 〔'dɛləkɪt 〕	A pianist or a violinist must have a ***delicate*** sense of touch. 鋼琴家或小提琴家都必須有靈敏的觸感。	*adj.* 細緻的;靈敏的;精密的 同 crude

Exercise 22.1　從第一部分中選出最適當的一個英文字,填入空格內。

1. Scientists sometimes need very _____ instruments.

2. Resting in bed will often _____ a cold.

3. The mistakes you made _____ me that you had not studied your lesson.

4. He sent the written request to _____ his telephone order.

5. The captain of a ship _____ all the officers and men.

【解答】

1. delicate　2. cure　3. convinced　4. confirm　5. commands

✦ 第二部分

dip
〔 dɪp 〕

She *dipped* her hand into the pool to see how cold the water was.
她將手浸入泳池看水有多冷。

v. 沾；浸
同 immerse

drain
〔 dren 〕

You should dig trenches to *drain* away the water. 你應該挖水溝以便排水。

【記憶技巧】
d + *rain*（雨）

v. 排水
反 irrigate

emphasis
〔'ɛmfəsɪs 〕

Some schools put special *emphasis* on language study.
有些學校特別注重語文學科。

n. 強調
動 emphasize
同 stress

estimate
〔'ɛstə,met 〕

The gardener *estimated* that it would take four hours to weed the garden.
園丁估計要替那座花園除草需要四小時。

v. 估計
同 evaluate

figure
〔'fɪgɚ,
'fɪgjɚ 〕

I saw a *figure* approaching in the darkness.
我在黑暗中看見有人影接近。

n. 數字；畫像；
人物；人影

foul
〔 faʊl 〕

We opened the windows to let out the *foul* air.
我們打開窗子，讓污濁的空氣流出。

【記憶技巧】
和 fowl（鳥；家禽）同音。

adj. 污穢的；
有惡臭的；
污濁的
反 clean

Lesson 22

gem 〔dʒɛm〕	Diamonds and rubies are well-known *gems*. 鑽石和紅寶石都是大家熟知的寶石。	*n.* 寶石 同 jewel
hail 〔hel〕	The crowd *hailed* the new boxing champion. 群眾向新的拳擊冠軍歡呼。	*v.* 歡呼 同 cheer
horizon 〔hə'raɪzn̩〕	We saw a small ship on the *horizon*. 我們看到地平線上有條小船。 Traveling can broaden our *horizons*. 旅行可以拓展我們的眼界。	*n.* 地平線 *n. pl.* 知識範圍
indicate 〔'ɪndəˌket〕	The arrow on the sign *indicates* the way to go. 告示牌上的箭頭標示應走的方向。	*v.* 指出；顯示 同 designate

------【記憶技巧】------
in (towards) + *dic* (proclaim 宣稱) + *ate*
(*v.*)

Exercise 22.2 從第二部分中選出最適當的一個英文字，填入空格內。

1. A writer sometimes underlines important words for _____.

2. He _____ his spoon into the soup and began breakfast.

3. The wall was covered with _____ of birds and flowers.

4. The air in this room is _____; open the window!

5. The crown of the queen sparkled with _____.

------【解答】------
1. emphasis   2. dipped   3. figures   4. foul   5. gems

✦ 第三部分

interrupt
〔͵ɪntə'rʌpt〕

Don't *interrupt* me when I am busy.
在我忙時，不要打斷我。

> 【記憶技巧】
> *inter* (between) + *rupt* (break)（從中間破壞，就是「打斷」）

v. 打斷

kneel
〔nil〕

She *knelt* down to pull weeds from the flower bed.
她跪下去拔花圃中的雜草。

> 【記憶技巧】
> *knee*（膝蓋）+ *l*

v. 跪下

lessen
〔'lɛsn̩〕

The child's fever *lessened* during the night. 那孩子的發燒在晚上減輕了。

v. 減輕
反 increase

magic
〔'mædʒɪk〕

In fairy tales, witches often use *magic* to change persons into animals or birds. 在童話故事中，巫婆常使用魔法將人變成動物或鳥。

n. 魔術；魔法
同 witchcraft

mend
〔mɛnd〕

My brother *mended* the broken doll for me. 我哥哥替我修補破損的娃娃。

v. 修補；改正
同 repair; fix

moist
〔mɔɪst〕

The thick steam in the room had made the walls *moist*.
房間裏大量的水蒸氣使得牆壁潮濕。

adj. 潮濕的

nest
〔nɛst〕

Most birds lay their eggs in their *nests*. 大部分的鳥在牠們的巢中下蛋。

n. 巢

Lesson 22

official
〔 ə'fɪʃəl 〕

The letter should be written in an *official* style.
這封信應寫成公函的形式。
The President is the most powerful government *official*.
總統是最有權力的政府官員。

adj. 正式的；
官方的；
公務上的
n. 官員

package
〔'pækɪdʒ 〕

He carried a large *package* of books.
他帶了一大包書。

n. 包裹

┌─【記憶技巧】─────────────┐
pack（包裝）+ *age*（表「一組」的字尾）
└──────────────────────┘

payroll
〔'pe,rol 〕

Don't do the work until he puts you on the *payroll*. 直到他把你的名字寫入發薪名單上後，你再做那件工作。

n. 發薪名單；
員工名冊

Exercise 22.3 從第三部分中選出最適當的一個英文字，填入空格內。

1. He made a trip to Tainan on _____ business.

2. The birds build their _____ with twigs and leaves.

3. Her eyes got _____ when she heard the bad news.

4. I don't want to be _____ in my business.

5. I _____ down and gave God thanks for my recovery from sickness.

┌─【解答】───────────────────────────────┐
1. official　2. nests　3. moist　4. interrupted　5. knelt
└──────────────────────────────────────┘

✦ 第四部分

pile
〔 paɪl 〕

The room was full of *piles* of old books. 這房間裏擺滿了一堆堆的舊書。 *n.* 一堆

The snow *piled* so high in front of the door that we couldn't go out. 門前積雪太高，因此我們出不去。 *v.* 堆積
同 heap

practical
〔'præktɪkḷ〕

His plan was interesting but not *practical*. 他的計畫有趣，可是不實際。 *adj.* 實際的

prompt
〔 prɑmpt 〕

His *prompt* action prevented serious trouble. 他立即的行動避免了大禍。 *adj.* 立即的
同 immediate

refer
〔 rɪ'fɝ 〕

If you don't know what this means, *refer* to the dictionary. 如果你不知道這個的意思，就查字典。 *v.* 提到；參考
< *to* >

represent
〔,rɛprɪ'zɛnt〕

On the map, blue *represents* water and brown *represents* land. 在地圖上，藍色代表海，棕色代表陸地。 *v.* 代表
同 symbolize;
stand for

【記憶技巧】
先背 present（呈現）。

righteous
〔'raɪtʃəs〕

He is a *righteous* man; he always behaves justly. 他是個正直的人；他一向行為公正。 *adj.* 正直的
同 just

【記憶技巧】
right（正確的）+ *eous* (*adj.*)

sandwich
〔'sændwɪtʃ〕

He ate *sandwiches* for lunch. 他午餐吃三明治。 *n.* 三明治

Their house was *sandwiched* between two tall buildings. 他們的房子被夾在兩棟很高的建築物中間。 *v.* 夾在中間

Lesson 22

secure
〔 sɪˈkjur 〕

He hoped for a *secure* old age.
他希望有一個無憂無慮的晚年。

We must *secure* ourselves against
the dangers of the coming storm.
我們應保護自己，免得受到即將來臨的
暴風雨之害。

He's lucky to have *secured* himself
such a good job.
他獲得這麼好的工作，真是幸運。

adj. 安全的；
　　　無憂慮的
同 safe
v. 1. 保護
同 protect

2. 獲得；為…
　　取得
同 get; obtain

---【記憶技巧】---
se (free from) + *cure* (care)（沒有憂慮的，
表示「安全的」）

shortage
〔 ˈʃɔrtɪdʒ 〕

The rice crop will be poor because
of the *shortage* of rain.
因為缺雨，稻米將會歉收。

n. 缺乏
同 lack
反 surplus

smart
〔 smɑrt 〕

Both of his children are very *smart*.
他的兩個孩子都非常聰明。

adj. 聰明的
同 clever

Exercise 22.4 從第四部分中選出最適當的一個英文字，填入空格內。

1. You'd better _____ to the dictionary for the meaning of the word.

2. The red lines on the map _____ railways.

3. The fort was _____ against any surprise attack.

4. I expect your _____ answer to my question.

5. There is a _____ of grain because of poor crops.

---【解答】---
1. refer　2. represent　3. secure　4. prompt　5. shortage

✦ 第五部分

spill 〔 spɪl 〕	The child ***spilled*** the milk on the floor. 那孩子將牛奶灑在地上。	*v.* 灑
statesman 〔'stetsmən 〕	Winston Churchill was a famous English ***statesman***. 溫斯頓・邱吉爾是有名的英國政治家。	*n.* 政治家 同 politician

【記憶技巧】
state（州）+ *s* + *man*（人）

struggle 〔'strʌgl 〕	The widow ***struggled*** to send her six children to college. 那寡婦努力送她的六個孩子上大學。	*v.* 奮鬥；努力； 掙扎
sway 〔 swe 〕	The branches of the trees were ***swaying*** in the wind. 樹枝在風中搖擺。	*v.* 搖擺
	The ***sway*** of the pail caused some milk to spill out. 擺盪的桶使一些牛奶溢出。	*n.* 搖擺

【記憶技巧】
s + *way*（路）

term 〔 tɝm 〕	The President is elected for a six-year ***term***. 選上的總統任期六年。	*n.* 1. 期間
	Are there any examinations at the end of this ***term***? 這學期末有任何的考試嗎？	2. 學期 同 semester
	The author uses many technical ***terms*** in this book. 那位作者在本書中用了許多專門術語。	3. 名詞；術語 同 word
	The ***terms*** of the contract are unfair. 合約的條件不公平。	4. *pl.* 條件 同 conditions

Lesson 22

toil
〔tɔɪl〕

He succeeded after years of *toil*.
他在多年的辛勞後成功。
The family was caught in the *toils* of povery. 這個家庭陷入貧窮的困境。
They *toiled* with their hands for a living. 他們爲生計而用雙手辛苦地工作。

【記憶技巧】
t + *oil* (油)

n. 1. 辛勞

2. (*pl.*) 無法擺脫的困境

v. 辛苦工作

tune
〔tjun〕

There are *tunes* that are easy to remember. 有些旋律容易記住。
A man is *tuning* the piano.
有個人正在爲鋼琴調音。

n. 曲調；旋律
同 melody
v. 調音

vice
〔vaɪs〕

He loves drinking beer; it is one of his *vices*.
他喜歡喝啤酒；這是他的惡習之一。

n. 邪惡；罪行；惡習
同 evil
反 virtue

weep
〔wip〕

He lost control of his feelings and began to *weep*.
他無法控制自己的感情，開始哭泣。

【記憶技巧】
sweep (掃地) 讓人 weep (哭泣)。

v. 哭泣
同 cry

zone
〔zon〕

Don't come into the danger *zone*.
不要進入危險地帶。

n. 地帶；地區
同 area

Exercise 22.5 從第五部分中選出最適當的一個英文字，填入空格內。

1. Who has _____ the ink on my notebook?

2. We honored him as our leading _____.

3. She _____ to get on the bus during the rush hours.

4. In spite of the police, there is usually a certain amount of _____ in all big cities.

5. Do you know the _____ of this song?

【解答】
1. spilled　2. statesman　3. struggled　4. vice　5. tune

成果測驗

I. 找出一個與斜體字的意義最接近的單字：

( ) 1. a famous *statesman*
 (A) lawyer   (B) soldier
 (C) businessman   (D) politician

( ) 2. a *smart* boy
 (A) dirty   (B) swift   (C) clever   (D) small

( ) 3. a *secure* position
 (A) safe   (B) good   (C) modest   (D) bad

( ) 4. a *righteous* man
 (A) practical (B) just   (C) clever   (D) fierce

( ) 5. to put *stress* on something
 (A) spot   (B) emphasis (C) emotion   (D) trust

( ) 6. to *cure* illness
 (A) vanish   (B) repair   (C) heal   (D) diminish

( ) 7. to *stand for* something
 (A) hail   (B) refer   (C) confirm   (D) represent

Lesson 22

(　　) 8. a safety *zone*

      (A) area   (B) rule   (C) vest   (D) device

(　　) 9. to *repair* something

      (A) reduce   (B) mend   (C) respond   (D) refer

(　　) 10. to *convince* someone

      (A) interrupt   (B) approve   (C) convert   (D) assure

II. 找出一個與題前中文意思相同的英文字：

(　　) 1. 潮濕的

      (A) modest   (B) moist   (C) moderate   (D) dim

(　　) 2. 立即的

      (A) prompt   (B) foul   (C) fierce   (D) smart

(　　) 3. 官員

      (A) senator   (B) mayor   (C) instructor   (D) official

(　　) 4. 企圖

      (A) refer   (B) toil   (C) attempt   (D) pile

(　　) 5. 寶石

      (A) gold   (B) gem   (C) silver   (D) cell

III. 找出一個與斜體字意義相反的單字：

(　　) 1. *virtue*

      (A) spider   (B) lack   (C) leisure   (D) vice

(　　) 2. *crude*

      (A) weak   (B) delicate   (C) safe   (D) moist

Lesson 22

(   ) 3. *foul*

       (A) dirty   (B) clean   (C) dry   (D) damp

(   ) 4. *obey*

       (A) reduce   (B) interrupt   (C) command   (D) yield

(   ) 5. *surplus*

       (A) shortage   (B) leisure   (C) evil   (D) wage

IV. 完整拼出下列各句中所欠缺的單字，每一格代表一個字母：

1. My high school puts great e_ _ _ _ _ _s on studies that are practical in our daily life. （強調）

2. Please c_ _ _ _ _m your telephone number. （確認）

3. It is not polite to i_ _ _ _ _ _ _ _t when someone is talking. （打斷）

4. The poor beggar had to s_ _ _ _ _ _e for a living. （奮鬥）

5. It took many hours to c_ _ _ _ _ _e John of his wife's guilt. （使相信）

V. 選出最適合句意的一個單字：

(   ) 1. She _____ for joy when she won the award.

       (A) piled   (B) struggled   (C) confessed   (D) wept

(   ) 2. Leave me alone! Mind your own _____.

       (A) affairs   (B) defects   (C) dignity   (D) virtue

(   ) 3. A colonel is an officer who _____ a regiment.

       (A) confines   (B) assaults   (C) commands   (D) obeys

( ) 4. He had the _____ of his skate sharpened.
    (A) slopes   (B) backs   (C) tunes   (D) blades

( ) 5. The prisoners _____ to escape but failed.
    (A) swayed   (B) attempted
    (C) exclaimed   (D) intervened

( ) 6. Parents try to _____ their children of bad habits.
    (A) cure   (B) dissolve   (C) drain   (D) yield

( ) 7. He has _____ himself that his method is the best.
    (A) convinced   (B) restrained
    (C) indicated   (D) represented

( ) 8. We _____ that it would take three months to finish the work.
    (A) attempted   (B) estimated
    (C) converted   (D) interrupted

( ) 9. The _____ machine can record even very slight changes.
    (A) dull   (B) fierce   (C) foul   (D) delicate

( ) 10. She went into the church and _____ down to pray.
    (A) melt   (B) piled   (C) knelt   (D) spilt

Lesson 22

【解答】
  I. 1. D 2. C 3. A 4. B 5. B 6. C 7. D 8. A 9. B 10. D
 II. 1. B 2. A 3. D 4. C 5. B
III. 1. D 2. B 3. B 4. C 5. A
IV. 1. emphasis 2. confirm 3. interrupt 4. struggle
    5. convince
 V. 1. D 2. A 3. C 4. D 5. B 6. A 7. A 8. B 9. D 10. C

Lesson 23

✦ 第一部分

acid
(ˈæsɪd)

Some *acids* burn holes in cloth and wood.
有些酸性物質會在布料或木頭上燒出洞。

adj. 酸性的
n. 酸性物質

---

approach
(əˈprotʃ)

As we *approached* the man, we saw that he was blind.
當我們接近那個人時，發現他是瞎的。

v. 接近
n. 方法

【記憶技巧】
ap (to) + *proach* (near) (向～靠近，也就是「接近」)

---

battle
(ˈbætḷ)

It is interesting to watch a *battle* between two lions.
看兩隻獅子搏鬥是有趣的。

n. 戰役；戰鬥

【記憶技巧】
bat（打擊）+ *tle*

---

bough
(baʊ)

The *bough* bent under the weight of the snow. 那樹枝因雪的重量而彎曲。

n. 大樹枝
同 branch

---

capable
(ˈkepəbḷ)

Mr. Smith is a man *capable* of doing anything.
史密斯先生能做任何事。

adj. 有能力的
同 competent; proficient

---

choke
(tʃok)

The smoke from the burning building almost *choked* the firemen. 著火的建築物冒出來的煙，幾乎使救火員窒息。

v. 使窒息
同 suffocate

Lesson 23

comrade
('kɑmræd)

The two boys were close *comrades* and did everything together. 這兩個男孩是親密的夥伴，做任何事都在一起。

n. 夥伴；同志
同 companion;
 fellow

【記憶技巧】
com + *rade* (行動的人) (一起行動的人，也就是「同志」)

consult
(kən'sʌlt)

Have you *consulted* your doctor about your illness? 你已向醫生請教過病情嗎？

v. 請教；查閱

credit
('krɛdɪt)

If you pay your bills on time, your *credit* will be good. 如果你能按時付清帳單，你的信用將會很好。

n. 信用；信賴
同 trust;
 confidence

declare
(dɪ'klɛr)

When will the results of the election be *declared*? 選舉結果何時宣布？

v. 宣布
同 announce

【記憶技巧】
de (fully) + *clare* (clear) (向大家表示得十分清楚，也就是「宣布」)

Exercise 23.1 從第一部分中選出最適當的一個英文字，填入空格內。

1. The rabbits hid under a pile of _____ cut from the tree.

2. As winter _____, the weather grew colder.

3. Some airplanes are _____ of flying 1,000 miles an hour.

4. You'd better _____ a dictionary for the meaning of a new word.

5. Fighting had been going on for a year but war had not yet been _____.

【解答】
1. boughs   2. approached   3. capable   4. consult   5. declared

✦ 第二部分

destroy
〔 dɪ'strɔɪ 〕

Careless children **destroy** all their toys. 粗心的孩子會破壞所有的玩具。

【記憶技】
de (down) + **story** (build) (使建築物倒下，也就是「破壞」)

v. 破壞
同 demolish
反 construct
名 destruction

disturb
〔 dɪ'stɝb 〕

She opened the door quietly so as not to **disturb** the sleeping child. 她靜靜地開門，以免打擾睡覺的孩子。

v. 打擾
同 bother
名 disturbance

effective
〔 ɪ'fɛktɪv 〕

His efforts to improve the school have been very **effective**. 他為改善學校所做的努力，非常有效。

adj. 有效的
反 ineffective

entire
〔 ɪn'taɪr 〕

The **entire** country was surprised at the news that an earthquake had happened. 全國的人民對地震發生的消息都很驚訝。

adj. 全部的
同 whole; total; complete

expert
〔 'ɛkspɝt 〕

She is an **expert** in teaching small children. 她是教導小孩的專家。

n. 專家

favor
〔 'fevɚ 〕

A mother shouldn't show too much **favor** to one of her children. 母親不應該太偏愛某一個孩子。

【記憶技巧】
用 <u>favor</u>ite (最喜愛的) 來背。

n. 恩惠；偏愛

flutter
〔'flʌtɚ 〕

The wings of the bird still *fluttered* after it had been shot down.
鳥被打落後，翅膀還在拍動。

v. 拍動（翅膀）；飄揚
同 flap

-----【記憶技巧】-----
fly（飛）前要 flutter（拍動翅膀）。

fur
〔 fɝ 〕

The *fur* coat will keep you warm during the winter.
毛皮大衣在冬天能使你溫暖。

n. 毛皮

grateful
〔'gretfəl 〕

I am *grateful* to the friends who have helped me. 我非常感激曾幫助過我的朋友。

adj. 感激的
同 thankful

hell
〔 hɛl 〕

Wicked persons are said to be punished in *hell* after death.
據說壞人死後會在地獄受處罰。

n. 地獄
反 heaven

Exercise 23.2 從第二部分中選出最適當的一個英文字，填入空格內。

1. He did all he could do to win her _____.

2. The new system of taxation will be _____ from next May.

3. Our hope of a picnic was completely _____ by the heavy rain.

4. She was wearing a very expensive _____ coat.

5. The curtains were _____ in the breeze.

-----【解答】-----
1. favor 2. effective 3. destroyed 4. fur 5. fluttering

✦ 第三部分

immense
〔ɪ'mɛns〕

An ocean is an ***immense*** body of water. 大海是一片汪洋。

adj. 廣大的
同 huge
反 tiny

【記憶技巧】
im (not) + ***mense*** (measure) (大到無法衡量，表示很「廣大的」)

instant
〔'ɪnstənt〕

The medicine gave ***instant*** relief from pain. 這種藥能立即減輕痛苦。

adj. 立即的

join
〔dʒɔɪn〕

Those two towns are ***joined*** by a railway. 這兩鎮由一條鐵路連接。

v. 加入；連接
同 combine; unite

lash
〔læʃ〕

The prisoner received ten ***lashes***.
囚犯被打了十鞭。

He ***lashed*** the horse until it ran.
他鞭打馬直到牠跑為止。

【記憶技巧】
l + ***ash*** (灰)

n. 鞭打

v. 鞭打
同 whip

lodge
〔lɑdʒ〕

We ***lodged*** in a hotel on our trip.
我們旅行時，住在一間旅館裏。

v. 投宿；住宿；
供 (人) 住宿
同 reside; dwell

mast
〔mæst〕

The ship has four ***masts*** for its sails.
那條船有四根桅桿掛帆。

n. 桅桿

mirror
〔'mɪrɚ〕

A woman usually carries a small ***mirror*** in her bag.
女人通常在手提包裡攜帶一面小鏡子。

n. 鏡子

nail
〔nel〕

Many women have long ***nails*** for beauty. 許多女人為愛漂亮而留長指甲。

He hammered some ***nails*** into the piece of hard wood.
他將一些釘子敲入那塊堅硬的木頭裡。

n. 1. 指甲

2. 釘子

Lesson 23

observe
〔əb'zɝv 〕

Did you *observe* anything strange in that boy's behavior? 你觀察到那男孩的行為有什麼奇怪的地方嗎？

A careful driver *observes* the traffic rules. 謹慎的駕駛人會遵守交通規則。

v. 1. 觀察

2. 遵守

名 observation

--- 【記憶技巧】---
ob (over) + *serve* (watch) (「觀察」有看守、監視之意)

outlook
〔'aʊt,lʊk 〕

From my study window I have a pleasant *outlook* over mountains and valleys. 從我書房的窗口，可以看到山谷美麗的景色。

n. 看法；景色

同 scene

Exercise 23.3 從第三部分中選出最適當的一個英文字，填入空格內。

1. Please _____ the rule about not walking on the grass.

2. The driver saw in his rear-view _____ that a police car was following him.

3. One of the sailors climbed up the _____ to see what was on the horizon.

4. The shipwrecked sailors were _____ in the hotel.

5. The horse didn't run very fast, so he _____ it over the back with his whip.

--- 【解答】---
1. observe   2. mirror   3. mast   4. lodged   5. lashed

✦ 第四部分

passage
〔'pæsɪdʒ 〕

The old bridge is not strong enough to allow the *passage* of heavy trucks.
舊橋不夠堅固，無法讓重型卡車通過。
The *passage* between the two houses was blocked.
那兩棟房子間的通道被阻塞了。

n. 1. 一段文章

2. 通過；通道；道路
同 path; route

---

perish
〔'pɛrɪʃ 〕

Hundreds of people *perished* in the earthquake.
那次地震死了好幾百人。

v. 死亡
同 die
反 persist

【記憶技巧】
per (thoroughly) + *ish* (go)（完全地離開世上，就是「死亡」）

---

politician
〔ˌpɑlə'tɪʃən 〕

Politicians are very busy when the election time comes.
選舉期間，政治人物都非常忙碌。

n. 政治人物

---

primary
〔'praɪˌmɛrɪ 〕

His *primary* reason for studying was to get a better job. 他唸書的主要原因是想獲得一份較好的工作。

adj. 主要的
同 principal; chief

【記憶技巧】
prim (first) + *ary* (*adj.*)（排在第一順位，表示「主要的」）

---

purple
〔'pɝpḷ 〕

The artist likes to use *purple* in his paintings.
那個畫家喜歡用紫色畫畫。

adj. 紫色的
n. 紫色

reflect
〔rɪ'flɛkt〕

The sunlight was *reflected* from the water. 陽光從水中反射出來。
Take enough time to *reflect* before doing important things. 在做重要的事之前，要花充分的時間考慮。

v. 1. 反射；反映

2. 考慮
同 think
名 reflection

> 【記憶技巧】
> *re* (back) + *flect* (bend) (曲折而回，也就是「反射」)

require
〔rɪ'kwaɪr〕

Every foreign student is *required* to take an English examination.
每一個外國學生都必須考英文。

v. 需要；要求
同 need;
　 demand
名 requirement

> 【記憶技巧】
> *re* (again) + *quire* (seek) (一再地尋求，就表示很「需要」)

risk
〔rɪsk〕

There are always some *risks* in every adventure. 每次冒險總是會有一些危險。

n. 危險
反 safety

sauce
〔sɔs〕

The vegetables were eaten with a cheese *sauce*. 蔬菜被沾著乳酪醬吃。

n. 醬汁

seek
〔sik〕

She managed to calm him down and *seek* help from a neighbor. 她設法使他平靜下來，然後向一位鄰居求助。

v. 尋找；尋求
同 search;
　 look for

Exercise 23.4 從第四部分中選出最適當的一個英文字，填入空格內。

1. The police opened a _____ through the crowd for the President.

2. The _____ cause of Tom's failure is his laziness.

3. After _____ for a time, he decided not to go.

4. All passengers are _____ to show their tickets.

5. Fishermen face a lot of _____ in their daily lives.

【解答】
1. passage　2. primary　3. reflecting　4. required　5. risks

✦ 第五部分

shriek
〔ʃrik〕

The girls were all ***shrieking*** with laughter.
女孩們都邊叫邊笑著。
A ***shriek*** of pain came from the wounded man. 受傷的人發出一聲痛苦的尖叫。

v. 尖叫
同 scream
n. 尖叫聲

snatch
〔snætʃ〕

The thief ***snatched*** her handbag and ran away. 小偷搶了她的手提包跑走了。
He made a ***snatch*** at the rope but missed.
他試著抓住繩子，可是沒抓到。

v. 搶奪；抓走
同 seize
n. 抓住

【記憶技巧】
諧音；死拿去，死要拿走，就是「搶奪」(snatch)。

spine
〔spaɪn〕

His ***spine*** was broken in the accident.
他的脊椎在那次意外中折斷了。

n. 脊椎

stem
〔stɛm〕

The ***stem*** of a tree supports its branches and leaves. 樹幹支撐著樹枝和葉子。

n. 樹幹；莖

stumble
〔'stʌmbḷ〕

He ***stumbled*** over a stone on the rough path. 他在崎嶇的路上被石頭絆倒。

v. 絆倒

sweep
〔swip〕

While her mother was cooking, Mary ***swept*** the floor. 當瑪麗的母親煮飯時，她掃地。

v. 掃；沖走
同 clean

Lesson 23

territory
〔'tɛrə,torɪ〕

The explorers claimed the land as British *territory*.
探險家們宣稱這塊土地是英國的領土。

n. 領土；地方

> 【記憶技巧】
> *territ* (earth) + *ory* (*n.*)（所擁有的土地就叫「領土」）

torture
〔'tɔrtʃɚ〕

Most of the civilized nations do not *torture* prisoners.
大多數文明的國家不會折磨犯人。

v. 折磨；刑求

The sight of his sick brother was an unbearable *torture* to him. 看到他弟弟生病的樣子，對他是一種無法忍受的折磨。

n. 折磨
同 torment

> 【記憶技巧】
> 諧音：脫白，是身體受「折磨」。

twin
〔twɪn〕

I can't tell one *twin* from the other; they look just alike. 我無法分辨出這兩個雙胞胎；他們長得幾乎一樣。

n. 雙胞胎之一

vine
〔vaɪn〕

Melons and pumpkins grow on *vines*.
甜瓜和南瓜長在藤蔓上。

n. 葡萄藤；藤蔓

whip
〔hwɪp〕

The boy was *whipped* for telling a lie.
那男孩因說謊而被鞭打。

v. 鞭打
同 beat; lash

It is cruel to use a *whip* to punish a little child. 用鞭子懲罰小孩是殘忍的。

n. 鞭子

Exercise 23.5 從第五部分中選出最適當的一個英文字，填入空格內。

1. He was _____ by his father for bad manners.

2. Much _____ in the northern part of Africa is desert.

3. Many bridges were _____ away by the floods.

4. If you are not careful, you'll _____ over that box.

5. The boy was _____ from his home by two armed men.

> 【解答】
> 1. whipped   2. territory   3. swept   4. stumble   5. snatched

成果測驗

I. 找出一個與其他三個不相關的字：

(　) 1. (A) lodge　　(B) dwell　　(C) reside　　(D) exist

(　) 2. (A) route　　(B) zone　　(C) path　　(D) passage

(　) 3. (A) primary　(B) principal　(C) practical　(D) chief

(　) 4. (A) seek　　(B) require　　(C) need　　(D) demand

(　) 5. (A) seize　　(B) snatch　　(C) grasp　　(D) confirm

(　) 6. (A) fellow　　　　　(B) comrade
　　　(C) delegate　　　　(D) companion

(　) 7. (A) capable　　　　(B) prompt
　　　(C) proficient　　　(D) competent

(　) 8. (A) terror　　(B) danger　　(C) risk　　(D) peril

(　) 9. (A) unite　　(B) combine　　(C) join　　(D) command

(　) 10. (A) whole　　(B) complete　　(C) vast　　(D) entire

Lesson 23

II. 找出一個與題前中文意思相同的英文字：

( ) 1. 專家
  (A) expert   (B) comrade
  (C) companion   (D) statesman

( ) 2. 領土
  (A) margin (B) property (C) horizon (D) territory

( ) 3. 掃
  (A) seek (B) sweep (C) sway (D) lash

( ) 4. 偏愛
  (A) emotion (B) trust (C) favor (D) comrade

( ) 5. 有效的
  (A) candid (B) effective (C) practical (D) clever

III. 找出一個與斜體字意義相反的單字：

( ) 1. *hell*
  (A) shortage (B) horizon (C) virtue (D) heaven

( ) 2. *construct*
  (A) bother (B) destroy (C) acquire (D) establish

( ) 3. *risk*
  (A) safety (B) favor (C) comfort (D) grief

( ) 4. *perish*
  (A) dwell (B) stumble (C) repair (D) persist

( ) 5. *tiny*
  (A) entire (B) primary (C) immense (D) effective

Lesson 23

IV. 完整拼出下列各句中所欠缺的單字，每一格代表一個字母：

1. We must try to o_ _ _ _ _e many kinds of regulations.（遵守）

2. If you drive carefully, there is no r_ _k of accident.（危險）

3. Mirrors r_ _ _ _ _t our faces.（反映）

4. You'd better c_ _ _ _ _t a doctor when you are sick.（請教）

5. I felt i_ _ _ _ _t relief from pain after taking a dose of medicine.
（立即的）

V. 找出一個與句中斜體字意義最接近的單字：

(　　) 1. The building was completely *destroyed* in the fire.
　　　(A) defended　　　　　　(B) reflected
　　　(C) choked　　　　　　　(D) demolished

(　　) 2. Do you give *credit* to his account of what happened?
　　　(A) confidence　(B) favor　(C) emphasis　(D) interest

(　　) 3. The bird *fluttered* its wings in the cage.
　　　(A) snatched　　　　　　(B) flapped
　　　(C) lashed　　　　　　　(D) reflected

(　　) 4. He *choked* when a piece of meat stuck in his throat.
　　　(A) struggled　　　　　　(B) cried
　　　(C) stumbled　　　　　　(D) suffocated

(　　) 5. Do not *disturb* the baby; he is asleep.
　　　(A) bother　　(B) whip　　(C) approach　　(D) insult

(　　) 6. He *declared* himself a member of their party.
　　　(A) indicated　　　　　　(B) announced
　　　(C) consulted　　　　　　(D) convinced

Lesson 23

(   ) 7. The boys *shrieked* when they saw the terrible accident.
  (A) hailed
  (B) disturbed
  (C) approached
  (D) screamed

(   ) 8. The police *tortured* the man to make him confess the crime.
  (A) lashed   (B) required   (C) tormented   (D) whipped

(   ) 9. We saw the *immense* statue of the hero, thirty times life size.
  (A) entire
  (B) huge
  (C) divine
  (D) magnificent

(   ) 10. I feel *grateful* for your help.
  (A) competent   (B) nervous   (C) proud   (D) thankful

VI. 將題前的斜體字轉換為適當詞性，填入空格中：

1. *require*   Experience in a related field is a _____ for this job.

2. *reflect*   He gave much _____ to the problem but still had no answer.

3. *observe*   This telescope is used for the _____ of distant stars.

4. *disturb*   You can work in here without any _____.

5. *destroy*   The fire caused the _____ of two buildings.

【解答】

I. 1. D   2. B   3. C   4. A   5. D   6. C   7. B   8. A   9. D   10. C

II. 1. A   2. D   3. B   4. C   5. B

III. 1. D   2. B   3. A   4. D   5. C

IV. 1. observe   2. risk   3. reflect   4. consult   5. instant

V. 1. D   2. A   3. B   4. D   5. A   6. B   7. D   8. C   9. B   10. D

VI. 1. requirement   2. reflection   3. observation   4. disturbance
    5. destruction

Lesson 24

✦ 第一部分

acquire 〔ə'kwaɪr〕	He ***acquired*** the money for his trip by working at night. 他晚上工作以獲得旅行所需要的錢。 【記憶技巧】 *ac* (to) + *quire* (seek) (去尋找，就會「獲得」)	*v.* 獲得 同 gain; obtain 反 lose

apron 〔'eprən〕	Wear an ***apron*** over the front part of your clothes to keep them clean while cooking. 烹飪時，在衣服前面穿上圍裙，以保持衣服乾淨。	*n.* 圍裙

bead 〔bid〕	She was wearing a string of green ***beads*** around her neck. 她在脖子上掛了一串綠色的珠子。	*n.* 有孔的小珠；珠子

boundary 〔'baʊndərɪ〕	The new ***boundaries*** were fixed after the war. 戰後規定了新的邊界。 【記憶技巧】 *bound* (被綁著的) + *ary* (*n.*)	*n.* 邊界

career 〔kə'rɪr〕	What made you decide on a ***career*** as a vet? 是什麼使你選擇獸醫這個職業的？	*n.* 職業；生涯 同 occupation; vocation

chop 〔tʃɑp〕	He was ***chopping*** wood into small, short pieces for burning. 他將木頭砍成小而短的木片，作爲燃燒之用。	*v.* 砍；劈；剁碎 同 cut

conceal
〔 kən'sil 〕

He *concealed* himself behind a large tree.
他藏在一棵大樹後。

v. 隱藏
反 reveal;
　　disclose

contact
〔 'kɑntækt 〕

If you bring fire into *contact* with gunpowder, there will be an explosion. 如果你讓火和火藥接觸，就會發生爆炸。

n. 聯絡；接觸

【記憶技巧】
con (together) + *tact* (touch)

creep
〔 krip 〕

We *crept* through the bushes towards the enemy. 我們悄悄地走過灌木叢，朝著敵軍的方向前進。

v. 爬行；
　　悄悄地走

decline
〔 dɪ'klaɪn 〕

I said I would give him ten thousand dollars for the horse, but he *declined* my offer. 我說我會以一萬美元的價格買那匹馬，可是他拒絕了我的提議。

v. 拒絕
同 refuse; reject
反 accept;
　　consent

【記憶技巧】
de (down) + *cline* (bend)（「拒絕」別人的請求時，會彎下身子向對方說對不起）

Exercise 24.1　從第一部分中選出最適當的一個英文字，填入空格內。

1. He tried to _____ the fact that he broke the window glass.

2. Churchill's _____ proves that he was a great man.

3. To bring fire into _____ with gasoline may cause an explosion.

4. The cat _____ quietly nearer to the bird, but the bird flew away.

5. I am sorry to _____ your invitation to dinner, but I have
to study for the examination.

【解答】
1. conceal   2. career   3. contact   4. crept   5. decline

✦ 第二部分

| **detail** | Everything in her story is correct | *n.* 細節 |
| ('ditel) | to the smallest *detail*. 她的故事完全 | 同 particular |

是真的，即使是最小的細節也不例外。

【記憶技巧】
de (entirely) + *tail* (cut) (將一件事徹底
分割，就是「細節」)

| **ditch** | A *ditch* is a long, narrow place | *n.* 水溝 |
| (dɪtʃ) | dug in the earth to carry off water. |

水溝是在地上挖的細長構造，可用來
排水。

| **efficient** | Our *efficient* new machines are | *adj.* 有效率的 |
| (ə'fɪʃənt) | cheaper than old ones. |

我們有效率的新機器比舊的便宜。

| **entitle** | The author *entitled* his book | *v.* 定名 |
| (ɪn'taɪtḷ) | "Treasure Island". |

作者將他的書定
名為「金銀島」。

【記憶技巧】
en + *title* (名稱)

| **experiment** | Scientists test out theories by | *n.* 實驗 |
| (ɪk'spɛrəmənt) | doing *experiments*. |

科學家藉由做實驗充分檢驗理論。

favorite (ˈfevərɪt)	What is your *favorite* flower? 你最喜歡什麼花？ Among those records, Beethoven's Fifth Symphony is one of my *favorites*. 在那些唱片中，貝多芬的 第五號交響曲是我最喜歡的之一。	*adj.* 最喜愛的 *n.* 最喜愛的人或物

【記憶技巧】
favor（偏愛）+ *ite* (*adj.*)（特別偏愛的，
就是「最喜愛的」）

foam (fom)	The breaking waves make *foam* near the coast. 碎浪在海岸旁激起了泡沫。	*n.* 泡沫
furnace (ˈfɜnɪs)	An oil *furnace* heats our school buildings in winter. 我們學校大樓在冬天使用油爐取暖。	*n.* 火爐；熔爐； 暖氣爐
grave (grev)	We visited her *grave* and put flowers on it. 我們探望她的墳墓， 並放一些花在上頭。	*n.* 墳墓 同 tomb
herd (hɝd)	We saw a big *herd* of cattle on the farm. 我們看到農場上有一大群牛。	*n.*（牛）群

【記憶技巧】
和 heard（聽到）同音。

Exercise 24.2 從第二部分中選出最適當的一個英文字，填入空格內。

1. We found a(n) _____ of elephants running together.

2. We buried the dead cat in a little _____ dug in the backyard.

3. Some people learn by _____ and others by experience.

4. A(n) _____ worker deserves good pay.

5. _____ are usually used to irrigate fields and carry off water.

> 【解答】
> 1. herd   2. grave   3. experiment   4. efficient   5. Ditches

✦ 第三部分

| **import**
〔 *v.* ɪmˊport 〕
〔 *n.* ˊɪmport 〕 | The United States ***imports*** coffee from Brazil. 美國自巴西進口咖啡。 | *v.* 進口 |
| | Last year we reduced the amount of ***import*** and expanded that of export. 去年我們減低了進口量，並增加了出口。 | *n.* 進口；
輸入額 |

> 【記憶技巧】
> ***im*** (in) + ***port*** (港口)

| **instinct**
〔ˊɪnstɪŋkt 〕 | He has an ***instinct*** for always doing and saying the right thing. 他有說話和做事永不出錯的本能。 | *n.* 本能 |

> 【記憶技巧】
> ***in*** (on) + ***stinct*** (prick) (被刺激，才能發揮出「本能」)

| **joint**
〔 dʒɔɪnt 〕 | The ***joints*** of the chair were very loose. 那把椅子的連接處非常不牢。 | *n.* 關節；
連接處 |

> 【記憶技巧】
> ***join*** (加入) + ***t***

| **latter**
〔ˊlætɚ 〕 | Of these two men, the former is dead, but the ***latter*** is still alive. 這兩個男人當中，前面那個已經死了，後面這個還活著。 | *n.* 後者
反 former |

lonesome
(ˈlonsəm)

The old woman was **lonesome** without children.
那位沒有孩子的老太太很寂寞。

> 【記憶技巧】
> 字尾-*some* 表「有…傾向的」。

adj. 寂寞的

---

masterpiece
(ˈmæstɚˌpis)

All of his paintings were considered **masterpieces**.
他所有的繪畫作品都被認為是傑作。

> 【記憶技巧】
> **master**（大師）+**piece**（一件作品）（大師的作品，就是「傑作」）

n. 傑作

---

miserable
(ˈmɪzərəbḷ)

The child is hungry, tired, and homeless; he is a **miserable** child.
那孩子又餓、又累，而且無家可歸；他是個可憐的孩子。

adj. 悲慘的；
（天氣等）令人討厭的

---

naked
(ˈnekɪd)

Some **naked** boys were swimming in the river.
一些沒穿衣服的男孩正在河裏游泳。

adj. 赤裸的；
光禿禿的
同 bare

---

obtain
(əbˈten)

It is necessary to **obtain** a permit to hunt or fish in this state. 在這一州，打獵或釣魚都必須獲得許可證。

> 【記憶技巧】
> **ob**(to)+**tain**(hold)（擁有就是「獲得」）

v. 獲得

---

output
(ˈautˌput)

What is the daily **output** of automobiles in this factory?
這家工廠的每日汽車產量是多少？

n. 產品；產量

Exercise 24.3 從第三部分中選出最適當的一個英文字，填入空格內。

1. _____ during the last five years were greater than exports.

2. He fell and put his knee out of _____.

3. Most animals have a(n) _____ to protect their young.

4. The _____ sailor was all alone in a strange town across the sea from his home.

5. Cold weather caused the leaves to fall and left the trees _____.

【解答】
1. Imports   2. joint   3. instinct   4. lonesome   5. naked

✦ 第四部分

passionate 〔'pæʃənɪt 〕	They soon fell in *passionate* love with each other. 他們很快就陷入熱戀。	*adj.* 熱情的； 熱烈的
permanent 〔'pɝmənənt 〕	After doing temporary jobs for a month, he got a *permanent* position as a clerk in a store. 做了一個月的臨時工後，他找到了一個當店員的固定工作。	*adj.* 永久的 同 perpetual 反 temporary

【記憶技巧】
per (through) + *man* (stay) + *ent* (*adj.*) (一直停留，就是「永久的」)

populous 〔'pɑpjələs 〕	China is one of the *populous* countries. 中國是人口稠密的國家之一。	*adj.* 人口稠密的

principle
〔'prɪnsəpl̩〕

The *principle* was established that the chairman should change yearly.
主席應每年更換的原則已確定。

n. 原則；原理

pursue
〔pɚ'su〕

The police are now *pursuing* the escaped prisoner. 警察正在追捕逃犯。

v. 追求；追捕

【記憶技巧】
pur (forth) + *sue* (follow)（跟隨自己的目標前進，就是「追求」）

reform
〔rɪ'fɔrm〕

The new president promised to *reform* the government.
新總統保證要改革政府。

v. 改革；
使改過自新

【記憶技巧】
re (again) + *form*（形成）

rescue
〔'rɛskju〕

The passengers were *rescued* from the sinking ship.
乘客們從即將沉沒的船上被救起。

v. 拯救；解救

【記憶技巧】
re（加強語氣的字首）+ *(e)s* (out) + *cue* (shake)

rival
〔'raɪvl̩〕

The two boys were *rivals* for the first prize. 這兩個男孩是爭取頭獎的對手。

n. 對手

saucy
〔'sɔsɪ〕

The girl was *saucy* to her mother.
那女孩對她的母親沒有禮貌。
The girl was wearing a *saucy* new hat.
那女孩戴著一頂俏麗的新帽子。

adj. 1. 無禮的

2. 俏麗的

seize 〔 siz 〕	Mother *seized* the child by the arm. 母親抓住孩子的手臂。	*v.* 1. 抓住

The weapons hidden in the house were *seized* by the police. 藏在屋中的武器被警方扣押。

2. 扣押；沒收
同 confiscate

【記憶技巧】
size（尺寸）+ *e*

Exercise 24.4 從第四部分中選出最適當的一個英文字，填入空格內。

1. Brick walls are more _____ than wooden fences.

2. A _____ country has many people per square mile.

3. The flow of water in a river is explained by the _____ of gravity.

4. We should try to _____ criminals rather than punish them.

5. The fireman tried to _____ the child from the burning house.

【解答】
1. permanent   2. populous   3. principle   4. reform   5. rescue

✦ 第五部分

shut 〔 ʃʌt 〕	*Shut* the gate so that the dog can't get out. 關上大門，以免狗跑出去。	*v.* 關上 同 close 反 open
soak 〔 sok 〕	She *soaked* the clothes before washing them. 她在洗衣服之前，先將它們浸在水裏。	*v.* 1. 浸泡

Use this cloth to *soak* up the spilled milk. 用這塊布將灑出去的牛奶吸乾。

2. 吸收
同 absorb

Lesson 24

spirit
(ˈspɪrɪt)

Though he is dead, he is with us in *spirit*.
雖然他已死，但他的精神與我們同在。

n. 精神
反 flesh

stepmother
(ˈstɛpˌmʌðɚ)

Mary didn't get along with her *stepmother*. 瑪麗和她的繼母處得不好。

n. 繼母

stupid
(ˈstjupɪd)

It was *stupid* of you to run away from the accident.
你從意外事故中逃跑，真是愚蠢。

adj. 愚蠢的

swell
(swɛl)

Wood often *swells* when it is wet.
木頭潮濕時常會膨脹。

【記憶技巧】
s + well (井)

v. 膨脹
同 expand

theme
(θim)

The *theme* of his talk was the need for education.
他演講的主題是「教育的需要」。

【記憶技巧】
them (他們) + e

n. 主題
同 topic;
subject

tough
(tʌf)

Only *tough* breeds of sheep can live in the mountains.
只有強壯品種的羊才能生活在山區。

adj. 困難的；
強壯的

twist
(twɪst)

She *twisted* her hair round her fingers to make it curl.
她將頭髮纏繞在手指上，使之捲曲。

v. 扭曲；
纏繞

violence
(ˈvaɪələns)

The policeman had to use *violence* to arrest the murderer.
警察必須使用暴力來逮捕兇手。

n. 暴力

whirl
(hwɝl)

The dancer suddenly made a *whirl*.
舞者突然轉了一圈。
The leaves *whirled* in the wind.
樹葉在風中迴旋。

n. 旋轉

v. 迴旋

Exercise 24.5 從第五部分中選出最適當的一個英文字，填入空格內。

1. He _____ his eyes and tried to sleep.

2. The _____ is willing but the flesh is weak.

3. John's real mother died last year, and now he lives with his
   _____.

4. Her ankle _____ up after she fell down.

5. Patriotism was his _____ when he spoke at our school.

【解答】
1. shut   2. spirit   3. stepmother   4. swelled   5. theme

成果測驗

I. 找出一個與其他三個不相關的字：

(   ) 1. (A) enduring (B) permanent (C) instant   (D) perpetual

(   ) 2. (A) chase   (B) pursue   (C) seek   (D) seize

(   ) 3. (A) acquire   (B) obtain   (C) save   (D) gain

(   ) 4. (A) theory   (B) theme   (C) topic   (D) subject

(   ) 5. (A) silly   (B) efficient (C) stupid   (D) foolish

(   ) 6. (A) unclothed   (B) passionate
         (C) bare   (D) naked

(   ) 7. (A) scheme   (B) vocation   (C) career   (D) occupation

Lesson 24

( ) 8. (A) entitle (B) name (C) designate (D) reside

( ) 9. (A) miserable (B) populous (C) wretched (D) pitiable

( ) 10. (A) resolve (B) decline (C) reject (D) refuse

II. 找出一個與題前中文意思相同的英文字：

( ) 1. 有效率的
(A) magic (B) efficient (C) clever (D) instant

( ) 2. 實驗
(A) instrument (B) expedition
(C) project (D) experiment

( ) 3. 傑作
(A) expert (B) master (C) masterpiece (D) feast

( ) 4. 原則
(A) principle (B) principal (C) subject (D) theme

( ) 5. 本能
(A) emphasis (B) instinct (C) emotion (D) passion

III. 找出一個與斜體字意義相反的單字：

( ) 1. *latter*
(A) former (B) better (C) lower (D) slower

( ) 2. *temporary*
(A) lonesome (B) cold (C) immediate (D) permanent

( ) 3. *reveal*
(A) disclose (B) conceal (C) obtain (D) improve

(　) 4. *flesh*
   (A) principle　(B) brain　(C) spirit　(D) instinct

(　) 5. *lose*
   (A) obtain　(B) perish　(C) tight　(D) unite

IV. 完整拼出下列各句中所欠缺的單字，每一格代表一個字母：

1. The stream forms a b_ _ _ _ _ _y between your land and mine.
   （邊界）

2. Who is your f_ _ _ _ _ _e American singer?（最喜愛的）

3. Have you been in c_ _ _ _ _t with your sister recently?（連絡）

4. The fathers of our country were p_ _ _ _ _ _ _ _e believers in freedom.（熱烈的）

5. I have to d_ _ _ _ _e your invitation because my mother expects me at home.（拒絕）

V. 選出最適合句意的一個單字：

(　) 1. The poet has ＿＿＿＿ fame all his life, but has never experienced it.
   (A) concealed　　　　(B) declined
   (C) acquired　　　　(D) pursued

(　) 2. He ＿＿＿＿ my hand and said how glad he was to see me.
   (A) seized　　　　　(B) twisted
   (C) pursued　　　　(D) required

(　) 3. The boy's eyes were ＿＿＿＿ with tears.
   (A) choked　(B) drained　(C) swollen　(D) swept

Lesson 24

(   ) 4. He _____ a good knowledge of English by studying hard.
    (A) disturbed   (B) acquired
    (C) revealed   (D) demanded

(   ) 5. He _____ the block of wood in two with a single blow.
    (A) twisted   (B) snatched   (C) chopped   (D) crept

(   ) 6. It is interesting to read about the _____ of great men.
    (A) beads   (B) boundaries   (C) purples   (D) careers

(   ) 7. What is your _____ food?
    (A) passionate   (B) favorite
    (C) populous   (D) effective

(   ) 8. The burglar _____ into the house and up the stairs.
    (A) rescued   (B) whirled   (C) crept   (D) declined

(   ) 9. Birds do not learn to build their nests but build them by
    _____.
    (A) instinct   (B) passion   (C) principle   (D) theory

(   ) 10. They started their holiday on a _____ day; it was cold
    and the rain never stopped.
    (A) stupid   (B) saucy   (C) wilful   (D) miserable

【解答】

  I. 1. C   2. D   3. C   4. A   5. B   6. B   7. A   8. D   9. B   10. A
  II. 1. B   2. D   3. C   4. A   5. B
  III. 1. A   2. D   3. B   4. C   5. A
  IV. 1. boundary   2. favorite   3. contact   4. passionate
     5. decline
  V. 1. D   2. A   3. C   4. B   5. C   6. D   7. B   8. C   9. A   10. D

單字索引

單字索引

單字索引

單字索引

單字索引

單字索引

單字索引

All rights reserved. No part of this publication may be reproduced without the prior permission of Learning Publishing Company.

本書版權為「學習出版公司」所有，翻印必究。

Vocabulary fundamental
基本字彙

附錄音 QR 碼　售價：280 元

修　　　編 / 劉　毅
發　行　所 / 學習出版有限公司　　☎ (02) 2704-5525
郵 撥 帳 號 / 05127272 學習出版社帳戶
登　記　證 / 局版台業 2179 號
印　刷　所 / 裕強彩色印刷有限公司
台 北 門 市 / 台北市許昌街 17 號 6F　　☎ (02) 2331-4060
台灣總經銷 / 紅螞蟻圖書有限公司　　☎ (02) 2795-3656
本公司網址 / www.learnbook.com.tw
電 子 郵 件 / learnbook@learnbook.com.tw

2022 年 1 月 1 日四版一刷

ISBN 978-986-231-468-5

版權所有，本書內容未經書面同意，不得以任何
形式複製。

一個人成敗的關鍵，
在於是否願意和單字
長久地作戰。

儲存單字量，
比儲存財富還要有價值。

背了會忘是自然的，
要持之以恆。

背完本書，要繼續挑戰
Vocabulary 5000、
Vocabulary 10000，
和 Vocabulary 22000。